THE DEVIL'S DUE: JOURNEY TO THE WHITE CLOUDS

THE DEVIL'S DUE: JOURNEY TO THE WHITE CLOUDS

WALLACE J. SWENSON

FIVE STAR

A part of Gale, a Cengage Company

PASADENA LIBRARY, FAIRMONT
4330 Fairmont Pkwy
Pasadena, TX 77504-3306

GALE
A Cengage Company

Farmington Hills, Mich • San Francisco • New York • Waterville, Maine
Meriden, Conn • Mason, Ohio • Chicago

LIBRARY OF CONGRESS CATALOGING-IN-PUBLICATION DATA

Names: Swenson, Wallace J., author.
Title: The devil's due / Wallace J. Swenson.
Description: Waterville, Maine : Five Star Publishing, 2018. | Series: Journey to the white clouds
Identifiers: LCCN 2018000904 (print) | LCCN 2018004928 (ebook) | ISBN 9781432844684 (ebook) | ISBN 9781432844691 (ebook) | ISBN 9781432844837 (hardcover)
Subjects: LCSH: Frontier and pioneer life—Nebraska—Fiction. | BISAC: FICTION / Historical. | FICTION / Westerns. | GSAFD: Western stories.
Classification: LCC PS3619.W4557 (ebook) | LCC PS3619.W4557 D49 2018 (print) | DDC 813/.6—dc23
LC record available at https://lccn.loc.gov/2018000904

First Edition. First Printing: July 2018
Find us on Facebook–https://www.facebook.com/FiveStarCengage
Visit our website–http://www.gale.cengage.com/fivestar/
Contact Five Star™ Publishing at FiveStar@cengage.com

Printed in Mexico
1 2 3 4 5 6 7 22 21 20 19 18

THE DEVIL'S DUE: JOURNEY TO THE WHITE CLOUDS

PROLOGUE

If he gets back up I'm going to have to kill him. The certainty of the thought, the finality of it, made Buell Mace lose focus for an instant. He regained it by concentrating on the long barrel of the Remington .44. It held steady, aimed at a man on his haunches, shoulders slumped forward, open hands pressed in the dirt. It was not something Buell wanted to do. As a matter of fact, all he wanted was to walk away, leave the dim confines of the barn, and maybe swing past Luger's for a whiskey. Anything but another shooting. There'd been way too many already.

Bright rays of winter sunlight pierced cracks in the walls of the stable, and sliced through the fine dust hanging in the frigid air. Breathing took conscious effort in the cold, yet surprisingly a bead of sweat started to creep down his spine. Maybe, just maybe, he'll see he's beat and stay down. The hope, a wish really, was denied when the man took a shuddering breath of air, and his splayed fingers slowly curled into massive fists.

The downed man raised his head. His right eye glistened through a narrow slit, the brow swollen and seeping blood from the welt raised by the barrel of Buell's gun only a minute or so before. His left eye grew wide as the concussive effects of the pistol whipping faded. Then a look of resolution built as his gaze settled on the muzzle of the revolver.

The fine hairs at the base of Buell's neck bristled. "Don't get up, Gus," he said loudly, silently prayed he wouldn't, and took a step back.

A chilling shriek was his answer, and the single step rearward his salvation. Contorted features and grasping fingers disappeared in a cloud of smoke and sparks. The man pitched face-first into the dirt, blood splattering Buell's boots. "Goddammit, Gus, I *told* ya not to." A horse slammed back and forth in a stall for a few seconds, and then stood snorting, taking quick looks over its shoulder. Buell knelt, glanced at the top of the man's head, and immediately stood again.

The man-door at the front of the stable opened and Simon's head appeared. "Buell?"

"Get outta here, Simon. Go get Doc Princher."

"He dead?"

"Git!"

"You can go back home, but the folks ya knew ain't there no more," an old-timer had once told Buell. It had bothered him at the time, and he'd spent quite a few dark hours pondering it. His best friend, Simon Steele, and he had left Carlisle, Nebraska, in 1869. Nebraska had been a state for less than two years. They'd wound up working at a roadhouse outside of Fort Laramie, in Wyoming Territory. Simon kept the books and Buell kept order. Simon liked to call it a restaurant, but he knew better. Hell, they were both only nineteen, but, in spite of their age, damned if they hadn't managed to bluff their way through.

There, thoughts of home brought only the misery of knowing they'd been forced to leave, so the memories were pushed back. They faded even more when they went their separate ways five years later. Simon off to some godforsaken valley in the middle of nowhere. Buell to the gold fields around Idaho City and two years of hard lessons. Fate had eventually brought them together again, and seven years after they'd left Carlisle, they'd come back and proved the old-timer right.

The door opened again and Doc Princher huffed through, pulling it shut. He scowled as he shuffled over to the sprawled figure. Kneeling, he put his bag on the floor, bent over the man's head for a moment, and shook his own. With a deep sigh, he slipped the two clasps on top of the bag, opened it, and took out a stethoscope. Then, with another glance at the dead man's head, he threw the instrument back into the bag. "Shit! What's the use? I don't need to tell you, *Sheriff*, you've seen mor'n your share of these lately." He then grunted to his feet.

"He didn't give me any choice, Doc."

"There's always a choice, Sheriff Mace."

"But—"

"I was against it when the council hired you." The doctor glanced at the prone form. "This just confirms my fears . . . again." He clapped the bag shut with an angry snap and picked it up.

"I suppose the street is full?" Buell ventured.

"Course it is. You're a circus, Sheriff, and folks love a good show." He sniffed. "It stinks in here."

Buell followed him to the door, and Princher opened it to a tight cluster of townspeople. A cloud of frozen breath hung over them. Simon stood front and center, and his furrowed brow irritated Buell. An expression of sadness? For whom? Or was it regret? If so, for what?

"Don't you people have places to be . . . *jobs*?" the doctor bawled. "Get the hell out of the way." He swung his bag and the crowd split like a dropped melon. Buell followed him through the gap.

"Couldn't you have just avoided him?" Simon called out.

Buell stopped halfway across the street, and turned to face

him. "No! He didn't give me a choice." The crowd at the barn had turned as one to watch.

"That's not what I . . . he said he was leaving, Buell. It was none of your business."

"What?" A tingling sensation flashed across his scalp. "Say that again, Simon. I wanna make sure I heard ya right."

Simon blinked against the angling sun and his Adam's apple bounced the knot on his necktie as he approached. "He was leaving of his own accord. We had an agreement."

"That was not your place, grocery boy. I'm the law here until your lip-lickin', side-steppin' friends say I ain't."

Simon recoiled like he'd been slapped. "Well, they may do just that. You're too quick, Buell, you always have been."

"Quick or gut-shot. I've seen gut-shot, Simon. It ain't for me."

Simon glanced at the onlookers. "I'm not going to stand here in the street and argue this."

"Then get the hell outta here . . . it was *you* stopped *me*, remember?" Buell left him there, his supplicant hands out. The tight knot of people at the barn door started to shove and pull to be the first inside. No tickets required for the last act.

He'd been there before, smiling at the devil while everyone else hid and watched. Why was it he couldn't let others fend for themselves? Gus Swartz was a crook—thief, liar, bully, and what else? Was he a back-shooter? And Simon? If he had made a deal, had he also told Gus to come see him one last time? The thought made him sick, and he cursed his doubts. Surely, not Simon.

A bleary-eyed drunk sat staring at an empty beer mug as Buell banged open the door at Luger's Saloon and stormed in. He brought a blast of late February with him.

Jake Luger winced as the door slammed shut, and with a puff

through pursed lips, reached under the bar and brought out a half-full bottle. "I gather he found ya?" he said as he filled a double-shot glass.

"Christ, Jake, I'm runnin' out of people I know. Simon made a deal with Gus Swartz."

"I'm completely flap-jawed ya didn't know that. I mean, I just assumed ya did. Here, on the house." He slid the over-full drink across the bar.

"God, Jake, yer a case. That's *my* bottle. I reckon I've paid for it ten times by now." Buell had grown up with Jake Luger. Jake, Simon, and he used to spend a lot of time in the saloon's back room. His eyes went to the place where the door used to be, now long gone thanks to several expansions and additions. Jake's mistake with the bottle had been exactly that, an oversight— there wasn't a deceitful drop of blood in his enormous body.

"Oh, yeah, I forgot." Jake wrinkled his nose, and took an absent swipe at a slick of spilled whiskey. "I heard one shot. Did ya . . . is he?"

"Yeah." Buell felt weary.

"Hey!" a slurred voice called from across the room. "*Servish* over here."

"Shut up!" Jake said without so much as a glance.

"Helluva way to run a saloon."

Buell looked over his shoulder, and the man's attention instantly shifted to the tabletop.

"I ain't walkin' over there fer a dime," Jake muttered. "He can come get it, and the dumbass knows that. 'Sides, he'll wanna put it on his ticket anyhow. I don't know why Pa puts up with it."

" 'Cuz he knows how to run a saloon." Buell carefully picked up the whiskey glass and took a sip. The fumes cleared his head, and liquid heat exploded down his aching gullet. "Looks like I'll be unemployed again," he said with a dismissive snort.

"That job didn't last long."

"I think as long as a couple of them meant it to last. That council's got the spunk of a neutered tomcat. I s'pect half of 'em wear dresses at home."

"Reckon they mean it?"

"Reckon I *give* a damn?" Buell lifted his glass and studied the color of the whiskey. It occurred to him that it was the same as the bar top, exactly the same.

Jake cleared his throat. "Ya know, Buell, I was plumb tickled when you showed up back here. When you left, both of ya—you *and* Simon—the whole damn place slowed down. Ya know, ya didn't even say 'so long.' Have I ever mentioned that?" His gaze shifted to the ceiling for several seconds, and his upper lip curled in concentration.

"Yeah, Jake, ya have. I was in a hurry."

Suddenly Jake's eyes were looking past Buell. "Here comes the first batch of gawkers."

Buell turned to face the tall front windows. *They look like a flock of quail chicks, Sherm Pederson out in front like their mother,* he thought. He tossed the remainder of his drink against the back of his throat. It burned. "I ain't got time for this, or the patience, Jake. I'm gonna use your back exit. I'll see ya later."

"Yeah. Come by my place, and we can talk old times some more. Yer always welcome, ya know."

"I do, Jake, and thanks." Excited voices reached him as he stepped through the door. The ex-mayor's nasal whine cut off as Buell closed it.

He hurried down the narrow alley until he reached the street, where he glanced at the cluster of people near the stable. He then crossed the street and walked up to the jailhouse. The heavy oak door swung easily on the well-oiled hinges, and Buell stepped into the slightly smoky warmth of his last sanctuary. Undecided whether to throw the bolt or not, he leaned his back against the stout wood, and absently bumped his head against it two or three times.

A squat, black-iron stove on the right wall faced a cluttered desk on the left. The empty springback chair behind it sat cocked to the rear. To the side of the desk, the seat of a four-legged stool showed signs of its actual use, the wood thoroughly boot-scuffed. The two cells in the rear of the room invited entry, the steel-lattice doors opened all the way. That's where Gus Swartz should be, he thought, waiting for a ride to Lincoln and prison. He pushed away from the door and turned toward the desk.

Suddenly, Sheriff Staker was sitting there, a half-smile on his face, and memories of the past year made the room entirely too small. Forcing the image out of his head, Buell stepped around the desk to settle onto the polished seat. There he leaned back, shut his eyes, and tried to keep the memory of Gus Swartz's head out of his own as he recalled the last tumultuous nine months.

CHAPTER 1

Buell stepped out of Moir's barbershop and started down the boardwalk. Today was his second day back in Carlisle, and though he found a lot of it familiar, a lot was also new. He studied the opposite side of the street as he walked: a new hotel, two new dress shops, the butcher shop he'd known had spilled next door into the business he remembered as a shoemaker's place.

"Hello, Buell. Heard you were back." Loren Staker's deep baritone startled Buell, and he turned. The lawman stood in the doorway of the jailhouse. "Been avoiding me?"

The sheriff's half-smile evoked memories of Buell's younger years, and apprehension tightened his scalp for an instant. Staker's calm, knowing eyes had always reminded him of a stalking cat. "Habit, I guess."

"Now why would you say that?"

"We *never* got along, now did we?"

"I'd like to think you've learned a few things since then, Buell. Come on in, and let me chew on your ear a little."

"Sure. Why not?" Buell followed him inside, and the twin cells at the back of the room grabbed his attention. He clearly remembered the last time he'd been in one. Even though the steel door had been left open, and he hadn't actually been under arrest, he'd still felt the threat of isolation. But that was then. The sheriff motioned to a stool by his desk. "I'll stand," Buell said, and leaned lightly against the wall by the open door.

"Still got that edge, I see." Staker settled into a creaky spring-back chair. "You can relax in here. Nobody chasing you that I know of."

"That you know of? You checked?" Buell felt anger rise.

The sheriff slid a desk drawer open and fumbled around in it. "Not in any formal sense." He waved a buff-colored envelope. "More a follow-up from an inquiry a year ago."

"From who?" Buell shook his head. "Lemme guess . . . Sheriff McFee, in a place called Idaho City?"

"That'd be him." Staker unfolded a sheet of paper and scanned it.

Buell recalled McFee's bushy mustache and his restless eyes. "I kinda liked him—for a lawman."

"It'll probably hurt your feelings to know he thought likewise." Staker flicked the edge of the letter with his second finger. "He says here that he offered you a job, as a deputy . . . on merit."

"I don't think he was serious."

"Serious as snakebite. The first query was just a telegram to see if you were wanted for something here."

Buell remembered another visit to this same office, one that had occurred just before Simon and he left in sixty-nine. Staker had asked to see Buell's pistol. He pictured the scene, the sheriff pretending to study the Remington, but watching him the whole time. He was doing the same thing now as he studied the letter.

"I got this dispatch about a week before you and Simon showed up," the sheriff continued. "I've got something for you to think about."

"Not my strong suit, Sheriff—thinkin'."

"That won't wash, Buell. Remember, I watched you grow up."

"I've only been back two days. I haven't given a thought

16

about what I'm going to do. Or, for that matter, if I'll even stay here."

"All the more reason to listen then." He laid the letter on the desk, leaned back in his chair, and gave Buell his full attention.

Stalking cat. Buell felt vaguely threatened. "All right. I'm listenin'."

"I'm sixty-five years old this fall, I'm tired, and I'm getting slow."

Buell chuffed lightly. "From what I've seen so far, you don't need to be all that fast here in Carlisle."

"That's because the problem isn't here . . . it's about four miles downstream, on Sandy Island."

"Never was anything on Sandy Island . . . too much sand." He smiled. Staker did not. "So, what's there now?"

"Herders."

"Cowhands?"

"I like *herders* better. They share about one brain for every three of 'em. Most have come in with a herd, and then stayed around with a fresh memory of how hard the trail is. Now they got nothin' to do but cause trouble."

"If they're as dumb as you say, I don't see a problem. Throw a couple in jail for a week, and the rest will avoid ya."

"I've done that, but they weren't even missed. At any given time, there's about twenty-five of 'em, and all together—there's more farther down the Platte, and more still about six miles above the island—there could be as many as fifty."

Buell let out a low whistle. "That's a small army."

"Still think you don't need to move fast around here?"

"Maybe so, but I don't see how it's any of my business."

"You have family here—*that* makes it your business."

"Never saw myself as a deputy, Sheriff Staker."

The lawman leaned back and laced his fingers behind his head. "I don't want a deputy, Buell. I got two."

"Then what?" Buell glanced down at the heavy pistol he carried. It was a Remington 1858, .44 caliber, nickel-plated weapon with carved ivory grips. "I'm done with hiring out this gun—I did that—"

The sheriff raised his hand. "I'm offering you *my* job—as sheriff."

Buell almost laughed, but the look on the lawman's face stopped him. "Is that the way it works here? You hire whoever you want? McFee was hired by a town council."

Staker rocked forward in his chair and laid his hands palm down on the desk. "Same here, but they'll do what I ask. Will you think about it? That's all I ask for now. Just think."

"It ain't gonna do any good, Sheriff, but I'll keep it in mind."

"That's good enough." Staker winced as he stood up. "Saw yer pa yesterday. All he could do was sputter about how you'd grown up, and how good it was to have ya back home." He reached around and rubbed his lower back. "He's changed some, too, don't ya think?"

"Tell ya something odd. I've seen some folks that're exactly like I remember 'em, while others are so different I have to—it's as if they're not the same people." And Buell was looking at one who hadn't changed a bit. The remark about his father was meant to pull something out of him. What, exactly? "Gotta git. I'm gonna meet Simon, Pa, and Mister Steele at Missus Luger's kitchen for lunch." Buell pushed away from the wall and made for the door. The sheriff appeared to be of two minds—hurry around and offer his hand, or just let Buell go. Buell made up the sheriff's mind for him. "Be seein' ya," he said as he stepped briskly through the door.

"Think on what I said," Staker called after him as he walked away.

★ ★ ★ ★ ★

Loren Staker stared at the open door for a couple of minutes, then picked up the letter from McFee and read the second page again. Natural lawman. When he'd read those words the first time, he'd almost spit out his uppers. Buell Mace had hated the law and all lawmen since he'd been old enough to pee standing up. He'd killed a man with a single shot through the head when he was sixteen. Staker had hauled Buell to jail for it, but the dead man had been a hired gunfighter and had drawn first.

And Staker knew it was Buell who'd shot David Steele. Doc Princher had seen what a doctor needed to see, a fatal head wound. Staker had seen what a lawman would see, how the death was dealt. In David's case, a bullet through the back of his mouth, easily missed when the dead man was an animal like David. Few men had the nerve to face David Steele, *and* the skill to place a shot like that. Was it justifiable? Staker had decided at the time he could live with it.

His current problem lay with the band of troublemakers on Sandy Island—a problem Staker knew would eventually overwhelm his ability to control it. He'd tried to be reasonable with them, but they'd taken that as a sign of weakness. One Saturday in February, about fifteen of them had ridden into town. They'd stayed at a small saloon out by the feedlots northwest of town—welcomed by the proprietor. Several times before, the owner had patched up what the drunks had smashed, but cheated them enough to make it worthwhile. Staker had left them alone, half relieved. But trouble began early Sunday morning when they moved into Lancer's place on Main Street. Problem being, Lancer's was closed for the night. Staker knew he'd been lucky to get the drop on two of the leaders, knocking one senseless with the butt of his shotgun. He and his two part-time deputies had managed to get three of them to jail, and the rest out of Lancer's.

Now it was just a matter of time before they'd come again. It sickened him to think he had to let them have their way, or confront them and be beaten. He'd considered approaching Paisley Mace. At one time, Mace—Staker had a hard time calling him anything but Mace—was a prime candidate. He was fair, honest, and unshakable in the face of a threat. Then Mace had married Matt Steele's widow, and a good man was swamped in compromise.

Staker had been prepared to go to his grave defending the twenty-two-hundred citizens of his town, knowing full well they deserved better protection. He'd been resigned to it until he'd received the letter. He looked at it again. McFee said Buell had the nerve of a badger but with a bonus—he didn't bluff. The first part was the Buell he knew. On the second point, Staker had questions. He'd never met a man who didn't bluff once in a while. Was Buell, at twenty-six, man enough to do what was needed? The sheriff put the letter down and heaved a sigh. "I'm up against it. The whole town is, they just don't know it yet," he said out loud. "What would make Buell Mace mad enough to fight for us?"

One of Buell's favorite people when Simon and he were growing up was Freda Luger. There was never any doubt in townspeople's minds where they stood with her. It was simple: they were all in her way and needed to move. He had understood that and stayed clear, where a lot of folks didn't. As a consequence, she tolerated his presence, which meant he was often the first to sample the food she'd put out every day for her husband's saloon. She'd always been a good cook, so it was no surprise to learn that she now also operated a small café next door to Luger's Emporium. What did come as a surprise was that Pa suggested they meet in her café, rather than the saloon.

When he entered, the sight of the three of them waiting

brought him to a halt. Paul Steele, his hair now graying at the temples, still had the friendliest smile of any person Buell had ever met. But instead of the patched flannel shirt and threadbare overalls he used to wear, he now dressed in a white cotton shirt with a stiff collar, and his dark trousers were supported by a belt *and* suspenders. Simon was his father's image: round, open face with a well-defined jaw, and broad, solid-looking shoulders. He'd also inherited the smile.

Buell's father had changed the most physically. His blacksmith's arms were still thick, but the muscles no longer stood out. And the flat stomach he used to invite Simon and Buell to punch—as hard as they dared—now hung over his broad belt.

"Good to see you today," his father said.

"Time was when we'd stumble over you to get to the food, Buell," Paul Steele said. "Been sightseeing?"

"Guess you could say that, Mister Steele. Hi, Simon."

"Hey, Buell. What do you think?"

" 'Bout what?" He sat on the empty chair.

"Everything. The size of the town, your pa's new business—all of it."

Paul chuckled softly. "According to Paisley, Buell has spent a lot of time out and about."

"Paisley?" Buell wrinkled his nose and looked at his father, head cocked slightly.

"Ruth insists folks call me that," his father said. "She says calling a person by just their last name doesn't show proper respect." The elder Mace frowned, then tried to make a smile of it. For years, Mace, as he was universally known, had carried a torch for Ruth Steele. He married her when she was widowed by her husband's suicide.

"But everyone except her called you Mace. You insisted," Buell said.

"Well, not any more. Paisley it is. I don't mind." A slightly furrowed brow contradicted his tight smile. "Let's order something, I'm starved." He raised his hand, and Freda Luger immediately started across the room. Shifting her ample rear from side to side, she negotiated the cramped space between tables.

"Well, und look vat wind has blowed in," she said and put her hand on Buell's shoulder. "*Und* not too soon." She pinched the muscles beside his neck. "Food, you need more, *ja?*"

"Exactly what I thought," Paisley said. "Today's Wednesday, son, and that means pot roast and spuds. Remember the cold roast beef she used to put on the bar?"

"I sure do." Buell recalled how he and Simon were allowed to go into the saloon at noon to have something to eat—but only in the back room with Jake Luger. On the bar there would be a large platter, overflowing with meat of some kind, cheeses, a special sauce made with mustard, and pickles—a two-gallon crock of dark-green, knobbly dills. He looked up at the dour-faced woman. "You still make them big pickles?"

Her thin lips submitted to the faintest smile for a moment. "*Ja.* For sure," she said brusquely. "Good they sell. Pot roast then you have?"

"Good for me," Buell agreed, and the others nodded.

"Good," Freda said and turned to leave. "*Und* you for pickle, Buell," she added as another slight smile violated her sour face. She bustled off.

"So, what'd ya do this morning?" Simon asked Buell.

"Stayed in bed till about ten. Then I went and got a haircut— guess what? Mister Moir's still telling the same jokes. Not a new one in the bunch, and he never stopped talking."

"I haven't seen him yet." Simon tugged at the hair on the back of his neck. "Probably ought to. Ya seen Jake?"

"Not yet. I went to Lancer's first last night and never managed to get out. I thought you'd have been in."

"His mother wasn't going to let him out of her sight," Paul said. "And his brothers about wore his ears off. He's got some hair-raisin' stories."

"Yeah, I heard a couple."

"Well, how 'bout you?" Paul asked. "Working in a gold town in Idaho Territory had to be interesting. You gonna share a few of your adventures?"

"Not much to tell, Mister Steele." Buell looked at Simon. "I was just talking to Sheriff Staker."

"Already?" Simon said, and everyone laughed.

"Not about anything I done, asshole," Buell said with a fake scowl.

"You don't need to cuss," Paisley said.

"Huh?" Buell stared at his father for a moment, and then glanced over his shoulder.

"No need to swear," his father said again. "I asked ya last night."

"That was a slip, in front of . . . of—"

"She's your stepmother. Call her Mother, or Ruth."

"But she ain't here," Buell said. "Ain't *no* women here." He couldn't decide if the embarrassment on Paul Steele's face was for him or his father. No cussing? What the hell is that all about? He looked to Simon for help.

"What did Staker have to say?" Simon stepped in.

"You won't believe it. He offered me a job as the *law.*" Buell laughed out loud, and then stifled himself as several heads turned to look.

"What's so strange about that, son?" Paisley asked. "You've always been able to use that pistol of yours." His tone sounded critical.

"True. And who taught me trees have bark for a reason? If I think I'm right, I'll argue the point." He locked eyes with his father.

"You notice that a lot of men don't carry sidearms anymore?" Paisley stared back.

"I do. What you gettin' at?"

"Nothin'," Paisley muttered and looked down at the table. "Just talkin'." He looked back up briefly. "But sometimes that can get more done than the other way." The last part sounded halfhearted. Then he shook his head. "Anyhow, I think he'd make a good sheriff, don't you, Paul?"

"Loren Staker's a better judge of that than me," Paul said. "And if he thinks so, I'd go along with it."

Buell looked across at Simon just as his friend's eyes found the tabletop irresistible. He felt his face flushing. "Ya know, I ain't got much of an appetite just now." He slid his chair back and stood. "I'm gonna go next door and get a beer."

"Buell?" Simon's voice sounded strained.

"I'll see ya soon." He gave Simon a dismissive wave, and then looked at Paul Steele. "Good to see you, Mister Steele."

The three sat with open mouths as Buell walked out of the café.

CHAPTER 2

Buell shoved open the restaurant's screen door, swung left, and ran head-on into the solid body of a large man: "Watch where the hell yer—"

"Well, if it ain't one of the runts," Gus Swartz said, and easily pushed Buell back. "Heard you'd come crawlin' home."

Buell's eyes met the pig-like squint of the other man. "Don't mess with me, Gus—I ain't in no mood."

"And your moods are s'posed to concern me?" Gus snorted. "Not till fish fly."

Gus Swartz's father owned Carlisle's older general store. Buell had seen the new store across the street. Gus had always been a blowhard, but one with a very large body. He was dressed in overalls, flannel shirt, thick-soled shoes, and a ragged cloth cap. He was not the well-dressed son of a successful shop owner Buell remembered. And he was unarmed. "Keep your hands to yourself, Gus, or—"

"Or what? You'll shoot me?" His eyes went to Buell's pistol. "With that Nancy gun of yours? Not anymore, unless you want to go to prison. Now, move." Gus took half a step sideways and shouldered his way past.

Buell, jaws clenched, watched him for a moment, and then walked the short distance to the door of Luger's Emporium. The high ceiling and smooth hardwood floor were instantly familiar, as was the man charging around the end of the bar. In half a dozen strides, Jake Luger had pushed his way past a dozen

25

startled customers, his arms outstretched.

"Buell, ya ugly, skinny, sumbitch!" Jake grabbed him in a suffocating bear hug, pounding the air out of Buell's lungs with several stunning blows to his back. "Damn, is it good to see you again." He let go and stood back. "Look at ya!"

Buell shook his head and flexed his shoulders. "Do you always try to break bones, or is that just fer special?"

"Jist for special." Jake grinned. "Heard you and Simon come home. Git on over there and let me buy you a beer or something." He motioned to the bar, and made his way around the end. "Where's Simon?"

"He's next door at your mom's place. When'd that start?"

" 'Bout a year ago." Jake picked up a patron's beer glass and set it farther along the bar. "Move down here," he told him, and before the man could protest, Jake signaled the bartender at the far end. "His next one's on me," he said, and pointed at the surprised customer.

Buell glanced at the man, and then put his foot on the brass rail. "I gather yer pa still owns the place, then?"

"Sure. And I'm still workin' my ass off for nothin'. Beer? Or something with a little more hair?"

"Well, at least ya ain't forgot that part." Buell scanned the backbar. "Whiskey. Looks like ya got the good stuff."

"Oh, we got it, all right." Jake selected a bottle with a deceptively plain label and poured two drinks. "I don't usually, but this don't happen ever' day." He slid the glass across the polished wood and picked up his own. "To friends and whiskey—two good things that get better with age."

They touched glasses, then Buell took a careful sip. "Soon as I'm settled, I'm gonna have you keep a bottle of that for me."

"Settled? That mean yer gonna stay awhile?" Jake glanced down the counter. "Don't answer that just yet." He jerked his thumb at the bartender. "He's gettin' behind. Be right back."

26

He hurried down the forty-foot bar, replenishing drinks as he went, and soon returned. "Okay, you gonna stay?"

"Fella once told me that where yer at's usually as good a place to be as any. Turns out, he's probably right. People are pretty much the same wherever you go. Speakin' of which, I met Gus Swartz outside."

"Worthless bag o' guts," Jake muttered. "He don't come in here much. Pa'll run him out if he's here. Never did say why. I don't care much, he's mostly fart and fluster."

"Does his pa still run the Carlisle store?" Buell took another pull on his drink.

"Nope." Jake finished off his and then wiped his mouth with the back of his hand. "He went bust. First, his suppliers wouldn't carry him from order to order, then the freighters started demanding payment up front. Finally, Simon's pa opened a store, and folks started doing their trading with him. Old man Swartz sold out and went to Omaha. Gus works at whatever pays best for the least amount of effort. Meaning, he steals a lot."

Buell chuckled. "Remember that stink just before we left? Swartz accused Simon of stealing from the cash drawer, and Sheriff Staker found the money where Simon kept his store-workin' clothes? Maybe ya didn't know."

"Sure I knew. Hell, everybody did. Wasn't s'posed to get out, but I think Gus blabbered. A few said Simon might have done it—damned few, I might add—and the rest said ol' Swartz cheated Simon." Suddenly, Jake's face lit up. "*You* did it, didn't ya?" He lowered his voice when several heads turned their way. "I'll be dipped in snoose. You boys got ol' Swartzy back 'fore ya left, am I right? He damned near had a heart attack that morning when he found his cashbox empty. Wanted Staker to swear out a warrant for the both of ya. Staker wouldn't, and that got Swartz madder than ever." Jake shook his head and poured another shot into each glass. "Well, did ya or didn't ya?"

"If I told ya I did or I didn't, one would be a lie. We'll leave it at that."

"Well, shit, Buell, that don't mean nothin'." Jake scowled, waited a few seconds, and then sighed. "So, tell me about that place you was in. Last time you come home we didn't get much of a chance to talk, with yer pa's weddin' 'n all."

"Not much to say, Jake." For the next half hour, Buell described Idaho City and what the country around there looked like. He recalled a bit about some of the people he'd met, and his job as a guard on a gold claim. "In short, it was just a gold town with lots of people lookin' to find some, and even more lookin' to take it when they did. Can't say it was all that good an experience. All history now. So, *you* tell me what's happened here. Lots has changed."

"Yep, and still changin'. Simon's pa has more to do with it than most, him and Mister Lindstrom, the lawyer. Between them, they own half this town. Yer pa ain't done bad."

"Who bought Swartz's store?"

"Paul Steele. What the hell does he want two general stores for? There's more to that than just business, I think." Jake winked. "Know anything?"

Buell recalled the conversation he'd had with Simon just before they'd left Carlisle. Gus Swartz had been cheating his own father, and had managed to get Simon blamed for it. Sheriff Staker tried to keep it away from the public, but Simon had been convinced everybody knew, and was talking about him behind his back. Buell realized that Jake was staring at him. "Nothing that would make any difference, Jake." The screen door squawked open just then, and he glanced up at the mirror. "Wait a second and ask the man who knows." He turned around. " 'Bout time," he said to Simon.

"That was a little awkward, don't you think?" Simon took a

place at the very end of the bar.

"What?" Jake shrugged his shoulders and looked back and forth between the two friends.

"He got his feathers ruffled next door," Simon said.

"Feathers!" Buell protested. "They both as much as accused me of being a shooter, and you had *nothin'* to say."

Simon shook his head. "That's not what I heard."

" 'I'd have to agree with Loren and go along with whatever he says,' is what your pa said. Not exactly the best praise I've heard. And *my* pa wasn't any better."

"We talked about it after you—"

Buell snorted. "Why don't *that* surprise me?"

"And they both said it come out different than they meant," Simon pressed on. "They did not mean to diminish you, Buell."

"Diminish?" Jake said.

"Make me littler, Jake. Can't ya talk plain ol' American, Simon?" Buell said.

Growing up, Simon had been their schoolteacher's dream: eager, resourceful, and intelligent. She'd even managed to gain him access to the local judge's library, and by the age of eighteen, Simon had been better educated than most adults.

"Well, the truth be known, I think you'd make a fine lawman," Simon replied.

"Lawman?" Jake blurted, and then lowered his voice. "Like, sheriff? They want Buell to be the sheriff?"

"Staker mentioned it, Jake," Buell said. "Just asked if I might be interested—that's *all.*"

"You know how to use that pistol—"

"That's been pointed out quite plain, Simon," Buell said sarcastically.

Simon sighed. "And *you* are overly sensitive. We all change, and that includes you, whether you believe it or not. Even if you've been what I thought was more harsh than necessary a few times, I've never seen you be unfair."

"Wouldn't *that* be somethin'?" Jake said. "Buell Mace, Sheriff of Carlisle, Nebraska. What was that cowboy's name, Buell, the one that taught you how to shoot? Lasley 'r somethin' like that."

"Pat Lacey," Buell said and chuckled. "Yeah, he'd get a tickle out of that."

"Did ya ever hear from him again?" Jake asked.

"Nope." Buell knew where any other answer might lead.

"Well, ya gonna take the job, Buell?" Jake looked eager.

"It ain't been offered. He just said I should think about it. Right off, I'd say it ain't something I'd wanna do."

"An offer would have to come from the city council, anyway," Simon said.

"Ha!" Buell snorted. "That's exactly what I told Staker."

"And guess who heads the council?" Simon asked with a satisfied smile.

Buell shook his head and frowned.

"Yeah . . . my father. Now does his comment make a little more sense? He'd defer to Sheriff Staker's experience on such matters."

"That means he'd do it if Staker said so?" Jake asked. "Defer?"

Buell scowled at Simon again. "Plain American, okay?"

"If you wanted the badge, it's pretty much yours for the asking, that's all I'm saying. That, and I think you'd do a damned good job."

"All right, I got a little hot." Buell was getting tired of discussing it. "I'll think on it."

"Good. Now, how'd you sleep last night? Feathers and clean sheets are nice, huh?"

"As a matter of fact, I slept where I used to sleep."

Simon cocked his head slightly. "The stables?"

"Yep."

"That part of the livery is the same, Simon," Jake said, "Ma—uh—Paisley left it like that when he moved up to the new house. He never said why."

"Well, I'm glad he did," Buell said. "Ruth forbade me to smoke, drink, or cuss in the house."

"No?" Simon furrowed his brow. "Just like that? Doesn't sound like my Aunt Ruth."

"Not *exactly* like that, but the same thing."

"Well, what *did* she say?"

"She asked if I minded not doing it."

Simon groaned and shook his head. "So you left?"

"Well, hell yes. That's Pa's house—he has the say."

"So, what did *he* say?"

"That's the problem. Not a damn thing."

Jake had a slight smile on his face, and Simon looked perplexed. "You gonna stay there?" Simon asked.

"As long as I stay here," Buell said. "I can smoke, cuss, fart, and drink all I want, and when I come home at two o'clock in the morning, the horses ain't gonna say a damn thing about it."

"He's got a case there," Jake said.

"But I think your new—my aunt—your step—"

"My pa's wife, Simon. And she'll get used to me the way I am, cuz I ain't gonna change."

"Everybody changes," Simon replied. "Remember what Tay Prescott said, 'The forest is littered with trees that won't bend a little'?"

"He was talkin' about not lettin' stuff get to us at Fort Laramie. Entirely different thing, and you damn well know it."

"Who's Tay Prescott?" Jake asked.

"What's different, Buell? The place, that's all."

"It's all different."

"It's not *all* different. We've only been here two days, Buell . . . give it a chance. Give yourself a chance. And go back to

31

your new home."

Buell picked up his drink, untouched since Jake had poured it, studied it for a moment, and then tossed the whole thing back. His eyes instantly glazed, and he puffed air between his lips. "I'll stick around awhile, Simon, but I'll stay where I'm at. And we'll see what bends and what don't." He raised his eyebrows at his friend.

"Well, who *is* Tay Prescott?" Jake repeated.

Tay Prescott. Buell, and Simon had just arrived at Fort Laramie, Wyoming Territory. They rode across the wide parade ground after spotting from the hill above what had to be the trading post. They'd decided it would be the best place to ask about finding a job. The sutler was busy when they went in, arguing in sign language with a half-naked Indian, so they watched and waited.

"They're hagglin'," a man's voice surprised them from behind. He wore a hat made of animal fur and felt. Misshapen and filthy, it perfectly suited the face below: dark eyebrows and tan-weathered skin frosted with short whisker-stubble. A dingy union suit peeked ruddily through the worn elbows of his shirt. For all that, it was his eyes that struck Buell. They sparkled, and the creases around them could only have been caused by the friendly, open smile he offered them. It looked as natural as breathing. "Name's Prescott, Taylor Prescott. Folks call me Tay," he'd announced and stuck out a grimy hand.

Tay Prescott impressed Buell as few men had, and judging by the comment about the fallen trees earlier that day, it seems he'd had some effect on Simon. Most of what Tay said, Buell had to think about later. There always seemed to be another meaning hidden just beneath the obvious. But Buell remembered Tay saying the forest was littered with trees that *can't* bend, not *won't*. Or had he heard what he wanted to hear? Buell sniffed dismissively. He'd been through "can't or won't" arguments more than once. Now, he wished he could saddle his horse and ride over for a visit. His talks with the old man had always managed to take the edge off Buell's mood. But that was then.

"He's one of those characters old men talk about," Buell said.

"Like at Moir's barbershop?" Jake asked.

"Exactly. Men who'd made a difference to them."

"Tay did that," Simon said. "And Walks Fast."

Jake curled a lip. "He walked fast?"

"An old Indian, Jake. So old he knew Lewis and Clark. Remember them from school?"

"Yeah. Kinda."

"I can see where this is going," Buell said, pushing away from the bar, "and I already know the story. I'm going back to my place and take a nap."

CHAPTER 3

His afternoon nap had felt good, but he'd also missed getting something to eat. Now he sat contemplating the pantry, which most likely didn't contain much. Maybe he'd go see Freda. And explain why he'd skipped her offer of pot roast and a pickle? Less trouble to sit here. His gaze swept the familiar room.

A Spartan place, he'd grown up knowing nothing else. Just him and his pa, they had what they needed: a stove, table, a couple of wooden chairs, and two soft ones for relaxing in. Through one door was the stable and blacksmith shop, through the other, a small bedroom. Not much, but he felt at ease in it.

"Buell? Ya home?" Simon's muffled voice called.

He got up and opened the stable door to see Simon standing in the livery's filtered light with a woman: Sarah. Buell's mouth went dry, very dry. "Yeah, I'm here."

Sarah Kingsley, only child of Judge Hyrum Kingsley, and Simon Steele, eldest son of a hardscrabble farmer, were born to be together. Everyone had believed that—almost everyone. They were the same age within a week, inseparable from the first grade, and both bright beyond fairness to their peers. Yet she had rejected Simon when they were nineteen. The episode had triggered Simon's decision to leave home.

"May we come in?"

Sarah's perfect diction jerked him back to the present. They had crossed the dirt floor without him realizing it, and he hastily stepped away from the door. "Sure. Da—dang, Simon, uh,

Sarah, I'm not really ready for company, the place is dusty as—it's a mess."

Sarah laughed out loud. "You've not changed a speck. Come here, you lout, and give me a hug." She opened her arms wide.

Buell reflexively took a swipe at the front of his shirt, glanced at his hands, and stepped into her embrace. Her lips brushed his recently shaved cheek as softly as a butterfly's landing, and his breath left him.

Then, as quickly as she'd kissed him, she stepped back and looked into his eyes. "On second thought, Buell, you've turned into a handsome man." She turned to Simon. "Don't you think so?"

Simon snickered. "If I did, I dang well wouldn't say so."

"Well, in any regard, it's wonderful to see you. And don't worry about a little dust," Sarah said as she swept past Simon and into the room.

Simon shrugged his shoulders and followed her, with Buell right behind. Before Sarah could sit, Buell took a cursory swat at the chair cushion, and then puffed as a cloud rose. "Aw, hell, you can't sit in that. There." He pointed at a chair by the table. "At least that one ain't got an inch of dirt on it."

"Nonsense," she said and plopped down in the chair where he'd been woolgathering, her full skirts smothering anything that might float free.

Buell took the one he'd pointed out to her, and Simon sat across the table from him. "I can make us some coffee," Buell said, then glanced at the stone-cold stove and shrugged.

"We didn't come to stay," Sarah said. "I just know you well enough not to expect a visit from you any time soon."

"I'd have *seen* ya," Buell protested.

"Maybe passing on the street, the same as I found Simon just a few minutes ago."

"We've only been back a couple of days. I ain't hardly seen nobody."

"I know. I'm simply setting some priorities for you—a woman's prerogative." She gave him a smile and then paused, her head tilted slightly.

"Yeah, yeah, I know—uh, yer right at the front of the line."

"Good. We have an understanding then?"

Buell turned to Simon for some clue, and got nothing but a shrug. He looked at his feet a moment, and felt the heat in his face. It had always been this way when he was around Sarah—her appeal powerful. He'd tried to avoid her, but when Simon had taken that as a sign of disapproval, he'd treated her coolly, which hadn't sat any better. It was a problem he'd never come to grips with. "You say when, and I'll be there," he muttered finally. He felt as unsure as a new colt.

"There, settled," Sarah said, and stood. "We'll go then."

Simon scrambled to his feet as she made for the door. She paused as he opened it, and stepped back. "Simon says you intend to stay here." She waved her hand vaguely around the room.

"Uh, yeah. I—"

Sarah looked directly at him. "I understand that completely," she said, and stepped past Simon.

Buell stood rooted by the table, unable even to nod as Simon gave him a perfunctory wave, and followed Sarah into the stable. Had he seen what he *knew* he'd seen on her face? Was that fleeting pucker of her lips meant to be his? And what *exactly* did she understand about him staying here? He went to the open door and looked out just as she and Simon stepped into the street, hoping she'd look back. She didn't.

Simon pushed the stable door shut, caught Sarah's hand, and started up the street. "There, are you happy? Embarrassed the man to death," he said.

"Nonsense. Besides, in all the time I've known him, I've never seen where he lived. Now I have." She looked at him and wrinkled her nose. "It's very masculine."

"If you didn't notice, Buell is too," Simon said wryly. "Which reminds me. What was that about him being so handsome?"

"Do I detect a little jealousy?" She squeezed his hand.

"It's not me I worry about, it's Buell. The thought of being married terrifies him, always has."

She stopped to face him. "And how do you know that?"

"He's told me so—several times."

"That he's afraid of me? That's hard to believe."

"He's not afraid of you, he's afraid of a commitment. Think back—he never had a girl."

She tilted her head to one side, and paused for several seconds. "I never really gave it much thought when we were younger. There was always just us. I sensed his discomfort, and I thought it was because he didn't like me a lot."

"Nope. And when we worked at the restaurant in Fort Laramie, all he did was play cards, practice shooting . . . and sleep."

"But you said he worked for a woman in that gold camp."

"He did, but as far as I can tell, she was older, and all he did was guard a claim for her. He doesn't have a lot to say about Idaho City, and I've asked him."

"Maybe, when we get him over to dinner, he'll tell us some more." She poked him in the ribs. "But you'll have to admit, he is handsome," she teased, then picked up her skirt and ran.

Towards evening, Buell's need for food drove him to Lancer's Saloon. In the few days he'd been back in Carlisle, he'd discovered that Lancer's place suited his tastes more than Luger's, his friendship with Jake aside. The customers were earthier and there *were* some women. And Art Lancer allowed things to get a little more exciting than did Fred Luger. Now if Art could only improve on the bar food a bit.

Tonight, the excitement involved the problem the sheriff had described. They stood at the far end of the bar: four loud and obnoxious waddies, hell bent on being noticed. Buell, sitting with the woman he'd spent some time with upstairs, tried to disregard the noise. He hadn't missed two of them heading his way, but ignored them until they stopped across the table from him.

"Ya done with her, Slick?" The speaker stood about six feet tall, and had a shape that reminded Buell of a worn-out splitting wedge. Enormous shoulders topped a torso that tapered to more average hips, all supported by a pair of bandy legs. He peered at Buell with bleary blue eyes set too close together. He stank of stale sweat and bad teeth. A young, wiry black man stood to one side and half a step behind him, smiling.

Buell slid his chair back and positioned his feet outside the front legs. "What ya want with *her*?" He looked past the tall man and caught the attention of the grinning Negro. "Looks like you already got a boy." The black man's smile vanished, and his right hand disappeared behind his back.

The white man blinked slowly two or three times, and then he leaned over the table, his grubby hands catching the edge. "What'cha mean by that?"

"Means ya weren't invited, Toad. So *git!*" The last word was loud enough to attract the attention of the men at a nearby table. Chairs scraped as the men got up as one and headed for the bar.

"Ya got a mean mouth," Toad said, and upended the table, shoving it toward Buell as he did so.

Buell shot to his feet, moving right before the man's face disappeared behind the rising furniture. Toad's arms were still raised over his head when Buell's fist slammed into the vulnerable kidney. A rush of foul air flew from the man's mouth, followed a second later by a howl of pain as Buell's bootheel slammed into the side of the man's knee. The leg gave way with a loud pop, and Toad went down hard, clutching it with both hands.

"Look out!" a woman's voice screamed.

Buell's pistol cleared its holster as the black man's knife started through a low, hip-high arc. He jammed the muzzle of the .44 under the man's jaw while ratcheting the hammer back, all in one fluid, practiced move. The knife stopped in mid-swing. "Drop it!" Buell prodded, and the crude blade clattered to the floor. Buell kicked it away and stepped back. "Git hold of yer partner and git outta here," he said, waving the pistol toward the door.

The man's eyes squinted defiance as they locked on Buell's for a second. "One time mebbe you don' have no gun, 'n then ol' Ned, he gon' cut yo pride off short." With a smirk, he turned his head toward his friends standing at the far end of the bar, and nodded.

Buell raised his pistol to shoulder height, his teeth set and his eyes focused. When the Negro turned back, Buell took one step forward, and smashed the long barrel of the Remington across the bridge of the man's nose. The dull crunch preceded the spurt of crimson by a heartbeat, and the man dropped to the floor like he'd been poleaxed. "Just a taste of what you'll git, ya come after me with a knife—*Ned.*" Buell jammed his pistol back into its holster.

Only then did Art Lancer come hurrying around the end of the bar. "Good!" he wheezed. Art Lancer had suffered a serious case of consumption for fifteen years, and for ten, each year had been predicted to be his last. He spoke in single words whenever possible to avoid a coughing fit. "Out." He pointed at the door.

"Me?" Buell asked.

"Them." Lancer pointed at the men on the floor, and then at their two companions at the bar. "You."

The pair hadn't made a sound or a move since Toad had spoken the first time. "It ain't *us*," one of them offered. "Roscoe and Ned did it."

Buell pointed at Lancer. "He wants all four of ya out of here. So do I."

The two hurried across the floor. One grabbed the black man by the arm and dragged him toward the door. The other helped the crippled one to his feet. "I'll see you agin," the injured man said through gritted teeth, and then, moaning loudly, he leaned on his companion as they went out into the street.

"Well," Lancer took a shallow breath, "done." He wiped his hands on the dirty towel tied at his waist, and went back behind the bar.

"That's been a long time coming, Mister Mace," a man said. "They're trouble every time they come in."

"First time anyone has stood up to 'em," added another.

A man shouted from down the bar. "Yer pa used to handle 'em like that!"

"Carved from the same stump, I'd say," the man beside him echoed.

"Young fella'd make a good sheriff."

"Kin I buy you a drink, Mister Mace?"

The evening air had a bite to it by the time Buell shut off the shouts of goodwill by closing Lancer's front door. He hiked the collar of his coat, and started the two blocks to the livery barn. The flurry of violence had left him both exhilarated and drained. Two years ago he would have killed the two of them, and then sat back down to finish his conversation with the woman. Two years ago he would have seen a fleeting image behind his eyes, a

40

vague shadow that gained definition as death was being dealt. But that was two years ago, and that had to stay behind him.

Next morning the sound of banging on the door roused Buell from deep sleep. After the dustup the night before, he'd come back to the stable, saddled his horse, and ridden into the prairie south of town. It was something he'd done as a boy—only then, he'd walked. It was nearly three a.m. before he rode back, built a fire in the stove, and went to bed. "Mace? Mose says you're in there." Mose had to be Moses Adler, the blacksmith who worked out front, and the voice belonged to Sheriff Staker.

"All right!" Buell shouted, and then winced as he opened his eyes to bright sunlight. He swung his feet out of the bed and took a long, deep breath. "Gonna have to get a bottle of Jake's good stuff over to Lancer's," he muttered to his bare feet.

The door to the stable shuddered again. "Well?" Staker hollered.

"Come on in," Buell shouted back and winced again.

The door opened and closed. "Want coffee?"

"Yeah." Buell fought his feet into his pants and stood. "Stove still hot?"

"Will be in a minute."

The sound of a damper screeching open made Buell grit his teeth. He grabbed his boots and stepped into the outer room.

"Is this drinkable?" Staker asked, and held out a blue and white spotted coffeepot.

"Will it still pour?" Buell sat down at the table and retrieved socks from inside his boots.

Staker chuckled. "You look like shit, ya know that?"

"Late night." Buell looked at his socks for a moment, and then stuffed them back in the boots. "Hell with it," he muttered.

Staker passed his hand over the stovetop, set the kettle on a

41

spot near the front, then turned around and leaned against the oven side of the stove.

"This ain't social, Sheriff," Buell said. "Somebody belly-achin'?"

"Just the opposite. Art Lancer is pleased as Grant's whiskey drummer. He spoke a *whole* sentence about it this morning."

"He did? What time is it?"

"After eleven." Staker gingerly tested the side of the cof-feepot.

"The ugly one tipped my table over," Buell said.

"Mister Ugly is Rudy Rosser. Folks call him Roscoe. You may have ruined his knee—ya know that?"

"Nope." Buell looked up at the lawman. "Should I care?"

"And the Negro can't see out of either eye." Staker glanced around the room. "Where's your cups?"

"In there." Buell pointed at a small cupboard to the left of the stove.

Staker found two, filled one, put a couple swallows in the other, and set them on the table. He pressed his hand into his lower back, groaned slightly, and sat. "It ain't very hot, but I can't stay."

Buell picked up his cup and drank nearly half of it. "Better than nothin'," he said, "but just barely."

"Have you been thinking about my offer?"

"Sure." Buell sniffed. "Constantly." He studied the sheriff over the rim of his cup. "But that ain't what yer after."

Staker chuckled. "I noticed that when you were just a youngster, Buell. You seemed to know when others were not quite upright, or that they were up to something. Special trait in a lawman."

"Nothin' special about it, Sheriff. I coldcocked a man last night. You're the law. Simple."

"Are you familiar with the term 'assault and battery'?"

"Yep."

"Well, then, do you know the difference between the two?"

Buell put his cup down and the corners of his mouth curled up slightly. "Sure. 'Bout one step."

Staker's mouth worked like a fish out of water for several seconds, and then he slammed his palm on the table. "Damn it, Buell, this is serious," he sputtered.

"I'm glad you think so. I did too, at the time."

"But Art said you had the drop on the Negro, and Roscoe was on the floor."

"All true."

"Then why did you hit him in the face, dammit? All you had to do was send for me. Both them yahoos have been in jail more than once."

"And a lot of good it did, right? Jail's a safe, comfortable place to sober up. I've used it myself mor'n once." Buell looked at his cup, grimaced, and pushed it into the middle of the table. "The man threatened me with a knife. *Nobody* threatens me and walks away feeling easy. *Nobody.*" His eyes locked on the sheriff's.

"I know that," Staker said, suddenly very quiet. "And I knew that seven years ago, and we'll let this pass just like then—but only because of the *scum* involved. Don't make me regret either decision."

Buell could not get enough air. "You knew about it then?" Buell gasped. "*All* of it?"

"Knew some—guessed the rest." Staker got to his feet and went to the door. "Justice done is justice." He left Buell staring at the closed door, his mouth half open.

Staker strode across the dirt to the front of the stable and stopped. He'd gotten the answer he'd come for—Buell *would* fight. In the letter, Sheriff McFee had told Staker that at first

Buell had been deadly when riled, but something had changed in him after the death of his friend. He'd become more reserved, almost reluctant to use force. A good thing, according to the Idaho City lawman. And Staker agreed—to a point. What he needed right now was someone who would be feared, if not respected. Obeyed, if not liked. Could Staker persuade Buell Mace to become that? Encourage his darker side? The callousness of it all made him wince. He pushed the man-door open and left the stable.

CHAPTER 4

Buell sat at the small table, too stunned to blink. Staker *knew*? Then, who else? Simon, because Buell had told him. Doc Princher? He would have raised a stink—so probably not. Sarah? The sheriff had guessed it, had she? Buell stared at the tabletop until the smooth surface slipped out of focus, and he was again waiting in the trees by the road west of Carlisle.

David would be along sooner or later, and Buell wanted a word with him before leaving town. He'd threatened Buell's father, and he needed to understand that any action on the threat would bring Buell back to town, ready to kill. That's all Buell wanted, an understanding. But things had gone insanely wrong, and David lay dead in the road, the back of his head blown away. Staker had questioned Buell, but it had looked like a bushwhacking, a robbery, and Staker couldn't prove anything. What Staker didn't know—something only Buell and Sarah shared—was why David Steele had deserved to die like a rabid skunk. Buell had kept the secret for nearly five years and finally told Simon the awful truth. David had raped Sarah, and worse yet, she had accepted the blame, her guilt the reason she'd rejected Simon.

Buell reached across the table for his half cup of tepid coffee. Sheriff Staker had just walked out knowing more than he knew coming in. Buell had learned early that an angered man tended to say what he thought, and Staker had angered him. Was he really concerned about Roscoe and Ned? Somehow Buell doubted it.

A cold sweat chilled him. He got up from the table, went into the bedroom, and found a clean shirt. A few minutes later, he gave Mose a casual salute on his way out of the livery, and headed for Freda Luger's café.

His father sat at the far end of the room, in a single table alcove. "Son," he said as Buell approached.

"Mornin', Pa." He took a seat, then nodded his head when Mrs. Luger raised both an empty coffee cup and her eyebrows.

A few seconds later, she put a cup and saucer in front of him. "Breakfast you didn't get," she informed him sarcastically, and then poured the cup full. "You have for eat same as you father?"

Buell nodded and she left.

"Ruth is very upset you've decided to stay at the livery."

"It's best." Buell took a cautious sip of the steaming brew.

"But it doesn't look right. Folks are already talking."

"Let 'em. It's always been *something*, Pa. You know that."

His father sighed and sat back in his chair.

And that's the truth, Buell mused. From the time he'd been old enough to choose, Buell had been defending his choices. He'd only called two people *friend* in his life, and even they had been at odds with him more often than not: Simon and Arley. He stole a glance at his father. His stern face had eyes that showed something else. And then Buell could see Arley. Arley had killed his stepfather—a desperate act after years of horrible abuse—and had then sworn never to harm another person. That conviction had gotten him mortally wounded. But even with that, he'd tried to convince Buell that violence only bred more of the same. Buell had grown up thinking his father had had that same sense of right and wrong. But now?

Paisley cleared his throat. "You have to agree that she's never been anything but good to you. She's made a nice place for you, and we'd like—"

"I'm staying where I am, Pa. I found out a long time ago that the only person who can stand to be around me *is* me. So leave it."

Paisley sighed. "Well, it just don't look good."

"Let it alone, Pa."

"Have you thought about work?"

Before he could answer, Freda came back. "Liver *und* onions with fried spuds," she said to Buell. "*If* today you think you stay."

"That sounds good." He winked at her. "And for a pickle, I'll eat here every day."

"*Unsinn,*" she said. *Nonsense,* and hurried off.

"You can come to work for me. Lord knows I need some help."

"I shoveled enough shit growin' up."

"I'm not talking about that. The sign says 'Mace's Transportation and Portage.' There are lots of jobs besides that. And don't cuss."

"That *ain't* cussin', dammit. I don't wanna get into nothin' with ya, Pa, but you never used to be so—"

"I heard about last night, Buell."

"And?"

"I was hopin' you'd got over that kind of foolishness."

"Foolishness? I was mindin' my own business when two no-count sons'o'bitches decided to—"

"Let's not talk about it, son. I just wish you'd try to control that temper of yours a little."

"But dammit, Pa, I—"

Paisley held up his hand. "Just try, okay?"

Buell looked down at the table and clamped his teeth together.

"Good. Now, about a job." Paisley fiddled with his fork for a few seconds, and then looked directly at Buell. "I'll come right out with it. Do you have *any* money?"

"You say that like you'd be surprised if I did."

Paisley sighed deeply. "Why do you take everything as a challenge?"

"Are you saying it's not?"

Paisley winced.

"I'm sorry, Pa, but you ought to see your face. Yes, I have money. Yes, it's legal. Yes, it's enough."

Paisley glanced around the rapidly filling café. "I want you to stay here, son," he said in a lowered voice. "I've worried about you for seven years, and I'd like to see ya safe."

"I'm full growed, Pa."

"Ya are now, sure, but for nearly twenty years, it was just me and you."

"Well, now you got someone else."

"You're still my only son."

"I'll do just fine. One day I'll tell you about Arley, a drifter I met out in the middle of nothin'. He reminded me some of you—part of the reason him and me partnered up, I think. He died, and left me what he had. Turned out, it was quite a bit."

"I could still use some good help." Paisley worried his fork some more, and then added: "Just as well tell ya the rest." He leaned across the table and whispered, "I want to run for mayor."

"You! You always hated politicians! Called 'em axle greasers."

Paisley grimaced. "Don't talk so loud. It's important to keep it quiet for a bit."

"But what the hell's that got to do with—"

Paisley put his finger to his lips. "Shhh, here comes Freda."

She unloaded two plates from the tray, and then put a small bowl containing two pickles in front of Buell. "There is pickle. Now you every day eat here, *ja*?"

"Hard to turn that down, Missus Luger," Buell said, and using his knife and fork, eagerly separated the onions from the liver.

"If you lived at home, you wouldn't be this hungry at noon," Paisley said.

Buell carefully put his utensils down and leaned back. "I don't and I won't, Pa. We've never chewed on our words much, so here it is. I'm livin' where *we* used to live, I don't drink or cuss any more than *we* used to, and you're lettin' folks call you a name I *know* you hate. So, I have to wonder—what else has changed?"

"I always looked out for our interests. You can't say I didn't."

"And I ain't sayin' different. I am sayin' I don't see that now. I think you're more worried about what other people think than how I might feel."

"But—"

"Before you deny it, let me finish. There's nothing wrong with that if it's what *you* want—I've learned a little, Pa—but it is wrong if you try to punch it down *my* gullet."

"I was an uneducated blacksmith, son. Now folks see me different."

"Marryin' Missus Steele didn't make"—Buell pressed his lips together and grimaced—"No, that's all I've got to say, Pa. I'm gonna eat this liver and onions, and then I'm gonna go next door and see Jake, and maybe even have a beer. You're welcome to come with, but if ya don't, I'll understand that too." Buell picked up his knife and fork, and with one stroke split the dark meat down the middle.

Half an hour later, Buell watched his father cross the street to the bank, and then turned to enter Luger's. The place was nearly empty with only Jake behind the counter. "Hello, trouble," Jake greeted.

"The news gets around." Buell headed to the right end of the bar.

"That kind does. You just missed another mess of it by about an hour."

Buell snorted. "I don't usually *miss* it. Just ask my pa."

"I saw him cross the street. You ate at Ma's?"

"Yeah. What kinda mess?"

"Three of those hard cases, friends of Roscoe's, was in."

"Lookin' for me, I suppose."

"Didn't say as much, but I expect they had a reason for being in *here*. This ain't their usual. Wanna beer?"

Buell turned and looked out the window. "Where on Sandy Island do these yahoos camp?"

"Ya ain't thinkin' about goin' out there, are ya?"

"Sure. They wanna talk, I'll be neighborly and oblige 'em."

Jake shook his head slowly. "Not a good idea, Buell."

"Upstream end or down?"

"Most of 'em on this end, so I hear. I ain't never been curious enough to go see. Ya sure about this?"

"I feel I'm gettin' sucked into a game I don't like. I wanna meet the rest of the players." Buell pushed away from the bar. "I'll drop by when I get back. Save my spot." He left a worried-looking Jake at the bar and headed for the stable.

Buell's horse, Shadow, sensed his presence as soon as he opened the stable door, and greeted him with a lip-flapping snort. An Appaloosa, a light shade of gray colored his front quarters, then turned subtly darker toward his rear. Dark spots and speckles covered his haunches, and, except for a few light streaks, his short tail was crow black. Simon had given him to Buell when they were working at Fort Laramie.

"Lookin' for a run, old boy?" Buell slipped a single rail from

50

its slot and cleared the way for the horse to back out of the stall.

The door to the blacksmith shop opened and Mose looked in. "Oh, it's you, Mister Mace. Want me to saddle him for ya?"

"Nope. I'll do it."

"Okay." Mose closed the door.

An hour later, Buell sat on a low rise overlooking mile-long Sandy Island. A scruffy-looking stand of cottonwoods covered it, most dense at the quarter-mile-wide upstream end below him. Three-quarters of the river it split flowed along the far side. The shallow channel nearest him appeared to be about twenty yards across. From the spring-green trees, three distinct columns of smoke lifted into the air. He leaned forward and patted the horse's neck. "Campfires in the afternoon. Pretty good sign there's not a lot goin' on."

He watched for several minutes, and then spotted three riders coming from the west, single file along the bank. A fourth horse lagged behind at the end of a lead rope: pack animal. The three riders seemed oblivious, until they came within a hundred and fifty yards of him. The one in front reined in sharply and looked back. The rider behind him pointed up and they talked for a few seconds. Then the man leading the packhorse turned down the bank and rode into the water. The other two charged up the gentle incline toward him, both of them whipping their horses with short quirts.

The leader, riding a rangy buckskin, got well ahead of his partner, and rode to within ten feet of Buell, where he slid to a stop. Pushing his sloppy hat back on his head, he exposed a mop of damp coal-black hair. He had small, shiny eyes, made even smaller by his wide ears. His nose twitched above a nervous mouth. Buell almost smiled. A weasel.

The man sat quietly and studied Buell until the laggard ar-

51

rived a minute later. The reason for his delay became apparent: the man was shaped like a rain barrel, and probably weighed three hundred pounds. A weasel—and a groundhog.

"Fine lookin' horse yer ridin'," Weasel said, and glanced sideways at his fat companion.

"Speakin' of horses"—Buell glared at Groundhog—"ya tryin' to kill that one?"

"Huh?" Groundhog's dull eyes blinked slowly, and he drew a filthy sleeve across his sweaty forehead.

"It's his horse," Weasel said, and gigged his mount a little closer to Buell's. He then rested both hands on his pommel.

"Don't make it right for him to abuse it," Buell said easily.

The Weasel looked past Buell for a moment. "You from 'round here? I don't reckon I've seen ya before."

"Don't get around much."

"But enough to get ya up here, lookin' over our camp. Somethin' partic'lar interest ya?"

"Nope. Just lookin'."

"Well, we don't like people sneakin' around." Groundhog glanced nervously at his partner. "Right?"

Weasel nodded and shifted in his saddle, easing his holstered pistol away from his body. "Just what is yer business, then?"

"I heard there was a bunch of drovers out here, and where there's drovers, there's Texans. I kin hear you're from there, or near there."

"And what's yer interest in Texans?" Weasel asked.

"Met a couple some years back and always meant to look 'em up one day—honest, straight-talkin' men."

"Well, we ain't them," Groundhog said.

"That'd be my guess," Buell replied, his eyes on the other rider.

Weasel's back stiffened and his right hand came off the pommel.

"It's been tried, Rooster," Buell said. "And by better men, I'd say. But you do what you think you can."

Groundhog licked chapped lips, and held his hands conspicuously high. Sweat popped out on his forehead and ran down his face.

Weasel put his right hand back on top of his left and squared himself in the saddle. "You're welcome to ride on down and ask around."

Buell gave him a slight smile. "Don't reckon I'll do that today."

"I can put your name around—never can tell."

"Do that. Name's Buell Mace."

Groundhog's head snapped around to look at Weasel. "Roscoe!"

"And Ned," Weasel said, and then smiled back. "Should've known. Yer kind push."

"Some."

"This ain't done." Weasel picked up his reins, and eased his horse back.

"Probably not," Buell replied, as the two men slowly turned their mounts and started back down.

CHAPTER 5

"What'n hell did you mean to accomplish by doing that?" Sheriff Staker leaned over his desk and glared at Buell. "You lookin' to get killed?"

Buell had just told the sheriff about his encounter with the two men above Sandy Island. The sheriff told him the slim one was named Bachman, the fat one they called Meat. Staker thought Meat was the more unpredictable and dangerous. "There was just two of 'em," Buell said.

"Thought you said three," Staker challenged.

"I said one rode onto the island. Had they all come up, I might have left early."

"That *don't* answer my first question. I want to know *why.*"

Buell had just turned sixteen when he'd asked himself the same question. He, Simon, and some Texans they'd worked with one summer had stopped at an adobe shanty-town for a drink. Some needling by a young soldier had gotten out of hand, and in the grimy confines of a dirt-floored saloon, Buell learned that he was capable of killing. Only the bartender's shotgun stuck behind Buell's ear saved the trooper's life. From that day forward, Buell had never walked away from a fight. Irritation sent an angry chill up his spine, and his eyes met Staker's: "I just wanted to make it plain—I'm not someone they can push around."

"Christ, Buell, how plain did you make it to those two at Lancer's? That wasn't a gentle reminder—Roscoe can only just

54

stand and Ned's got 'bout half an eye."

"I don't like worryin' about my back."

"And that helps?" Staker sat back with an exasperated gasp. "Damn it, Buell, you can't carry on like that anymore. Those days are over. Did you know that the city council is considering an ordinance banning pistols in saloons?"

"Yer nudgin' bullshit. They can't be *that* stupid."

Staker squinted at him for a second and then raised his eyebrows. "Why do you need a gun if nobody else carries one? Go to Omaha, or Des Moines—you rarely see an armed man, unless he's the law."

"Well, this ain't Omaha, 'n they forgot to pass out balls to Iowa clodhoppers."

Staker slowly got to his feet, color rising in his face. "You're right, Buell, this isn't Omaha—and we aren't in Iowa. You're in Carlisle, Nebraska—*my* town. By God, you'll respect that, or I'll clap your smart ass in jail so fast your legs won't find it fer a week," Staker bellowed. "Is that *plain* enough for ya?"

Another sheriff in another town had made that same threat: McFee, in Idaho City: "Now get the hell out of here, Mace, or by God I'll throw you in jail just for the sheer pleasure of seeing you sit there." There were only two men, besides his father, who could talk to him like that and not suffer some consequence, and both were lawmen—the irony was not lost on Buell. "Yeah, Sheriff, plain as a goat's asshole."

"Damn good thing. One last point—if you're not going to consider my offer, I'd suggest you take up your father's. Don't look so surprised—I knew about it. Paisley's a good friend, has been since I came to Carlisle. Now get out of here, and keep your nose clean." Staker sat down, picked up some papers, and studiously ignored him until Buell turned and left.

★ ★ ★ ★ ★

Staker waited until he heard boots on the boardwalk before he looked up from his desk. Had he overdone it? He'd taken a risk by encouraging Buell to take a job, but one he was willing to take—he *needed* Buell to stay. And he'd just learned some more about the youngster: the risks he took were calculated ones. Most folks didn't give Buell much credit for being smart, and they were all wrong. A ripple of exhilaration flashed through the lawman. Maybe, just maybe, Carlisle stood a chance.

For six weeks, Buell's nose did, in fact, remain clean: sweat running off it continuously saw to that. The day after his conversation with Sheriff Staker, Buell accepted his father's offer and immediately set about learning the freighting business.

"Hey, Buell."

Buell turned around to see Simon standing in the shade by the freight depot. "Hi, Simon." He raked his arm across his forehead. "Yer pa let you come out to play, 'r do ya need something?"

"You should talk. I've been watching you for ten minutes. Slow down a little—or does yours whip your butt if he catches you slackin'?"

"Do it now, or do it tomorrow. What'n hell's the difference."

"Guess there isn't any. Get off there. I want to talk to ya." Simon pointed to a bench by the building. "C'mon."

Buell turned back to his loading crew. "All right, everybody, sit for fifteen minutes." Two men climbed off the load and joined three others in the shade of the wagon. Buell jumped onto the dock, and sidled over to slump down beside Simon. "I'm not so sure I like this workin' idea."

Simon chuckled. "It's something you're not used to, I know that."

"What do ya mean? All you did at Laramie was sit in that office and order stuff." Buell glanced at the half-loaded wagon. "And when it came time to shift it, guess who'd disappear?"

Simon sniffed. "And watching over a saloon with that Sharps rifle is your idea of hard work?"

"Hey! We all have our talents. Don't be gettin' preachy—again."

Simon punched Buell on the arm. "Oh, quit pawin' the ground. I'm glad to see you've taken hold and decided to do something."

"It was this, or take care of the stable. I've cleaned stalls before, remember."

"Like you said, talents." Simon sniggered, then stood up to dodge Buell's fist.

"Smart ass grocery boy."

Simon tipped his head back and laughed.

"What?" Buell cocked his head.

"Remember when we'd argue about who was going to shine the last piece of harness brass at your pa's place. There always seemed to be an odd number."

"Damn, that was a shitty job, wasn't it?" Buell chuckled. "And if I remember it right, it was usually me that did that last one."

"That *is* the way *you'd* remember it. Them were fun times, huh?"

"Oh, yeah. I've spent a lot of hours rememberin'." Buell sighed and looked down at the wooden deck. "A lot has changed."

"Yup. And some things never will."

Buell's head snapped up. "Like what?"

Simon put up his hands. "Whoa there. It's not what you're thinking at all."

"How do you know what I'm thinkin'?"

"I've seen that look before, Buell—hundreds of times."

"Don't mean a damn thing, either. Never did."

"Then you know the look I'm talking about?" Simon paused for a few seconds when Buell just stared back. "You can't bullshit me." Simon sat back down on the bench. "We've been friends, best friends, for twenty years. Right?"

"Yeah."

"Well, that's the reason I came over today. I want you to be the first to know about me and Sarah."

Buell shifted to face Simon. "It's about damned time. A dozen people have asked if I knew anything. Worst kept secret in Nebraska."

"It's not been a secret. We just decided last night—for sure."

"So you finally got the question out, did ya?"

The year they'd left town, Simon had made several miserable attempts at proposing to Sarah. Each episode had been the subject of long conversations between Buell and Simon down by the river and in Luger's back room. Conversations that always ended with Simon vowing to get it right the next time, and Buell secretly seeing each failure as a triumph. And after every attempt, Buell would suffer pangs of guilt, and swear not to enjoy Simon's failure the next time. The last occasion was the fateful day Sarah had denied Simon *before* he'd actually voiced the proposal.

"It was easy," Simon said cheerfully—all the past frustration apparently forgotten. "We were sitting in the glider on her folks' porch, and I just asked her, 'Sarah, will you marry me?' and she said, 'Yes.' Simple as that."

"Some things are meant to be, Simon, and you and Sarah are one of 'em. Folks have been saying that forever."

"Thanks, Buell. We're going to tell Judge and Missus Kingsley today at lunch, and Sarah and I would like for you to be there."

"Oh, I don't know. You know me and things like that. I don't even have a decent suit to wear. I don't think I—"

"Sarah said you'd say that. It's outdoors, in the back garden—informal picnic. That means you don't have to wear anything special. Your pa and Aunt Ruth, my folks, John Lindstrom—*Uncle John.*" Simon smiled. "And I asked Jake to come too. He was there when I told you that I was going to marry Sarah one day. Remember that poem you made up and recited in the back room?"

"What poem?"

"I didn't think so. I went home that night and wrote it down. I showed it to Sarah last night."

Buell's memory drew a blank, and he shook his head.

"I'll be damned," Simon said. " 'Here's to freedom from worry and strife. To play when I want, without askin' a wife, to drink with my friends and stay out all night, still standing up straight when they turn out the light.' "

"I recited *that*? Bullshit!"

"That you did—rattled it off like you'd spent a month memorizing. I was impressed." Simon grinned. "Sarah said you'd have to define 'play.' "

"I don't remember it, but it sounds like—naw, it don't. Congratulations, Simon. It's been a long time comin', and you'll make lots of folks happy. Now, I gotta get back to work, even if you don't." He punched Simon on the arm, and hollered at the other workers who watched them from the shade of the wagon box.

The Kingsley residence used to be the last house on the east side of town, as well as the largest and most imposing. Now it blended well with those that had joined it over the years. The white picket fence was no longer the only one, but the large oval of etched and beveled glass that adorned the front door was still one of a kind. Buell could see his reflection as he stood nervously waiting for someone to answer the bell he'd just rung. He glanced over his shoulder at the two carriages tied to the hitching rail and debated the wisdom of being the last to arrive.

Suddenly the door opened, and the space filled with billowing skirts. Irene Kingsley, with her clear skin, high cheekbones, and luxuriant sable hair, had always turned Buell's head, and she was old enough to be his mother. The yellow silk of her dress turned her blue eyes azure, and made the dazzling smile she offered him even whiter.

Informal, my ass. Buell glanced down at his unpolished boots and plain corduroy pants.

"We're so pleased you decided to attend, Buell," she purred. "Come in. The rest are in the back—talking about you."

He winced.

"Serves you right for being late." Another bright smile.

Buell couldn't suppress a sigh.

"Just teasing," she said and squeezed his arm. "C'mon." She made a swishing turn, then walked through the parlor and into the kitchen. Simon's mother, Ana, stood slicing a ham at a counter. "Here he is, Ana, just as I said he'd be."

"Hello, Buell," Ana said. She hesitated a split second, then stepped around the end of a large table and crossed to him. "Let me give you a hug—like I used to." She wrapped her strong arms around his waist, pressed her face into his chest for a moment, then leaned back and touched his cheek. "I'm so pleased you've decided to stay."

The scent of her—cinnamon, soap, fresh bread—kitchen aromas—took him back ten years. Buell had been in Simon's house hundreds of times, and had always been welcome. In stark contrast to Buell's home with just his father, Simon's place was crowded, full of chatter and good cheer—and touching. Buell had seen Ana touch Simon's face, as she'd touched his just now, and every time he'd seen it, he'd felt pain. Her hands were gentle, the gesture sincere, but she wasn't *his* mom—who'd died giving him life—he'd killed her, and Ana's touch was his punishment.

His father had done the best he could, and Buell felt the love, but he had sensed something just below the surface—the affection wasn't quite complete. Always, there was the thin barrier that went up, and it wasn't just his father—almost everybody did it. It was as though they sensed his badness.

"Couldn't miss a grand occasion like this," he said with a wide smile—one he didn't feel.

"Oh, piffle," Mrs. Kingsley scoffed, "a simple picnic. Nothing grand abou—" She whirled on her heel and rushed to the back door. "Sarah! You little vixen. What do you and Simon have up your sleeves?"

Buell grimaced, sidled over to counter by the stove, and started to pour himself a glassful of lemonade from a pitcher.

"Buell!" Sarah shouted from the garden. "Buell Mace, you come out here."

Ana shook her head as he walked past, and offered a wry smile. "I'm going to assume that was just a slip of the tongue," she said.

Slip? Of course it was a slip. Wasn't it? A familiar feeling swept over him and he shrugged. Outside, the carefully cut grass provided a perfect carpet for the two, long, umbrella-covered tables. His father and Ruth sat at the end of one with Judge Kingsley. At the other end sat a surprised-looking Simon. Beside him stood Sarah, hands on hips.

"You told!" She glared at him.

"I . . ." He looked at his father and Ruth, then at the judge and Mrs. Kingsley. "She—I guess I did."

"And I'm glad," Simon said. "Saves me the fidgets I'd have until Sarah told me it was time. We've decided on a December wedding. The twenty-fourth, the day after my folks'."

"Hurrah!" Paul shouted and everyone applauded.

"Bravo," a deep voice said behind him, and Buell turned to face John Lindstrom. Tall and dressed in his habitual black frock coat and brilliant white shirt, he posed a striking figure.

John had been an eastern lawyer who'd come west to drown his past in alcohol. Paul and Ana Steele, and Buell's father, had been the only people in Carlisle who'd treated him with any respect at all. In return for the Steele's kindness, John had staked the Steeles to sixty dollars in gold. It came to light later that John was in fact a very wealthy man. Over the course of years, and sober, he had become a part of the family, and a vital part of all the Steele-Mace business enterprises. He also had the respect and admiration of the whole community.

Mrs. Kingsley went to her daughter and took her by the hand. "He didn't actually *say* the words, Sarah," she said. "He said he was here for a grand occasion, and your announcement is as grand as I can imagine."

"Always knew it would happen," said Judge Kingsley. "I recall all the hours you spent with those books in my library—the dull ones. Remember, Simon?"

"I do, sir. And it turns out the dull ones had the best information."

"Information he was always willing to share—asked or not," Buell scoffed.

Sarah crossed the grass and took Buell's arm, his slip apparently forgiven. "If I thought you did that on purpose, I'd"—she finished in a voice only he could hear, her face turned away from the rest—"I'd have to wonder why, would I not?" She squeezed his biceps, her fingernails digging through his long-sleeved shirt.

Before he could respond, his father and Ruth approached. "We're very pleased for you both, Sarah," Paisley said and nodded at Buell. "Glad to see you here, too, son."

"Indeed," Ruth said, and then turned to Sarah. "Congratulations, dear. Anyone would be proud to claim you as a daughter."

Mrs. Kingsley tapped a silver bell. "All right, everybody, let's eat."

They all lined up, Simon and Sarah first, and attacked the food arranged on the second table. The array started with the ham Ana had been carving, followed by a plate of cold fried chicken, potato salad, warm biscuits, butter, three kinds of jam, pickles, deviled eggs, sugar cookies, and a chocolate cake. Already at work on it, half a dozen yellow-jackets grudgingly gave way to the hungry people. Buell recognized most of the dishes as Mrs. Luger's cooking.

Before Buell realized it, noon had shifted into late afternoon, and his father and Ruth were standing in front of him, already having said their goodbyes to the Kingsleys. John Lindstrom had left early, and Jake had never arrived.

"Paisley tells me you're learning quickly," Ruth said.

"Yes'm. But loadin' and seein' a wagon full of oats go east to Mercer or out to Langdon ain't that hard."

"Oh, I think you do more than that," she insisted.

"Not really. I don't even drive. One of the muleskinners does that."

"You're doing a good job, son," Paisley said, and then nudged Buell in the ribs. "Actually, we're a little insulted you haven't come out for supper yet." Paisley winked. "Just rustlin' ya a bit. You come when you want."

Buell's discomfort was alleviated when Paul and Ana stepped up from behind. "Clear the way folks—Ana's got chickens to tend, and knittin' to do." Paul's cheerful teasing made Buell smile.

Ruth and Ana were sisters, and Ruth's first husband, Matthew, was Paul's brother. Ana had once worked sixteen hours a day tending a small flock of hens, and struggled to keep five children fed, clean, and decently dressed. At the same time, Ruth had lived sumptuously on the original Steele farm with Matthew. John Lindstrom's generosity and perceptive business advice had made Paul's poultry farm thrive and put an end to Ana's drudgery. After Matthew's death, Ruth had married Paisley Mace. Buell smiled to himself and thought—one big, happy family.

"Paisley said you're the best help he's had in years," Paul said.

"What else is he gonna say, Mister Steele?" Buell regretted the remark instantly.

"We must go, Paisley, before the mosquitoes eat us alive," Ruth said curtly, and steered her husband around the corner of the house toward the front.

Ana sighed and put her hand on Buell's arm. "It is good to have both of you home," Ana said. "Please feel welcome at our place any time."

"Thanks, Missus Steele. I'll make it a point to come by for a cup of your famous coffee."

She squeezed his arm, and then she and Paul followed the Maces.

Buell turned to find Simon and Sarah sitting with Judge and Mrs. Kingsley. "Come join us, Buell," Mrs. Kingsley said, and patted the chair beside her.

He shrugged and walked across the garden. "I should leave, too. I reckon you folks have a lot to discuss."

"Don't be silly," Sarah said. "Mother and I have months to plan. We want to hear of your adventures. Simon has told us some really frightening stories, and insists yours are even more so."

Buell caught Simon's eye and rolled his own. "Wasn't much exciting that Simon didn't see. He'll tell ya all about them—

he's a much better storyteller than me."

Sarah put on her best pout. "But he wasn't with you when you were working for that woman in the gold camps. And you actually lived with Chinese?"

"Maybe we'll all sit down some afternoon, and I'll do the best I can. But not today. Today is about you and Simon." He glanced at the walkway leading to the front of the house. "I'll just thank you for the nice—uh, time, and git back home. Got a busy day tomorrow."

"Tomorrow's Sunday," Simon said and grinned. "You're stuck."

"Oh, leave him alone," Sarah said, and got up to stand beside Buell. "I'll walk him to the front. You keep my parents company for a few minutes, Simon."

"Good afternoon, Missus Kingsley." Buell bowed awkwardly, and then turned to the judge. "And you too, sir. I'm glad I came."

"As are we," Mrs. Kingsley said as Buell and the judge shook hands.

Buell felt Sarah's gentle but firm pull on his arm, and he followed her lead across the garden. Lavender scent, her scent, filled the air along the stone walkway, and he couldn't resist inhaling deeply. At the front edge of the house, a large lilac offered a bower, and there Sarah stopped and turned around. She stepped close. "Have you been to the river since you returned? To the place where we all used to picnic and swim?"

Her perfume confused his thoughts, and he found himself studying her soft brown curls. She was as close as she'd ever been to him, near enough for him to see errant wisps of hair shift slightly in the soft still air—spider threads.

"It's still there, you know," she said and looked up at him. "I've been back many times." Her eyes fixed on his, and he marveled at the tiny lines that fanned out at the corners. The same soft lines that creased her lips, lips that trembled ever so slightly before she continued: "It's still green, cool—and private. Just like it was."

Simon! Buell thought, and gasped. "Damn, Sarah, this ain't right." He stepped back until the lilac bush stopped him. "It's you and Simon." He glanced nervously toward the rear of the house. "Always has been." Pushing away from the branches, he stepped around her and into the clear. "I like ya 'n all, but what I think yer thinkin' is wrong." His heart pounded as hard as he could remember, worse than in any barroom fight. "I'd better go." He turned away, and ignoring the gate, straddle-jumped the picket fence. She followed him to the edge of the yard.

"Sometimes wrong can feel so right, Buell," she said as he stripped the reins out of the hitching post's iron ring.

He didn't dare look back as he threw his leg over the saddle. Shadow shouldered Simon's mare out of the way and turned into the road. Buell's heart still raced wildly and he pointed Shadow east, lashing the ends of his reins across the horse's withers.

CHAPTER 6

The Appaloosa had the speed Buell felt he needed. Leaning over the eager horse's neck, he urged the animal down the middle of the road. They barely avoided a carriage that pulled out from a side road, and in less than a minute, passed the last house east of town. Then Buell spotted the Steeles' surrey a quarter of a mile ahead, and without slowing, he eased his right knee into Shadow's shoulder. They shot off the road to the left, leaped a barbed wire fence, and landed in a new wheat field. He guided the horse north, jumped the fence on the far side, and then turned west, into the setting sun. On open ground, Buell gave the horse its head, his own pressed tight against Shadow's neck. Flecks of froth dotted his face and the heat of the animal's breath matched that of his desire.

Paul Steele caught movement out of the corner of his left eye, glanced over his shoulder, and then reined his surrey's horse to a stop.

"What is it?" Ana asked.

Paul turned in his seat. "That's Buell's horse. What's he doing in the middle of the wheat?"

"Are you sure?"

"No doubt about it. He's running like the devil's after 'im."

"I worried about him before the boys left, and I still do," Ana said, craning her neck to get a look. "My, that animal can run."

Paul snorted. "Not doing that spring wheat any good, I can

tell you that. He should know better." They watched until the horse jumped the north-side fence and turned west. Paul flicked a ripple down the reins, and they continued toward home. "Did you get a chance to talk to him at the Kingsleys'?"

"Just for a little bit—in the kitchen. Irene has a knack for saying it all for everybody. I'm sorry, that was shrewish."

Paul chuckled. "Well, someone had to say something. Ruth was sure quiet."

"She's having a hard time understanding why Buell stays in the stable. And I can't say that I blame her. She completely redecorated David's old room for him." Ana shrugged. "I don't know what to tell her."

"He's always been a loner, you know that. I also get the feeling he's kind of disappointed in Mace."

"Paisley, you mean."

"*Mace*, M-A-C-E. He'll always be Mace in my head. You should have seen the look on his face when Buell found out folks called him *Paisley*. Poor boy about choked. I felt sorry for him."

"Because Ruth insists on Paisley? That's silly. What's it matter? Paisley doesn't mind."

"That's where you're wrong. He does."

"Really?"

"Uh-huh."

"Then for goodness sake why doesn't he say something? You would."

"I think that's exactly what Buell was thinking. That the old Mace would have, too."

"Well, I'm just happy Simon is fitting right back in. Have you decided to let him try to do something with Swartz's old place?"

"I think I'll let Simon run it as a store."

"But we don't need two general stores."

"Who said they both have to be general stores? How many

times have you complained about waiting for something to come from Chicago or St. Louis? Like the new sheets and pillowcases you've got on order."

"You think Carlisle could support a store that sold nothing but soft goods?"

"Who better to ask than yourself?"

They rode in silence for a bit, and then Ana asked, "Have you mentioned it to Simon?"

"Not yet." Paul chuckled. "After today, I'm not sure he'll be able to think of anything but December."

Buell let Shadow run for a mile, then slowly eased him into an easy lope. Another half-mile took them to where he and Simon used to practice shooting, and he turned the horse into the trees that lined the river. Apparently the place still served that purpose. Several stumps supported the remnants of shattered bottles, and the glint of empty twenty-two shells marked the firing line. A circle of smooth rocks formed a fire ring off to one side. The area was worn bare except for a few small patches of green close to the water. Buell led the sweating horse to the sparse grass, swung down from the saddle, and dropped the reins on the ground. The dense shade of a sycamore drew him, and he sat down with his back against the blotchy bark. At last, he thought, a familiar place where he could sort some things out, line them all up and take them down one shot at a time.

Nothing in Carlisle had been as he'd expected. He sniffed at the simple thought, picked a thumb-sized branch off the ground, and tested it until it snapped in two. Shadow lifted his head for a moment, then went back to grazing. Everyone Buell had met since he and Simon had returned home had been trouble. Staker was pushing like he always had, but this time Buell was convinced there was something in it for the sheriff. Exactly what that might be was still unclear, but the simple fact that the sheriff wanted to *use* him made his teeth grind.

His pa—*Paisley*—let Ruth Steele, except it was Ruth Mace now, walk all over him at home, like he was a hired hand or something. Buell envisioned his father at the forge, wearing a sleeveless shirt, his arms shiny with sweat, and his brow furrowed in concentration as he danced a heavy hammer on a ringing anvil—*that* was his pa. "Now look at him," Buell said out loud "He doesn't talk, he whines." Ruth had taken over his father's life and left no room for Buell. He skidded the pieces of stick across the bare dirt.

And Sarah. "Green and private," she'd said. He pursed his lips as he mouthed the word "private" and anger warmed his neck. She'd breathed the word, like a saloon whore proposing an upstairs deal. But this was Sarah! Prim-and-proper Sarah, who read small books of poetry. Church-all-day-Sunday Sarah, whose perfect voice in the choir silenced bawling babies and woke old men. Loyal Sarah, who had devoted all her attention to Simon until David's unwanted attention.

Buell leaned his head back against the bark. What happens when Simon finds out—and he will! Buell would offer Sarah no encouragement, but would Simon understand that? Had she given some sign, a hint of some kind? What had he missed in the past? But what if she had? She was Simon's, then and now.

He desperately needed to talk to someone. Simon's mother was out of the question, and his own father had never been able to discuss anything but what Buell *shouldn't* do. That was it, two people, and he could approach neither. He felt left on the outside again, isolated.

Maybe the best thing for him to do was to leave, go down to Texas and see if he could find Lacey or one of the other Texans. He'd come home with Shadow, Arley's mule and camp gear, and the money Arley had left him: over eleven thousand dollars in cash and gold. He could buy into a saloon somewhere. He'd seen a couple of people make good money at that—his kind of people, just-over-the-line-from-respectable kind of people.

Buell looked around the clearing. The shadows had lost their definition in the flat light of the faltering sun. Summer leaves hung limp in the still air, awaiting a breeze to dance on. The nearby river whispered to the shoreline as it passed. Quiet, still, and alone, he swallowed hard and set his jaw against what he felt.

On his way home, Buell circled numerous grain fields and approached Carlisle from the west. He'd seen gaslights in Ogden, Utah, and again in Cheyenne, but the sight of them in the streets of Carlisle still gave him pause. And the brightness inside the saloons was almost an invasion of privacy. He figured it was a little after ten and was surprised at how few people were in the streets. In Idaho City, a man couldn't ride a straight line at this time of night.

He rode past Luger's and took a look inside the nearly deserted room as he did. The sheriff's office across the street showed no light at all. At the next corner he could hear the piano at Lancer's, but not much else. He turned right and rode the half block to the stable.

Inside, Buell lit a lamp, pulled off Shadow's saddle and blanket, and slipped the bridle free. He stood back while the horse shook. "Feels all sticky don't it, boy? Stand there a minute and I'll get a curry comb—loosen that up a little." He lugged his gear into the tack room, found a comb and brush, and went back to the horse.

"Where ya been?" The voice shot a charge up Buell's spine, and he reached for where his pistol usually hung. Simon stood in the doorway of Buell's room.

"Jesus, Simon, scare the hell outta me, why don't ya?" Buell let his breath go with a puff. "Ya coulda said something when I came in."

"I was half-asleep in your chair. I didn't hear ya till something banged on the tack room wall. Hope ya don't mind me goin' in."

"Hell, no. Any time—you know that." Buell went to his horse, stuffed the brush handle in his back pocket, and started to rake Shadow's side with the teethed steel hoops. "What's on your mind?"

"My folks saw you hightailing it across a wheat field right after they left the Kingsleys'."

"Yeah, I guess they did. That field didn't used to be there."

Simon came over to where Buell was working and sat down on a short bench. "And there's something else."

Buell stopped combing and laid his arms across Shadow's back. "Isn't there always?" He studied his friend's face in the lamplight.

Simon looked down at the dirt floor for several seconds, wet his lips, and took a deep breath. "Did you and Sarah have words out front?"

"Like *words*—words?"

"Yeah. When she came back to the garden, her face was red as a sunburned pig. Even her father noticed."

"Nope."

"Don't start your one-word bullshit, Buell!" Simon stood up. "Answer me."

Buell stared at him a moment. "I did, Simon. I'd have thought a simple *nope* was enough—but I can see you ain't gonna be happy with that. She asked if I'd been to the river where we used to go. I told her no. She said she had and it was just like it used to be. Just friendly talk. Then I said I had to go, and I did. Now if she was thinkin' about some of the stuff that went on down there, and got a little wet over it, I don—"

"Wet! Damn it, Buell, this is *Sarah* you're talking about." Simon stood, glaring, jaw thrust forward. "I don't like your—"

Buell abruptly ducked under Shadow's neck to stand face-to-face with Simon. "That's why I like single word answers, Simon. As a matter of fact, it ain't none of your goddamn business what she said to me, and if you weren't my friend"—Buell stuck the curry comb in Simon's face—"I'd probably split yer lip fer askin'."

Simon pushed the tool out the way. "Well, it *is* my business. When the woman I love looks like she—"

"Stop!" Buell put his face inches away from Simon's. "If you say one word that even *hints* I did something I need to be ashamed of, you can quit calling me *friend* in the same breath. Goddammit, Simon, you know I don't get along with women. I don't understand 'em—I don't like 'em around—they've never give me nothin' but trouble 'less I paid for it."

Simon's mouth gaped, and then he swallowed hard. "I was wrong," he muttered.

"*Wrong?* Say it again, Simon, so I can hear ya."

"You've never felt about any woman like I feel about Sarah. I feel I have to protect her—against *anything*. I don't really know what she was—"

"Exactly my point, Simon. You . . . don't . . . know. So guess what? You have to trust I'd never do anything to hurt her. Not because she's Sarah, but because she's yours, and I think of you like a brother."

Simon plopped down on the bench again. "It's hard to keep up with, isn't it?"

"Yep." Buell tossed the comb in the air, caught the handle, and started to work on Shadow again.

"Did you go to the river?" Simon asked.

"Yep."

"To where we used to swim—and stuff?"

Buell chuckled. "You just can't leave it be, can ya? I went to where we used to shoot. The place is just like it was: splattered bottles, the old fireplace, right down to that big sycamore. I sat for a while and thought."

"About what?"

Buell moved to the horse's other side. "Leavin'."

Simon started. "Not *now*, Buell. We just barely got here."

Buell shrugged his shoulders. "And I ain't felt right since we got off the train. I thought it would be good to come home, Simon, I really did, but"—he held up a single finger—"one, my pa ain't the same. Two, you're all tied up with *your* pa's business and Sarah. Three, a man can't stand up for himself without Staker kickin' in the damn door to tell ya about it." A fourth finger joined the other three. "And four, I just think I'd be better off back in Idaho somewhere, or maybe up in the Montana country."

Simon shook his head slowly. "We've done enough of that, don't you think? This is where I need to be, Buell. That's one of the things I learned while we were gone."

" 'Man shouldn't be where he ain't happy, 'cuz there's just too many other places he *can* be.' Remember who said that and why?" Buell asked.

Simon gave him a half-smile. "Tay. I was thinkin' about leaving Laramie when things got a little out of hand. But it's not the same."

"Sure, that's what you'd say when it don't hold up what yer preachin'."

"But I stayed, didn't I—for another year."

"Because what was makin' you unhappy went away. I don't see that happenin' for me here."

"What if it did, Buell? What if things changed just a bit, and you found out you could like it here?" Simon stood up and put his hand on Buell's shoulder. "You said you saw us as brothers.

74

You know I've always felt that too. So I'm asking you like one. Stay here, Buell, at least for a few more months. Let things work themselves out. I feel good about this place. In time, you will too."

Buell leaned his head momentarily against Shadow's neck. "I'll tell ya straight out, Simon, I don't see it. But I'll give it a try."

Chapter 7

The Kansas Jayhawker, the right side of his head bloodied, led the mob. Right behind him, two Indian men, one armed with a shotgun, screamed and shook their fists. Struggling to keep up, a man in miner's boots, his groin and right leg wet with bright blood, cursed and pointed to a mangled body at Buell's feet. The carnage on the floor had been a young Indian boy. More men, their faces vague in the uncertain light, shoved and pushed the rest from behind. They had come for him, and this time he knew they'd have him—knew, because he'd already killed each of them once. He reached for his pistol and fear made his body shrink inside itself—he was stark naked.

"Wha—wha!" Buell bolted upright in bed, the night air instantly cooling his sweat-soaked skin. "Holy shit," he muttered, and swung his feet out of bed. He sat for a while in the darkness. When his heart had slowed to normal, he lay back down. *They never come twice in the same night,* he mentally intoned to the dark room. *They never come twice in the same night.* Over and over he repeated it until the person praying found the courage to sleep again.

Next morning, Sunday, Buell slept until noon, got up and had some coffee and a little hardtack, and then went back to bed for a nap.

Monday morning, he was Mrs. Luger's first customer, and she appeared in the kitchen door the moment the screen door shut behind him. She took one look, went back in, and a minute later set a cup of coffee in front of him. "Thanks, Missus Luger."

"*Ja,* not to church you went Sunday, I think."

"Not for years, Missus Luger. Do you still make buckwheat cakes?"

She rolled her eyes—"The Pope is Catholic, *ja?*"—then crossed herself.

"Those, with ham, and three . . . no, four eggs."

"*Ja, das is gut.*" She squeezed his upper arm and shook her head. "*Der* mouse can have you."

The front door opened to let Sheriff Staker come in. He strode across the floor. "Coffee, Freda, when you bring his food. I've already had breakfast. Can I use the other half of the table, Buell?" He sat before Buell could answer. Mrs. Luger headed back to the kitchen.

"Bit early."

"Saw you come in. Last Monday of the month is city council meeting day. Today's June twenty-six."

"They meet in the mornin'?"

"Nope, this evening. But they expect a report from me." Staker pursed his lips. "Whether anything's happened or not."

Buell sagged back in his chair, his coffee cup cradled in both hands, and shook his head. "Tell 'em no, Sheriff. Buell Mace ain't gonna be the law in Carlisle."

"And you're sure that's why I came in here?"

"Tell me it ain't and I'll believe ya."

Staker chuckled. "I don't know where you got your brass, but it's bright."

"I've been here about six weeks, and after that little disagreement at Lancer's, I ain't seen or heard any trouble."

"Could that be because you haven't been where the trouble is?"

Buell sat forward, nearly spilling his coffee. "Well—I'm—I'll be shot fer lookin'. Who was it come bangin' on my door fer settin' them two camp squatters straight? *You!* And now yer mewlin' 'bout me *not* bein' there. I'm work—"

"All right, all right," Staker said. "You've made your point. I'll just say what I need you to hear. Roscoe was in Lancer's Friday night along with four others from the island. He was talking about what he intended to do when the two of you met again."

"So what's that mean to me? Just proves he's short on memory or long on stupid."

Staker leaned forward and lowered his voice. "This isn't easy to say, Buell. But Lancer sent for me after the five of 'em threatened to shoot the place up. I went over," he paused for several seconds, "and got my bluff called."

"If you *were* just bluffin', serves ya right," Buell said.

"That's exactly what I thought you'd say."

"Then I don't see your point—tellin' me this."

"You're not making it easy. Is that on purpose?"

"It wasn't me that brought it up. How can it be on purpose?"

Staker's eyes narrowed. "It's your nature, son. I don't know why, but you like to see people squirm. You gonna tell me *you* never bluffed?"

"Sure I have."

"Then why are you looking down your nose at *me*?"

"When I bluff, Sheriff, I'm ready to have it called. You weren't." Buell waited for the sheriff to respond, but Staker simply sat there. "Pa used to say, 'Don't kick off the brake unless yer ready to roll,' and I've always tried to remember that. I've seen what can be done with that shotgun you carry—a ten gauge is a lotta bluff. And you said there were five of 'em, together. I reckon you weren't ready. The question is, why?"

"I care for the folks in this town, Buell. Can't you believe that?"

Buell shrugged.

"Doesn't matter if you do or don't—fact is, I do. And that's the reason I've been hounding you about taking my job. It's not for me—or you—it's for them."

Before Buell could respond, Mrs. Luger burst out of the kitchen, her behind banging the door open. She hustled over to the table, put two overfilled plates in front of Buell, and a cup of coffee before Staker. "Eat before is *nicht* hot, *ja*," she said, then turned and left.

Buell picked up his fork, then put it back down. "I don't think I owe this town a damned thing. Maybe you've forgotten how I was treated before Simon and I left. I haven't. Simon seems to be okay with it, and that's his business. He's always been the forgive-and-forget kind. I'm not. I've been thinking about that city council of yours, and their stupid idea to take away a man's pistol. Do they think for one second that bunch from the island is gonna give 'em up? Every one of the dumb bastards on that council needs his nose bent by a couple *citizens* like Roscoe and Meat." Buell snatched up his fork. "There, I've said enough to last me all damn day, and now I'm gonna eat this."

Staker sat for a few seconds, and then stood. "Someday, you're gonna need someone, Buell. Who're you gonna call on?" He dropped a dime on the table and left the café. Buell never looked up.

Buell tried to use the day's work to forget the sheriff's last words, but they were still very much on his mind when he ticked off the final freight item. A stocky man loading the wagon put the keg of nails down and looked back hopefully. "That's it, Walt. Lift the tailgate and close it up. Looks like we can get this off to Bedell's ranch today." Buell went to the office at the end of the dock and stepped inside.

Paisley sat at a large oak desk, sleeves rolled up to his elbows, studying a newspaper. He looked up when Buell entered. "Problem?"

"Nope. Got Bedell's stuff loaded."

Paisley glanced at the wood-cased clock on the wall. "It's only nine-thirty. Did you get it all?"

Buell dropped the two-page order on the desk. "I guess you can go check."

"No, no—I just mean, that's real fast. There was just you and Walt, right?"

Buell picked up the order again. "Do you want it to go today?"

"Well, yeah, if you're willing to ride along. The first of the other five outfits isn't due back till about noon so there's nobody to help Walt unl—"

"I'll go. Nothing to do here until I have a wagon."

Paisley's chair creaked as he leaned back in it. "You get a lot more work out of them than I can, son, I'll give ya that."

"We just move a piece at a time, Pa."

"Well, proof's right there." Paisley pointed at the order. "Bedell was expectin' that tomorrow, and the other crews are on a run—all of 'em. First time that's happened. Keep that up and I'll have to buy another couple rigs." He chuckled, and then his expression changed. "How's it goin', son? A person would never know we work in the same place as often as we talk."

"Goin' all right. I work and sleep. Not much to talk about."

"I told ya I was gonna run for mayor. Maybe you could tell me what ya think of that."

"I already said I was surprised." Buell shrugged. "Can't say much more."

"Well, then, maybe we could just talk about you and me."

The look in his father's eyes made Buell uncomfortable. "Tell ya what. If I get back early enough, I'll come out to the house, and we can sit outside and rag on a bone."

"Really?" Paisley smiled. "I'll ask Ruth if she'd mind frying some chicken, and maybe make that gravy you like. Remember—"

"Don't have her make anything. I just want to sit on the porch and talk a little bit."

"But Ruth—"

"We'll just sit. Okay? On the porch."

"Sure, son. Just sit and talk, like ya say." Paisley nodded, his smile a little tighter.

Buell took his pistol belt from a peg on the wall and buckled it on. "I'll git out to Bedell's then," he said and left.

Outside, he found Walt sitting on the dock having a smoke. The man grabbed his hat off the bench and stood. "Looks like you and me," Buell said as he climbed into the driver's seat. Walt scrambled up beside him. "Show me where that Bedell outfit is, Walt. I need to get out of this goddamn town—at least for a while."

CHAPTER 8

The Bedell ranch lay fourteen miles east of Carlisle and three miles south of the Platte River. Ruben Bedell ran cattle on a twenty-five-hundred acre ranch that he'd established when Nebraska was still a territory. He'd acquired the land by helping his hired hands file for homesteads, on which Bedell would then build a line shack and dig a well. They'd partially seed each plot with Timothy grass, then graze it, or cut and store the hay, thereby "proving" the claim over the required five years.

As soon as the land office granted a patent on the property, Bedell would offer to buy the land for what a cowhand could earn in three years. Not one had ever turned him down, and many still worked on the ranch. Buell had only seen Bedell once, at the office in Carlisle. Though they hadn't spoken, Buell had taken a liking to him. He was from New Mexico Territory, but his brusque and direct manner reminded him of the Texans he'd known as a youngster.

The compound lay in the bottom of a shallow basin. A small stream ran in from the south, flowed down the east side, and into a reservoir half a mile north of the house. The main buildings covered about two acres and consisted of six structures: a west-facing two-story stone house, a blacksmith's shop with a bunkhouse west of it, and a large stable with two enormous lofted barns a hundred yards northeast. Flower beds graced the sides of the residence, and young maple trees grew alongside the quarter-mile lane leading into the front yard. Walt swung the wagon in a wide-looping turn and pulled to a stop at the porch steps.

Ruben Bedell waited for them on the veranda. The confidence in his stance made him appear taller than the five-foot-seven he stood. Hatless, he was dressed in worn corduroy trousers and a collarless, blue cotton shirt. Only his boots suggested his status: dark brown and highly polished, intricate stitching peeking from below his trouser cuffs. "Didn't expect to see you till tomorrow."

"We got a good start, sir."

"All right." He pointed at the wagon bed. "About a quarter of that goes in the house, so leave it parked where it is." Bedell looked toward the blacksmith shop and let out a shrill whistle. A moment later, a man wearing a leather apron stepped into view. "Find a couple hands and unload this wagon," Bedell shouted, and then beckoned to Buell. "Climb down, and come sit on the porch."

"I'll help unload this, Mister Bedell. It all comes with the deal."

"Bullshit, you're Paisley Mace's son. That makes you the straw boss. C'mon." Bedell nodded his head. "I don't get to talk to you town folks much."

Buell climbed down the wheel and followed the rancher along the covered porch to the shade on the north side of the house. There, Bedell sank into one of a pair of wide leather chairs that flanked a low table, and pointed to the other. "Take a load off."

"This feels pretty good after fifteen miles on that wagon." Buell stretched out his legs.

"A ride like that will try your patience."

"Didn't know if you'd remember me or not."

"Oh, yeah, I remember seeing you. Your name's Buell. A couple of my men were in Lancer's place when you stood up to those two island misfits. Not many have tried *that*." Keen interest showed in Bedell's eyes.

"So I've heard," Buell said quietly. "Pa said you come from New Mexico. What's it like there?"

"Hot. Desolate. I don't recommend it."

"Then why'd ya go there?"

"My folks were on their way to California when their oxen got into some bad water and died just outside of Albuquerque. They didn't have the money to buy a new team, so they stayed. I was born there in twenty-one. I understand you've seen some pretty wild country, too."

"A little. A friend and I went to Fort Laramie for a while. We worked for a fella that run a whorehouse and saloon for about five years. Then we split up, and I went to a gold town in Idaho Territory for a couple years."

"Just a minute." Bedell reached back and banged on the wall. "Wu!" he shouted. A few seconds later, a stooped and wrinkled Chinese man hurried out a side door to stand before them. Dressed in a dark smock and cloth slippers, he bowed slightly at the waist. The man's black eyes lingered on Buell for a moment before he turned his attention to the rancher. "We need something to drink," Bedell said. "What'll you have, Buell?"

"Lu cha', da' xie'," Buell said.

The Chinese man started, then stared at Buell for a couple of seconds before letting go a burst of firecracker Chinese, gesturing wildly.

"Whoa," Buell said and put up his hands. "I used half the words I know in Mandarin."

Bedell chuckled. "Serves you right for showing off. But I'll admit, you impressed the hell out of him. What did you say anyway?"

"I said I wanted green tea."

"Cha' is light, he ask tea," the Chinese man said, and dipped his head toward Buell. "He say Chinese!"

"Coffee for me, Wu," Bedell said.

The small man gave Buell a wide smile, and hurried back into the house.

"I gather there were some Chinese at that camp?"

"Quite a few. I learned to like their food."

"Whorehouse at Fort Laramie, mining town in Idaho— couple of rough places. Is that where you got to be so handy with that fancy Remington?"

"Don't know that I'm all that handy."

"Oh, you're quick. Word gets around." Bedell leaned back and studied him.

The scrutiny made Buell uncomfortable. "It's not something I set out to learn."

"But it made the difference at Lancer's, didn't it?"

"Ya might say. Look, Mister Bedell I—"

"Call me Ruben."

"I don't look for trouble like—"

"But according to the boys, you didn't so much as blink."

"When it gets like that, blinkin' ain't a good idea."

Bedell laughed out loud and slapped his knee. "Not a good idea." He continued to chuckle—all the while studying Buell. "No indeed. Have you thought about doing anything here besides the freighting business?"

"Nothing wrong with what I'm doing," Buell said more sharply than he meant to.

"I'm not sayin' there is, but a talent like that can be very useful out here."

"Seems lots of folks think that."

"You know what makes a hen cluck, Buell. Can I call you Buell? She knows there's something goin' on, but can't get her eye on it. I've got that kind of trouble. If you hadn't come out with this shipment, I was going to come in and talk to you. I'm losing about a dozen head a month on my east range. I sent some riders out last month to stop it, and lost two of 'em—one dead. The county sheriff's not much good because he really doesn't care to be, and Sheriff Staker doesn't have jurisdiction. I need some help—your kind of help. I can pay real good."

"What do you mean the sheriff doesn't *care* to?"

"Just that. We managed to catch one of them rustlers. He told us some real interesting things before he . . . ran out of breath. It appears the sheriff's good offices have been bought and paid for by someone. I haven't figured out who, though I think I know why. It means protecting what I have is up to me."

Wu pushed open the screen door and came out with a tray. He set it on the table, unloading two cups and saucers, a silver sugar and creamer set, and two pots. "Cha'," he said to Buell, and pointed at the squat, white one. He then put down two spoons, gave a quick bow, and left.

"One other thing," Bedell said as he picked up the taller pot. "Last winter we lost a supply shipment just before the snow set in. The men with it said six riders stopped them in the road, told 'em to get down, and then drove off with the wagon. I've got a good idea where it went, but no way to prove it."

"You figure that bunch on Sandy Island took it, don't you?"

"You know the place?"

"I know of it. Looked it over after my little talk with those two at Lancer's."

"Then you can see why it wouldn't be smart to go see for myself."

Buell picked up the teapot and poured his cup full. It smelled good. "I can. I met two of them. Hard-lookin' men." He took a sip.

"Well, what do you say?"

"Not my fight, Mister Bedell."

"Damn, I was afraid you'd say that. Don't take me wrong— but is it because you don't care for cowmen?" Bedell fixed his eyes on Buell when he asked the question.

"Hell, no! Why would you think that?"

"The farmers here'bouts don't care for us ranchers."

"I ain't heard that. Why?"

"We both need the ground, and they think grazing cows on land that can be plowed is a waste."

"This is a big place."

"That's how I see it too. They don't."

Buell took another drink and then set his cup down. Memories of Idaho City flickered in the back of his mind. "Still ain't any of my business. Once before I got between some folks with serious differences. Got nothin' from it but bad memories. I swore I wouldn't do it again."

Bedell sighed, glanced at his coffee, and then ignored it. "I guess I can see your point. I was just hopin' to find . . . I don't know, someone with the *cojones* to back me up."

"I've seen half a dozen men since I got here. You don't need any help."

"They're not gunfighters, they're cowmen."

"And I'm a freighter, Mister Bedell. I've seen too many *dead* gunfighters."

"Wasn't any harm in askin', was there?"

"No, sir. There wasn't."

"Will you stay for dinner? Wu is a good cook."

"Thanks fer the invite, but we've got some eats in the wagon. I'd like to get back well before supper."

"Let's finish our coffee, then, Mister Mace." Bedell picked up his cup and saluted Buell. "It's always good to sit and talk to someone new."

CHAPTER 9

As he'd hoped, Buell made it back to town before supper. By seven o'clock the horses had been unharnessed and put away in the barn south of the stable. His back hurt, his head ached, and his clothes looked like he'd spent the day in a badger's hole. Even his teeth felt dusty. He crossed the paddock to the livery, took off his shirt and hat, and dipped his upper body in the horse trough's tepid water. Submerged, he scrubbed his head and shoulders vigorously for as long as he could hold his breath. With a gasp, he stood, slicked the water out of his hair, and went inside.

Half an hour later, Buell pinned the last elusive bean to the rim of his enameled plate, smashed it with a piece of bread, and ate it. He didn't feel like going out—he eyed the soft chair for a few seconds, and then went into the stable. Shadow turned to look. "Is it worth putting a saddle on you?" Buell went over to his horse and patted him on the rump. "We'll go for a ride tomorrow—promise."

He strolled the half-block to Main Street and turned left, sweat already sticking his clean shirt to his back. By the time he'd covered the first block, he was reconsidering his decision to plod the three-quarters of a mile to Matt Steele's farm. He could not yet think of it as his father's.

At the corner he paused and looked towards Lancer's. A dozen horses, heads drooping, dozed while their swishing tails kept a swarm of flies in the air. He was about to move on when one animal snorted and backed up a little. He recognized the tawny, long-legged buckskin; Bachman, the Weasel, was in town. *Mind your own business,* his common sense warned. *Just today you told Bedell it wasn't your fight.* He let the thought linger, hating the feeling that he was walking away from something, yet relieved he had no obligation to go challenge anyone; not his fight.

Fifteen minutes later he stopped in the road, the old Steele homestead silhouetted in the bursting orange of the setting sun. Two stories tall, a covered porch protected the first-story windows on the north side of the house. When he'd left seven years ago, it had been painted all white. Now, at least five colors made the exterior glow: red, brown, moss green, and yellow with purple accents in the gingerbread trim at the eaves. Light from inside the house spilled onto the porch through two five-foot windows. The left one illuminated his father sitting in a rocking chair beside a round, cloth-draped table. Buell went up the flagstone walkway and climbed the stairs. "Hi, Pa."

"I'm glad you came out, son. Sure a nice night, and the mosquitoes haven't found out yet. Come and sit down." He motioned to another rocker, and then turned his head toward the open door. "Ruth, Buell is here."

A moment later she hurried out of the house. "Oh, it's nice to see you again," she said with a smile. "I only wished you'd let me make supper for all of us. It's no trouble, really."

"I'm grateful for the offer . . . uh—"

"Call me Ruth, Buell, like your father does."

"Okay—Ruth. I'm not used to much more than a plate and a fork. In fact, I ain't been in a proper home for years. Let some of my bad manners wear off a little, and I'll take ya up. But not just yet."

"You're being silly, but I can wait. It's just that I loved cooking for David"—her face changed—"before he was taken from me," she quietly finished.

"But, I *love* your cooking," Paisley protested.

"I know you do." She waved her hand at him. "But you don't count."

Buell sought the word that could describe her manner, and his scalp tingled when it came. Toleration. *She barely tolerates him.*

"I'll go get you something to drink," Ruth said, and went back into the house.

Twitches in Paisley's lower lip belied the cheerful words that followed a few seconds later. "So, how was the trip out to Bedell's?"

"Like I expected. Long, hot, and dusty. He was friendly enough."

"Oh, he can be that when he wants to. He can also be hard as flint." His father's mouth tightened.

"In his business, that can be the difference 'tween standin' up and layin' flat on yer back."

"Times have changed, son. He's got to learn to share. Not everybody can live on the same patch of dirt."

"He's not exactly on the *same* patch, Pa. He's another hour past where you and Simon's pa grazed those cows for the army."

John Lindstrom had seen an opportunity to buy cattle: herds blockaded by the Union Army in southeast Kansas during the war. He had them trailed into Nebraska, beating by months the Texas herds the army usually bought. The scheme had worked, and the result financed the beginning of Paul Steele and Paisley Mace's success.

"It's not that patch I'm concerned with. It's that piece he managed to buy just outside town. It's perfect for grain and corn, and the farmers ain't gonna be happy when he puts a four-hundred-acre feedlot in it. Neither are the folks who live on the northwest side of town."

"If he owns it, how can anyone stop him, Pa? He's a *cattle-man*."

"And that's the *problem*!" Paisley spit out the last word. "And I don't need another problem. Speaking of which"—Paisley leaned forward and lowered his voice—"don't bring up David again."

"Huh? *I* didn't."

"Shhh." Paisley shook his head emphatically. "Doesn't matter—it upsets Ruth."

Buell slumped back in his chair.

Paisley continued: "I think there's room for both sides. Bedell should be allowed to conduct his affairs like every other landowner. Enough of that. Has Simon told you Paul's going to let him run Swartz's old place?"

"Nope. When's that gonna happen?"

"I'd think pretty soon. Carlisle is doubling every two years. We need businesses, and Simon seems to have a knack for running one."

"I can vouch for that. He took a three-whore crib and turned it into a fancy saloon that made his boss a rich man—and he did it in five years."

"He said it was a restaurant."

"That's Simon. What the hell would you expect him to say?" Buell grinned.

Paisley grimaced and glanced at the open door.

"Is she *that* tender, Pa? I said hell, not *Goddammit* to hell."

"Buell!" Paisley said in a harsh whisper.

"All right. I'll work on it. But it's ridiculous. How's your mayor thing workin' out?"

"Oh! You really want to know?" Paisley scooted his rocker around to face Buell more directly. "I think I've got most of the important folks leanin' my way. Doc Princher is being salty, but he always is . . . about everything. I'm a little surprised Paul hasn't come right out and told me he's on my side. But then again, he's always been cautious. I get the distinct impression he's waiting to see what Lindstrom says. What do you think, Buell? Your grimy old iron-bender pa the mayor of Carlisle? Never mind, I know what you think."

"Do ya, now? Dammit, Pa, does everybody know what I'm thinking *all* the time?" Buell snorted. "Staker knows I'd make a good sheriff, Simon knows I'll grow to like it here, you know what I think about everything—and even today, a total stranger asked me to work for him, knowin' I wouldn't. What the hell is it about me that I can't have a *private* thought?"

"Do you really want me to tell you?"

"I suppose you might as well—I can't know for myself."

Paisley chuckled. "How many talks have we had that ended about here? Dozens? Hundreds? The difference then was, you wouldn't say five words. I had to try and figure out what you were thinking. I got real good at it. Since you were old enough to talk, you haven't. Words dribbled out of you a word or two at a time. Simon had to do the same thing—figure what you was thinkin'—and so did the sheriff. Everyone did."

"I learned to talk listening to you. Ya never had much to say to me."

"I suppose you're right. But we did have a feel for each other, didn't we?"

"I could tell when you were gettin' mad." Buell smiled. "I worked real hard on that."

"Those were simpler times, son. Sometimes I miss 'em."

"Miss what?" Ruth said as she backed through the door. She carried two tall yellow-tinted glasses and a matching pitcher. "I made some fresh lemonade." She set the glasses on the table and poured them full before handing one to Paisley. "We're almost out of ice."

"Thank you, Ruth. We were jawing about when Buell was a

youngster. How he didn't say much when there was just me and
. . . I'll remember the ice tomorrow." Paisley tipped his glass
and took a long drink.

"I'll leave the pitcher." Ruth turned on her heel, and went
back inside.

"Damn, Pa. Is it like that all the time?"

Paisley peered over the glass for several seconds, sighed, and
put it on the table. "Some days. I think you and Simon coming
home set it off bad."

Buell reached for his drink. "I'm sorry. You seemed so happy
when I come home for the wedding."

"We were. And are," he added hastily. "What blows in, blows
out eventually."

"I take it she won't be back out then?"

"I expect not. Best just leave things as they are for now."

They sat in the cool of the evening and talked. More exactly,
Paisley talked and Buell listened. The strain of growing with a
business when he was ill-prepared for the job weighed heavily
on Paisley Mace. Most of his decisions had been made only
after consultation with John Lindstrom or Paul Steele, or both.
But, running for mayor was all Paisley's idea. His election was
almost assured, because talking to people was what Paisley
Mace did best. And first and foremost in Paisley's mind was the
prospect that Ruth would be proud *with* him. His father was
still the honest, hardworking man Buell had known. But now, it
seemed his father's own sense of worth took second place to
rebuilding Ruth's.

Buell stifled a yawn. "I'm about shot."

"And I've sat here and bored a hole in yer head."

"No. I've enjoyed it, but I'd better get back."

"It has been nice, son. Let's do it again soon."

Buell stood and put his hat on. "Well, if nothin' else, ya
convinced me to vote for ya." He went down the steps, along

the walkway, and then turned to give his father a brief salute before stepping into the road and heading for town.

Ruth looked up from her tatting as Paisley gently closed the screen door. "Well, you *two* seemed to enjoy yourselves."

He didn't miss the emphasis. "Truth be known, I'd say one of us enjoyed it." He lowered himself into his soft chair.

"I simply can't understand what that boy has against me." Ruth dropped both hands into her lap, holding her work tightly.

"Oh, Ruth, I've told you a hundred times, he's that way to everyone—always has been. I thought maybe being away from here might have knocked some of the rough edges off. It seems he's just toughened up more." He looked at her and shrugged. "That doesn't make him a bad person, does it?"

"I've known tough men with rough edges, Paisley, lived with them—in spite of them, even. Were they bad?" She looked down at her hands and took a deep breath. "I won't say," she said as she raised her head. "I will say this—I won't tolerate men who're like them."

Paisley's scalp reacted to the chill that crept over it. Ruth's son, David, had been a brute. He'd almost killed her once, and beaten her more times than Paisley dared to guess. Her husband had been David's very able mentor. Mathew had never harmed her physically. Worse, he'd constantly belittled, insulted, and browbeat her, slowly but surely destroying her soul. His early grave had been a blessing for everyone, no exceptions. "Buell will come around, Ruth. He has a good heart. It's just hard for him to show it sometimes."

"I'd settle for once," Ruth said, and picked up her needlework again.

Buell had gathered a lot to think about over the last three hours, and used the quiet stroll from his pa's place to do just that. He did notice that the streets of Carlisle were empty again, and soon turned the corner to walk the short distance to the stable. Apparently his father missed the closeness they'd had in the two small rooms they'd once shared. Buell reached the front of the building and paused. Maybe his father's silence about the mother and wife they both missed—for markedly different reasons—was simply self-defense. He had the distinct feeling that his father was being overwhelmed by something, and had just asked for help. He lifted the latch and pulled the door open.

He felt the weight of his pistol leave his hip, and at the same time, pain, as someone knocked his hat off and grabbed a handful of hair. A moment later he lay prone on the dirt floor with someone sitting on the back of his head, his face forced into the dust. Rough hands yanked his own behind his back. "Tie the bastard good, Ned."

Soft leather bit into his wrists, and then came more pain as his elbows were bound tightly together. Someone at his feet did the same to his ankles. Bright light flashed behind his eyes and his ears started to ring as his breath ran out. Consciousness started to fade, and then they jerked him off the floor and dragged him across it to a center post.

Hemp rope burned his skin as they lashed him, arms and legs, to the heavy timber. He gasped as cold water hit his face, and his eyes flew open. They clamped shut instantly against the sting of the grit that invaded them. Blinking furiously, he struggled to make sense of his situation. Then he heard the squawk of a lifting lantern chimney, and saw the flare of a match.

"Told ya I'd see ya agin," Roscoe said, and poked Buell hard in the stomach with the barrel of the Remington. "Remember?" The hammer ratcheted back, and Buell's head snapped to the rear as the muzzle dug under his upper lip. "Sure a purty pistol ya got here. Ivory grips 'n all." Roscoe's breath reeked of sour beer and tobacco.

Buell fought to see past the tears of his dirt-filled eyes, and for a second felt panic. Over Roscoe's shoulder he made out a blurry Ned, and one other man. Then he felt rage at his own stupidity. He'd seen a horse he'd recognized. He should have gone to Lancer's and at the very least taken a look. Instead, he'd decided to keep his nose out of Staker's business, and now that *business* was about to get even.

"Ned here wants to cut your nuts off, cowboy." Roscoe twisted the barrel and the front sight cut into Buell's gums. "Whatcha think?"

Buell's vision improved as the tears flowed, and he could see the smiling face of the black man. "Tol' ya one day you don' have no gun. 'At's today." He chuckled softy, and showed Buell a knife—the same crude blade he'd seen before.

"Bachman said you was real interested in coming out for a visit. We waited, but ya never showed up. Not very friendly, Mace." Another jab with the cold steel.

"Why don't we take him with us now," the third man said. He stepped closer to the lamp where Buell could see him more clearly. Young, probably not more than sixteen, and his eyes glinted eagerly in the yellow light. "We could have some fun." He licked his lips, and then wiped them with the back of his hand. "Ned says he's skinned a feller before. I'd like to see that."

"Shut up, Scrawny," Roscoe growled, "before ya piss yerself." He lowered the pistol, then drew it back and laughed out loud when Buell winced. Roscoe turned to Ned. "See, the son of a bitch can blink, jist like the rest of us. What ya wanna do, Ned? Mess him up here, or throw his cocky ass on that fancy horse of his and take him to the island?" Roscoe squinted at the Negro and then sniggered. "You really skinned a man before?"

For the first time, fear crept into Buell's consciousness, and he turned his face away from it. Arley had told him of a miner the Blackfeet had caught stealing a horse. The Indians had staked the man spread-eagle in the sun and sliced inch-wide strips of skin from his shoulders to his groin. Then, they'd cut his eyelids off and left him. Arley had found the remains after several eagles had taken what they wanted, which included the man's eyes. The image brought on a numbness that dimmed his vision and dried his mouth.

"Drop the pistol, Roscoe." Staker's voice was calm and perfectly clear.

Buell's head snapped around and he nearly choked at the sight of the sheriff's massive, twin-barreled shotgun. The Remington thudded into the dirt.

"You should have closed the door," Staker said. "Ned, same with the knife. And you, Colson, turn around so's I can see you clear."

The skinny kid's hands shot over his head, and he spun to face the sheriff. "We ain't done nothin', Sheriff—*I ain't.*"

"I told ya to shut yer mouth, Scrawny!" Roscoe barked at him.

"Likewise, Roscoe," Staker said and took a step forward. "I've half a mind to just shoot ya—all three of ya. Now get away from him before I quit *thinkin'* about it."

Roscoe and Ned backed up several steps to stand beside the boy. Staker, his short-barreled weapon never wavering, went over and picked up Ned's knife. A second later, Buell's hands slipped free, and then his arms. His fingers started to tingle, and he rubbed his palms together. "Gimme that shotgun, and I'll watch 'em while you get my feet."

"I've got my eye on 'em," Staker said and squatted.

Buell's body flashed cool as he stepped away from the post. He picked up his pistol.

Staker grabbed him by the arm. "I *can* shoot 'em, Buell—you can't."

"They had every intention of spillin' my guts!"

"And didn't. Are you hurt? Your mouth's bleeding a little."

"No. But—"

"Then it's common battery, same as a saloon fight. We can feed them for a week, or—"

Buell jerked his arm free, and leveled his Remington at the boy. "That crazy little bastard there wanted to see me skinned. And that black sumbitch was gonna do it!"

"Wanted and was . . . didn't happen. I can go out and come back later, Buell." Staker, shotgun still trained on the three men, stepped in front of him. "Git outta here, Roscoe, and the next time I see you, you'd better be sober and on the other side of the street."

They slowly backed to the open door where the boy bolted, leaving Roscoe and Ned to saunter into the darkness.

"You know they're gonna try that again!" Buell shouted. "Christ, Staker, we could have had it out right here."

"It's not *we*, Buell. I'm the law, and I stopped what I saw. I can't do more than that. Count your blessings. I'm not usually out and about this time of night. Now I'm going to go home." He slung the shotgun under his arm and headed for the door. His hand on the latch, he turned around and let out a deep sigh. "And you're welcome." He stepped into the night, leaving the door open.

CHAPTER 10

In the ten days following his confrontation with Roscoe, Buell had made it a point to be in Lancer's every night for a couple of hours. Three or four rough-looking men had come in, caught his eye briefly, but nothing had come of it.

Tonight, he stood at the bar in Luger's, the saloon nearly empty, usual, as he'd learned, for Thursday after about ten-thirty.

"Wanna go fishin' with me Sunday?" Jake asked, and leaned his elbow on the bar, chin in hand.

"I ain't done that since we was kids," Buell replied. "I don't even have a pole that I know of."

"I got several. What do ya say?"

"You still go by that big cottonwood snag?"

"Nope. That finally washed out, but I found another place just as good for shade and grass."

"Ya catch many?"

"Never."

"What'n hell ya go for then?"

Jake curled his upper lip as his eyes sought the ceiling. "To fish?"

"I guess makin' kindling ain't always the reason for splittin' wood."

"Huh?" Jake grunted.

"Something someone told me once. Didn't make sense till just now." Buell shook his head and chuckled quietly as he remembered Tay Prescott's wise face. "Yeah, I'll go fishin', Jake. Maybe we can get Simon to come along."

"Ya think he'll wanna bring Sarah, like he used to?"

"I don't think so."

"Good. She was always a pain in the ass—to everyone."

"Now why do you say that?" Buell said, too quickly.

"Didn't mean no offense."

"I know that, and ain't none taken, but I never got that idea. Everyone?"

"Everyone we went to school with. You didn't see that?"

"I guess I never bothered to look."

"She jerked Simon around like a mutt on a sock." Jake glanced down the bar and stood. "I'll be right back."

Like a mutt on a sock. A mutt? Buell pictured a prim Sarah Kingsley. She had been as pampered as Simon had been deprived. As a matter of fact, back then, there were only two kids besides Sarah who had more than one pair of shoes: David Steele and Gus Swartz. So why had Sarah been attracted to Simon? He was interesting, and smart as hell, but of all the kids in school, he stood the least chance of being someone. And even then, to Buell's way of seeing things, being important mattered to Sarah. Buell smiled to himself. Being someone important—ain't. Tay Prescott speaking again.

Then Jake returned. "I'm gonna close up—those two down there are done."

Buell glanced up at the mirrored backbar as two men left the saloon. "Yeah, good idea. I've got two wagons to load tomorrow. I'll talk to Simon, Jake. Might be good to spend a day on the river." He pushed away from the bar and headed for the door.

"Ain't no such thing as a bad day fishin'. 'Night, Buell."

★ ★ ★ ★ ★

Buell had just checked off the last item on an order when Simon bounded up the steps to the dock. "Have you heard?" he asked breathlessly.

Buell wiped his brow with his sleeve. "I guess not."

"General Custer got killed Monday—his whole command was wiped out! Several thousand Sioux and Cheyenne ambushed them in Montana Territory. I thought we had a peace treaty with the Cheyenne!"

"So did the Cheyenne. You know how that works, Simon."

"You'd think they could find a better way to settle things than just killing each other."

"Still lookin' for the posies in the pig shit, aren't ya? The Indians are a nuisance, and the damned army don't like nuisances. They thought I was one, remember?"

"Still, makes me sick."

"Do they have the details yet?"

"Not all. The army was trying to get the Indians back on their reservations, and the Seventh Cavalry under Custer were all killed in one battle. Reports say they fought against ten *thousand* Indians."

"Now even *I* ain't *that* dumb, Simon. Remember that beating I told you about. When that saloonkeeper caught me asleep in the way station at Eagle Rock? I told you six or seven men come after me with wagon spokes or something. Well, it *felt* like seven—more than likely it was two or three. And I know it sounds contrary, but anybody who can kick the army's ass has got my nod."

"I wouldn't say that too loud, Buell. Folks are upset about this."

"They don't ask, I ain't gonna volunteer an opinion."

"I wouldn't, if I were you."

"And you ain't." Buell then quickly added, "So who's got the luck?"

Simon started to speak, stopped, and then smiled: "That's a tricky question."

"Ain't it. I was gonna come find you today anyhow, so it's handy you stopped by. I'm going fishin' with Jake on Sunday—all damn day. Wanna come?"

"Oh." Simon winced. "That might pose a problem. I usually go to church at eleven with Sarah."

"Usually? That means you ain't said for sure."

"Well . . . no."

"Good. You can come with us, then. Settled."

"I better ask her if—"

"*Ask?* I don't remember exactly what that poem I was supposed to have wrote said, but ain't there something in there about 'without asking a wife'? You ain't married yet, Simon. Ya better stomp a few anthills while ya still got yer balls."

Simon grimaced, looked into the street, then at his shoes.

"Well, grocery boy, make up yer mind." Buell leered at him. "Ya gonna fish 'r fornicate?"

"Damn it, Buell! We're not—"

"Aw, hell, I know yer not. Don't be so proddy. C'mon, we'll bring a couple buckets of beer, some cigars, and I'll have Missus Luger make us some of her ham and pickle sandwiches."

"Okay. That sounds like fun. Let's bring something to shoot too. Yeah, this is sounding better and better."

"Good. Come by my place about eight, and I'll have a rig ready."

"A wagon?"

"Ever tried to carry a bucket of beer on a horse?"

Buell had always maintained that Sunday mornings were made for sleeping. That's what he was doing, solidly, when his bed covers flew off. He bolted upright.

"Ya lazy dog," shouted Simon. "Have a rig ready, you said. Git up!"

Buell sank back against his pillow and dug knuckles into his eyes. "Ain't no call for that, Simon. Shit!"

"Simon's right," Jake hollered from the other room. "Let's get going."

Buell swung his legs out of bed, and Simon threw a pair of pants at him, followed by a shirt. He stifled a yawn and stood.

"We'll be over to Missus Luger's," Simon said. "Too late to make coffee here."

"You two ain't gonna help me harness the horse?" Buell protested as he hopped on one leg to get the other into his pants.

"Nope. C'mon, Jake."

"This is bullshit and you know it, Simon!" Buell shouted as the door shut.

Five minutes later he barged out of the stable to find Simon and Jake waiting in the wagon outside.

"For being late, you get to ride in the back," Jake crowed.

"The beer?"

"Got it, and our lunch, the poles, a couple rifles—everything. Git on," Simon said, and then hefted a tall, square-sided enameled cup. "Got you coffee and some biscuits."

Buell hopped over the short tailgate and scooted to the front. "I guess I owe you a thanks."

"Damn right ya do," replied Jake. "Ready?"

Buell stretched his legs out and leaned against the side. "Yeah, let's go fishin'."

The place by the river was new to Buell. A gentle slope led down to a flat and grassy bottom, shaded by healthy cottonwoods and willows. The river eddied in a sharp bend, the perfect place to slowly circle a cork bobber. The fishing had been as Jake promised, futile. They took full advantage, talking constantly throughout the morning. When the sun was well past overhead, they'd eaten Mrs. Luger's enormous meal, drunk a bucket of beer, and stretched out in the shade for a two-hour nap.

Buell sat up and stretched just in time to see Jake striding towards him along the riverbank. "Where's Simon?" He got to his feet.

"Moving the horse." Jake jerked his head toward the trees behind them, and then pointed at four dangling horseshoes. "Forty paces. If that's too far for ya, I can move 'em in a little." He grinned.

"That'll do." Buell picked up one of the two rifles leaning against a tree. It was a new Remington. "Whose is this?"

"Simon's. Mine's the Springfield."

"I haven't shot it yet," Simon said, just then walking into the clearing. "Picked it up yesterday at Pa's store." Buell held it out to him. "Nope," said Simon. "Remember that old thirty-six navy you got when you weren't supposed to have one? The one we got caught shooting?"

"Like it was yesterday." Buell chuckled. "Hell to pay for that, huh?"

"Well, you did me a favor and let me shoot it first." He nod-ded at the new rifle. "You can do that one."

"That wasn't a favor, Simon," Buell said in a serious voice. "That was an old, used gun, and I wanted to see if it would blow up."

Jake snorted.

"Damn it, Buell, I can never be sure if you're just yankin' my clanger."

"Frustratin', huh?" Buell drew back the hammer and lowered

104

the block. "Gimme a shell, then."

Simon shook several from the box and gave one to Buell. A few seconds later, the small rifle cracked, and one of the shoes responded with a clear ring. "Right where ya point it. Here ya go. I'll watch." He handed the rifle to Simon as Jake stepped up beside them.

"Start with the left one and turn it around," Jake said. "I'll try to turn it the other way."

Before long, all four shoes were wobbling and rotating slowly. They loaded and fired as fast as they could until they'd shot an entire box of shells. Jake stepped back, propped his long-barreled rifle against a tree, and shook his arms. "Can't hold it steady no more." He sat down on the ground beside Buell.

"Me, either," Simon said, and put his gun down. "I'm gonna go get the beer."

It wasn't real cold, but it was wet, and they took turns soothing their parched throats, both inside and out—drinking beer from a bucket.

Jake burped forcibly and sighed. "This is nice."

"I'll let ya have that, Jake. This was a good idea," Buell said.

"I told ya you could like it here," Simon added. "No trouble, and there's plenty to do in a growing town."

"Well, not exactly *no* trouble," Jake said, and gave Buell an impish wink.

"What's he mean?"

Buell frowned. "Nothin' much."

"Ain't what I heard," Jake said.

"Damn bartenders. Only thing worse is a barber."

"Well, he obviously knows something, Buell. Spit!"

"Had a little run-in with Roscoe Monday night. I—" Buell held up his hand to Jake. "All right! Roscoe and the nigger jumped me. They tied me up, and were about to do what I don't know, but it wasn't gonna be good, and Staker showed up with that hand-cannon of his. Untied me—and then let the sonsabitches go. Can you believe *that*?"

"He doesn't want to start a feud with the ranchers," Simon said.

"So he lets 'em threaten to gut *me*? What'n hell's that got to do with ranchers? And how do you know that?"

"What do you know about the upcoming election?"

"What you'd expect me to know—nothin'."

"You do know your pa's thinking about running, don't you?"

"Maybe."

"Well, we think he is."

Buell cocked his head. "Who's we?" Simon held his gaze for only a moment, and then irritation tightened Buell's mouth. "I know that look, Simon. Show me the cookies."

"I think Sherman Pederson's done a good job and deserves to keep it," Simon muttered.

"He delivers *ice*—in someone else's wagon," Buell said derisively. "You'd choose him over my pa?"

"So he is running then?"

"I didn't say that."

"Uh, yup, I think ya did, Buell," Jake said.

Buell glared at him for a second, and then looked back at Simon. "That don't make sense. Pa's got a good business, knows everybody—probably done a favor for everyone in town at one time or another."

Simon sat silent, unable to meet Buell's stare.

"Well, ain't he?"

"He ain't a member of the Progression Project," Jake said.

"*Simon?*" Buell felt his anger rise. "Don't play me the fool."

"Ask your pa about it. It's not my place to speak for him."

"I'm asking *you*. What's this progression thing?" Then Buell looked at Jake. "You tell me."

"Ain't no secret. And don't drag me into this. I like my life simple—I fish where there ain't none, remember? The Progression Project is a bunch of business folks who think the farmers are the way this place will grow. They want to make the ranchers move north or south, and they don't care which way. They think the Sandy Island bunch works with the ranchers."

"Is that it, Simon?"

"More or less. Your pa doesn't see it that way."

"And that surprises you? Who the hell do you think got both my pa and yours going?" Buell glanced at Jake. "And yours! Texas cows, brought by Texas cowmen—not a bunch of sodbusters from Illinois. Hell, Simon, we rode herd with that bunch!"

"The ranchers can graze cattle just as well fifteen miles north—and ship them from there as well."

"But their ranches are here and so is the feedlot. That just ain't fair."

"Sometimes it isn't practical to be fair," Simon said.

"I can't believe what I'm hearing. But it sure puts some light on Ruben Bedell's offer."

Simon's eyes lit up. "What did he want?"

"Me." A chill tugged Buell's ears back. "And my pistol."

"You'd side with the scum that was going to cut your throat?"

"At least they were willing to look me in the eye while they did it."

"Now what the hell is that supposed to mean? This is politics, Buell. It has nothing to do with your father personally, and you know that damn well."

"I'll take you at your word," Buell said and studied his friend's face. "But you're lookin' around the backside on this. You're assumin' Roscoe and his friends are in cahoots with the ranchers. I think you're wrong, and I know it ain't personal with Pa, but ya don't take sides against yer friends, either."

Simon glared. "Well, what would you have me do?"

"Stay the hell out of it," Buell shot back.

"Will you?"

"Yeah, Simon, I will."

"Hey, any of that beer left?" Jake asked with a shrug.

The ride back to town was a quiet one.

CHAPTER 11

In time, tall, dark-green stalks of grain turned lime-yellow, then golden, and finally bowed their heavy heads to McCormick's machine. With every available wagon pressed into service, their iron wheels churned the dirt roads to powder as the grain came in. Buell ordered the tired horses away from the wooden silo and into the road.

Saturday ended a grueling week of fourteen-hour days in strength-sapping heat, breathing air full of dust and chaff, and with no time to pause from sunup to dark. The sun burned its way into the western horizon. Long shafts of fire shot into the gathering dusk as Buell turned his team into the paddock, and climbed down. Mose grabbed the lead horse's bridle and led the teams into the barn.

Buell ached from his elbows to the middle of his back, and he could barely feel his legs. He went into his place, gathered up a complete change of clothes, and walked to the bathhouse behind Moir's barbershop. An hour later, bathed, shaved, and wearing clean clothes, he headed for Mrs. Luger's.

He pulled the screen open and stopped in the doorway. The air vibrated with the sound of busy cutlery, clattering dishes, and forty men talking at the same time. Three harried women shuffled from table to table with pitchers, pots, and platters. He couldn't see one empty chair. A waitress spotted him and zigzagged across the floor until she was close enough to be heard. "Be about twenty minutes or so," she shouted and shrugged.

Buell nodded and went back outside. He hadn't eaten since eleven, and that had been some bread and cheese washed down with tepid, linen-flavored water from a muddy, canvas bag. He thought about Lancer's, and the two-block walk for a few seconds, then went next door to the saloon. About half the tables were occupied, and a dozen men stood along the bar, the right-hand end empty. Jake didn't notice him until Buell was standing at the counter, and then he hurried over. "Yer slicked up like a drummer, Buell," he said. "Goin' somewhere?"

"Just tired of goin' to bed feelin' like a gopher. It's been a hell of a week."

"Let me get ya a drink."

"What I need is something to eat. Your mom's place is packed. You got anything left over from lunch?"

"Pickled stuff and a few hard rolls." Jake shuddered. "Not very high on the hog, huh?"

"Pickled what?"

Jake stepped back and looked under the bar. "Eggs, them little sausages, pigs' knuckles; somethin' that looks like carrots, onions and cauliflower. Oh, some hard sausage too. The sausage ain't too bad."

"Put the eggs, pickles, and bread up here, and the hard sausage. And a beer—the beer first."

Jake filled a large schooner full, set it in front of Buell, and went to the middle of the bar, returning with a shallow dish. "If I put those jars on the counter there won't be any for lunch tomorrow—Ma would skin my ass and Pa'd hold my ankles." He stooped, and Buell heard the tops being levered off. A few seconds later, Jake put an overflowing bowl on the bar.

Buell disposed of four eggs between three long chugs of beer, put the empty glass back on the bar, and belched. Jake picked up the beer mug, filled it again, and left to attend to several waving hands down the counter. Silently and methodically, Buell ate the rest of the bar-food, and drank half of his beer before Jake came back. Buell burped again. "My gut thanks you, Jake, but tonight my nose may not. How much do I owe ya?"

"Four bits for the beer, same for the eggs—Ma'll never miss the rest."

"Ya sure?"

"If this place was mine, wouldn't cost ya nothin'. But it ain't."

Buell dug a dollar out of his shirt pocket and laid it on the bar. "Not very busy in here tonight." He looked around the saloon.

"Most of our customers are next door—farm help mostly. They'll be along. Lancer's will be full of cowboys and such by now."

"I've noticed that. How long has that been going on? Never was that way before."

"Ya know, I'm not sure. Slowly the farmers 'n the cowboys just separated, and this place got real quiet. But this *was* where the drovers came, remember? Lancer's was always just a little rougher. But you know that." Jake raised one eyebrow.

"Do people still remember that, Jake?"

"Like it was last week. I know I'll never forget it. And like everything else, folks took sides."

"How could there be sides? That foul-mouthed son of a bitch went too far, and he meant to shoot first. Who in hell would take his side?"

"Some did."

"Who?"

"Doc Princher, for instance—but ya gotta figger that, he hates guns. And old man Swartz. There were a few others."

"That just don't make any sense. They'd just as soon see a

bastard like that do whatever—" Buell puffed his exasperation.

"There are more like them now. This place is getting downright civilized. Oops. I spoke too soon." Jake nodded at the front door.

Gus Swartz and a man who Buell thought would be invisible in a garbage heap paused for a moment, spotted Buell and Jake, and headed their way.

"I'll take care of him, Buell. Okay?" Jake said quietly.

"How's the delivery boy," Gus said to Buell, and leaned his bulk side-on against the bar. His companion stood to one side—he reeked of old sweat.

"Ya want a beer, Gus—or directions outta here?" Jake said.

"Don't get yer nuts in a knot, Jake. I just want a coupla words." Gus looked directly at Buell. "*You* got a problem with that?"

"If you can get it done before I run out of breath." Buell blew a puff of air through pursed lips.

Jake glanced over his shoulder at Buell. "Still quick with the mouth aren't ya, Mace?"

"Say your piece, Gus, and leave, or go sit down and mind your business." Jake moved to the end of the bar near Buell.

"You've always wondered whether you could take me or not, haven't ya, Jake." Gus stood up straight.

"No doubt here." Jake reached under the bar.

Gus stared at a three-foot axe handle. "One day we'll find out." He looked at Buell. "Word is you wanna be sheriff, Mace. I'm here to tell you we think that'd be a bad decision."

"I'd like to know who *we* are, Gus. It can't be you talkin', and it sure ain't that bunch on Sandy Island—you're *all* so dumb, you've gotta be watered." Buell's hand dropped to his pistol.

"Don't!" Jake said, then stepped around Buell and away from the counter. He pointed at Gus with the hickory handle, and then nodded at Buell. "Either of ya." Everyone in the saloon stopped talking, and turned to look. "You've had your say, Gus. Leave."

Buell took his left hand off the butt of his pistol, and hooked his thumb in his belt. "He invited you out, Gus," he said with a smile.

"You heard what I said, Mace. Best pay attention." Gus stepped back, then turned and stormed out of the saloon.

"Whew!" Jake stepped back behind the bar and put away his persuasion. "You sure know how to rile a man. I thought I was gonna have to whack 'im."

"So did he—that's why ya didn't. Gus is a sneak and a coward, always has been. Who was that with him?"

"Don't know. Never seen anybody quite that filthy though— he'd run flies off a gut-pile."

A man seated near the door with several others caught Buell's eye. Vaguely familiar, he stood and started across the floor. "Who's that?" Buell whispered to Jake.

"Blake Waldon. Used to run the tannery—he does land deals now."

"Remember me, Buell?" the man said as he approached.

"Yes'ir, you're Mister Waldon."

Waldon looked back at the others he'd left and smiled. "I saw how you handled Gus Swartz, and I've heard how you showed a couple of others the error of their ways. I'm impressed."

"You weren't watchin' close enough, Mister Waldon. Gus did the handlin'."

"From where I was sitting, Swartz's eyes were on that pistol of yours. Don't be so modest."

"That's something I've never been accused of."

"And you still speak your mind, I see. That's good."

"Is it? For who?"

113

"Could be for all of us, Buell. Can I call you by your first name?"

"You have been."

Waldon's face colored slightly. "I have *some* influence in Carlisle, and I'm offering to use it for you if you decide to take Loren Staker's place."

"Who said I was offered that?"

"Word like that moves quickly, Mister Mace. We also understand that Ruben Bedell offered you a similar position. We can pay whatever he might." Waldon raised both eyebrows expectantly and gave Buell a practiced smile.

"First, can't anybody around here talk for themselves? Always *we*. Who is this *we* that understands, and *who* can pay?"

The businessman's smile vanished. "Why, Carlisle, of course. I'm a member of the city council."

"Well, you've got it wrong, councilman. Mister Bedell wanted to hire my gun. It's not for sale—to him, you, or anyone else. Tell *we* that next time you see them."

"I was hoping to do us both a favor." Waldon huffed. "I was mistaken."

"And I'm doing you one by saying no."

Blake Waldon looked confused as he went back to his table. Buell watched him until he sat, and then turned to Jake. "I think Simon told me his pa is the head of the city council. Is that true?"

"Yep."

"So there's him, Waldon, and who else?"

"Doc Princher, Art Lancer, and Jude Cody—he owns the jewelry store."

"And how many of them are in the progress thing?"

"Steele, Cody, and the doc."

"Do you see how crazy this looks?"

"I try to keep it simple," Jake replied.

"The ranchers—Waldon—want me to be the law, and Gus, who runs with the Sandy bunch if we can guess by his partner tonight, wants me to stay out of it. Does that mean Gus sides with Paul Steele and his friends?"

"That *ain't* simple, Buell. But Paul Steele is *no* friend of Gus Swartz, I can tell you that. He holds Gus responsible for Simon going away."

"I'm going over to Lancer's, Jake. Maybe all this will make sense if I'm drunk."

"Ya can't do that here?"

"I don't like me drunk, Jake, and you wouldn't either. I saw the size of your attitude adjustor." Buell drained the last of his beer, now flat, and pushed away from the bar. "I'll see ya later."

CHAPTER 12

Buell had no sooner walked through the door than Art Lancer waved him over to the only empty spot in the place, a small table at the end of the room. The saloonkeeper met him there with a bottle and two glasses.

"Good see," Art said over the din, and settled onto one of the two chairs. Without asking, he poured two glasses full, slid one across in front of Buell, and picked up his own. "Mud," he said, and tossed it back.

"Thanks, Art." Buell lifted his glass. "What's the occasion?"

"None—yet," Art replied and winked.

Buell nodded and drank half of his whiskey. "Full house tonight. What's going on?"

"Three outfits. Feedlots."

Buell mentally interpreted Lancer's short speech. Three ranchers had moved their cattle into the feedlots, ready for the fall shipment to the eastern packers. He looked at the tables nearby, and saw at least one bottle on each. "Bonus time for cowboys then."

"Me too." Lancer grinned widely, poured himself another drink, and tipped the bottle toward Buell.

"I'm okay with this."

"You law?"

"So that's what this is about?"

Art nodded.

"Well, at least you're up-front about it. I've considered it, but you have to remember what happened right over there." Buell nodded toward the bar.

Art nodded. "Good."

"A lot of folks didn't think so, and a lot of them are still here."

"Don't count."

"Course they do."

"Got votes. Me, Blake . . . and Paul."

"Are you sure about Paul Steele? Simon told me about the progressive bunch. Mister Steele is in on that."

"Paul, Lindstrom—smart."

"Livin' in a town is a lot different than I'm used to, Art. You folks have a way of climbin' all over a man. Do ya all go to a meeting someplace where you plan this?"

Art chuckled carefully, his hand with a hanky hovering just above the tabletop. "We plan. Good for town."

"And for me, while yer at it, right?"

"Good you . . . too." Art gripped Buell's forearm. "You see." He glanced at the packed bar—"Work."—then slid the bottle across the table. "Yours." He got up, stood for a minute breathing shallowly, and then left.

Buell watched Art for a few minutes as the older man expertly worked the customers down the bar. They were mostly slouch-hatted, dusty men with big bandanas tied around sun-darkened necks. All wore plain cotton shirts—working cowboys. A shout from the table next to him took his attention away from the bar. Two men, sleeves rolled up to expose pasty skin from their tanned wrists to their bulging biceps, were arm wrestling as a group of about ten watched. Buell finished his whiskey and settled back to watch.

One contestant had copper-colored hair, and his forearm was sprayed with freckles. The other man, black hair cropped short, stared with unblinking eyes at his opponent. Weathered hands, thumbs locked, were motionless in an upright position, each man's elbow firmly set on the table. Neither man showed any emotion, nor would anyone know the contest had started except for the slight quivering of taut tendons.

A third man watched intently. "Keep your wrists straight, boys," he ordered quietly.

"Flatten 'im, Andrew," an onlooker said. "Got four dollars on ya."

"Four you lose," another replied, and the group laughed noisily.

The silent battle raged as the rigid arms remained fixed in place. Then the black-haired man's jaw muscles flexed, and in the same instant a barely perceptible smile started to form on Red's face, his eyes narrowing slightly. A second later the locked fists tilted a half-inch in favor of the redhead, and determination furrowed the other man's brow. The sinewy triangle shifted again, ever so slightly, and sweat popped out on Blackie's upper lip. Stoically, Red stared as the other man clamped his teeth even tighter. Another half an inch, and both men's arms started to tremble. Red's lips pressed hard together, and the cords in his neck pulled taut. Bang! Two interlocked fists crashed onto the tabletop and a shout went up from the crowd.

Blackie's head drooped for a moment, and then he stood and extended the arm that had just failed him. "Ye've got gristle thet don' show, Paddy," he said in a broad Scots accent.

Red shook his hand. "Ya bet an Irishman a bottle, Jocko, you'll not beat'm till ya hear the queen fart." The entire bunch erupted, pounding each other on the back, and shrieking with laughter.

Buell laughed with the cowboys as they threw arms over familiar shoulders, yelled their appreciation for each other, and sloppily recharged their whiskey glasses. Buell felt at home for the first time since he'd returned, and suddenly missed Arley so much his chest hurt. He poured himself another drink, but then sat and stared at the amber liquid, willing the pain to ease.

"Jake said you'd be here," Simon said.

With a start, Buell spilled half his drink on the table.

Simon stood to Buell's right. "Caught you dreamin' did I? I was watching you watch them." He nodded at the boisterous cowboys.

"Yeah, I guess ya did. Sit down. Art's buying. I'll get you a glass." Buell started to get up.

"Sit still. I'll get it." Simon went to the bar, hailed one of the bartenders, and came back with a glass and towel. "There." He pushed the glass across the table and wiped up the spilled whiskey.

Buell poured him a shot. "What brings you in here?" He picked up his drink.

"Felt the need for some company." Simon rested one arm on the table.

"Where's Sarah?"

"Not that kind." Simon raised his whiskey. "Our kind . . . you know what I mean. Here's to Laramie and the folks at Amos's place."

"Amos, and others." They touched rims and drank. "I was havin' the same thoughts before you showed up. Let's hear yours."

Simon dragged a knuckle across his lips. "Pa and I were talking after supper, about how Carlisle's growing, and how I can grow with it. It's a conversation I've had at least once a day since we got here, and with a dozen different people. I got to thinking how simple it was at Amos's saloon, and in that empty valley I found later. I had some tough times, both of us did, but the problems there were easy to see, and even if coming up with a fix was going to be hard, it was always clear what I had to do."

"And here?"

"Here, I get the feeling that no matter what I do, it's not gonna be good enough. Somebody is going to be disappointed with it."

"Like who?"

"Everybody—and nobody specific. Pa has expectations, as does Sarah, and Uncle John. And then there's my ma, and the Kingsleys, and the mayor . . . and me."

"Damn, Simon, you gotta bad case of black-ass, don't ya?"

Simon shrugged.

"What do *you* want to do?"

"That's the worst part, Buell—I don't have any idea. I was hoping you would." Simon sagged back in his chair.

Buell felt a bit annoyed, and at the same time a little pleased. "So the naggin' about me staying wasn't *all* about me, was it?"

Simon's eyes went wide and he leaned forward. "That never occurred to me, but you could be right," he said in a lowered voice. He picked up his drink and took a sip, then another. "I can remember half a dozen times where I simply took for granted that you'd be there to help me out. I depended on it." He toyed with his glass before meeting Buell's eyes. "I've always depended on it."

"I'd like to fatten up my head and agree, Simon, but what about that place you built in the mountains? You did a lot there, and did it alone, from what you've said."

"I had to. Had to or die. And that was different."

Buell puffed his lips. "I can't see how."

"Just different. The threats were clear. Build a cabin or live in a tent, kill an animal or eat corn mush, cut wood or freeze. Simple decisions. Here, I feel uneasy most of the time, and I don't know why."

"And having me around makes it better? I ain't your wife, Simon."

Simon shook his head and snorted. "I knew that was coming.

120

Yeah, knowing you're around makes it better, even with smart-ass remarks like that."

"Well, I'm truly flattered." *And you've done it again, Simon,* Buell thought. He got satisfaction from knowing he saw it coming.

"So now that I've bucked you up, I can renege—"

Buell's eyebrows shot up.

"I can go back on a promise, kind of."

"How do you *kinda* go back on a deal?"

"By making you do the same."

"I'm not gonna get into this political thing, Simon." Buell shook his head emphatically. "There's nothing but trouble to be had."

"Look at it this way. Family comes first, right? Of course it does. So, you're as obligated to support your pa as I am mine. We have to. Friends come second, and then the politics. We're friends. We can support each other by not fighting with each other. Agreed?"

"Damn you, Simon, you're talking around me again. I'm going to agree and not know what I agreed to until you tell me later. Ya son of a bitch, you've done that all our lives."

"And I've never caused you any harm, have I?" Simon's brow furrowed. "Straight common sense."

"How the hell would I know? Your common sense is about as straight as titmouse tracks."

"Let me say one more thing. Then we can sit here and drink all Art's whiskey and remember Fort Laramie. Okay?"

"Like I can stop ya."

"You support your pa for mayor, and I'll do the same for Sherm Pederson. Whoever wins, you take Staker's job when he quits, and do what the council needs you to do. Everybody's happy. Or at least happier. How's that?" Simon said it all in a rush.

"Pa don't stand a chance and you know it."

Simon looked down at the table for a split second too long.

"But we *are* friends," Buell said, "and I understand that you have to help your pa."

"Does that mean you'll take Staker's job then?"

"No, it doesn't. Now let's hurt that bottle."

Fortunately, the bottle Art supplied hadn't been a full one, and by the time it was gone, so was Buell's desire to get drunk. Simon, on the other hand, had to make three attempts to get to his feet. "I've enjoyed our night, Buell," he said, enunciating each word carefully. "I'm now going home."

"You're gonna try. Want me to—"

"Don't be 'diculous." Simon squinted at the front door. "See ya t'morrow." Weaving his way across the floor, he paused at the door, gave Buell a lopsided grin, and left.

The two arm wrestlers were the only ones remaining of the dozen that had swarmed around the table three hours before. Both were so drunk they could no longer fill their glasses, and were taking turns swigging directly from a bottle, giggling like children. A subdued game of dominoes carried on at the far end of the room, and two men stood talking by the front door. Art leaned over the bar, half-asleep.

Buell stared at the empty bottle he held cupped in his hands. Simon had done it again. He never meant to do it the dozens of times he had, but the result was the same—Buell was committed to something *Simon* needed. He'd always been aware of Simon's dependency. It had been a burden he'd easily carried. Simon's friendship came without reservation, and Arley was the only one who'd ever matched it—and Arley was dead. That left Simon.

Buell knew his father faced a crushing defeat and everyone but Mace—it would never be Paisley—could see it coming.

There was no doubt in his mind that his pa could make a great mayor—he acted like a mayor. But the reality of the town businessmen lining up behind Sherman Pederson made it clear he wouldn't get more than two out of five votes. What was Buell going to do about that?

The two drunken cowboys struggled to their feet. Leaning heavily against each other, they started for the front door, then veered off to the right. Art paralleled them to the end of the bar and opened the door to the alley. "Night, boys." The redhead attempted to say something, then waved his hand vaguely in Art's direction instead. Both men stumbled into the dark. Art shut the door.

Buell sat for another minute and then stood. "I think they had the right idea, Art. Nothin' as depressing as a quiet saloon." He headed for the back door. "I'm gonna take the shortcut, too." Art nodded and gave him a perfunctory wave. Stepping into the warm September night, Buell pushed the door shut. Moving carefully in the dark alley, half-shuffling his feet to avoid tripping, he willed his eyes to adjust.

Then he heard a noise ahead, the sodden thud of fist on flesh and air being expelled from a man's lungs. His hand found the lapped wood of the building to his left and he hurried up. Another dull thud came, closer this time, and he squinted into the darkness. Vague shapes appeared across the alley and another fifteen feet away. He drew his pistol and crossed diagonally toward the dark shape of an alcove on a building opposite. He stepped past the opening and stopped. Three men, one unusually large, stood over what looked like another man on the ground. He pointed his pistol at the large man. A metallic crackle filled the night as he cocked it. "Git away from him!"

Brilliant light filled Buell's head, and his pistol bucked in his hand as it discharged. He tried to move away, and then his legs collapsed beneath him.

The smell of antiseptic medicine turned his stomach, and he cracked his eyelids against the light. Doc Princher stood over him, a half-smile, a smirk maybe, on his lips. "He'll be all right. Good whack on the head is all."

"What do you make of those scars?" It was Staker's voice.

"Gunshots. Small caliber. The other could be anything, knife, but it's not very clean—ragged cut—hard to tell."

Buell opened his eyes all the way. "They were beatin' some-one."

"*They* are in jail." Staker stepped into view.

Buell raised his head and looked around the room—an infirmary. There was another bed to his right and a tall cabinet with glass doors stood against the wall beyond that. Pain radiated across his head from the right side. His careful fingers found a ridge running from behind his right ear to the corner of his brow. He looked at Doc Princher. "What happens if I get up?"

"You'll likely fall down. Let me take a closer look." The doctor stooped over, forced one of Buell's eyes wide open and stared into it, then did the same to the other. "Slight concussion. From what I feel around that right eyebrow, you've had one of those before. Does that eye bother you?"

"Some."

"I recommend you stay here tonight. I'll come by and see you late morning. If you have to urinate, use this." He held up a glass beaker, and then put it on the table beside the bed.

"Do you want me to go tell Mace?" Staker asked.

"God no," Buell said. "I mean, there's nothin' he can do. I'll go see him later. Who was gettin' beat up, Sheriff?"

"Bedell's famous Celtic pair. They're all right, sleeping it off."

"Who's the bastards ya got in jail?"

"Why, them, of course."

"But it wasn't—they weren't—they was the ones gettin' beat on."

"I thought they were at each other."

"They were so drunk they couldn't *see* each other, much less take a swing. No, there were two other men, plus the one that hit me from behind."

"Art didn't see anyone. He heard a shot and come out. You were flat on your face beside one of the cowboys. The other was sitting up holding his head."

"There were more, I'm tellin' ya."

"We'll leave it for now, Buell. It's after two. Those boys are safe in jail, and you're not bad hurt. We'll talk tomorrow."

Buell raised his head as far as the pain would let him, and spotted his boots, shirt, and gun belt. "Where's my pistol?"

"Still in the alley would be my guess—in amongst the trash behind the hat shop. I'll go look, first light."

Buell slowly lowered his head. "First thing, Sheriff, okay? That Remington is special."

"Obviously. I'll go look."

Doc Pincher reached over and turned the light down to a dim glow. "I wouldn't get up if I were you."

"We'll sort all this out in the morning," Staker said, and together with Doc Princher, left the room.

CHAPTER 13

Buell could stand, but not without pain, and Staker's news a minute before hadn't helped. He leaned against the bed while he buttoned his shirt. Whoever had hit him in the head had also delivered a kick high on his right butt cheek.

The anger he directed at himself only made it hurt more. Twice in as many months he'd let his guard down, daydreaming about the good old times that in fact weren't. He'd endured two years in a wide-open mining town, and survived several attempts on his life with hardly a scratch. He'd survived because he'd been careful. Wouldn't Tay Prescott get a laugh if he could see this? Banged up like a common drunk in a lazy place like Carlisle? And that's the problem. It's not as sleepy as it seems. Hadn't *he* said the same thing?

Buell grimaced at Sheriff Staker. "The son of a bitch kicked me." He gingerly prodded the spot. "Did ya look real good?"

"Found your hat, no pistol."

"Dammit."

"Why so special, other than it's a fine-looking piece?"

"It tried to kill me one night. I feel better holdin' onto the handle."

"You've covered a lot of ground for your age, Buell."

"And still ain't learned enough to stay out of dark alleys," Buell said wryly. "Have ya let those cowboys out yet?"

"I let 'em go, but they're broke and stuck. Whoever roughed them up took their horses too. They said someone would come looking for them."

"Don't you find that a little odd? The cowboys were headed for the stable. That means Gus took their horses out of twenty others in a corral. He knew which ones."

"Hmmm," Staker murmured and nodded. "Gus, ya say? Who said it was Gus?"

"I did. And I'll make him admit it when I see 'im." Buell put his hat on, and yanked it off again. "Bastards," he muttered. He slung his empty gun belt over his shoulder and glanced at the wall clock. "I'm gonna go buy them boys some breakfast. Ain't no need you telling pa. He'll hear soon enough."

"Doc said to go a little easy today."

"Eatin' a couple eggs ain't gonna strain much."

"You know what I mean," Staker said.

Buell had found the cowboys at the train depot half-asleep on one of the high-backed benches. They'd jumped at his offer of breakfast and they'd gone to a small place the cowboys knew of—Mrs. Luger didn't open on Sunday. The black-haired one was a Scotsman named Andrew McCulloch, and the other man an Irishman who answered to Red, or, he'd admitted with an engaging grin, Paddy.

The Irishman slid the last two eggs off the platter, right on top of the last two pancakes, and then looked sheepishly at Buell and Andrew. "Kinna let it go to waste, now can we?"

"God's truth, Paddy, ye've eaten six o' the bleedin' things already—and as many griddle cakes. Be'jesus, where's it goin'?"

Red smiled easily, and cut into the stack with his fork.

Andrew sat back in his chair. "Ye said ya had a reason, Buell?"

"Do ya know Gus Swartz?"

"I've heard the name—don't know the man."

"He was the one workin' yer guts over last night."

"Can't say one way 'r tuther. I don't really remember a lot."

"No one mentioned a name?"

"I wouldn't remember. We were nay fit t' bury."

"It seems they knew you well enough to recognize your horses."

"T'weren't our horses," said Red around a wad of pancake. "We were usin' Mister Bedell's."

Andrew answered Buell's question before he asked it. "Ours were used up. If them fellers knew we were Bar-M, the horses wer'na hard to find."

"Why do you think they picked you two?"

Before Andrew could answer, the front door opened, and Ruben Bedell came in.

"Mornin', boss," Andrew said.

"You two boys okay?" Bedell strode across the small room.

"Me guts are a wee bit tender," Andrew replied.

"You?" Ruben looked at Red.

"I'm fine. They took a likin' to Andrew." The Irishman chuckled.

"Sorry about your head, Mister Mace, and I really appreciate you givin' them a hand."

"Didn't do much."

"We'll never know that, thank God. Staker says they took the horses." Bedell pulled out a chair, sat, and looked at Andrew. "Were you robbed?"

"I hope that was the reason they took us, cuz they got nothin'. You know what happens when you're with Paddy."

"Me!" Red said with a snort. "Who supplied the bottle of whiskey?"

"You were broke then?" Bedell continued.

Andrew shook his head. "Not a copper."

"One of them was Gus Swartz," Buell said.

"Are you sure?" Bedell asked.

"I grew up with the bastard, Mister Bedell. I sat behind him in school, watched him throw his weight around for years. I know him when I see him, dark or not."

"But what would Swartz do with two Bar-M horses?" Bedell said. "There's not a man within two hundred miles who doesn't know that brand."

"Could it be he's helping the rustlers who're taking your cattle?"

"By damn, you might have something there."

"Maybe they're puttin' them on one of the islands down the river a bit," Andrew offered. "Gather up enough to make a ride into Kansas worthwhile."

Red put his fork down on the empty plate. "I'd be up to takin' a look," he said. "There's several of us who've talked that over a bit, boss. If it was that island bunch, our horses just might be there now."

"He's right," Andrew said. "You kin see most of the island from the bluffs above. They're not gonna keep a herd of cows there, but two extra horses in the herd would ne'r be noticed."

"If you decide to take a look, I'd like to go." Buell gingerly finger-traced the lump on his head.

"A couple horses are not worth a man's life, boys, no matter how good it might feel to get 'em back."

"A couple? Why not take 'em all?" Buell asked. "I've seen how they're laid out. The horses are a good quarter-mile away."

"That's rustling, Mister Mace." Bedell frowned at the big grin showing on Red's face. "Exactly what's causing the trouble."

"It's not rustlin' if you don't keep 'em," Buell said. "Leastways, not to my way o' thinkin'. Get yours back, and run the rest into the prairie."

"What d'ya say, boss?" Andrew's eyes sparkled.

"Stay away from there, boys. I've lost one man. I ain't gonna lose another." Bedell's voice sounded stern. "Now, if you two are ready, the spring wagon is in front of the sheriff's office. Wait for me there."

Bedell waited until Andrew and Red left, and then turned to Buell. "How serious is your father about being mayor?"

"Couldn't be more so. Why?"

"Do you know about the little piece of ground I bought northwest of town?"

"Not so little, I've been told."

"Then you *do* know. Can you tell me how your father views its . . . uh . . . development?"

"Does he want to see a feedlot there?"

"You are current." Bedell raised his brow. "Yeah, what might he think about that?"

"Why don't you ask him?"

"Because you're sitting right in front of me. If you don't want to say so, say so."

"He thinks how you do business is your business."

"I'm pleased to hear that. How much support does he have in town?"

Buell snorted. "He's gonna lose."

"No doubt?"

"Far as I can see . . . unless his horses can vote."

Bedell's eyes met Buell's. "Tell your father he has my support." Then he chuckled. "*And* that of my horses." He stood and offered his hand. "You're as good a man as I thought when I met you, Mister Mace. Those boys are like the sons I never had—I hate to see them hard done by."

Buell felt the warmth in the small man's hand, and the strength. "I don't like bushwhackers, Mister Bedell. And call me Buell."

"All right, Buell. And don't give up on your father—just yet."

★ ★ ★ ★ ★

October twenty-first delivered winter's first promise of misery. Hard bits of snow blew against Buell's right cheek and made his eyes water. Shrugging his collar tighter against his neck, he extended his new pistol at arm's length. Carefully sighting on a brown bottle, he pulled the trigger and the top half disappeared. He thumbed back the hammer and lined up on the bottom piece.

He'd tried Sam Colt's newest offer, the 1873 Army, but Remington's pistol felt better. Both were cartridge weapons, and he didn't miss fussing with loose powder and percussion caps, but he was nowhere near as handy with the new gun. He fired the last round, ejected the six empties, and reloaded. He was improving.

Still half-frozen from his shooting session, Buell dropped more coal into the glowing firebox and set the lids back in place. The left side of the stovetop showed a dull red. He'd come back hungry as well, but the thought of visiting Mrs. Luger's was promptly dismissed by the sound of the howling wind. With a butcher knife, he hacked a cross in the top of a can of beans, bent back the four points, and shook the contents into a pan. He set the pot on the far right of the stove, then sat down in an easy chair and pulled his boots and socks off. His feet felt dead. Putting one palm below his toes, and the other on top, he rubbed them vigorously. His thoughts flashed back to Idaho City, and another pair of hands that used to massage his feet the same way. Before the woman's face could appear, someone knocked on the door.

He glanced at the newly cleaned pistol that lay on the small table beside him. "Come in." The door opened so slowly that Buell's hand went to the butt of the Remington. "Come on in," he said louder.

The black eyes of a Chinese man met his for an instant, and then engaged the floor. The man shut the door. "Wu Le, Luben Bedell cookman say, me see you."

"Ruben Bedell's cook, Wu?"

The man looked up and nodded.

"*He'zai?* Why?"

A flash of pleasure lit the man's face for a moment. "Wu say, he know you gun. He tell place." He mimicked stroking along his hand. "Nice gun."

Buell glanced at his Remington.

"No that." The Chinaman held up one finger. "One gun. *Di yi.*"

Buell scrambled to his feet, and the startled man reached for the latch. "Number-one gun?" Buell asked. "He knows who has it?"

"*Wei.*" Yes.

"*Shei?*" Who?

"Wu say come. Lanch mens go find."

"When?"

"Tomollow. Lanch mens wait island." He bridged his fingertips, making a rough oval. "*Wei?*"

Buell pointed east. "Big island?"

The man nodded.

"I'll be there. Thank you, uh . . . Mister—"

The man flashed him another smile, put one hand over his mouth, and pointed with the other.

Buell followed his look. "Shit!" He hurried to the stove, grabbed the boiling pot, and promptly dropped it, shaking his fingers. "Goddammit." He turned around just in time to see the latch drop into place—the Chinaman gone. Using a sock, he retrieved the pan of beans from the half-empty coal scuttle, and put it on the table. Leaning over, he sniffed. Opening the cupboard door, he took out another can, found another pot, and was soon back in the chair, rubbing his frozen toes—and watching the stove.

That the Chinese man had this kind of information had surprised him only for a moment. He'd seen several around town, mostly when they visited the general store, always carrying wicker baskets, their eyes on the boardwalk. Idaho City had a large Chinese population, and Buell had come to accept that they had some secret way of communicating. They never seemed surprised at anything unusual. Even news from distant places seemed to reach the Chinese before anyone else. He'd never figured out how they did it, but he'd learned to trust that they did. The Chinaman knew who had his pistol—Buell's fingers pressed the tender spot on the side of his head. That person was going to wish he'd thrown it in the river.

He smelled beans.

CHAPTER 14

Stepping out of his warm room into the stable's open space made Buell glad he'd put on a heavy wool coat. Frost puffed ahead of him with every breath. He went to the tack room, gathered up his gear, and then went to his horse. After patting the Appaloosa on the rump, he dropped the poles in the rear of the stall and backed the horse into the open. Shadow shook his head up and down, pawing the dirt floor. "You like the cold, don't ya? Dumb ass." Five minutes later, he slid the double door shut and climbed on the prancing animal. "All right, let's go raise some hell."

A skiff of grainy snow covered the ground, unmarked as yet by Sunday churchgoers or anyone else. Shadow needed little urging to slip into an easy lope, hooves drumming the partially frozen ground. All the houses east of town were still dark, except for the window in Judge Kingsley's study; but then, it seemed he was always awake. A few minutes later, Buell passed the Steeles' place and then another half-mile down the road, the cluster of buildings that marked the original homestead of Simon's family. The old sod house was now haven for a milk cow. The sharecropper who ran the chicken farm lived in a small house nearby. Three more places, and Buell was clear of town.

He rode to the bluff where he'd first seen the rowdies' camp, keeping back far enough to remain out of sight. Finding no one there, he continued at a walk downriver until he spotted a thin wisp of smoke, barely visible in the early dawn. Twenty minutes later, he hauled Shadow to a stop, climbed off, and walked the last fifty yards to the crest of the low rise. He searched the downslope for a minute, and then smiled. The straight lines of a rifle barrel stood out clearly at the edge of a small clump of trees. Twenty yards beyond, the hidden sentry's horse stood, its rusty-red rump in plain view. Buell walked back to Shadow, mounted, and rode over the ridge and down.

He guided his horse to within ten feet of the hidden guard. "Nice sorrel ya got there," he said, and then turned in his saddle to look directly at the startled man. "I'm Buell Mace," he added quickly as the man raised the old Spencer to his shoulder. "You with Bedell's bunch?"

"Uh . . . yeah. Mace—I heard ya comin'." The man squinted in the low light.

"Yep, I can see that. Do I just ride in?"

"Jist a minute, I'll get my horse."

Andrew McCulloch stood with seven other men around a small, hot fire. Buell dismounted and threw Shadow's reins across a picket rope. "Pleased to see ya, Buell," Andrew said. "Come warm yer hams a wee bit—cold as a whore's heart this mornin'."

"Did you stay here overnight?" The fire felt good on Buell's legs.

"No. We've been here 'bout an hour."

"So whatcha got in mind?"

"How much did the Chinaman tell ya?"

"He said to meet you here, at least by the island, and that Wu knew where my pistol was." Buell glanced around. "Is he here?"

"No. Ya kinna git a Chinaman on a horse. The man he described was a feller named Bachman. Do ya know him?"

"Looks like a polecat?"

"That be the man. The island bunch have a Chinese cook."

Andrew shook his head. "Somehow he got word to Wu that Bachman was showin' that fancy pistol around, and braggin' how he took it off ya."

"Why didn't the Chinaman just tell me that?"

"Ya said if we was gonna pay them laddies a visit, you'd like to come along. Red and I reckon we owed ya."

Buell looked around. "Where's he?"

Andrew nodded north, toward the island. "Him and another fella are over there havin' a peek. They'll be back directly."

"What changed Bedell's mind about this?"

"Don't know that he did. He's in Kansas City, and will be for another week or so. We'll git done what we want to do, and n'er a soul will be the wiser."

"This ain't gonna stay a secret."

"I look forward to handlin' any complaints." Andrew's eyes sparkled. "Are ya game then?"

"Hell, yes." Buell turned his back to the fire and folded his arms across his chest. "What exactly are ya gonna do?"

"Like ya suggested. Push their horses up on top and then run 'em for as long as we can in three groups, each in a different direction. They'll play the dickens findin' even half of 'em." Andrew winked at him. "I like yer thinkin', Buell—ye've got a streak of the devil in ya."

Fifteen minutes later, Red and his companion came back, both grinning like well-fed coyotes. "They ain't stirred yet," he said. "I saw the cook, but that's all." He climbed off his horse, tethered it, and joined the rest at the fire.

"Do they have horses near?" Buell asked.

"Three, and one of 'em is that buckskin of Bachman's. They're in a rough corral about seventy yards east of the camp." Red smoothed a place in the dirt with the sole of his boot and squatted. "Let me scratch a map."

As he explained it, the camp was a cleared area in a thick

stand of trees. Eleven bedraggled huts lined the west and northern edges of the clearing. A bark shanty stood near the middle; probably their supplies, because east of it a square fire-pit served a two-gallon coffeepot. A lidded kettle hung on an iron rod. The cook was busy there.

Red poked his stick into the center of the map. "He was slicing spuds into a deep flat-bottomed skillet—or maybe it was rutabagas."

"That means about an hour before they eat," Buell said. "How long ago did you see this?"

"Fifteen minutes at the most." Red chuckled. "And here's the best part. The rest of the horses are all bunched at the skinny end of the island in a rope corral. The south side runs into the water. All we've got to do is cut that one rope and push them across the channel. We could do it quiet if we've a mind."

Buell turned to face the fire. "It's yer shivaree, Andrew." Heat rushed through his body. "What do ya think?"

"I say we raise a ruckus. The sooner they know they're in the shit, the better for me. What about the rest of ya?" Andrew looked around the circle of smiling faces, every man nodding. "Good then. What is it you plan to do, Buell?"

"How long did it take you to get from the camp to the horses, Red?"

" 'Bout half of that fifteen minutes."

"Were you riding?"

Red shook his head. "Walking my horse, quiet. I could have ridden. There's a plain path, and it's all dirt."

"Will you go back with me?"

"Sure. They ain't gonna get up till that Chinaman hollers—I know I wouldn't."

Buell turned to Andrew. "Me and Red will let the three horses near camp go, maybe lead them away. If it's done quiet, and they're not on to us, Red will leave with them. I'm going to stay and try to find Bachman."

"You don't look any more convinced than I feel, laddy," Andrew said. "How kin ya find Bachman? Stick yer head in and ask?"

"Maybe." Buell smiled. "And maybe not."

"They'll see ya," one of the cowboys said.

Andrew looked Buell up and down. "And what'll they see?" He grinned. "Another cowboy. I think we can do it, Buell." Excitement filled his face. "Ya ready boys?"

Three or four of the animals snuffled their curiosity as the cowboys rode up and dismounted. Four led their mounts around to the east side of the corral.

"I'll wait on top and make sure you've made it out," Andrew said, his face serious.

"I don't want ya to do that. I'd just as soon not have to think about where you are."

"Ya sure? I follow yer thinkin', but I'd be glad to stay."

"I can see that, but you've got your men to look after. I've been in tighter spots than this."

"Why do I find that so easy to believe?" Andrew clucked at him and went to join the four waiting men.

A few minutes later, Buell and Red lifted crossed pieces of deadfall out of two tree crotches, clearing the corral opening. More than twenty saddles and a tangle of bridles, halters, and leads hung on the rough fence. The three animals stood quietly.

"Looks like they'd be easy to catch," Buell said.

Red shook his head. "Lookin' at the trail, I think if we head them east, they'll be pleased to go where the feed is. I'm gonna stay and make sure you don't get yer arse kicked."

"You heard what I told Andrew?"

"I did." The Irishman smirked at him. "I'm stubborn."

The three horses moseyed out of the corral, turned down the well-trampled path, and kept going. "What'll Andrew do when you're not with those horses?"

"Cipher two 'n two—Andrew and me have ridden a long ways together."

"All right. Let's put our horses between the camp and the channel," Buell said quietly. "I want up that bank as fast as we can get there."

Keeping well out of sight, they circled their mounts around the camp and tied them to a sapling. They hurried back at the edge of the clearing, only this time on the south side. "Still nobody but that Celestial," Red whispered. "What ya gonna do?" He kneeled, the butt of his rifle on the ground.

Buell hunkered beside Red and studied the camp for several seconds. On the west side, there were three huts, big enough for three or four men, followed by a line of three smaller ones. On the north side, five more structures stood, also big ones. Roscoe would have a hut all to himself. One of the smaller ones. Would Bachman? Buell shook his head, then abruptly stood. "Wait here and watch. I'm gonna go ask the Chinaman."

"Are ya bloody daft?" Red's eyes showed white. "I thought you were foolin'."

"How else?"

"Ya jist as well be bangin' on the bleeder's door." Red glanced at the huts. "If they had a door."

"Keep your eye on me. If shove comes to shootin', empty that Winchester. Put a shot into those pots hangin' over the fire, then a couple more into the coals—after that, shoot anything but me, and shoot low. Right?"

"Ya got a pair o' brass ones." Red winked. "I'll be watchin'."

Buell stepped around the last covering tree, and strode directly toward the campfire. The Chinaman, oblivious until he was within a few feet, looked up. His eyes widened, and the spud he held dropped into the pan.

"Chūjiāo, Wu Le." Buell pointed at his own chest. *"Bū el."*

The man glanced over his shoulder, and then nodded. "You see." He stood and strode to the fifth hut in line. After a slight bow at Buell, he touched the top of the crude affair and, without a backward glance, disappeared into the trees. Buell strode across the distance, drew his pistol, and stooped over to slip past the canvas cover.

The stench inside cut off his breath for a moment, and he opened his mouth to breathe. To his left a blanket-covered man lay flat on his back on a low bed, his head toward the west end of the cramped space. He was snoring. Crouched, Buell remained still until his eyes adjusted a bit to the faint light. A second rough cot on the right stood empty except for a rumpled blanket and a hat. Buell moved closer, and searched until he saw what he wanted—a gun belt, and the long-barreled Remington with the gleaming ivory grips. It hung from a peg driven into one of the shaggy roof logs. Stuffing his new gun behind his belt buckle, he carefully drew the shiny pistol from its holster.

Bachman's breathing stopped . . . then exploded with three loud hacks. Buell dropped to his knees, the Remington ready. After a few muffled coughs, the man's breathing became even again, and the snoring continued. Smiling, Buell rose back into his crouch, and moved to the sleeping man's side.

Bachman! With his mouth half-open, the polecat's throat rattled with each intake of breath, and the air above his face filled with the stink of him. Buell raised the pistol shoulder high, and then whispered loudly. "Bushwhacker!" Bachman's breathing faltered, his eyelids fluttered, and then popped open. Buell hit him hard, the barrel striking Bachman just above the right ear. Bachman grunted, lifted slightly in his bed, and then sagged back. "Son of a bitch." Buell poked him in the cheek with the gun barrel, and Bachman's head rolled loosely to the side.

Hustling to the canvas opening, Buell lifted one side. Nothing moved but a thin column of smoke from the fire. Stepping out, he hurried toward Red's position and breathed a sigh when he spotted the Irishman, rifle at the ready. Right behind him stood the Chinaman.

Red shrugged. "He just showed up."

"I go you," the man said and motioned toward the camp. "Bad for me."

"I 'spose he has a point," Red said. "They're gonna find him gone and come lookin'."

Buell nodded at the Chinese man. "*Duō xiè.*"

Red grimaced. "Ya speak that monkey talk. Sounds funny comin' out a white man's mouth."

"I told him thanks." Buell turned to the Asian. "You ride with him." He pointed at Red. Then, stuffing his pistol in the holster, he looked at the cowboy. "Let's git out of here—this was too easy." Buell took off for the concealed horses, and hadn't taken five steps when he felt a vibration in the ground. "Run!" he hissed.

At the hiding place, Shadow stood perfectly still. Buell ripped the reins loose, clambered on, and turned toward the channel. Red tried to do the same, but when he jammed his rifle into the boot, the horse turned, its eyes rolling wildly at the Chinaman.

"Stand still, ya stupid beast." He slapped the horse in the ears, and hauled back on the reins. Head held low, the horse submitted to the small man leaping onto its back.

"Go!" Buell shouted and dug his heels into Shadow's flanks. In three long strides, they hit the icy water, spray blasting into the air. The horse lunged across to the south side. Dodging several trees, Buell reached the base of the bluff and angled Shadow east. He heard Red come out of the water, the Irishman cursing the horse.

Buell gritted his teeth as they raced out of the trees and into the open. A spurt of dirt erupted just in front of him, and a second later, the report of a pistol shot reached him. He leaned over Shadow's neck, and the Appaloosa responded with a burst of speed. More shots rang out as they struggled to the top, and then they were over it. He drew the horse to a sliding stop, and spun him around to watch.

Red's brown, nostrils flared, surged over the crest and Buell burst out laughing. The Irishman leaned far to the right, nearly off his horse. To the left of the lunging animal's shoulder, flopping like a string doll, the terrified Chinaman clutched at the arm wrapped tightly around his neck. Red pulled his mount to a stop beside Buell, and dropped the man with a disgusted snort. "What the hell you laughing at? He's thick as a pork pie." He glared at the cook. "Climbed up me spine like a scared cat, he did."

The ruffled Asian stared back defiantly. "He clazy," he shrieked. "Chen Li not die now."

"For a few seconds, I didn't think you'd make it." Buell snorted. "God, what a sight." Then he pointed east. "There's a batch of horses and three riders. I'm going to get out of here before that hornet's nest figures out what happened. Tell Wu I'm grateful for what he told us." He looked down at the China-man. "Chen, you go with Crazy?" Buell pointed at Red. "Or to town with me?"

"No Clazy. Go town. Chen walk."

"Chen better run unless he wants a bullet in his yellow arse," Red said, and leered at the small man. "We'll see you in a couple weeks, Buell. This was a good one." The Irishman gigged his horse and headed to intercept the herd galloping south a half-mile away.

"Climb up, Chen," Buell said and extended his hand. The

Chinaman shook his head. "Those men are coming, and they aren't happy. Get up here."

Again the man shook his head. "Chen go." Then, with a short bow, he turned and took off running, his short legs lifting the dark-blue shirt that hung to his calves. Buell followed at a lope, glancing over his shoulder from time to time, half-hoping two or three might give chase.

Forty-five minutes later, the Chinese man hurried up the main street until he turned left past Lancer's place—Buell rode his horse toward the stables. He needed a nap.

CHAPTER 15

Buell walked out of the freight-holding shed and onto the dock—Paisley was standing there. "Can you break for a minute and come with me?"

Buell shrugged, put a sheaf of papers on top of a stack of lumber, and secured them with his gloves. He followed Paisley down the plank deck to the office. Inside, Sheriff Staker stood looking at the ivory-handled Remington hanging on the wall.

"Want to tell me the story?" Staker didn't turn around.

"Nothin' to tell. I found out where it was and took it back."

"All by yourself?" Staker turned around.

"I didn't need any help. Bushwhackers are usually lazy."

"Two questions then—who had it, and who told you?"

"What difference does that make, Loren?" Paisley said. "They took his property, assaulted him doing it, and he went and got it back. That sounds fair."

"We're not talking fair. What do you folks hire me for?" The sheriff raised his hand to Buell. "And you don't want to say what you're about to." His eyes narrowed.

"Would it make a difference if I told ya I was outside of Carlisle?"

"Not one damn bit, and you know why."

"Trouble outside Carlisle is not your . . ." Paisley paused and flushed slightly. "You don't have jurisdiction, Loren."

"Until that trouble comes to Carlisle."

"And did it?" Buell asked.

"You *know* it did. How could it not?"

"I'm not following this at all, Loren," Paisley said, and turned to Buell. "Has there been a . . . did you—"

"Nobody's dead—yet." Staker glared at Buell and waited. When Buell remained silent, Staker went on. "Ike Bachman came in on a wagon late last night, the right side of his head cracked like a clay pot. Doc Princher can't say if he'll make it or not. Did you do that, Buell?" Staker's brow furrowed, and he took a step forward.

Paisley moved between them. "You don't have to answer that, son."

Staker's face flooded red. "No, he don't *have* to."

"Let's be reasonable," Paisley said. "We've always been able to talk."

"We have, Mace," Staker said. "Buell's another matter."

"Then let's talk—you and me. Calmly. Okay?" Paisley pointed at the leather couch that stood along the wall. "Sit, and let's see what we have."

"I'm too—I don't wanna sit." Staker went to Paisley's desk and leaned against it. "It's plain as a bloody nose, Buell. Bachman comes to town with his nut busted, and you've got your pistol back." Staker tightly gripped the edge of the desk with both hands, the cords in his neck taut. "I'm saying straight out, I think you did that to him, and if he comes to enough to tell me so, I'm going to have to arrest you for it."

Paisley threw his hands up. "This is all backwards, Loren. That bunch is nothing but trouble, and the first person who steps up and does something about it is—"

"Stop right there," Staker barked. "You know damn well how many times I've thrown the serious troublemakers in jail."

"And what did it get us? A couple months' peace? Maybe a cracked skull will make 'em think twice about coming back for more." Paisley pointed at Buell. "Maybe his way *is* the right way."

"Which means you think he did it too."

"So what? Where the hell has a man's right to protect himself gone to?"

"I usually leave disputes like these alone, Mace, and you know it better than most." Staker's expression was challenging. "But this situation is no longer about him and a couple of the Sandy Island bunch." Staker's fierce gaze settled on Buell. "Am I right!"

"Buell?" Paisley looked confused.

"Tell him," Staker said. "I know some, and I *will* find out the rest."

"I'm tellin' ya, Sheriff, I did what I did alone."

"You walked into that camp—there must be close to thirty men there—just strolled in, and picked up your pistol? I've been there, Buell—there isn't enough room between those shacks to ride a horse. And I know damn well someone went in with you." Staker stood up straight. "Deny it!"

"I don't like being called a liar, Sheriff."

"Their horses were run off, Buell—every last one—scattered across the prairie like flushed quail. I saw the tracks. One man can't do that."

"If their horses were gone, how'd they get to town—with a wounded man?" Paisley asked.

"A team and wagon. Roscoe said—"

"Roscoe!" Buell almost shouted. "You're taking his word over mine?"

"He's right," Paisley said and jutted his jaw. "I want you to tell *me* what the hell you're after and why." He paused and swallowed hard. "Or get the hell outta here." His voice trembled slightly.

Staker's face paled, and he leaned heavily on the desk again.

Surprise drove anger out of Buell's mind as he watched both men struggle for composure. Paisley took half a step toward the lawman, and then stopped when Buell shook his head. Staker sighed deeply and looked at Paisley. "Let me lay it out, Mace," Staker said quietly and deliberately. "Buell—and I suspect Ruben Bedell's hands—rustled that mob's horses. That leaves two dozen cowboys on foot with winter about two weeks away. Bachman aside, that makes for some very dangerous men—men looking to even a score. They know who did it because Bachman made no secret where he got the fancy pistol, and who they roughed up in the fight."

"So this isn't *all* about Buell," Paisley said.

Staker shook his head slowly. "No. And I should have said so right off—I'm sorry about that. It's just that I'm running out of ways to keep the lid on this. There was a Bar-M burned into the wagon seat, and the team carried it, too. The rig is out to Venable's stable by the feedlots—they'll see that Ruben gets it back." Staker looked at Buell. "So what *do* you have to say?"

"I turned three horses loose. That's not rustling."

"Buell," Staker said quietly, "I need some help. I'm *asking* for some help." He met Buell's eyes for only a few seconds, and then his gaze shifted to the floor.

"I'm not seein' what I can do. The only score I settled was my own."

"That whole bunch is going to see this town as the source for all their grief, whether the bunch that run off their herd was Bedell's outfit or not. They're without horses—you know what that means to a cowboy."

"You're talkin' to the wrong man about their horses. I'll say it once more. I went into that camp alone."

"There's going to be hell to pay, Mace," Staker said to Paisley.

"Then I'd go see Ruben Bedell," Paisley replied. "This is not Buell's fight."

147

"I don't think Ruben even knows about it." Staker looked at Buell. "Does he?"

Buell shrugged.

"And even if he did, I'm not sure he'd do anything. His concern is for the ranch and *his* men. This town hasn't been very friendly towards them."

"You've thought about the county I sup—" Paisley stopped and winced. "Never mind. Maybe it's time to go back to the city council and ask for another deputy."

"Paul Steele is the only one who sees any danger, Mace. The rest follow Doc Princher's lead, and he figures if we leave the islanders alone, they will us too."

"Maybe he's right."

"He's not," Buell said. Both men looked at him. "If the five I've met are like the rest, don't count on them figgerin' anything. Their kind don't think, they just do what makes 'em feel good—and that usually means someone else is gonna feel bad."

Staker pushed away from the desk. "Then you understand what I'm up against?"

"I've never said I didn't understand the problem. I just said it's not mine."

"If they can't find you, they're gonna come after your pa and this." Staker waved his hand around the office.

"Then I'd make 'em pay."

"Of course you would, and rightly—" Staker grimaced.

Buell gave him a tight smile. "Rightly so—like I did Bachman."

"I'm wasting my time," Staker said to Paisley. "I'll bring this up tonight at the council meeting. Maybe with the election a week away, I can stir somebody up."

Paisley put out his hand. "I'll support whatever you decide to do, Loren. I always have."

Staker shook Paisley's hand and then glanced at Buell.

"What he does is his decision," Paisley added. "Has been since he was about thirteen."

Staker closed the door, and his footsteps faded down the dock.

"I've never seen him beg," Paisley said. His face looked sad.

"I was glad to see him beg," Buell replied.

"What! How can you say such a thing?"

"I left Idaho because of a deal a lot like this one. I didn't know who to trust, who had his bet where, who was lyin', or who was honest. I needed to know where Staker stood, Pa—now I do." His father looked perplexed. "I've been here six months and only found out just now that I can trust you."

"Buell!" Paisley's face crumpled with hurt and confusion. "I'm your father."

"Who didn't want to hear what I had to say until Staker said some of the things he did. This town is going to learn a hard lesson, Pa. I saw it as soon as I arrived. Folks who shouldn't have secrets, sneakin' around. Old friends talkin' about each other, takin' sides when there ain't no reason to, and lookin' twice in the mirror, hopin' to see somethin' different."

"I offered—I asked you out to talk."

"You asked me out to listen. You asked me out to get my support. That was an insult."

"I'm sorry, son. That's not—"

"I know you didn't mean it. You didn't even know you was doin' it. That's how the whole town is."

"Where did you get all this, Buell? Where did you learn to see life like this?"

"When you've got no friends, you learn to watch everybody. When you're not sure what folks think, expect them to look to themselves. I've had two friends I trusted with my life. I killed one, and the other is lookin' to trade his soul for somethin' shiny—crow bait."

"So what are *we* gonna do. I mean, you and me and Ruth."

"Maybe nothin'. I know Staker has run out of rope, and if I have to do something, he's not gonna look too close." Buell smiled.

"What? Why you grinning?"

" 'The good of the why kinda balances the bad of the how.' A man told me that after I'd—I had a—I did what I needed to do one time. It wasn't pretty, but I was right."

Paisley shook his head, a frown forming. "I'd try to understand if ya wanted to tell me."

"You don't need to know. We'll get through this. I've got a wagon to load." He went to the door, opened it, and then turned back. "And I appreciate you stickin' up for me."

Buell hauled down hard on the rope, threw two half hitches around a stanchion, and tucked the tag end under the canvas cover. "That's got it, Walt. Knock off for today. With a forty-mile round trip, you're gonna have a long one tomorrow."

"You don't have to say that twice, boss." The burly muleskinner climbed down from the loaded wagon and pulled his gloves off. "Kin I ask you a question?"

"You kin always ask." Buell enjoyed working with the easygoing man. Walt was about the same age as he, but had not grown up in Carlisle. A hard worker, he never complained and talked very little. He did say enough that Buell knew he had a wife he cared for deeply, and two young girls he doted on.

"A bunch of us had a rhubarb session at noon. Me, Mose, and, well—you know—the regulars."

"Someone not happy? You know I work fer the company jist like you do."

"It ain't nothin' like that. We heard about what ya did to them outlaws downriver and—"

"What did you hear and from who?"

"Heard that you and a bunch of cowboys run their horses off, and damn near killed Ike Bachman. That big fella you crippled last spring, Roscoe, was talkin' about it in the saloon last night."

"So what's your question?"

"Is there gonna be trouble? Is that bunch gonna come to town and tear things up? They've done it before, ya know."

Walt's face showed concern but no fear. Just the way he stood, shoulders square, and feet set apart, made Buell smile to himself. "Let me ask you one before I answer—what'll you do if there is?"

"Go home and protect my family." Walt leaned forward slightly. "Anybody coming through my gate without an invite won't leave standin' up."

"What do the rest think?"

"They think you'd make a good sheriff. Not sayin' that Sheriff Staker *ain't* a good one, but—well, we hear things."

"I'm a workaday freight hauler. I've got no interest in being a lawman."

"Too bad, I think."

"What else do ya hear? I don't mix much—you've noticed, maybe?"

"About what?"

"Stuff. The election, treasonous Democrats, price of coffee." Buell ticked off each topic on his fingertips as he spoke. "Stuff."

"I'm gonna vote for yer pa. So's lots of us plain folks."

"Why?"

"For one, he ain't a liar. He's always willin' to help out. Even livin' out there in that fancy, gingerbread house—no offense— he'll still say howdy to us."

"How many of you do you think will vote for him?"

Walt paused for a few seconds. "Most of the people I 'sociate with, twenty-five or thirty."

"Do people usually vote?"

"Those that live in town? Like a religion. Ya didn't answer my question."

"Where people are, trouble is too, Walt. It's just a matter of how bad."

"And that's what's worryin' some of us. How bad?"

"That we won't know till it's over. Go home. We'll handle what comes our way."

The round-faced clock read two forty-five when Buell pushed open the office door and went in.

Paisley looked up. "Problem?"

"Nope. Got that load for Langdon ready to go. I sent Walt home."

"Good. He's one of the best we got, and that's a long trip."

"I'm gonna take off too, okay?"

"Sure, son." Paisley squirmed a little in his seat. "Uh, jist wonderin'—you registered to vote?"

Buell chuckled. "I've never voted in my life."

Paisley raised an eyebrow.

"Can't a person do that on election day?"

"You can, but they appreciate it if you do it before. I would too."

"Where do I sign up?"

"The Methodist Church." Paisley smiled. "And thanks."

"Don't mean I'm voting for you—axle-greaser." Buell dodged out the door and slammed it as a pencil flew across the room.

CHAPTER 16

The church smelled of floor wax and camphor, a comforting scent. Two ladies Buell didn't recognize sat in the foyer at a small table. They eyed him as he pulled the door shut and took off his hat. "Is this where I register to vote?"

Both women nodded in unison, and then the one with an open ledger in front of her spoke: "Your name, age, address, and occupation, please."

"I'm Buell Mace. I'm, uh, twenty-six. No, twenty-seven, and I haul stuff."

"Oh, yes, you're Paisley's son," she said as she wrote. "Ruth is a member here." She dipped her pen and looked up at him. "I know already, but you have to state your place of residence." The lady's smile was tightly officious.

"I live at, uh—I stay in the stable, Mace's Transportation, Third Street."

Two left hands flew to two mouths. "Oh," the ledger-keeper said, shaking her head. She wrote some more in the book. "There—you're registered, Mister Mace." The smile appeared even more tightly controlled.

"Thank you, ma'am," Buell said as heat crept up his neck to his ears. He hurried out the door and stood on the porch for a moment, looking back, annoyed that he felt a bit ashamed. Dammit! He started down the steps just as a one-horse, covered carriage pulled to a stop in the street. He started to walk around it.

"Why, Buell, what on earth?" Ana Steele said.

"Hi, Missus Steele. Guess I wasn't payin' much mind." He backtracked to stand by the wheel.

She smiled warmly. "You registered, didn't you? Good." She turned to the young man beside her. "Eric is old enough to vote this year. I can hardly believe that."

The driver was a young Paul Steele: capable hands, intense eyes, and a shock of sandy-brown hair. "Good to see you again, Buell," the young man said as he climbed out the far side and came around. They shook hands.

"Go on in, Eric—they'll help you out," Ana said. Eric nodded, went up the steps and inside. "I'm so glad to catch you like this," Ana continued. "I came with him to pick up a few things at the store. I'm making my cobbler—remember it?"

"Oh, yes, ma'am. Your cobbler's one of the things I'd remember when I was gone and home come to mind."

"Then you have to come out for supper—tonight!"

"Well, I don't—"

"It's Monday, Buell. *Nothing* happens on Monday. I insist."

"But—"

"You promised me the end of June that you'd come out for coffee—my famous coffee you said."

"I guess you got me. I'd be pleased. What time?"

"We eat at six. And no need to dress up, really. We're still soddies at heart."

"Six it is, then." He touched his hat brim, and walked away.

That evening, Buell chuckled to himself as he tied Shadow to the iron post outside the gate. Soddies. The two-story house had been built before he and Simon left Carlisle, but now it was a home. The well-planned flower beds—tilled patches of bare earth now—promised a glorious display in the spring. The picket fence, plumb-bob straight, tips perfectly even, gleamed white in the low light. Four lace-hung, eight-pane windows in front flooded the porch with light.

He pulled the gate shut, and went up the steps to the door. A "T" handle protruded below the oval window. An agitated buzz sounded inside when he turned it. A moment later the door swung open, and to Buell's relief, Simon stood there in faded trousers and an old shirt. "Hi, Buell." He stepped back. "C'mon in. We're all in the kitchen."

Ana stood at a gleaming black- and nickel-plated stove, whisking something in the bottom of a large roaster that sat on top. To one side, Paul worked at reducing a pair of golden-brown chickens to neat slices of white meat and chunks of dark. The room was as impressive as Buell remembered it: a smooth plank-wood floor, tall yellow-pine cabinets, gleaming gaslight fixtures, the whole dominated by a polished pine table and eight cane-backed chairs. Eric and a beautiful young girl sat together on the far side of it. Buell found himself staring at her.

"Mom," the girl said. "He doesn't remember me." She laughed and stood. "I'm Abby, Buell—grown up."

"I never would have recognized ya, Abby. I guess I come in expectin' to see little ones."

Ana turned from the stove. "They even get away from me sometimes, Buell," she said. "Go sit—supper's ready as soon as I finish this gravy."

"Sit by me, Buell!" Abby insisted. "I have dozens of questions."

"Where are Ax and Abe?" Buell made his way around to her.

"Both in school." Paul set a platter of chicken on the table. "Both gonna be lawyers, looks like."

Buell glanced at Eric.

"Me and school don't get along," Eric said flatly, and looked directly at his father.

Buell chuckled. "I remember feelin' the same way."

"I suppose he can learn the way I did," Paul said. "The hard way."

"Hard lessons stick," Buell said, and immediately wished he hadn't.

"Have you had some hard lessons?" Abby asked.

He turned to answer and found himself looking directly into her eyes. Soft brown and full of eager curiosity, they held steady on his own until she blinked, showing him perfectly curved eyelashes. To his mind, the reflex lasted seconds. Her gaze seemed to mirror the soft smile that formed on her lips. Buell felt panic. "A few, I guess," he muttered.

Paul cleared his throat, and Buell tore his gaze away from Abby to find himself looking at the top of Steele's head. He folded his hands in his lap and bowed his head. "Dear Lord," Paul prayed, "Bless this gathering of family and a very welcome guest, bless our country and her leaders, watch over our boys at school, and bless this food to our bodies. We ask in Jesus' name, Amen."

Buell mouthed the closing as he'd done all his life, somewhat embarrassed every time he felt required to do it. The room burst alive with the sound of silver against porcelain as serving dishes circulated around the table. Creamy mashed potatoes, gravy, squash, canned corn, ruby-red beets, sweet pickles, hot biscuits, butter, gooseberry jam, and chicken. Buell's mouth watered as he loaded his plate.

"Simon said that at Fort Laramie you had Indians nearby." Abby started immediately. "Did you ever have to fight them?"

"Abby!" Ana declared. "Let him eat something first."

Buell flashed Ana a tight smile of thanks, and started in on his meal. Out of the corner of his eye he caught Abby's glances, aware of her body heat and floral scent. "So, Simon, what's this nonsense about Indians?" he blurted.

Simon stopped mid-chew, then swallowed, nearly choking.

"Uh, I told them about Walks Fast. And uh, about how I got Spud."

"Where is that old dog?" Buell asked quickly. "I don't think I've seen him twice since we got back."

"Spends most of his time with Eric, running around the farms. He has a place in the barn."

"Simon said you were attacked by Indians." Abby's eyes sparkled. "Tell us about that, Buell." She glanced at her mother.

"Simon's story about one sneakin' up on him is better." Buell began: "Happened at night, and Spud saved his hide." Simon's annoyed look made Buell feel much more at ease, and he reached to spear a beet slice.

"You never mentioned that, Simon," Ana said.

"Because it was nothing. I never got a scratch."

"Only because of the dog," Buell said around his food, and grinned. "Quite a story, really."

"Simon?" Ana cocked her head.

Simon put down his fork. "I left the restaurant after work one night"—he shot Buell a warning glance—"and just as I stepped up on the porch of our little place, I heard, or more likely sensed, someone coming. I was a little startled, I guess. I turned to see and luckily I put my arm up. It was an Indian—we decided later that he had been robbing us—and we both fell to the ground. Right then Spud, who had been out taking a last run before bed, came charging back and knocked the man off of me, and chased him away. There—the nighttime Indian story."

"Did he have a tomahawk?" Amy's eyes opened wide.

"No, he did not," Simon said firmly.

"He had a long, sharp dagger instead," Buell added. "Long as that carving knife your dad used on this chicken—stuck the poor dog with it." Simon's narrowed eyes and tight lips made Buell chuckle out loud. "Well, he did, Simon. I think it was a very brave thing you did—protecting our stuff."

"Good Lord, son," Paul said. "You actually fought an Indian with a knife—bare-handed?"

Buell nodded sagely. "Told ya. Brave."

Everybody looked at Simon, the meal forgotten. He glared at Buell. "That's ridiculous. It was over before I knew it. And yes, he did wound Spud, but I think all the man was trying to do was get away."

"Did he take your money and things?" Eric asked.

"Sure did," Buell said. "All of it. Simon went right to the Indian camp and demanded they point out the thief. Walks Fast, their chief, told him to come back the next day, and he'd have it all."

"Did he?" Abby asked breathlessly.

"Sure did. Plus, he gave Simon that horse outside, Shadow, and Simon gave him to me. I think because he felt bad about me almost losing all my stuff. Quite a brother you have there."

The look on Paul Steele's face suddenly changed from intrigued to amused.

"I gave you that horse because you liked him," Simon said emphatically.

"Then it is true, all of it!" Abby squealed. "Oh, what a wonderful story!"

Simon groaned. "Some of it's as he said. Most of it should be in a Beadle's dime novel."

"It's the way I remember it," Buell said. "Wonderful beets, Missus Steele—best I ever had."

The cobbler came last, along with hot coffee, and it was as good as Buell remembered. The clotted cream Ana scooped out of a crock partially melted and ran onto the plate. Warm slices of peach mixed with tender crust and the cool cream. Buell caught himself rubbing his knee with pleasure at the same time he saw Ana's satisfied look. "Oh, Missus Steele, a meal like this makes a man think twice about stayin' single."

"I can make this," Abby said, and blushed.

" 'Cept ya can't eat the bottom crust," Eric chided. "And that's if you can chisel through the crumble on top."

Abby hit his broad shoulder with the heel of her hand. "None for you next time, Eric!" She put on an obviously fake pout for a moment, and then smiled at Buell. "I'm learning."

A few minutes later Simon pushed his plate away and leaned back. "All right, everybody, now we hear a story from Buell." He tilted his chin up, plainly daring Buell to refuse.

"Oh, yes," Abby said.

"Sounds fair," Paul added and picked up his cup.

"I suppose you want Indians and shooting and—scalps!" He thrust his face at Abby and she squealed. Buell leaned forward, and put his folded arms on the table. "Me and a fella name Prescott decided to—" Buell stopped and looked at Simon. "No interruptions, Simon—this is like I remember it."

Simon slowly shook his head. "Oh, go ahead."

"Me and Tay—that's his first name—decided to go take a look at the Dakota country. Simon was busy with some German high muckety-mucks in velvet pants—they was hunting wolves or something with dogs, so it was just me and Tay. We rode four days to the north and finally come to the mountains that Tay knowed about. Just before we got there, Tay told me what we was gonna look for—gold! Now this was, what, seventy-one? Anyway, it was before the trouble that's goin' on up there now. Somehow ol' Tay knew where to go. Straight in we went, Indian sign everywhere, smoke signals billowing into the sky all day long. And at night, if you listened real close"—Buell lowered his voice to a whisper—"war drums." Abby swallowed hard.

"Well, we snaked our way in without being seen, and Tay found us a nice stream to work. He showed me how to pan for gold, and then sent me off in one direction, him goin' the other, plan bein' to test along the creek for what he called 'colors.' I didn't find much of anything. But on the second day, Tay said he thought the gold was up higher—in a dry, dead-end canyon. Goin' in there with no way out made us both plenty nervous. But I had been bit by the gold bug, just like Tay knew I was gonna be, and off we went.

"It was hard work without water, but about three days later Tay found what we wanted. Why, one shovelful of gravel sometimes had a dozen nuggets in it, most near the size of my thumb. We had two mules with us and loaded big saddlebags called *panniers* with the stuff we dug up"—Buell mangled the French word—"and took it to the water below to wash it out. We worked from first light till we couldn't see in the evening. Finally, we had a leather water-bucket plumb full of them nuggets."

"Full?" Eric whispered.

"Yep. Took us both to lift it." Buell slowly looked around the table before continuing in a lower voice. "And then." He paused, took a deep breath, and let it go with a slight shudder. "What we feared most come sneakin' up the canyon. At least they was tryin' to sneak. One of Tay's mules had been taught to smell Indians—from a mile away, or more. He'd paw the ground and kinda make a huff sound. Well, we was jist finishin' our supper when that mule started. Tay told me to dump the water bag and coffeepot on the fire, and git into the bushes." Buell hunched over the tabletop.

"So there we was, peerin' out of the weeds. I had my Remington and a Sharps rifle, Tay only had a muzzleloader, but"—Buell's eyes shifted from side to side—"he had a big ol' pigsticker." He described twelve inches in the air with his forefingers. "And Tay knew how to use it. Lucky for us, or so I thought at the time, there was a full moon and we could see clear across our camp—easy to spot the first heathen that come belly-crawling through the rocks below. I pulled down on him with my pistol, and then felt Tay's hand on my arm. 'Wait,' he whispered. 'And we kin git 'em all.' So I did, and sure enough, the rest of 'em came on—four, then six, then four more. Ten Indians in all. I did some fast cipherin' and knew we was gonna run out of bullets before we did Injuns."

"Oh, dear," Abby breathed.

"I was figgerin' what to do when they all stood up at once and charged into camp, screaming like Irish banshees and waving tomahawks—they *all* had tomahawks. I raised up my pistol and again Tay stopped me. 'Till you kin count their teeth,' he said. I can tell ya, I was gettin' a little nervous. But I trusted Tay, and I waited. The savages were now as close as the front door, and then *half* that—'Kill 'em all!' Tay cried and I started to shoot, just as fast as I could haul back the hammer. Tay's long gun exploded and the chief, right out in front, fell to the ground, his huge feather headdress lookin' like a pile of peacocks."

Abby's breath came in short gasps, her linen napkin a damp wad in her hand.

"Six times I shot, each bullet fetchin' an Indian square in the chest. And then I picked up my Sharps, and killed one more. Jehoshaphat, we were down to *two*. I stood up straight to fight the one comin' right at me. And just as I did, six more of the screamin' devils appeared—it was like they popped up out of the ground. I looked at Tay, and this time I was worried. He didn't even blink when he said, calm as a clam, 'There be mor'n we kin handle, I reckon.' " Buell stopped talking and bowed his head, shaking it slowly.

"Buell!" Abby cried and grabbed his arm. "What *happened?*"

Buell looked up, lips set in a tight line. "Tay was right, Abby—they killed us both and took the gold."

For several seconds, her face showed the struggle, and then

she started beating Buell on the arm with both hands. "You—
you!"

"Ten little Indians?" Simon asked, and started to howl.
"Good grief, Buell," he snorted, "That's terrible!"

Paul chuckled and Ana's shoulders quaked as she watched
her daughter.

Color fired Abby's face, and her eyes flashed. "That's *awful.*"
She hit Buell again. "I feel like an idiot!"

"It was a good story," Paul said. "Well told. Now admit it,
Abby, he had you completely."

"Me too," Eric said. "That's better than Beadles. I couldn't
see how you was gonna make it"—he leaned back in his chair
laughing, his arms holding his stomach—"And ya *didn't,*" he
hooted. They were now all laughing out loud—all except Abby,
who sat glaring at Buell.

In the darkness of his room that night, soft brown eyes, full of
eager curiosity, confused Buell's restless dreams.

CHAPTER 17

Buell remembered that election day in Idaho City had passed almost unnoticed, but in Carlisle the event took on the trappings of a national holiday. Townspeople, dressed in their best, filled the streets and boardwalks. Two competing brass bands punched the air with exuberant tubas and thundering drums, with fireworks exploding at random for emphasis. The saloons did a brisk business dispensing free beer, courtesy of various election committees.

Most businesses closed early or hadn't opened at all, Mace's Transportation and Portage included, so Buell was surprised when he found the office door unlocked. He went in to find Paisley, his face florid above a too-tight strip of celluloid, sitting on the couch with a whiskey glass in one hand and a bottle in the other.

"What're you doin' here, Pa?"

"I could ask the same."

"I needed to check something on the load to Hailey tomorrow. It'll leave before I get here in the mornin'. You're drinkin'."

"So's everybody." Paisley's speech sounded carefully controlled.

"Not sayin' ya shouldn't be, but why here? I saw ya this morning at Luger's, shakin' hands and havin' a good time."

"I got tired of hearin' them spoutin' one thing when I could tell they'd done somethin' else. But hell, that's their right. They can vote how they want." He splashed his glass half full. "Sit down, son. Better yet, get yer coffee mug and have a drink with me. Go on—get it."

Buell fetched it off the cold stove, sat down on the couch, and held it out. Paisley poured until Buell raised it. "Whoa."

"To a broke down old man," Paisley said, and lifted his glass.

"I ain't drinkin' to that. Ya ain't broke down or old."

"We was happy livin' over there in the barn, wasn't we?" Paisley took a swig.

"Yeah. I still am. And you should be." Buell shrugged. "Nice house, this business. I know for a fact the men who work for ya respect you a lot."

"But did they vote for me?" Paisley smiled crookedly.

"Yeah, Pa, I think they did. Is that what this is all about?"

"That and everything else. I liked Carlisle when it was small and I knew everybody. When Paul was flat broke and strugglin', and Ruth would come to me when she needed protection—did ya know that, son? She'd show me bruises in places that I wasn't supposed to see—ya understand what I'm saying? I miss just worrying about you being out on the prairie half the night, instead of buckin' scum like Roscoe and Bachman." Paisley's eyes glazed over. "I miss just bein' Mace." He lowered his head.

Buell sat, silently listening to the hubbub outside, until his father heaved a deep sigh and leaned back on the couch. "I don't have answers to any of that," Buell said, " 'cause I don't have enough years. But I do know my pa, and this ain't like him. I was out to the Steeles' last night for supper. We talked a lot about this election, and Paul come right out and said he was glad you were runnin' for mayor."

"Then why hasn't he said he'll vote for me?"

" 'Cause he probably won't. He thinks different about what the town needs. That don't mean you're wrong and he's right. He wanted you to run because it would make people think. It made good sense to me. Paul is still your friend—in fact he thinks you're his best friend."

"He say that?" Paisley leaned forward and put the bottle on the floor.

"He didn't have to. Hell, he remembers when he was broke. Matter of fact, we talked about that too. He's your friend, all right."

"I guess this gettin' whipped don't sit too good with me. I'm not used to it."

"I could tell ya it ain't over yet, but I won't. A fella told me once, 'Ya can't win if ya won't play, and you've lost for sure if you don't.' "

"Humph, never heard it put quite like that. I may have done it for the wrong reasons anyhow. This is usually what happens when you do that."

"Don't ya want to be mayor?"

"Yes—and no. At first, I thought maybe it would make Ruth happy. And then I thought I just might make a difference in the town. Turns out I'm not gonna find out, either. She's a strange woman, son. Sometimes I wonder why she married me."

Buell tipped his cup and drained it. "Let's get out of here. Go back to Luger's, or maybe go see how Lancer is doin'. Not good to sit here and grump about what ain't happened yet."

Paisley glanced at the clock. "Three-thirty—most of the folks who're gonna vote already have, I suppose. But you're right. Besides"—he reached down for his bottle—"I sit here much longer, I'll have to count on staying at your place." He stood up, went to his desk, and laid the bottle in a drawer. Smoothing out some of the wrinkles in his black suit, he offered Buell a reluctant half-smile. "So, I'll go grin, shake hands, and act like an axle-greaser." His light tone did not carry into his face.

They walked down the steps of the loading dock, and had just turned toward Main Street when Paisley stopped. "What in hell's that?" A steady stream of mounted men moved slowly along Main Street.

In the space visible between the corner buildings, Buell counted fifteen horses. The hair on his neck prickled until he realized they weren't islanders. "Looks like ranch hands. But why not—everybody took today off."

"But they can't vote," Paisley said.

"They can drink," Buell said and chuckled. "C'mon, let's go mix with some real folks." They carried on up the street as the parade continued. At the corner, the riders' destination became apparent. Dozens of horses clogged the street in front of and along one side of the Methodist Church. Lined up on the walkway, the cowboys stood in a single file that snaked all the way to the sheriff's office over a block away.

Buell spotted Ruben Bedell coming out of the church. A conversation he'd had with the rancher flashed into his mind: "Tell your father he has my support," he'd said. "And maybe that of my horses." His horses—his men. "They're voting, Pa."

"But they can't—they don't live here."

"Let's ask him," Buell said and pointed at Ruben. They stepped into the street and hurried across.

"Ruben!" Paisley shouted and waved. The rancher turned, raised his hand, and then headed their way.

"Afternoon, Paisley," he said as he approached. "Nice turnout you got here."

They shook hands. "But your men can't vote."

"How ya doin', Buell?" The rancher grinned broadly. "Thought you'd be out for some of Wu's cookin' by now."

"Been busy, Mister Bedell."

"So I understand."

"*Are* they voting, Ruben?" Paisley insisted.

"Sure. It's their constitutional right."

"But they're not registered—they can't be."

"They can register today—law says so. All they need is proof of residency."

"But they live out on ranches, and in line shacks."

"Look close," Ruben said and pointed at the line of dusty men.

Each man in the long queue had what looked like a small book—dime-novel size—some rolled up, some folded and stuffed in pockets, some actually being looked at. "What's that they have with them?" Buell asked.

"Seed catalogs. And every one addressed to the man holding it—through the Carlisle Post Office. I hope it helps, Paisley."

"They're not gonna let us get away with that." Paisley snorted. "Not a chance in hell."

"I don't see how *they* can stop it. I checked already. Their vote is as good as yours."

"I don't know what to say." Paisley's mouth opened and closed a couple times. "I'm—I—"

"How about offering to buy me a beer like any good politician?"

Paisley grinned, and this time his eyes joined in. "I could take that as an insult."

"Long as you buy the beer, you can take it any way ya want." Ruben clapped Paisley on the shoulder. "Let's go wait for the count."

Later at the city hall, Buell, Paisley, and Ruben forced their way through the crowded foyer and into the back of the meeting room. Buell climbed onto a chair for a better look at the front. The three members of the election board sat at a raised table, and a short, red-faced Sherm Pederson stood facing them. "It's plain dishonest—it's cheating!" Sherm shouted above the noise. "I want a recount. No, I want my opponent to concede. This is fraud!"

The chairman of the election board slammed his gavel onto

167

the tabletop repeatedly. "Order!" he hollered. "Everybody be quiet!" The noise level in the room rose.

"They're not gonna settle down any time soon," Paisley said to Ruben, and the rancher nodded.

Buell looked over the crowded room until he spotted Simon. He and his father were all the way across the hall. Simon saw him, too, and pointed toward the door. Buell nodded and got down. "I'm gettin' out of here, Pa. I hope the count stands." He offered his hand.

"Even if it don't, son." Paisley grabbed hold and squeezed hard. "This isn't going to be settled until the judge has his say. I guess I'll see you tomorrow morning."

Buell waited outside the door until Simon pushed his way through the crowd, and they stepped into the middle of the street.

"Well, that was a surprise," Simon said as they walked.

"Nobody more surprised than my pa. You should have seen him earlier."

"I did—over at Luger's. He looked fine."

"I found him in the office this afternoon with a bottle."

"What!" Simon stopped.

"Yep. He'd convinced himself nobody was gonna vote for him. I told him some of what we talked about last night. He found it hard to believe." They moved to the side for a passing buggy.

"*Exactly* what? We talked about a lot of things."

"About yer pa supporting him even though he was voting for Pederson."

"Pa and Mace are lifelong friends, Buell. He doubted that?"

"Like I said, he'd convinced himself of a lot of things. He was having doubts. Hell, we all have days like that."

"He won't have any more if that eleven-vote margin holds."

"What do you think, Simon?"

"Pa said it completely changed his perception of Ruben Bedell. Ordering seed catalogs for all the cowboys in the county was smart—sending them General Delivery at the post office was genius. Judge Kingsley is in his office reading election law right now. So, what do I think? I think we'll just wait and see." They stopped in front of Luger's. The air hummed with the noises beyond the closed door. Simon grimaced. "Do you want to go in?"

"Not really. C'mon over to my place. We haven't had a chance to talk since before harvest."

At his place, Buell picked up his sheepskin coat from the easy chair and chucked it into the bedroom. "Sit there and I'll get us a drink." He took two glasses out of the cupboard, blew in the bottom of each, and grabbed a half-empty bottle of brandy.

"Just a short one, Buell. I've had a snoot-full of that stuff today."

Buell pulled the cork with his teeth, poured a dollop in each tumbler, and handed one to Simon. Collapsing into the other soft chair, he jammed the stopper back in the bottle and put it on the floor. "What do we drink to, Simon?"

"Peace and quiet."

"That's for damn sure." They touched rims and took a sip.

Simon settled back. "Where did you get that story you told last night? That was absolute nonsense—brilliantly told—but pure bullshit. And to hear you talk for ten whole minutes—well, I've never seen that side of you."

"I just put some things together. Stuff I'd heard."

"And you completely turned the story about Spud getting stabbed on its ear. You should have heard Abby after you left. She thinks I'm Ulysses. And *you*, she thinks you're—" Simon stopped. "She's quite taken with you, Buell."

Buell gulped the rest of his drink and reached for the bottle.

"Ya hear me?" Simon asked.

"Where ya been keepin' her, Simon? Last night was the first time I've seen her."

"She doesn't spend a lot of time at Lancer's." Simon smiled.

"I did some figgerin' last night. She's nineteen, right?"

"Last May, a week before we got home." Simon leaned forward and cocked his head. "Don't be gettin' any ideas. Pa'd come after you with a whip, and Ma with a butcher knife."

"God, Simon, I was just askin'. It was *you* brought it up."

"Only to tell you she's spoken for—by Jeremy Princher."

"*That* little turd? I haven't seen him since we were in school. Always running down the street bawlin' about something."

"Bawlin' about you giving him a noggin-knuckle or worse. And the little *turd,* as you call him, is in his third year at medical school."

"You'd wish a Doc Princher on your sister?"

"He's not at all like his father. He was home for a while this summer—I think you'd like him."

"Believe me, Simon—I won't like Jeremy Princher."

"Well, if Abby should show more than just friendly interest, you are honor bound, as my friend, to discourage it." Simon grinned. "Or I'll have to kick your ass."

Buell huffed. "Don't let nothin' but fear and better judgment stop ya." He reached for the bottle. "She's safe with me. Now have another snort, and you can tell me who else I can't *con-sort* with."

The next day, Buell's head hurt with every step, so when Paisley came into the loading shed and hollered for him, Buell nearly went to his knees. "Three o'clock," his father shouted. "Judge Kingsley will be at City Hall at three with his decision."

Buell held up his hand. "Don't holler, Pa. My skull is about to split."

"The evils of drink, my son," Paisley said lightly. "Never touch the stuff myself."

"Right." Buell sat down on a bale. "So, are ya ready—either way?"

"After yesterday I am. You're a good man, Buell. As well as a good son."

"You like the cheap help. Ya ain't foolin' me."

"Where'd ya get the pop-skull?"

"Me'n Simon—at my place last night. I shouldn't keep that much around."

"So, what did he think of my chances?"

Buell grunted. "Typical Simon—'Wait and see.' What time is it?"

"About two-thirty. You comin' over?"

"Yeah. I'm just goin' through the motions here anyway."

The meeting room wasn't nearly as full as the night before, and the chairs had been lined up so everyone could sit. The election board sat at the front table along with Judge Kingsley. Sherm Pederson and his supporters sat in a group on the right. Sherm glared as they walked in.

"He ain't lookin' happy," Buell whispered. "Maybe he already knows."

"I doubt it. The judge and him don't see eye-to-eye on much."

They took their seats just as the chairman banged his gavel and stood. "Let's get to this business of the meeting right off. Mayor Pederson asked for a survey of the votes, as is his right. We, the election board, can report we have a final result." A murmur went through the crowd. "First, several—"

Judge Kingsley cleared his throat.

"First, thirteen votes have been voided."

"Only thirteen?" Sherm shouted.

The chairman banged the gavel again. "We'll have order." He

glared at the mayor. "Thirteen votes have been declared invalid." He paused for several seconds. "I'll let Judge Kingsley explain. Judge." He sat down as Kingsley stood.

"Concerning the case at hand, the election law of the State of Nebraska stipulates that proof of residency can be satisfied by a voter availing himself of a delivery box at a United States Post Office, or by receiving correspondence through General Delivery. I'd like to make the point here that eight of ten patrons in Carlisle proper receive their mail General Delivery. Therefore, the votes cast by *most* of the ranch labor and owners are valid and counted as such." As the muttering started, he raised his hand. "However, a cross-check of the names on the mail presented as evidence of residency against the registration rolls resulted in eleven votes from outside Carlisle being dis-counted—as were two from within. The final result is five hundred seven to five hundred five. Paisley Mace prevails."

Paisley's lips moved, but nothing came out. Then, dozens of men mobbed him, all seeking to shake his hand or slap him on the shoulder. Buell stepped back and watched for a few minutes before going outside. He looked up the street just in time to see Gus Swartz turn the corner and head toward Lancer's. Buell hesitated, then followed him.

CHAPTER 18

Buell pushed the door shut behind and spotted Gus just set-
tling down at a table with two others. Even without seeing his
face, Buell recognized the man who sat with his back to him.
Ignoring Art, who was behind the bar polishing shot glasses, he
strode across the nearly empty room, and stopped directly
behind Roscoe. "How's the leg?" Gus looked up and Roscoe
started in his chair. "Just sit still, Roscoe." Buell glanced at the
man sitting to Gus's left. "And you keep yer hands right there
on the table."

"Yer damned bossy fer just one man," Gus said.

"Roscoe don't think so, do ya?" Buell kneed the back of the
chair. "Last time I saw him, he wanted to skin me. Right?" He
jostled the chair again. "Right!" Buell slapped Roscoe's hat off
his head. When Gus made to get up, Buell's hand dropped to
his pistol. "Nobody here to stop me this time, Gus. And Roscoe
knows what I'm talkin' about, don't ya, Roscoe." Buell could
see his answer on Gus's face. "I bet ya had a good laugh about
that." He shoved the back of Roscoe's head. "Ya don't seem to
find it so funny now. Why's that?"

"Yer bitin' off a big wad," Gus said and glanced sideways.
The man to his left gave his head a slight shake, and spread his
fingers on the tabletop.

"I don't think so, Gus. If there were three like you, I might
ease back a little, but there ain't. Roscoe has a stripe up his
back a foot wide and yellow as piss in new snow." Gus glared

173

across the table at Roscoe. Buell chuckled. "See what I mean?"

"You got something to say to me, Mace, say it," Gus said.

"Sure. I come in here to see you until I saw lard-ass here. Then I thought I'd see if he'd give me a reason to bust up his other leg." Buell shoved Roscoe's head again, this time harder. "But I guess not." The front door banged open, and Buell glanced at the backbar mirror. Three men hurried in, saw Lancer's hand go up, and immediately went to the far end of the room.

Gus's jaw muscles rippled as he gripped the table's edge. "Speak yer piece," he muttered through tight lips.

"You had some words of advice the last time we talked. That was over at Luger's, remember, just before Jake *threw* you out?" The third man's eyebrows rose, and he looked at Gus. "Oh yeah, he ain't as mean as he'd like you to think," Buell said. "You was tellin' me what a bad decision it would be if my pa ran for mayor. I saw ya leavin' City Hall." Gus's slight twitch confirmed Buell's guess. "So I know ya heard the good news. Now, listen to *my* advice. You so much as blink twice at my pa, and I'll splatter what little brains you have all over the street. That's a *promise*, Gus." Buell reached down and caught the top of Roscoe's ear. "And for *you*, I'll need even less of a reason." He twisted his hand, and a gasp came from the other end of the room. "You'll be missin' mor'n yer horse between yer legs."

Buell stepped aside and stomped on Roscoe's hat. "Now you can stand up, lard-ass, and make yer case, or sit there and think about what you'd do if ya had help." Roscoe's eyes shifted to meet Buell's and immediately looked away. "How 'bout you?" Buell addressed the third man.

"Nothin' to do with me, Mister," he said in a nasal whine. "I jist come to town two days ago."

"You're in bad company," Buell said, and then looked at Gus. "You're thinkin' bad things again, Gus. Just remember, I

174

can make 'em a lot worse."

He kicked Roscoe's hat toward their table, then, keeping his eyes on the big mirror, sauntered over to Lancer. Gus had hold of Roscoe's shirtsleeve and was pulling hard on it. Buell couldn't hear what was being said, but the stranger at the table had moved his chair well back, eyeing the front door.

"Mace won," Lancer said, and smiled.

"Yep, he did—by two votes. Some folks ain't real happy right now."

Lancer glanced at Gus. "Like him." His hands came out from under the counter to pick up a whiskey glass and towel again.

"And the people who pay him. I wish I knew who that was. Any ideas?"

"Can't tell."

Buell looked directly at the bartender. "Can't—or won't?"

"Can't," Art said sharply, and paid for it with a deep, soupy cough. He looked pained.

"Sorry, Art," Buell apologized. "I hate an enemy I can't see."

Art nodded acceptance. "Drink?"

"No, I got a head 'bout to split in half and work to do."

Lancer glanced towards Gus.

"Him and me needed to understand each other," Buell said. "I think we do."

Art shook his head. "Roscoe?"

"Roscoe's a coward. I knew it, and now everybody does." Buell looked up at the mirror again. "Gotta git. Maybe I'll drop by after work." He reached up and pressed both thumbs into his temples and grimaced. "No—I won't."

"Welcome," Lancer replied.

Buell walked the half-block to Main Street and turned west. A few people nodded and gave him a high sign as they passed, but most avoided his eyes. As he passed Luger's, he heard laughter and recognized his father's. He hesitated a moment, then pushed the door open.

"C'mon in and have a drink with yer pa," Paisley hollered. He was standing at the bar with Blake Waldon and several others.

As Buell approached, Waldon slapped Paisley on the back. "Yer boy and I had a little talk a while back, Paisley. Maybe with you being mayor, he'll think about what I said." He looked at Buell with a smile. "What do ya say?"

"I'd say yer still lookin' to do *yerself* a favor."

"Buell!" Paisley stepped away from the bar. "Blake's been behind me all the way."

"I can see that."

"You're reading me all wrong," Waldon said. "Sure, I've got interests, but they're the same as yours—and your father's."

"He's right, son. This town is ready to grow and grow fast. All it needs is people like Blake to invest some of that hoard of money he's sittin' on, expand the gas works, convince the railroad to lay in an extra siding, build another ice plant—all kinds of things."

"And the right man to keep the peace," Waldon said to Buell. "The *only* reason I approached you that day." He smiled and gave a slight bow.

"There, Buell, ya see? Sometimes you look for things that aren't there. Now, have a shot with us." Paisley stepped back to the bar and made room.

"I don't think I better. Matter of fact, I'm gonna go back to my place and put my head down—slowly."

"Him and Simon Steele bucked the mule last night." Paisley jostled Waldon. "Not something we've ever done." They both chuckled and Paisley pulled out his watch. "Do that, son. It's after four. I'll swing by the office shortly and tell Walt to take care of whatever you had to do. I'll see you in the morning."

Mose looked amused as Buell shuffled through the stable. "Don't ask, Mose, but I'd appreciate it if you leave off any work on the anvil for the rest of the day."

The older man grinned, and pointed at the empty bottle on his bench. "Found that in the middle of the floor this morning. I'll be quiet."

Buell nodded, went into his sitting room/kitchen, and stopped just inside the door—the heat was palpable, and the acrid smell of scorched coffee filled the air. "Shit!" he muttered, then hurried to the stove and squawked the damper nearly closed. With a piece of kindling, he pushed the blue-speckled coffeepot off to one side. "I ain't cut out for this." He threw the stick of wood into the coal bucket and went to his bedroom, taking off his coat as he did. That room was hotter yet.

He dropped his sheepskin in the chair, unbuckled his gun belt, and hung it on a peg. Then he shrugged out of his heavy flannel shirt. Flicking the garment toward the single wardrobe, he sat down on the bed. There he struggled out of his boots, grimacing at the pain in his head. Finally, stripped of his heavy leather belt, he swung his feet up, and lay back with a deep sigh. The quiet reminded him of his room at the hotel in Idaho City, and the picture of it faded in and out as he drifted.

The closeness and privacy of the small rented room felt good, and he wondered what Emma was doing just beyond the door—probably reading. He slowed his breathing and listened. She was usually very quiet when she knew he was resting, but he could always count on a muffled cough, or the clink of a teacup to alert him she'd come home. He waited but heard nothing, and then felt a chill. Reaching over himself, he caught the edge of his blanket and pulled it over his upper body, slightly surprised that he was bare-chested. Had they?—he felt for his pants as he tried to remember. What time was it? The heavy blanket pushed his body's heat back, and he tucked both arms under it, content to just clear his mind and wander.

He caught a whiff of perfume and smiled to himself—Emma was there. They enjoyed this game: he'd pretend to sleep, and she'd act like she didn't know he was faking. Cool air settled over his skin as she lifted the blanket.

"More?" she whispered, her voice muffled.

"Um-huh," he breathed back. Her hand left his chest and the muscles in his belly trembled as her fingertips slipped beneath his waistband. His being centered on one thought, any second now she'd do it—he tilted his head back in the pillow and held his breath.

His body snapped taut with the sudden, cold shock of comprehension—Wrong! Her breasts were supposed to be next—smothering him—covering his face, her hands behind his neck, clasping him to her chest. He grabbed in the dark, caught her hair in his right hand, and yanked away.

"Buell!" There was pain in her voice.

With one kick, the wool blanket flew through the air, and he was on his feet. "What the!" he shouted, and backed into the wardrobe with a crash.

"Buell," Sarah whispered harshly in the darkness. "Keep your voice down."

"Are you gone mad?" he hissed. "Get *out* of here."

"Buell, please," she said, her voice a whimper, "Please."

"Go in the other room Sarah. Now!"

He waited until he heard her in the kitchen, then shuffled his feet past the blanket and to the table by his bed. There, he fumbled around for a match and lit a lamp. He kicked into his trousers and grabbed his shirt off the floor. After putting it on, he stepped through the door with the light. She stood in the middle of the room, clasped hands to her mouth. "Jesus, Sarah, what are you doing here? In pants!"

"I needed someone," she said, and tried to meet his eyes.

"You got Simon! You're taken, Sarah—married next month."

"I *know* that. And I'll do it, just like Simon is going to do it. Go through the motions, say the words, do what's expected. Exactly as it's always been."

"But you're a—him and you—we all—"

"You're doing it too. Listen to yourself. That's all I've heard my whole life. Nobody ever asked *me*. *You* didn't ask me, Buell, and you *knew*." Her eyes glazed over and she started toward him.

Dread clamped down on Buell's breathing, and he put his hand up. "Stay there! Knew what, Sarah?"

"You knew I was interested, but ignored me when others were around—I caught the secret glances. I saw your discomfort when Simon kissed me. Why didn't you do something, Buell? You were the strong one, always so collected when there was trouble, always the one in command—all you had to do was *take* me."

"I couldn't do that, Sarah—then or now. I want you to leave." He set the lamp on the table.

"I *have* to talk to someone. Or I'm going to do something awful—I can feel it."

Buell grimaced and shook his head before pointing to a soft chair. "Sit down." When she was settled, he sat in the other one. "You have to understand, Sarah, I *won't* do what you're asking, and you *shouldn't* do what you came here for."

"You won't? Does that mean you could if it weren't me?"

"Can't, won't—for us, it's the same thing, and for the same reason. Neither of us would be able to live afterwards."

"Then you admit you have feelings for me?"

"Had, Sarah—before I knew about myself. I'm not good for women. I'm not much good, period."

She leaned toward him for a moment, then lowered her head. "I'm not much good either, Buell. We're the same— circumstances, the twists of fate—our situation made us dirty. We didn't ask for it, you and I—we just happened to be there. If Simon knew, he'd agree."

Good God, he didn't tell her he knew! He still hasn't. "That's not true!" He heard panic in his voice. *Then what does she know? Be careful.* "You lived in the best house in town, had nice clothes, everybody enjoyed being with you. You were like an—"

"Please don't." Her eyes fastened on his, the lamplight dancing in them. "I know you know," she said, her voice barely a whisper.

The cold gripped him again, and this time the look in her eyes made lying futile. "When?"

"The day you left. Sheriff Staker knows too." Her brow furrowed, and then she covered her face with both hands.

"I'm sorry, Sarah." Her shoulders started to quake and he tried to swallow the ache starting to build. He wanted to touch her, but didn't dare to, and then the lump in his throat dissolved into tears. He hurriedly stood and turned his back to her. Almost grateful for her muffled sobs, he used the time to get control of his own emotions. Lust. Fornicatin'. How many people are ruined?

"So, don't you see?" Her voice startled him, but he couldn't bear facing her. "We're the best we're going to get, Buell. David sullied us both. You know what I am, but admitted you could have me were it not for Simon." He started to respond, then her hand touched his shoulder. "I know," she said and squeezed. "You didn't say that, but it's what you meant. I only wished I deserved that kind of respect. But I don't, even though Simon thinks I do. That's the sad part."

Buell spun around so quickly that Sarah jumped back and put her hands out. "You're wrong!" he nearly shouted. She blinked rapidly, confusion on her face. "Simon knows, Sarah. He knows *all* of it."

She collapsed in a heap, Buell just quick enough to catch her head before it hit the floor. Gathering her in his arms, he moved her to the chair, put her down, and then hurried to the sink to pump furiously for a splash of water on a dish towel. He went back to her, knelt beside the chair, and wiped her face with the wet cloth. A few seconds later, her eyes fluttered and then popped open. "You fell down, Sarah. Ya okay now?"

Her hand found his and stopped his anxious dabbing. "He knows?" Her lips quivered. "Simon knows what David did?"

"Yes, Sarah. I had to tell him."

"When?"

"At Fort Laramie."

"That long? He's known that long?" She struggled to sit upright, and took both of Buell's hands in her own. "Why'd you tell him?"

"He was gettin' eat up about you—started the day we left, and got worse and worse. There was a woman at Fort Laramie." Her hands gripped tighter. "Her and Simon were like sister and brother, Sarah. She finally made Simon tell her what he was feeling, and how you acted the month or so before we left. She guessed what happened to you and told Simon that might be the case. One day, him and me was havin' one of our arguments, and I told him I'd shot David. He jumped up on his preachin' stool, and I blew up like I always do. Mad, I told him *why* I shot him."

"And he still wants me to marry him?" Her voice was incredulous.

"He loves ya, Sarah. Always has and always will. I found him way back of nowhere in a cabin he'd built. It was set between twin spruce trees, a perfect matched pair. It was the reason he chose the place, but didn't know that till I pointed it out. I thought you knew. He told me he wrote you a letter. Didn't he?"

She shook her head slowly. "He said he knew David tried to hurt me, and that maybe I thought I had encouraged him. He said that was never the case. He told me it couldn't have been my fault, and that I was still the same woman he'd always loved. It was an unusual letter, not clearly written—not like Simon at all."

"Do you remember the last letter you sent? You told him you were happy with what you were doin'. He saw that as you wantin' to be left alone. And as much as he wanted to come back, he didn't want to cause you any more trouble. When I read that letter, I could've broken his jaw."

Suddenly, tears streamed down her cheeks, and she pressed his hands to her face. "I can only thank God that it was you I came to, Buell. I've made a terrible mistake."

"You *almost* did, Sarah. You said a bit ago that you didn't ask for it, you just happened to be there. That's exactly right—you had *nothin'* to do with it. Simon knows that. So do I."

"So what do I do—what do we do?"

Buell glanced at the slouch hat and heavy wool coat hanging on a kitchen chair. "You walk home, just like you got here. I'll follow along out of sight to make sure you get there safe. Then, come December, I'll give ya a kiss after your wedding, and we can both think about this when we're old."

"I can see why Simon loves you, Buell. Some woman is going to be very lucky."

He sniffed derisively. "Or they'll all be." He stood and pulled her to her feet. "Now go home."

CHAPTER 19

Buell's nose froze stiff as he breathed the icy air, and he controlled the reins only because he could see them, his sense of touch lost an hour out of town. He had the load because Walt was at home with the grippe, and opportunities to travel on a clear road could not be taken for granted much longer. The four-horse team blew clouds of steam into the air, and their backs grew frostier with every passing mile. He let them set their own pace, a steady fast walk, and lowered his hands into the scant protection of the buffalo robe that lay across his lap.

Smoke rising straight into the sky above Bedell's ranch brought a sigh of relief. Even the horses picked up their heads a little. He swung the wagon in a wide loop, then lined up with the barn doors. When two men slid them open, he drove into the relative warmth.

"Ya look plumb frozen, ya do." Andrew's smiling face looked up. "We gonna need the loft pulley ta git ya off there?"

"Could be." Buell forced a chuckle. "If I can get my ass unstuck."

"Yer gonna stay the night, sure?"

"I thought I might. It keeps goin' the way it has the last two days, tonight'll be cold enough to freeze fire."

Andrew nodded at the two men who'd opened the doors, and they started to unhook the team. "Git yerself down then. We'll see to the load and the horses."

Buell had to watch where he put his feet, holding tight to the wagon until he was on the ground. It hurt to move. "Damn it, I hope I ain't froze my toes."

"I'd say come on over to the bunkhouse—they keep that place hot'ern hell—but Mister Bedell will want to see ya for sure."

"Let me hobble around here a minute, Andrew. I swear I can't feel my legs from the knees down."

The Scot scrambled up the wagon wheel and lifted the buffalo skin out of the foot box. "Did ya use this?"

"Yeah, I had it across my legs the whole trip."

"Across? Ya gotta sit on it, ya ninny, then wrap it round yer legs." He climbed back down. "Move around a bit then, give yer blood somethin' to do."

Buell shuffled back and forth across the floor, and slowly the feeling started to return. The pain in his toes made him limp. He was near the door when it opened.

Ruben Bedell stepped in and put out his hand. "Good to see you, Buell."

Buell yanked off his glove. "Pa figgered we better git out here while we can."

They shook hands and Ruben grimaced. "Thought you might be feeling the frost a little, but that's like grabbin' hold of the pump handle. Come on in the house. Wu will get a footbath ready."

"Oh hell, I can't be soakin' my feet in your place."

"Sure ya can." The rancher smiled. "I do."

Buell's mind flashed back to Idaho City as he breathed the unique aroma in the room. The clean sharp bite of ginger and cassia blended with the crisp, edgy smell of crushed anise, both softened by the nutty scent of hot oil and soy sauce in the pleasantly smoky kitchen.

Wu stood by a large table. *"Huan ying,"* he greeted Buell, and gave him a half-bow.

"Ni hao, Wu." Buell dipped his head.

"Lia'ng hoa, da'xie Zuo xia." Wu motioned to one of the four chairs that flanked the table.

"You two are gonna have to stop that," Ruben said with a snort. "After you left the last time, it took me a week to convince him *I* wasn't gonna learn his lingo. So, what did you two just say?"

"It ain't that hard if ya listen, and they like to teach if ya wanna know. He said howdy when we come in, and I asked him how he was." Buell paused. "Not exactly that. I asked if he was well. He said he was and thanked me for askin'. Then he told me to sit down."

"So much noise to me. I make 'im speak English. Ain't that right, Wu?"

Wu smiled. "My Engrish good."

Bedell nodded at Buell. "He needs a footbath."

"I get." He pointed at Buell. "You sit. Boot off." He pointed at the chair again.

"I feel funny as hell takin' off my boots here in your kitchen."

"Sit down and git 'em off. You're not gonna drive back tonight, are ya?"

"If ya got a place in the bunkhouse, I'd be obliged."

"Nonsense! You can stay here—the place has four bedrooms. Wu will cook us some of that Chinese food you say ya like, and we can sit in by the fire and talk. How's that sound?"

"A lot better than riding in the dark."

"Good. Now take off your coat and gloves, and let Wu put 'em away. Then, git your feet in some hot water. I'm gonna make sure my whiskey order doesn't wind up in the bunkhouse. Wu will take good care of you." Ruben pulled on his gloves, shrugged his fleece coat tight around his shoulders, and went back outside.

Buell turned to find the Asian beside him, his hands out. "Coat," Wu said, "And gruuve."

Buell cautiously dipped his fingers into the pan of water—it felt cool—and then lowered one foot into the bath. He ground his teeth as the nerves responded. "Aww," he groaned and submerged it completely.

Wu bent over, studied the other foot for a moment, and then gently poked the big toe. "No floze." He looked up and smiled. "But feer rike summumbitch."

Buell burst out laughing and was still howling when Ruben came back in. "What the hell? I could hear you clear out in the barn."

Buell snorted and slapped a hand over his mouth, but continued to laugh, his head down.

"Well, what?" Ruben shrugged out of his coat. "You two tellin' Chinese jokes?"

"No," Buell finally managed to say. "I just heard how we must sound to the Chinese. I didn't think about it till just a couple minutes ago, but I never learned one Chinese cuss word. I don't know that they use them like we do." Buell looked at the confused Chinaman. "*Mingbai,* son of a bitch?" Wu started with a torrent of Mandarin. "Whoa, whoa," Buell insisted. "Talk English, Wu. Wu understand, son of a bitch?"

"No feer good, no rike food, no go town, wagon bloke, all bad, all same—summumbitch."

Ruben chuckled. "I see what ya mean, but I'd say he understands it just fine."

"I suppose he does that. Sure hit my silly spot when he said it."

"How's your feet?"

"He knows what he's doin'. The water's a little more than

warm now, and I've quit thinkin' about just cuttin' 'em off. I did this once in Idaho City, only it was my hands." Buell flexed his fingers. "They hurt for a month."

"Well, sit there and let 'em thaw. Your horses are fed and watered now, the wagon's unloaded, and the boys are settled for the night. I'll go get something I discovered in New Orleans last year. I think you'll enjoy it, and it's perfect for a night like this." Ruben left the room. He returned a couple of minutes later with a heavy mug in each hand and set them on the stove. He poured hot water into them, then turned to Wu just as the Chinaman stepped away from a tall cabinet. He handed the rancher two small slivers of reddish-brown wood. Ruben dropped one in each of the steaming drinks and brought them over to the table. "Here ya go. Take a sip of that and tell me what ya think."

The biting scent of cinnamon competed with the tangy aroma of cloves as steam lifted the bouquet off the oil-spotted brew. Buell took a cautious, hissing sip. "Umm. That's got lots of stuff in there. I was never one for sweet drinks, but that goes into a cold gut right nice. What's in it?"

"I have Wu mix it up in a small crock—dark sugar, butter, cloves, nutmeg, and cardamom. Pour a jigger of rum over a couple spoons' full of that, then add some boiling water and a piece of cinnamon bark. I keep it out by the fireplace when it's cold like this. Ya like it then?"

"Yeah, I like it lots."

"Drink that, and then join me in the big room. We'll find a couple of chairs that're a little more comfortable." Ruben picked up his mug and left.

By the time the hot rum was gone, Buell's feet had quit aching, and Wu brought him the socks that had been warming by the stove. Buell dried his feet, put on the heated stockings, and stood gingerly. He pointed at the closed door Bedell had left through earlier. "Big room?" he asked Wu. The Chinaman nodded.

Bedell sat at a five-foot-wide desk at one end of the huge space. A large ledger reflected the light of a double-wick oil lamp into his face. Ruben looked up. "Got yer pegs under ya, I see. Good. Take a seat by the hearth. I'll be done here in a minute or so."

An energetic blaze danced in the biggest fireplace Buell had ever seen—Wu could stand upright inside it. Made of irregular pieces of rusty-brown rock, Buell guessed the structure spanned twelve feet or so, and the chimney rose to the pitched ceiling twenty feet above. A shiny-haired moose hide covered the plank floor in front of it.

Buell settled into the fire-warmed leather of a tall-backed stuffed chair, and looked up at the soaring stone-works. Above a six-inch-thick wooden mantel, a pair of long-rifles—muzzleloaders—framed a well-worn wagon wheel. A log, twenty inches in diameter and three feet long, lay across triple andirons, flames flicking eagerly over the rough brown bark. Buell leaned his head back, folded his hands in his lap, and watched the cavorting fire.

"That chair suits ya," Ruben said.

Buell started forward, his hand reaching towards his hip. "Wha—"

Bedell chuckled. "Didn't mean to startle you. Ya ready to eat?"

The log in the fireplace was now a black cylinder, blue-tinged flames rippling back and forth along its length. "I guess I dozed off."

"Easy to do."

"What time is it?"

"Just at seven-thirty. Wu is chomping at the bit to feed ya. We can eat in the kitchen"—Ruben pointed at a long table with five chairs on either side—"over there, or right where ya sit."

"I don't know." Buell eyed the formal dining table.

"The look on your face gives ya up. We'll eat right here. I do it all the time." Bedell went to the kitchen door and pushed it partly open. "We eat in here, Wu."

A minute later, the Chinaman rushed through the door carrying a two-foot-square low table. He put it in front of Buell, hurried out again, and returned with another for Ruben.

"Told ya I do this a lot," the rancher said. "You don't play chess by any chance?"

"No sir. I saw Simon Steele and another fella play once. I 'bout went cross-eyed jist watching 'em."

"It can actually be quite exciting. It's a lot like what's going on in town right now."

"Ya mean the jostlin' 'tween the council, the money men, and such?"

"That, and more. To be good at the game you have to know where each piece is on the board, both yours and your opponents, and where each one can move to next. Then you imagine what it looks like after a move, and after the next one, and the next. The farther you can see ahead, the better player you are. I mention that because your father has just become an important piece."

"I never thought about a town's goin's-on quite that way, but I can see how ya could. I think that lawyer, Lindstrom, would know how to play the best. Him and Simon's pa, and maybe the judge. Seems they're big enough to do what they please."

"That's not how it works. To be real good, you have to be able to *force* the man to move the piece you want moved, and leave him convinced he *wanted* to do it. It's not a matter of being the biggest or strongest."

"Like settin' up a bushwhackin'?" Buell couldn't hide his distaste.

"It's a little bit like that, but your opponent can see the ambush. You appear to attack one of his pieces, but your eye is really on another, and you do it in such a way that he *has* to move something to protect it. He'll use the smaller pieces at first, but eventually he'll have to commit the more valuable ones. You keep doing that until he's got no way to protect the big prize—and then you take it. Mind you, he's trying to do the same thing."

"You just explained why I keep to myself." Buell settled back in his chair. Ruben looked at him for a few seconds, and then did the same, his hands across his stomach. The broken wagon wheel on the tall chimney caught Buell's eye. Missing four spokes, the wooden wheel had shrunk so badly, the rim was tied on with what looked like rawhide. He couldn't imagine it limping along a trail. "What's the story about that wheel?" He pointed.

"I like to think it's about getting somewhere. That wheel was on the wagon my folks drove from Pennsylvania to New Mexico."

"It's not gonna go much further."

"And raised around a blacksmith, you'd know that. My father was a gun maker—he made that pair of rifles up there—so he didn't know what a wagon wheel would or wouldn't do. Sure, he understood you needed to keep the iron rim intact—so he tied it on—and he knew the dozen spokes kept the wheel rigid, but saw it would work with less than twelve. He depended on the wheel to do what it was supposed to do—what wheels do best."

"If it lost one or two more spokes, it would have given up on him."

"But he didn't know that. So he kept going—and so did the

wheel." Ruben winked at him. "Sometimes not knowing it can't be done will get it done."

"You play that chess game real good, I bet."

"I do." Ruben chuckled. "And so would you, if you'd try it."

Before Buell could respond, the kitchen door burst open and Wu bustled through with a large tray that he put on the sideboard by the fireplace. From it he arranged silverware, two crystal goblets, and white linen napkins on the small tables in front of Ruben and Buell. In the center of each he set two shallow fifteen-inch porcelain bowls heaped with food. Then, he stepped back, bowed, and rattled off a string of Chinese.

The aroma wafting off the dish made Buell's mouth flood, and he realized how hungry he was. "Sweet chicken with black mushrooms," he said, more to himself than the Chinaman. Then he looked up at the beaming face. "Thank you, Wu. I ain't had that for more than a year. I won't ask you how you knew it's what I like best."

"He amazes me," Ruben said and poked at the ragged fungus. "I eat his food once or twice a week, have for over ten years, and I've never seen *that.*"

Wu bowed again. "Mo' food in kitchen. Eat prenty." He turned and left.

They called Wu twice over the next thirty minutes, and when the Chinaman came back of his own accord with another small bowl and two dessert plates, Buell raised his hands. "Not another bite. That was as good as I ever ate. Missus Luger ought to hire you away from here."

"Over my dead body," Ruben said, then looked at the Chinaman. "Good food. Thank you." Wu gathered up their dishes, leaving the wine glasses, and went back into the kitchen. "Sure I can't tempt you with the last of that bottle?" the rancher said, nodding toward the sideboard.

"No. Really, Mister Bedell. I can't hold no more."

"Ruben. Mister makes me feel old. How about a cigar then?"

"That I'd do."

Ruben hustled over to his desk and came back with two black, stubby cigars. He clipped off the end of one and handed it to Buell, then prepared his own before returning to his seat. Reaching into his vest pocket, he took out two stick matches and handed one to Buell. "Light that up, and we'll talk a little about what you're seeing in town."

Buell snorted lightly. "You're gonna tell me who the pieces are, right?"

"I'm gonna tell you who I *think* they are. You're a smart young man. Smart enough to know that Carlisle's got one, maybe two spokes to go. And in chess, the only thing that really counts is how you handle the end game."

Buell flushed cold as an image of his father appeared, bloody and trapped under a broken wagon, and himself, with nothing but his bare hands, struggling to free him.

CHAPTER 20

Buell's prediction of a cold night proved true. The thermometer showed seven below zero under a startling blue sky, an ineffectual sun struggling valiantly to be noticed. The skin on Buell's face tightened the instant he stepped out of the kitchen and into the morning air.

"Sure you don't want to wait another couple hours?" Ruben stood on the porch, shoulders hunched.

"I can either freeze my ass this morning, or later tonight. We have a load that has to go to Langdon, and the longer I wait here, the longer I have to work when I get back." They descended the steps and together they walked toward the barn. "I'm dressed for it, and I'll let the horses set their own pace."

"I sure enjoyed our visit—and our talk about where Carlisle is going. Think about what I suggested."

"I ain't got much else to do for the next four hours. I'll let ya know." Buell pulled open the man-door and went inside.

Andrew and Red stood by the team. "I'm glad it's you and not me," the Irishman said. "One of the advantages of cowboyin'—a warm bunkhouse in winter."

"We give the horses each a full gallon of oats," Andrew said. "That'll keep 'em till ya git to town. Remember what I told ya about that robe?"

Buell climbed the wheel to the seat, and settled down on the thick buffalo hide. Grabbing the edges, he whipped one across the other over his lap, protecting his lower back and legs. "All right, Red, open up and let me out of here," he said when he'd arranged the reins in his hands.

"Stop by the kitchen steps," Ruben said. "Wu has something for you." He slid one of the doors open while Red worked the other.

Buell kicked off the brake, flicked encouragement down the reins, and the four horses leaned into their collars. He rolled out of the barn and drove across the yard to the back steps, Ruben keeping pace alongside. As he pulled the wagon to a stop, Wu came out carrying three linen bags, one about the size of a fifty-pound bean sack, the other two, half that. Ruben handed the larger one up. Grasping the gathered neck, Buell's hand went underneath to support the weight. "What'n hell?"

"Hot locks," Wu said. "Put under lobe."

"He heats them up in the oven," Ruben explained. "Drop that one in the foot box and put your feet on it." Buell spread the robe open and lowered the bag into the folds at his feet. Ruben took the smaller ones from Wu. "Put these on either side of your butt, as close as you can stand. That big one will still be warm when you get to town." Ruben hoisted the two bags up, and Buell put them on the seat beside him. The heat rose immediately and he closed the heavy hide.

"*Duō xiè, Wu*," Buell said.

"Bu'ell wercome," the small man said with a bow. "Lide to town summumbitch."

Ruben laughed out loud. "Those will make it a lot easier. See ya next trip." He went to the lead horses and slapped the offside one on the rump. "Git on," he ordered, and as the wagon moved past, he waved at Buell.

Buell hadn't driven a hundred yards before he caught the edge of the wool scarf wound around his neck and lifted it to cover his nose. Lowering his head slightly, the brim of his cap kept the frigid air from freezing his forehead. He was glad he'd decided to wear the wool hat instead of the felt-brimmed one. The horses didn't seem to mind at all, moving along at a fast walk, gouts of steamy breath leading them. Frozen ruts shook the wagon relentlessly, and with the tailgate chains rattling and the floorboards creaking, he made the turn west and the ranch house dropped from sight.

He shifted his rear on the seat, moved the bags of hot rocks away a bit, and slumped his shoulders, preparing himself for the long ride home. Ruben had been as candid as Arley used to be, and in their talk the night before, Buell had learned a lot about who meant to gain what in the upcoming year or two.

Blake Waldon was as crooked as a dog's hind leg, and smooth as a cat's purr. John Lindstrom, the lawyer, could be trusted to act according to the law, but he would also take full advantage of it. Paul Steele wanted to create a business that would provide for all his children and theirs to come—he depended on Lindstrom's advice. The soon-to-be-ex-mayor was for sale to the highest bidder, and had been bought in the past by Blake Waldon.

All those things, Ruben said he *knew* for sure. Some things he suspected, and they were even more interesting. Gus Swartz worked for whoever paid him, and it wasn't always Waldon. When pressed a little, Ruben had not said any more about who it might be. Sherm Pederson owed Waldon a considerable sum. With no way to pay it back, his defeat as mayor was a blow. And last, Blake Waldon was scared to death of Buell Mace. Buell chuckled to himself. And just exactly what was Ruben Bedell's interest in all this?

For two hours Buell drove the winding road along the frozen Platte River, his mind now as numb as his face. Looking up every minute or so had exposed the strip of flesh between his hat and the bottoms of his eye sockets enough to numb it. He glanced up the road at a small grove of winter-stark sycamore and cottonwood trees. Maybe a short stop to build a fire and—he pushed the thought aside. Twenty minutes to get a decent fire going, another half-hour huddled over it to change numb skin to searing pain—not a good idea.

The rest of him really felt quite good, thanks to Wu and his rocks—now *that* was a good idea. Besides, the horses would cool off, and that couldn't be a good thing. He stole another look, shrugged off the last feeble argument for stopping, and dropped his chin into the frosty muffler.

Both lead horses snorted at the same time, and Buell's head jerked upright just as two men eased their horses out of the trees. The closest one was on his left, his wedge-shaped body appearing even bigger in a black bearskin coat—he was no more than ten feet away. Roscoe! The second, near as wide as the horse, stopped in the middle of the road. Both wore scarves wrapped around their faces and had their rifles pointed at him. "Whoa!" he shouted and hauled back on the reins. The horses stopped.

"Throw that robe back so I can see that pretty pistol of yours, Mace," Roscoe ordered, and showed Buell the half-inch bore of the short rifle. "You can try something if you'd like."

Buell dropped the reins and slowly opened the buffalo skin.

"Now, take it out using two fingers, hold it over the edge of the seat, and drop it."

"It's strapped in," Buell said.

"I know that. It don't take much to undo, stupid. Do it!"

Buell's hand went to the warm leather holster, and without taking his eyes off Roscoe's, he slowly slipped the loop over the curved hammer. He raised his hand again.

"Well, git the goddamn thing out then," Roscoe shouted, and moved his horse ahead a step.

Buell's team shifted uneasily, and the man in the road turned his mount sideways. "Let's just shoot the son of a bitch and be done with it."

"No!" Roscoe shouted. "He's gonna feel what it's like to be stuck out here without a horse. Git that goddamn Remington out of there, Mace!" Roscoe's horse started to prance and shift from side-to-side.

Something moved behind and to his right. He glanced over his shoulder to see another masked rider standing near the rear wheel. He carried a heavy-looking, long-barreled lever-action rifle. *How in hell did I miss him?* "All right," Buell said quietly. "No need anyone gettin' killed over this."

"That's up to you, meddler. I owe you a bum leg."

Buell reached into the thick hide, slowly withdrew the gun, and held it at arm's length, his eyes fixed on Roscoe. The big man's gaze never wavered as he expertly controlled the agitated horse and kept the rifle pointed. Buell flicked his wrist and threw the pistol to the side of the road. Roscoe moved his horse closer yet, and peered into the well at Buell's feet. "No rifle?"

"Do ya see one?"

"Now take off that sheepskin—and your hat and gloves."

"Yer gonna make sure, aren't ya?"

"Just git 'em off."

Buell settled his feet in the bottom of the foot box, put his hands on the seat beside him, and leaned forward to stand. Roscoe settled back in his saddle with a smile.

"Hey!" Buell hollered, and Roscoe's horse shied. In the same instant, Buell threw a fist-sized piece of angular rock as hard as he could. Before the chunk of granite found its mark, he was going headfirst over the side of the wagon, diving toward his pistol. The thick fleece coat absorbed most of the shock, and his hand was on the Remington as he crashed to the frozen earth.

Thumbing back the hammer, he rolled over to see the man in front of the team raising his rifle. Buell got a glimpse of the man's heavy wool coat over his front sight and pulled the trigger. Roscoe's horse reared and spun around, dumping his rider to the ground before taking off into the trees. The man he'd just shot slumped forward in the saddle, struggling to bring the rifle to bear. Buell cocked the Remington again, took deliberate aim at the scarf-bound head, and fired. The bushwhacker's weapon went off—the bullet blasting flint-hard dirt into the air—and the man slipped off his horse and onto the road as the animal lunged sideways.

Roscoe lay still on the ground, and Buell scrambled on hands and knees to the wagon's front wheel. Peering under the box, he could see the stationary legs of a sorrel horse with four white stocking feet. "I don't take no pleasure in this," he shouted. "Turn yer horse and ride out of here." The four hooves remained fixed to the ground. " 'Cause I don't like it, don't mean I won't do it, friend."

"Ya won't shoot me in the back?"

Buell recognized the high, nasal twang immediately. "I told ya you was in bad company. You'd serve yerself real good if you told the sheriff about this."

"I ain't goin' to no lawman. Ya sure ya won't shoot me in the back? I was jist lookin' for a place to winter-over. I wasn't gonna fire on ya, God's truth."

"Then git—I'm done talkin'." Buell looked under the wagon again. The horse moved back two steps, and then the front hooves dug sharply as the animal responded to the slap of reins on its hide. Buell waited for a moment, then stood. Tattered duster flying behind, the man bent low over the horse's neck and slapped savagely at the animal's haunches with the butt of the long rifle, urging it down the center of the road.

Roscoe lay flat on his back, a steady stream of blood flowing from a bone-deep cut on the side of his head. Buell prodded him with the toe of his boot. "Roscoe!" The heavy overcoat fell open, exposing a pistol underneath. He stooped over and pulled a brand-new Colt .45 out of its holster. "Now where'd you steal that?" He grabbed hold of the bearskin and tugged hard. "Hey! You gotta get up. I can't lift your fat ass into that wagon. Git up, or by damn I'll leave ya here like you meant to leave me." Roscoe's eyes fluttered open, stared straight past Buell for a moment, and then rolled back into his head again as the lids stuttered shut.

Buell went to the gunman in the road—the heel marks caused by the man's death throes told him all he needed to know. The horse was standing on its reins. Buell shouldered it sideways and led it to the rear of the wagon where he tied it on. He went back to the dead man and pulled the scarf down. It was who he'd thought it might be—Meat. The second bullet had hit him just below the left eye; the first, a chest shot, considering the amount of blood in the wool coat. He dragged Meat off the road, and then went back for the rifle, an ancient Spencer. He dropped it beside the body.

He strode back to Roscoe. "Hey!" He kicked him hard in the hip, and smiled grimly as the man stirred. "You gotta get up, ya bastard." Roscoe's eyes opened again, and this time they focused on Buell's face. "Ya shit on yer suspenders again, Roscoe. One of yer partners is dead, the other one turned tail, and you've got a cracked gourd. If I had a witness, I'd leave ya lay right where ya are. I don't, so you're gonna have to climb that wheel and git in the seat."

Roscoe's lips moved to form a reply and then stopped.

"Yer thinkin' bad again. You best put yer mind to gettin' on that wagon. It won't take much for me to jist drive off."

Resignation showed in the man's eyes, and he tried to roll over on his side. Buell grabbed hold and pulled. Slowly, Roscoe got his knees under him and made it to a kneeling position. "Can't." His voice was barely a whisper.

"Ya ain't gonna like the other choice." Buell stepped around him and caught hold of the bearskin at Roscoe's shoulders. Feet slipping, he managed to drag him to the front wheel. "Grab hold of the spokes." With Roscoe pulling and Buell shoving, Roscoe made it to the top, right hand on the seat, left on the foot rail. There, he lost his grip with his left hand, and fell into the bottom of the foot box with a loud grunt.

Buell climbed up, arranged the buffalo robe again, and heaved a sigh of relief as the heat of the rocks penetrated his body. Picking up the reins, he put his feet on Roscoe's back and clucked the horses into motion again. He hoped Roscoe lived, but just long enough to tell Staker what happened.

CHAPTER 21

"Goddamn you, Mace, let me out of here." The thick hair of the buffalo robe muffled Roscoe's voice, but Buell could hear the rage. He bore down on Roscoe's back with both heels. "I like you right where you're at, so shut up. Another hour, and you can talk all you want." Buell encouraged the horses with a light flick of the reins, and they picked up their pace.

They rumbled into Carlisle just after noon, and Buell circled a block to park the wagon directly in front of the sheriff's office. As soon as they stopped, Roscoe tried to get up again, and Buell tromped hard on his back. "If I have to shoot you to keep you there, I will," Buell shouted. Two passersby stopped abruptly and looked up at him. "Would you step into the jail and tell Sheriff Staker he's got a customer out here?" he asked one of them, and set the brakes. The man hurried into the jail, and a moment later Staker rushed out the door carrying his shotgun.

"Who're you gonna shoot?" he asked as soon as he saw Buell.

"I've got Roscoe here." He shoved down with his foot. "Him and a couple others ambushed me about halfway to Bedell's place."

"He's a liar!" Roscoe shouted, and struggled to get up again.

Buell threw back the robe and climbed over the back of the seat. Standing in the wagon bed, he drew his pistol. "All right, bushwhacker, get up."

"Put that away, Buell," Staker ordered. "Stand up, Roscoe,

201

where I can see ya." Groaning loudly, the man struggled to his knees, throwing the bulky buffalo hide out of the way. "Dammit all, Buell, do you have to hit *everybody* in the head?" Staker shouted. By now, there were over half a dozen people standing around watching, and a woman gasped.

"It's worse than it looks," Buell said, then went to the back of the wagon and climbed over the side. He hobbled over to stand by Staker.

The sheriff turned to the people standing around. "All right, everybody, get on with your business. Someone go by Doc Princher's office, and tell him I'd like to see him when he's got a minute." He waited until they moved away, and then looked up at Roscoe. "Get down, Roscoe, and go into my office."

"He ain't got no right to do this," Roscoe hollered. "He drove up on us and emptied that fancy pistol at me. We had no choice but to shoot back."

Buell lifted the Colt revolver out of his belt and offered it to the sheriff. "This is what he was using. It hasn't been fired."

Staker took the pistol, glanced at the front of the cylinder, and then gave it back to Buell. "Hold that. Now, Roscoe"—he raised the shotgun's muzzle—"climb down here and go inside. We've got a difference of opinion."

Buell stepped out of the way as the ungainly man climbed down. Then, with the sheriff two steps behind, Roscoe shuffled into the jail. Buell followed them into the stifling heat of the small room.

"Put that Colt on my desk, Buell, and yours too."

"Mine? I don't see—"

"I'm not askin'." Staker's grim face said the same.

Buell dropped the Colt on the desk, and then his Remington.

Staker stepped closer to Roscoe. "Turn your head and let me take a look at that."

"He tried to brain me with a rock," Roscoe whined.

"I thought you said he started shooting? I want you to go sit in that first cell. You got a hell of a lump, but it's not bleeding that bad."

"What about him?" Roscoe objected.

"Take off that overcoat, then turn around and put your hands on the wall," Staker ordered. Scowling, Roscoe did as he was told, and when he stood positioned, the sheriff put his shotgun on the desk. With a meaningful glance at Buell, he went over to his prisoner. "I wanna make sure you don't have a surprise hidden somewhere." He started to search.

Finished, he picked up his shotgun again. "All right, turn around and get in there." Staker motioned with the gun, and Roscoe stepped into the cell. The sheriff pushed shut the latticed iron door, then turned the key and took it out. "Now, Buell, I want you to sit down and tell me your side." He shoved the stool beside his desk toward him and sat down in his own chair. "You said there were three? I hope you're not gonna tell me he's the only one left."

"I'll tell ya, Sheriff," Roscoe shouted. "He shot Meat and Simpson. Killed 'em both like they was dogs."

"Shut up, Roscoe!" Staker ordered. "You'll get your turn."

Buell shrugged out of his fleece coat and hung it on a hook by the stove. "Do ya mind?" He pointed at the coffeepot. "I'm parched."

"No, go ahead." Staker reached over and picked up Buell's pistol.

"He killed a man and yer givin' him coffee," Roscoe protested. "I guess that's plain enough."

"One more time, Roscoe. Shut up!"

"Or what? You'll put me in jail?"

"I'll stuff a cleanin' rag in your mouth, and tie it there." The sheriff drew the Remington's hammer back a notch, slowly turned the cylinder, then reset the hammer and put the pistol back on the desk. "Let's hear it," he said as Buell sat down.

"I was right at halfway back when I come up on a small stand of trees. Meat pulled his horse into the road while Roscoe and a man I didn't recognize walked out on both sides of me."

"And that's all? They just stopped you?"

"See!" Roscoe hollered. "We weren't doin' nothin'."

"I warned you," Staker said. He opened the bottom drawer of his desk and took out an oily, powder-stained gun-cleaning rag.

Just as he stood, the door opened and Doc Princher barged in. "Soon as they said it, I knew." He glared at Buell for a second, and looked through the iron bars. "Open this up, Loren," he ordered.

Staker got up and went to the cell. "I'm not going to let him out, Doc. You go in and I'll watch from here."

Princher looked at Roscoe, and then nodded towards Buell. "Did he do this?"

"Does it matter, Doc? You gonna look or not?"

"If he did, why isn't he in there?" He pointed at the other cell.

"You do your job. I'll do mine."

The doctor glowered at the sheriff for a few seconds. "Open it up then." Princher went in, and Staker closed the door. Putting his case on the second cot, the doctor snapped it open, and took out a polished steel probe. Buell couldn't see exactly what he was doing, but for several minutes Roscoe let out a series of grunts. Finally, Princher stepped back, and put the instrument back in his bag. "I want him in my office as soon as you're done. That needs to be cleaned and the wound closed."

Roscoe smirked at the sheriff.

"Soon as I'm done, Doc."

"You treat people like animals, they'll act like them. How'd that happen," Princher asked Roscoe.

Roscoe looked heartened. "He threw a rock at me."

"That's enough, Doc." Staker opened the door. "I'll get him over there within the hour."

Princher picked up his satchel, stepped out of the cell, and stared directly at Buell.

Buell shrugged. "It was him or me—what would you do?"

"Within the hour, Loren," Princher said, and left, banging the door.

Staker rattled the cell door locked again. "Be warned, Roscoe, I've got that rag ready." The sheriff sat back down.

"Anyone can see he's lying," Buell said.

"You tell me what happened, Buell, and I'll do my best to figure that out. First, is there anyone out there that needs attention real quick?"

"No."

Staker shook his head in dismay.

"They stopped me in the road. Roscoe told me to take off my coat, gloves, and hat. Meat wanted to shoot me."

"That what you think?"

"That's what he *said.* Roscoe stopped him. He wanted me out there without my clothes, and I think he meant to bust up my leg."

Staker's eyebrows shot up.

"He said he owed me that. I reckon he meant it. My gun was on the ground—Roscoe made me throw it—so I spooked his horse and chucked a rock at him. I managed to hit him in the head and knock him out. He fell off his horse. Meat tried to get a shot at me, but I got to him first. Two shots. The other fella decided to run."

"And you let him?"

"I'm not a back-shooter." Buell's face flushed. "Never make like ya think that."

"Which way did the man go?"

"Back toward Bedell's. I dragged Meat off the road. He's in plain sight on the south side. Then I got Roscoe into the wagon and came to town. That's about it." Buell shrugged. "Now, I've got a tired team that needs lookin' after, so unless you—"

"Two things. Where in hell did you get a rock if ya never got off the wagon? And, why'd you bring Roscoe back?"

"I needed him in case you can't find that other fella, and I reckoned Roscoe would do exactly what he did. You can see he's lying, can't ya?"

"I think I can admit that. But what about the rock?"

"I had two bags of 'em, one on each side of me, under the robe."

"You just *happened* to have a sack of rocks?" Staker shook his head slowly.

"Bedell's cook put a bunch in the oven. Under that robe, they kept me from freezin' my ass. He heated a big one for my feet. Ask Roscoe, he laid on it for two hours."

"Do you know how lucky you are—three men and you with a bag of stones?"

"I reckon the devil wasn't ready for me, Sheriff." Buell pointed at his pistol. "Can I have that back?"

"Yeah, go ahead. You said two shots, and I can see two used caps."

Buell nodded towards Roscoe. "You gonna keep him in jail?"

"This time I will. Attempted murder, kidnapping, mayhem, robbery, eluding—I can think of several others."

"That's bullshit," Roscoe said. "I've got friends, and besides, it's my word against his."

"If that's the case, Roscoe, I'd be worried."

"You know someone sent them, don't you?" Buell said as he put on his coat. "They knew where and when."

"That occurred to me."

"Any idea who?"

"Not that I'm willing to share—until I know for sure."

"But you got an idea." It wasn't a question.

Staker picked up the keys and stood. "That's my job, Buell. Go take care of yours."

Buell poured about a cup of kerosene over the wood and coal he'd stacked in the firebox and dropped a lit match on top. The flame spread from end to end almost immediately, and he put the lids back on. His toes had started to ache while he'd been talking to Staker, and they were getting worse. He thought briefly about going out again for something to eat, but instead took a slab of bacon and four eggs from his pantry and found three hard rolls on a plate in the cupboard. By the time he had the meat sliced, the stove was starting to creak. He slid a skillet to the hottest part. Then, groaning, he went to his chair and pulled off his boots. Instead of feeling cold to the touch like he'd expected, his toes were hot. The cool air felt good. He went back to the stove and had just arranged the slices of bacon in the pan when someone knocked. "Come on in."

Simon's face was a mixture of concern and irritation.

"Don't start, Simon—my feet hurt."

"Sheriff Staker just came by the store. He had a new Colt's revolver, and wanted to know if we'd sold it recently. He said you took it off Rudy Rosser."

"Who?"

"Roscoe. Rudy Rosser."

"He told ya right. And good afternoon to you too."

"I'm sorry. If you *took* it off Roscoe, that means you had a confrontation—you got into it with him." He glanced down. "What's wrong with your feet?"

"They got cold. I drove out to Bedell's yesterday with a load. About froze the left one. Just about—it'll be all right."

"So what about Roscoe? And that pistol?"

"Let me guess. You sold it to someone other than Roscoe?"

"Of course. He doesn't have that kind of money. What disturbs me is who we *did* sell it to."

"Blake Waldon," Buell said as he shifted the skillet to the right a little.

"How in hell did you know that?"

"Just a guess. And a good one it looks like. How long ago?"

"Yesterday, in the morning. I sold it." Simon looked confused. "How can that be?" I saw Waldon not two hours ago—how could Roscoe have taken it from him?"

"He didn't. Waldon gave it to him—to kill me."

"That's crazy. Insane. Why—what? *Waldon?*"

"This whole place is about to come apart, Simon. I thought goin' out to the island, and stirring things up a bit would make them yahoos think twice about coming back for more. I was wrong—they're madder'n hell, and lookin' to get back at us."

"Us? I don't mean to sound disloyal, but you and Bedell's bunch did the stirring. I know, I know, it wasn't you directly, but the same as. Why are they angry at the townspeople?"

"How about if someone told 'em me and Bedell's cowboys were put up to it?"

"But you weren't—were you?"

Buell flipped the bacon strips over with a fork and snorted. "Of course not. You've been too busy in that store. If I can see it, someone as smart as you should."

"See what?" Simon threw his hands up. "What are you talking about?"

"Waldon needs something that Ruben Bedell has, and Ruben isn't going to part with it willingly."

"What?"

"I'm not sure. Do you want some bacon and eggs?"

"No!" Simon sighed. "I mean, no thanks. How can you be so indifferent after something like this?"

"Indifferent? That means I don't care, right?"

"Almost. It means you're not concerned one way or the other."

"Then say that, dammit. I am concerned. I just don't know what I'm going to do about it right now." Buell shoved the four slices of bacon to one side of the skillet. "You didn't tell Staker you sold that Colt to Waldon did you?" He reached for an egg.

Simon blushed. "No—I didn't."

"Why?"

"Somehow I knew you could make better use of the information than Staker. I hope I'm right."

Buell didn't answer while he carefully laid four eggs into the hot bacon grease and watched them for a while. Then he faced his friend. "Staker would have made good use of it, Simon. In his own time, after he'd tied up all the loose ends, and got all his clothes pegs standing up right, just so." He splashed some hot fat over the tops of the eggs. "But right now, or at the very least, in a few weeks, I can make better use of it."

"So you don't want me to tell him? I said I'd ask the clerks."

"That's what I want. And thanks for talkin' to me first—and trustin' me. My eggs are ready." He sniffed the air over the pan. "Ya sure ya won't eat a couple?"

CHAPTER 22

Buell vigorously rubbed his right eye and stared straight ahead. "Damn it all," he muttered as he took his hat off the hook by the door. He could smell hot charcoal as soon as he stepped into the stable, and looked around for Mose. He spotted him deliberately cranking the curved handle of the blower fan, intent on the fiery heap of fuel in the forge. Again, Buell stared straight ahead, this time looking across the twenty-odd feet to the blacksmith. Then, he slowly turned his head back and forth by degrees, twice, cussed again, and left the stable.

A few minutes later he walked into the stark white of Doc Princher's office. The stink of ether turned his stomach. A young lady sat at a desk just inside the door.

"Good morning, Mister Mace." She glanced down at a small ledger. "Is the doctor expecting you?"

"No. Do I need to fix that up before I can see him?"

"Usually." She gave him a bright smile, and then glanced at the door in the back of the room. "But I'll write you in now. His next patient isn't until nine."

"I don't reckon I know you, Miss—uh?"

"Oh, I know you. My name is Samantha. Abigail is my best friend."

"Abigail?"

"Abby Steele. She's told me all about you, and I've seen you on your wagon." She wrinkled her nose. "Abigail says you like to tease."

"Uh . . ." Buell looked at the doctor's door, and then pointed at the appointment book. "Shouldn't ya write my name in there?"

She blushed. "Yes, I suppose I should." She looked at the small watch pinned to her blouse, and wrote on the page. "Your appointment is for eight-fifteen, or as soon as he's done in there."

Buell saw three chairs on the other side of the door. "What time is it?"

"Just after eight."

"I'll just sit, then. And I'm pleased to make your acquaintance, Miss—uh?"

"Samantha Winberg, Mister Mace."

Buell had no sooner sat down than the examining-room door opened and a man with a bloody apron came out, followed by Doctor Princher. "That's going to get real sore, so don't fret a lot when it does. Come back Wednesday about this time." He looked pointedly at Miss Winberg, and she picked up her pen. "If it gets to looking bad, come on in and let me check it."

The man raised his bandaged hand. "Okay, Doc." He nodded at Buell, then opened the door and left.

"What brings you here?"

Buell turned to find Princher glaring at him, and flushed.

"He has an eight-fifteen appointment, Doctor." Miss Winberg tapped the entry with her index finger.

"Does he? Well, then, come in—you've been here before."

The bright white of the waiting room carried into the next—Buell recognized the tall cabinet and pair of beds. Princher pointed at a chair. "Sit down," he said gruffly, then hooked a tall four-legged stool with his toe and dragged it close. When both were seated, Princher folded his arms, and studied Buell's face. "What's your complaint?"

"I'm not here to complain. I want you to—"

"That's not how I meant it. What seems to be the matter? What's wrong with you?"

Buell glanced at the closed door. "I'm going blind," he said quietly.

"Good Lord, what makes you think that?"

"I can't *see*, Doc," Buell said sarcastically. "My right eye ain't working like it should."

Princher stood up and swung a gas lamp away from the wall to a position over one of the beds. "Come over here and sit on the edge." Buell did as he was told, and the doctor covered Buell's right eye with a card, leaned close, and then moved it. He then did the same to the left. Princher pointed across the room. "Look at that chart on the wall—can you read any of it?"

"Most of it."

"The fourth line down?"

"I can see the seventh line."

"Read it."

"F E L O P Z D."

Princher covered Buell's left eye. "Now?"

"Same."

He shifted the card to the right one.

"Same," Buell muttered.

"You can see fine. In fact, perfectly."

"But not off to the side." Buell raised his right hand to just in front of his chest, then moved it right a bit. "I can't see that." Buell turned his head. "Unless I look right at it."

"Look straight ahead again, and then slowly turn your head right without shifting your eyes. Tell me when you can see the door." Princher stood in front of him.

Buell looked straight at the doctor for a moment, and then slowly rotated his head right until: "There."

"About twenty degrees. How about the left?"

"It doesn't bother me that way, only on my right. It's gettin' worse."

"Since when?"

"I don't know. I got hit." Buell felt above his right eye. "Two or three years ago."

Princher shook his head. "I've seen your scars. One would think a person who'd been as abused as that would not want to inflict the same on others." The doctor touched Buell's right brow. "What were you struck with there?"

"Can't say about that one, I was sleeping. A doctor looked at it and said it would be all right."

"You're losing what's called peripheral vision. Most people can detect movement almost ninety degrees to one side or the other. You've lost most of that for some reason. I'm not as familiar with the eyes as I'd like to be, but there are doctors who specialize in it. I know one in Omaha, and St. Louis will have more."

"So I'm not goin' blind?"

"Not in the sense you mean, no. At least I think not. All I can do is look again in six months or so—or you can do it. Do what we just did from time to time."

Buell stood up. "Nobody has to know about this but me and you, right?"

"I don't discuss my patients with anyone but another doctor, and then only if he needs to know."

"Can I count on that, Doc?"

"You're questioning my ethics, Buell. You seem to make it a habit of challenging people."

"I just like to know where folks stand, that's all. Do I pay you or the girl out front?"

"Normally me, but there's no charge. I did nothing."

Buell shrugged and started for the door.

"A personal question, Buell—if you don't mind."

"I usually do, Doc, but go ahead."

"Does this have anything to do with your reluctance to take Sheriff Staker's job?"

Buell paused for several seconds. "No," he finally muttered, "it doesn't."

Buell's visit to Doc Princher had been a huge disappointment. Weren't doctors supposed to fix things? He walked down to the loading dock and into the office. "I'm going to take the day off," he said, and stopped just inside the door.

Paisley swung his feet off the deck. "Sure, son. After yesterday, I'm not sure I'd have got out of bed. How's yer feet?"

"They're all right. I went and seen Doc Princher."

"Good. You can't be too careful with that. Go on home, and put 'em up. We'll take care of things here."

"I'm gonna do that. I'll be back tomorrow." Buell turned to leave.

"Uh, something else, Buell."

He faced his father. "Yeah?"

"Ruth and me'd like to have you over for Thanksgiving dinner. Whatcha say?" Paisley stood and came around the desk.

"When's that?"

"Next Thursday, the thirtieth." When Buell sighed, he added quickly. "Say yes, son. We've got a lot to be thankful for, don't ya think? Ruth would be real pleased too."

"All right. I'll come."

"Aw, good!" Paisley stepped close to Buell. "She'll feed ya like you was a king." He clapped him on the shoulder. "She said we could have a drink or two—how's that?" he said with a big smile.

"Kin I cuss?"

Paisley's smile vanished. "I . . . uh, she—"

"I'm snappin' yer s'penders, Pa," Buell said, and punched his father lightly in the belly. "I'll be careful."

"Ya git me easy, Buell. I can never tell when ya mean it or not."

"What time?"

"She says we'll eat about twelve-thirty, so come out in the morning when ya feel like it." Paisley smiled again. "Now git out of here, and take care of them feet."

Paisley watched his son leave, and went back to his chair. He'd just told Buell a bald-faced lie. He wasn't at all sure Ruth was going to be happy about Buell being there for dinner, and the drinking was even more in question. But all that had to change. He recalled what had happened when he went to tell her the news on election day.

Paisley strode up the steps and hurried into the house. "Ruth," he called as he shut the door. "Where are ya?"

"In here," she answered from the kitchen.

He strode across the living room and stopped in the doorway.

Ruth stood, watering a houseplant in the window above the sink.

"I'm gonna be the mayor," he announced with a rush.

"Humph," she said without turning around.

A chill surged through his body. "Don't you care?" He swallowed hard and went to stand by the stove.

"Of course, Paisley." She tapped the tip of the spout against the rim of the pot, and turned around. "It's what you wanted. Congratulations."

He stared at her for several seconds, and then his shoulders slumped. "I don't understand, Ruth. I've tried my level best to do what I think will make you happy. We have money, a nice home, all—"

"What precisely did you add to my happiness?" Her voice

215

was sharp and she squared her shoulders. "What do I have now that I didn't have before?"

Anger rang in his ears. "You don't have bruises, Ruth. You don't have to hide in the house for weeks at a time. You don't have a man who wouldn't share your bed, or a son who—"

"Don't you say it, Paisley Mace—don't you breathe a word of what you're thinking. I'm sick to death of your mincing around. Yes, dear. No, dear. May I, dear." Her voice mocked him. "At least they had the brass to speak up—to assert themselves." Her eyes blazed. "They were *men*, Paisley." She threw the tin watering can into the sink and stormed past him. "Maybe your precious council will vote you a set of balls," she shouted, and then slammed the bedroom door.

Paisley's heart beat hard as he remembered her words. She had said what Buell had hinted at, and he'd realized that he'd become so soft that even Paul had lost some respect for him. In fact, almost everyone had. He loved her too much to just let it go. He'd always loved her, even after they'd both married others, and he didn't mean to lose her. So, two days after her challenge, he'd started to do things different. Thanksgiving Day with Buell would be the real test.

Buell sat in his chair holding a lukewarm cup of coffee, idly staring at the cupboard and turning his head slowly back and forth. Was it worse now than it was two hours ago? He started, almost spilling his drink, when someone rattled his front door with a vigorous knocking. "Buell?" Staker's voice came through.

"Come in." Buell put his cup on the side table.

Staker pushed the door open and entered. "Yer pa said you were here." He looked down at Buell's feet. "How's the frost-bite?"

Buell followed his gaze. "I'm not sittin' here 'cause of my feet."

"I can see that."

"I—"

"That's your business, Buell. You don't account to me."

"Oh, no? Yer here for something, and yer not smilin'."

"Right to it, huh? At least you're consistent." Staker unbuttoned his coat and took off his hat. "Nice and warm in here. Can I sit?"

"Sure." Buell nodded toward the stove. "Coffee there if ya like. I owe ya one. Clean cup there by the dishpan."

"Don't mind if I do." Staker went to the corner by the cupboard, picked up the heavy mug, and filled it at the stove. "We're missing a body," he said as he put the pot back down.

Buell sat straight up. "Roscoe?"

"Nope, he's still tucked away. The one you left by the roadside yesterday." Staker watched Buell closely.

"He *can't* be missing. You just didn't find 'im."

Stalker put his cup on the table by the second easy chair, shrugged out of his coat, and sat down. "I sent both deputies out yesterday. They found where you said you were stopped."

"Well, Meat's right there, not six feet off the road, south side."

"Nope." Staker picked up his cup, tested it with a short hissing sip, and then took a couple swallows. "They told me they can see where Roscoe's horse pranced around, even found where he hit the ground—some blood—but no tracks in the road, like you said—and no body."

"The tracks were ruined when I drove the team across them. And what about the man behind me—had to be tracks there?"

"Sure, like there are all along that road. I talked to Judge Kingsley, Buell, and he's not happy about this." Staker's eyes never left Buell's as the sheriff took another drink. "Roscoe's got a lawyer."

"Wha—where?"

"Yep. Smart too. Roscoe has recanted—Roscoe took back all he said yesterday. Lawyer says he'll have Roscoe out Monday."

"That's bullshit, and you goddamn well know it. That son of a bitch was lyin' as fast as he could move his lips—an idiot could see it."

"Whoa there, Mace, watch who you're calling names."

"Well, dammit all, you saw it." Buell slammed his fist into the arm of the chair. "He's lyin'."

"I know he is."

"Then why ya pissin' on *my* campfire?"

"I think that lawyer can cause us some problems. I needed to *know* you were telling me everything—feel right about it. You don't like Roscoe, and he feels the same—men have let grudges get in the way before."

"I can find that third man," Buell said flatly. "I'll bet he's back with that bunch on the island."

"You leave that to me, Buell—I mean it."

"Can you keep Roscoe in jail, or will Kingsley let him out?"

"I asked for a week—judge let me have it. Now, is there anything you may have remembered since we talked yesterday? Something that might help?"

"Ya got Meat's horse. Was there blood on it?"

"Nope." Suddenly, Staker's face brightened. "His rifle! Did ya throw it on the wagon?"

"Tossed it off the road. It was a beat-up old Spencer—I left it beside him."

"Damn." Staker drank the rest of his coffee and stood. "I've got until next Friday, plenty of time. I'll roust a couple of them this weekend and ask some more questions." Staker put his cup on the counter and put his coat back on. "One other thing. Did Roscoe mention that other fella's name—seems like he did, but

I can't recall?"

"Nope. And they were all wearing scarves over their faces."

Staker shrugged. "Take care of them feet." He clapped his hat on and left.

Buell stared at the door. *I should have finished it—like I used to,* he thought. *Now I've got to go find Simpson and give 'im a chance to be my friend.* He smiled tightly and took a swig of cool coffee.

CHAPTER 23

Buell pulled the door open and entered the store. The tangy scent of kerosene predominated, but just barely, as the aroma of fresh-ground coffee found him, followed immediately by a floral essence. The women he saw explained the latter. As cold as it was outside, their number took him by surprise, and standing in groups of three or four, they were all talking at once. He spun on his heel and grabbed the doorknob.

"Good afternoon, Buell."

He looked over his shoulder as Abby Steele walked away from two ladies. "Uh, 'lo Abby."

She stepped close, too close. "Simon is right over there," she said and pointed past the women she'd been with. "And he's busy, so you're going to have to talk to me—unless." She tilted her head.

"Oh, no—I mean sure." He stepped away from the door—and her, then snatched his hat off his head. "How are ya?"

"I'm fine. I heard about your terrible ordeal yesterday. The authorities simply must do something about those awful men." She looked down at his feet. "Simon told me—"

"They're fine now. I'm fine. Really wasn't that much to it." He cleared his throat.

"Exactly what I'd expect you to say. A little bird told me they were bad enough that you went to see the doctor."

"Is that bird named Samantha, by any chance?"

"Why, Buell, you remember her name," she said lightly.

"She'll be *thrilled*."

"It was just this morning, Abby."

"Still—she's very pretty, isn't she?"

"She's just a girl, can't be more that—I'm not lookin' to . . ." He glanced around the store and lowered his voice. "Dammit, Abby, ya got me stumblin' like a new calf."

She giggled. "I know. It's fun to pay you back." She cocked her head again. "Remember?" She looked triumphant.

Suddenly Buell's whole body felt hot, and he glanced through the window at the frosty street. "I think I'll come back when he's not so—"

"You're safe now," she said and smiled. "Here he comes."

Buell followed her gaze. Simon stepped around the end of the counter, and headed toward them.

"A man of leisure?" Simon said, then addressed Abby: "Hi, sis. Saw you when you came in, but as you can see." He nodded toward a large cluster of women at the counter and shrugged.

"I just had to get out of the house," she said. "I'll leave both of you to whatever it is men talk about." She laid her hand on Buell's arm. "Nice to see you. And you'll have to admit, Samantha is engaging." She turned and left before he could respond.

"Samantha?" Simon said. "Doc Princher's nurse? She's about *twelve*, Buell."

"Dammit, Simon." He glanced at the nearest bunch of women. "I went to see him and she was there. What do you want me to do about it? Abby's messin' with me, that's all."

Simon chuckled. "And doing a good job of it, looks like." He glanced around the store. "What brings you in here?"

"I need a spyglass."

"What on earth for?"

"Do you sell 'em or not?"

"It wasn't a nosy question. I don't have a telescope, and there are various kinds of binoculars."

221

"I want to be able to count deer a mile away."

"Then you want the stronger type, the military model. You're in luck, I have one." Simon glanced at the counter. "Let me help a couple of those ladies, and then I'll go get you what you need." He hurried off.

Buell moved to the rear of the store and stood under a long rack of rakes, forks, shovels, and other iron. He found the source of the fuel oil smell. A five-gallon barrel lay sideways on a sawbuck, a brass spigot releasing a drop at a time into a beer bucket on the floor. Feigning interest in the tools, he didn't miss the surreptitious looks the other customers sent his way. Only two or three were familiar faces, but their distaste was obvious, and he could only imagine what was being said behind the gloved hands. He endured it for a while, until finally, one at a time, he directly met each gaze—their interest fluttered away.

Then Simon was at his elbow. "This is what you're looking for." He handed him a strapped leather case. Unsnapping the top, Buell took out the twin-barreled telescope. "That right there"—Simon pointed at a knurled wheel between the barrels—"lets you change focus. Look through them, and then turn it till you see the *deer* clearly." He gave Buell a direct look. "They're from Germany and very expensive."

Buell reached for his purse. "How much?"

Simon grimaced. "Forty-six dollars."

"Goddamn, Simon, I ain't buyin' the store." Several heads swiveled around. "I don't have that much," he finished in a harsh whisper.

"Take 'em," Simon said. "Pay me tomorrow."

"I will." Buell put the glasses back in the case and snapped it shut. "I'll see ya later."

Simon grabbed his arm. "Hardhead," he muttered. "Come with me."

"Huh?"

"Into the back room. I want to know what you're up to."

Buell glanced at the front door.

"I'm not taking no for an answer. Now c'mon." Simon stepped around behind him.

Buell went past the end of the counter, pushed open the storeroom door, and went in. Simon followed. "I know you're going to spy on the island bunch. What for?"

"Did you tell Staker about the Colt?"

"I told him no one I asked remembered selling one."

Buell sniffed. "Same ol' Simon," he said and chuckled. "If that's what it takes."

"I could *tell* him," Simon said peevishly.

"No. And I appreciate that ya didn't."

"Then don't make snot-nosed remarks. Now, tell me what you're up to."

"The man I left out there was gone when Staker's deputies went lookin'. Roscoe has a lawyer and—"

"Where'd he get a lawyer?"

"Good question—I'd like to ask him. Anyway, he does, and without the man who run off, my side of the story can look a little suspicious. Judge Kingsley gave Staker until Friday to come up with a good reason not to let Roscoe out. It's my word against his."

"How's spying on the island gonna help?"

"I recognized the third man's voice, and I know his name."

Simon's face brightened. "Then tell Staker."

"My way is easier and more likely to get the man."

"So why the binoculars?"

"After we run their horses off, that bunch is gonna be hard to get close to. I expect they'll have sentries up on top, and for damn sure on the island." He hefted the case. "These will let me find out if he's there or not."

"And if he is?"

"Then I'll go get 'im."

"That's suicide."

"So is letting Roscoe go." Buell touched him on the shoulder. "Thanks, Simon." He lifted the glasses again. "For these, and for being a friend."

"You going today? It's freezing out there."

"I've got a week, and Mother Nature don't give a shit about me." He started for the door and then veered back. "Shorter this way." He pulled the back door open, and left Simon standing, hands on hips.

Nothing moved on the frozen prairie, and the brittle air kept the birds in the shelter of the trees. Well away from the river, Buell sat astride Shadow, scanning back and forth along the bluffs until he spotted the sentries. The one in the middle had been easy. Buell couldn't see the man, but he couldn't miss the wispy smoke from his fire. He found the next one, about a quarter of a mile east, and the third about half that distance to the west. He couldn't actually see the last man, but his ground-tethered horse stood almost out of sight below a bluff. It pleased him he could easily tell the color of the animal through the glass.

Carefully, he cased the instrument, dropped into a gully leading to the river, and easily rode past the man with the fire. After he'd tied Shadow up in a small patch of brush, he took a hair-on deerskin off the back of the saddle. He climbed to the top of the bluff and spread the hide out on the ground. With his glasses, he then located the man with the fire—huddled in a bright red blanket. He was either dead or asleep. Buell smiled to himself and turned his attention to the island.

The horses were where they'd been before, but the rope corral was now double stranded, and guards were stationed around it. He found their positions marked by three rough lean-tos. On the north side of the clearing, four men sat by a small stack of hay, smoking. He concentrated on the horses, nearly all of them standing at the rope barrier watching their guards and, he presumed, the food. Where had the fodder come from? He studied each animal until he found the sorrel with four stocking feet. With a grunt, he rolled over and looked toward the red-shrouded figure just west of his position—he hadn't moved.

He rolled up his ground cover and stole down the slope to Shadow. There he tied the deerskin back on the saddle, and then made his way to the trees lining the frozen channel. Stopping every twenty or thirty yards, he crept upriver, scanning the bluffs above until he saw the sentry's horse. He slipped into the cover of the cottonwoods. For the next hundred yards he moved from tree to tree until he reached the place he and the Irishman had charged across the water. Unconsciously, he loosened the long-barreled Remington in its holster before creeping up the slope. When he was high enough to see the two rows of huts and the center fire-ring, he sat down in a clump of brush and took out his glasses.

Eighteen men stood around the fire, and from where he hid he could almost see them blink. It took him only a minute to find Simpson, arms crossed tightly in front of his chest, shoulders hunched. And standing next to him was Bachman. The slim man held a cup in one hand and was talking. Suddenly, he stabbed a forefinger at three men, each individually, and then started gesturing wildly at the others, coffee splashing on the ground. The three he'd singled out looked back as he motioned vigorously, but most stared at the fire. With a shout Buell could hear, Bachman sloshed the contents of his cup into the fire, then stomped over to a hut and went in.

With Bachman gone, the rest of the men started talking back and forth, nodding and shaking heads, until the three men Bachman had pointed at turned and walked to the supply hut. They went inside to come out a moment later, two carrying shovels, and one a small pickax. They slowly made their way into the trees on the north side of the clearing, past a wagon that was almost hidden, and disappeared. "Gifts are always welcome," Buell muttered under his breath. He watched for a while as the remaining men huddled around the fire, stomping their feet, and smoking. Finally, he cased the glasses and made his way back to Shadow.

Back in town, Buell put his horse away and went to Staker's office. "I need to talk to you outside," Buell said.

"It's cold out there."

Buell pointed past him toward the jail cells and shook his head. Staker nodded, got up, and went to the coat stand. A minute later, they were standing outside. "We can go to my place, or to Pa's office," Buell offered.

"What do you have on your mind?"

"A lot more than I'd like. For one, I found your missing man."

Staker winced. "Let's go to your father's place. I've got a feeling he's going to need to know what's going on." They walked across the street and over to Mace's freight office. Staker followed Buell into the room.

"I thought you were home, son." Paisley looked at Staker. "Trouble?"

"Don't know. Buell's got something to tell us."

"Tell him about Roscoe, Sheriff," Buell said. "And his lawyer, and what the judge had to say. Then I'll tell you what I found out today, and what I suspect." He took off his shearling coat, hung it on the back of a chair, and sat.

Staker shrugged out of his wool one and took a seat on the couch. "We can't find the man Buell said tried to shoot him on the road to Bedell's."

Paisley started to get up.

"Wait a minute, Mace, and let me finish," Staker said. "Two deputies went to the exact spot, no doubt about it." He looked at Buell, who nodded his head. "So, Roscoe's lawyer—please, Mace, let me finish. As unlikely as it sounds, Roscoe has a lawyer, that new fella from Cincinnati, and he petitioned the judge with a habeas corpus writ. That means we have to produce proof that Roscoe committed a crime. Worse yet, the lawyer is seeking a warrant for Buell's arrest."

"I've heard enough!" Paisley said loudly as he stood. "There ain't no way Buell is going to jail for taking a swat at the likes of Rudy Rosser." He came around his desk and stood in front of Staker, his powerful-looking hands on his hips. "It's time we showed some proof of our own, yer corpus whatever be damned. I know yer a stickler for the law, and most times I'm right behind you, but there's folks who have had it in for Buell since he came back. I'm ashamed to say I didn't back him up the way a father should." He took a deep breath, let it out noisily, and then leaned back against his desk. "So, let's hear what he has to say, and then figger a way out of this mess. Buell?"

"I went out to Sandy Island today and I know where the body is."

Staker sat up straight on the edge of the couch. "Now why doesn't that surprise me one damned bit?" He shook his head. "Not one goddamned whit." He sank back in the sofa. "Go on."

"The man who was in on the ambush was named Simpson. I know, Sheriff, I said I didn't know. I recognized his voice from a little talk I had with him, Bachman, and Roscoe over at Lancer's. And Roscoe mentioned his name at the jailhouse."

"So where's the body?"

"On the island, north side of their camp."

"Damn it, son. You just waltzed in there and took a look?"

"I didn't. I used a spyglass. I went lookin' for Simpson or his horse—he rides a sorrel with four white feet. I reckoned I could get close enough to see the corral and the camp without them knowin'. It was pure luck Bachman sent them three men off with shovels and a pick."

"You say Bachman *sent* them?" Staker said.

"Yep, *sent.* He's in charge. I could see it."

"And you saw Simpson?" the sheriff asked.

"No doubt about it."

Paisley pushed away from his desk and went around it to sit down. "See there, Loren, what'd I tell ya—proof. All you have to do is go get this Simpson fella and make 'im tell the judge what he saw."

"Not as easy as that, Mace. I'm sheriff of Carlisle, not Lincoln County. I'll have to ask for a warrant, and then *they'll* have to serve it."

"We have three days, Loren. Buell says Simpson and the body are there. Can't you just get some men together and go get 'im? Judge Kingsley will see that's right when we have 'im— I'd bet on it."

"And you'd lose, Mace. It hasn't been that long ago that we had *no* law. The judge is not gonna let us slip back to those times. I'll send the telegram and we'll see what happens."

"But—"

"No buts. I think we can keep Buell out of jail, but that lawyer's going to insist on a charge of aggravated battery."

Buell's hand went to his head and his fingers probed the tender spot above his right ear. "If that's what the law means, I've seen about all I want of it."

"Now, Buell, don't lose sight of what we're doing here," Paisley said. "I believe you, and so does he." He looked at Staker and the sheriff nodded. "We just have to do what the law says and get this trouble over with once and for all."

"The trouble didn't start on that island," Buell scoffed. "Nobody sees that?"

"I don't get what you're driving at," Staker said. "*All* our trouble comes from there."

"That may be so, but that's not where it starts. I saw a stack of hay on the island, and I spotted the wagon that hauled it. You took the wagon they had—it was Bedell's. You said Venable was gonna see he got it back. Did he? And if he did, where'd they get another one, and the money to buy feed for nearly twenty horses?"

"I get the feeling you're going to tell us," said Paisley.

"You ain't gonna like it either. But before I say any more, I want to make sure of a couple of things."

"I don't want you interfering in my job, Buell," Staker said as he got off the sofa. "What's this you want to make sure of?"

"Don't you want to know if Venable got that wagon back to Bedell?"

"Of course. And *I'll* ask, not you. Keep your nose clean, Buell. Don't give that lawyer a reason to go to Judge Kingsley and get yourself slapped in a cell."

"He's right, son. We've got till Friday." Paisley got out of his chair and went to Staker. "Get the telegram off, Loren." He stuck out his hand. "I appreciate ya discussing this in front of me."

"You're gonna be the mayor in just over a month." Staker shook his hand. "I reckon getting this sorted out is gonna take at least that long."

"What?" Buell almost shouted.

"At least," Staker said firmly. "So it's important that you keep out of trouble."

"But a month? We go get Simpson, and dig up that Meat fella—it's all over."

"Not when you've got a lawyer involved. Times have changed,

Buell. We'll do it by the letter of the law. Agreed?" Staker wasn't asking.

"I'll stay off the island, Sheriff," Buell said. "They aren't goin' anywhere."

CHAPTER 24

As soon as Staker left, Buell went to the stable, saddled Shadow, and rode out to Venable's feedlot. He'd had no reason to go since returning home, so seeing a dozen holding pens surprised him. Aligned north and south along a passageway about two wagons wide, six on each side, were corrals capable of holding a hundred head each. Fifteen-foot-high stacks of hay stood along the west and north sides.

A two-story barn loomed east of the pens, and about sixty yards north of it stood a small structure with an east-facing door and a single window. Buell rode up on the south side of the barn and got off, letting both reins drop to the ground. He patted Shadow on the shoulder before he took a look around. In the back of the building, a single door opened on a path that led past the pens and around the haystacks. Past that door, a pair of closed sliding ones parted the center of the barn, a loft hatch above. He continued around to the north side and peeked through a window.

A black horse stood tied to a hitching post by the back door of the smaller building, he assumed an office. Unbuttoning his heavy coat, he angled across to the southeast corner of the building and looked around it to see a door with an uncovered porch and a four-paned window. The sign above the entry read "Venable and Associates." He stepped up on the porch, pushed open the door and went in.

An obviously startled Blake Waldon, hands held behind his

back, stood on the left in front of a black Franklin stove. "Well, well, Buell, come on in. Nice to see you." His wide eyes gave lie to his cheerful tone, and he started to flush. "What brings you out to Venable's?" He nodded toward a man on the other side of the room. "Jules, this is Paisley's boy, the one I've been tellin' you about. I guess you two have never met." Behind a cluttered table that apparently served as a desk sat a swarthy, black-haired man. "Jules Venable, meet Buell Mace."

"Heard some about ya," Jules muttered, but remained seated.

"Buell here is gonna be sheriff one day. His pa and me are gonna see to it. Ain't that right, Buell?" Waldon gushed.

"I don't know why my pa likes you, Waldon, but I don't," Buell said flatly.

"Huh?" Waldon looked like he'd been slapped, his face turning red. He shot a glance at Jules, who had a slight smile on his face. "Now listen here, Mace, that's the third time you've insulted me for no reason, and I'm tired of it. You have a bone to pick at, start pickin'."

"Soon as he answers a couple of questions," Buell said as he faced Venable.

Jules leaned back in his chair, the smile now a smirk. "Pushy young puker, ain't he?" he said to Waldon. "I said I'd heard a little about ya, Mace. Seems yer a real rooster when ya got a saloon full o' friends." He took an exaggerated look around the room. "Problem is, I don't see any here. As a matter of fact, there's some fellas outside who watched you ride up, and one for sure would really like to take a crack at ya." He glanced at the window.

"Ya mean those two out in the barn? Yer gonna have to wake one up, and Gus doesn't appear all that interested either. I wondered where he was stayin'. I left my horse on the south side." Venable licked his lips and fidgeted in his chair as Waldon moved away from the stove, closer to the back of the room. "So, my question," Buell continued. "Sheriff Staker brought a wagon out here a while ago. It belonged to Ruben Bedell. You told him you'd see Bedell got it back. Did he?"

"Yes."

"How so?" Buell stepped a little closer to the desk.

"Back about a week or so, two of his men was in for some oats. They took it with 'em."

"There—go take a look around, Mace. You won't see that wagon," Waldon said a little more confidently. "If that's all you needed, it's settled, 'cause it isn't here."

"That bone you mentioned," Buell said. "I took a brand-new pistol off Roscoe when he jumped me the other day—I can see you know about that—he couldn't afford that kind of gun if he starved for a year. Turns out you bought one three days ago. Did—" Buell glared as Waldon started to speak. "Don't bother to deny it. I know it for a *fact*! My question is, did you give it to Roscoe to bushwhack me, or were ya payin' him off for something else?"

"That's preposterous! If he had that Colt, he stole it." Waldon moved closer yet to the back door.

"Time was when I'd shoot you right here and now—time was. But I can't know for sure if you put Roscoe up to it or not, and for that you can be thankful. But—"

"I've had enough!" Blake strode over to Venable's desk. "Jules, throw this impudent ass out of here." Venable slowly stood, and then edged to the corner of the table. "Now! Jules," Waldon shouted and stepped back to let him pass.

Buell dug his left elbow into the edge of his overcoat and pushed it back, exposing his Remington. "He's a pushy puker, ain't he, *Jules*? How 'bout you?"

Venable glanced at the holstered pistol, stepped to his chair, and sat down. "This ain't my affair, Blake. I run this feedlot and that's all."

Buell moved back to the front of the room and took a quick look through the window. "I don't know exactly what you're up to, Waldon, but I know it's not good. You're greedy, and not near as smart as you think you are. Greedy *and* stupid will git ya a hole in yer hide." Watching both men, he sidestepped along the wall until he felt the doorknob in his back. Reaching behind, he opened the door and left.

He hurried across the yard and stood in the half-open barn door before Gus knew he had company. "This ain't no social call, Gus, so don't get up," Buell said quietly. The big man sat hunkered over a kerosene lantern, his ragged coat spread wing-like around it. His companion, a much older man, sat wrapped in a heavy wool blanket, slumped in a tilted chair. A sack of feed elevated his feet. With his head cocked back against a roof pillar, his slack mouth exposed teeth rotted to ragged stumps and stained a dark tobacco-brown. Buell kicked one of the rear chair legs and stepped out of the way as the man crashed to the ground.

"What'n hell!" He struggled to free himself from the tangle, and then stopped abruptly when he looked up at the muzzle of Buell's .44.

"Yer smarter than some I've known, mister," Buell said. "Keep them hands where I can see 'em, and we'll git along fine." The man nodded, and pulled the blanket up around his ears, grasping the edges with both hands. Buell looked at Gus, who hadn't moved except to close his overcoat and scoot the lamp away with his toe. "Figgered you had someplace to hole up, Gus. Haven't seen much of ya lately—what ya up to?"

"Mindin' my own business, Mace." He looked at the pistol and sneered. "And you can put that away—I'm not impressed." He opened his coat. "Or carryin' one. Never saw the need."

Buell shrugged, gave the man on the floor a look, and then

put his pistol away. "What does Blake Waldon have to do with Venable?"

"Yer funnin', right?"

"I just had a little talk with the two of 'em. Neither one is much for backbone."

"Waldon pays good," Gus said. "I ain't interested in the size of his balls."

"Pays you to do what? I haven't found out that he really *owns* anything."

Gus jerked his thumb toward the window. " 'Cause his name ain't on that office, don't mean he don't own it."

"What's he got on Venable then? It was clear to me that Waldon calls the shots."

"Why should I tell you anything? You've been a pain in my ass since you were old enough to chew."

"Maybe 'cause you've never been afraid to speak yer mind. Maybe 'cause you've always got the shitty end of the stick—like me. Maybe we're more alike than ya think."

Gus started to say something and then stopped. He sat looking up at Buell for several seconds before he smiled. "You always were a slick-tongued son of a bitch, Buell. I'm not gonna tell you a damned thing. I don't like you and never have."

"Plain enough." Buell took another look at the man in the blanket and snorted—mouth agape, the old guy was sound asleep again. "You can sure pick 'em, Gus. I'll leave ya to yer tendin'." He started to leave.

"What was you doin' here, then?" Gus stood up.

Buell turned back and stood silent for a few seconds. "Chasin' rabbit tracks, Gus. Remember when we used to do that down by the river? I learned back then there's always a big buck that the rest followed. Sometimes his tracks was clear and sometimes all messed up by the ones that followed."

"So what'n hell ya gettin' at? *Rabbits!*"

"I think I might have found the big buck, Gus."

"Me?"

"Yer big, Gus, but that's all. And one more thing—I owe ya for that night behind Lancer's." Buell turned on his heel and left as Gus's face delivered the truth.

Before Buell climbed on Shadow, he checked behind Venable's office again—the black was still there. A few minutes later, he pushed through the double doors at Lancer's and looked for the owner. There were only three other people in the place, and Art sat at a table playing patience.

Art looked up from his card game as Buell crossed the saloon and pulled out a chair. "Buell."

"Afternoon, Art. Real busy I see."

"Cold." He shrugged his shoulders. "Drink?"

"Naw. I come in to check on something. Finish yer game." Buell looked over the spread cards. "I'd say yer soon done with that one."

"Yep." Art turned over the last few cards he held in his hand, then gathered the rest, quickly sorting those that lay faceup from those facedown, and dropped the deck on the table. "So?"

"You know there's some bad comin' at us, don't ya?"

Art nodded.

"And I think you have a good idea who's behind it."

"Maybe."

"Then you're right where I'm at—not quite sure, yet."

Art nodded again.

"I was just out to Venable's. Never been there before—big. Blake Waldon was there. Is that unusual?"

"Daytime? Yep."

"Let me tell ya what went on when I barged in on 'em." Buell laid out Waldon's apparent dominance over Jules Venable and Venable's story about how the wagon was returned to Bedell. "What I need to know is, has any of Bedell's men been into town the last two or three weeks?"

"Nope."

"You sure?"

"Cold. No need."

"How about Bedell needing some feed?"

Art shook his head and smiled. "He sells oats."

"Thanks, Art. One more question. Am I on the right trail? I mean, is Waldon behind that mob on the island?"

Art nodded.

"But why?" Buell said more to himself than Lancer.

Art shrugged and shook his head.

"Well, have another go at the game, Art. I'll talk this over with Pa tomorrow at Thanksgiving dinner."

"Goin'?" Art's face lit up.

"Yeah. See if I can get to know Ruth a little better."

"Glad," Art said and picked up his cards.

CHAPTER 25

Thursday morning greeted Buell with leftover coffee frozen in the pot, the stove as dead as day-old meatloaf. Cursing under his breath, he shifted from one stocking foot to the other as he built a fire. As soon as it was crackling, he hurried back to his bedroom and got dressed. He was anxious to talk to his father. Well into the night, he'd moved the pieces of the puzzle around in his head until they nearly all fit—all but one.

At ten o'clock, Buell walked Shadow into his father's barn, loosened the cinch strap, and slipped the bridle off before putting him in a stall. Sliding the door shut behind, he ran across the yard to the house. Tugging off a glove, he was about to turn the doorbell when the door opened.

"Don't you even think about knockin' on this door," Paisley said and stepped back. "Get in here before the chickens get out."

"Mornin', Pa," Buell said, glancing around as he shrugged out of his coat. He'd been in the house right after his father's wedding and didn't recognize anything from then except the fancy gaslights. The furnishings, all polished wood and fancy upholstery, made him want to wipe his feet.

"We're pleased you decided to come today," Ruth said as she came out of the kitchen and over to him. "Let me have your coat and hat. You may put your pistol there." She pointed at an umbrella stand.

He handed her his coat and unbuckled his gun. "That doesn't

smell like turkey, Mis—uh—"

"Let's get that out of the way right now," she said with a smile. "I'm Ruth."

He nodded.

"No, say it. Ruth."

"That don't smell like turkey, Ruth." Buell felt the heat in his face.

"There. That's because it's a goose. Paisley told me you didn't like turkey, and I can't say that I blame you. You two go in the parlor and talk. I'll be busy for some time yet." She hung his coat on the rack by the door and left.

Paisley waited until Buell had the pistol put away. "You heard her, son . . . parlor." He beckoned with his hand and Buell followed him into the dark-paneled room. "Mahogany wood," Paisley said proudly. "I had it put in last year."

"It's beautiful."

"Sit there," Paisley said, indicating one of two oversized, leather-covered chairs. "Would you drink a whiskey?"

"In here?" Buell glanced at the French doors they'd just come through.

"New rules, Buell. Whadda ya say?"

"Well, sure. Little early, but it's Thanksgiving."

"Good for you." Paisley went to a low cabinet and splashed two fingers of rye in a pair of glasses. He handed one to Buell, then sat down in the matching chair. "I don't suppose you've heard anything about Roscoe's fate?"

Buell eyed the amber drink. "Nope."

"I had a little talk with John Lindstrom. Ya mind?"

"What did he have to say?"

"Do you know John's story? I mean, about what brought him to Carlisle?"

"Simon said he used to be a lawyer back east. Then he got caught up in somethin' bad, where some folks got killed—

burned, I think."

"You've got the gist of it. He swore off criminal law, and he intends to stand by that, so he won't get involved officially. But he's also a longtime friend."

"I remember you lettin' him sleep in the loft when he got drunk."

Paisley chuckled. "Time changes a lot of things, doesn't it? Anyway, if we need a lawyer, he'll ask one he knows in Kearney to come over. He doesn't seem to think we will."

"Sheriff Staker doesn't think that."

"You've got friends, Buell, lots of 'em. Most don't want to say so right out, but they're lookin' out for ya." Paisley took a sip. "You look like ya don't believe that. It's true. Waldon came by last night and we had a . . . what?" His brow furrowed and he shrugged.

Buell let out an exasperated sigh. "Waldon is poison. I *know* it. What did he want?"

"Same thing as you. Quiet."

"I had a run—"

"He told me, Buell. Complete misunderstanding. He said he blew up at you a little, but then you have that way about ya that brings it on."

Buell set his untouched drink on the table between them. "I've about got this whole mess figgered out, Pa, except for one little piece."

"Figgered how?"

"Blake Waldon wants something, a business, a ranch, another piece of Carlisle—something. That's a fact."

"And somehow that's wrong?"

"Listen to me. Gus Swartz works for him. He so much as admitted it. Waldon gave Roscoe that pistol." Buell held up his hand. "No-no. I *know* it. He said if Roscoe had a new Colt's pistol, he stole it. Nobody but Staker and I knew it was new or a Colt. So, both men work for Waldon, and both are mixed up with that bunch on Sandy Island. Who sells hay, Pa—besides us? Jules Venable. Did Waldon tell you where he and I had our little disagreement?" Buell paused as his father thought for a moment. "I didn't think he'd mention that. At Venable's. Starting to come clear?"

"Waldon has never done anything to me. He's always been straight."

"He's never had a reason to buck ya. He'd sooner hug ya to death than fight ya." Buell winced. "I know how it works, Pa. It was done to me."

Paisley leaned back in his chair. "Why does he want you to be the sheriff, then?"

"Because he thinks I'll follow your lead." Buell couldn't stop a smile. "And he thinks he's got you buffaloed."

"He doesn't know us that well, does he?"

"Nope. Well, does he—have ya buffaloed?"

"I guess he did, until today. You're dead sure of your facts?"

"No doubt. Now help me out with a couple things. What is it Waldon wants? And who has it now?"

"That could be complicated. Carlisle is growing like thistle. The man, or men, who own the land around us stand to make a killing. I know Paul has dreams of a couple more flour mills and several new silos. He's been angling for the ground, but the farmers and ranchers see the profit too. It's fairly certain that Waldon has a controlling interest in Venable's place, and it could expand. His problem there is he needs another railway siding, council permission, and the two hundred acres to the east that Bedell owns. Other—"

"Bedell!"

"What?"

"I thought Bedell's ground was farther north, by the river."

"Nope. Smack up against Venable's. Waldon has encroached

a dozen times, and Bedell has used Staker to move him off it. Been an ongoing thing for—I dunno, since Bedell got here I guess."

Buell picked up his whiskey glass and stared into it for several seconds. "Bedell said his family was from New Mexico. Has he ever mentioned a brother or sister—any kin?"

"He doesn't have any. Least, that's what he told me. Just him and his cowboys."

"The last piece just fell into place, Pa."

"Huh?"

"Yes'ir, I know who thinks he's the tall hog, and I know what he wants." He offered the edge of his glass to his confused father. "A toast. To good whiskey and wheels with strong spokes."

"Wheels and what? Never mind." Paisley shook his head. "And makin' good with what ya got, and by damn, we have." He touched Buell's glass.

"And how's that, Paisley?" Ruth said from the door.

"Ya caught us, dear. Preachin' and braggin'—'bout all we do. Ain't that right, son?"

"Mostly, I guess. More in self-defense than anything, though."

"What an interesting observation, Buell." She came over and sat on the arm of Paisley's chair. "The yams just went on the stove. All we do now is wait. What prompted you to say that? It's a defense."

"Just what I've seen. If a man brags it means he ain't got as much as he says he does. And if he preaches, he's wishin' he could be more like he ain't. In both cases, it's to keep others from gettin' a good look. Most folks see through both, so ain't nobody gettin' skunked."

"Now that ain't what I meant at all," Paisley protested. "I was just sayin' we got here by workin' hard—"

"Don't slip a cog, Pa. I know what ya are."

"And I'm finding out," Ruth said airily as she stood up. "And I like it." She stopped at the double doors. "There's fresh coffee in the kitchen if you'd like. I'm going to have a cup."

"Good idea. We'll be in shortly," Paisley said to her back and then looked at Buell and grinned. "Better?"

"Much."

The meal had been perfect, and Buell remembered Simon describing the ones the two Steele families used to share—before Matt Steele was killed. They were all three back in the parlor sipping something so sweet it made Buell's jaw ache. "It has been a real nice time, Pa—and Ruth."

"I am very pleased you've decided to visit," she said. "You're always welcome."

Paisley glanced at his wife, then added, "And if that stable gets a—"

"I like it there, Pa. It suits me fine." Buell emphasized the last word, and his father nodded. "I think the things you're gonna try to do as mayor will cock some hats."

"Maybe some hats need cocked." Paisley winked broadly.

"Paisley will be a good mayor," Ruth said. "Don't you think?"

Something struck the front door so hard the bell cover fell off on the floor. Buell was across the room before Paisley could get up. "Stay there," he ordered, and in three strides had his hand on his pistol belt. The door rattled again. "Mace!" someone shouted, and again hit the door. Buell moved the lace curtain aside and looked past the edge of the window. A horse stood at the gate, reins thrown over the top fence rail. "Mace, open up. All hell's broke loose in town."

"Open the door, son," Paisley whispered harshly.

Buell jerked the door open, and thrust the Remington's muzzle into the visitor's face. "What kind of hell?"

The man stumbled back. "God, I'm glad to see you, Mister Mace."

"You want me or him?" Buell jerked a thumb at Paisley.

"You. Staker asked for you. Hurry, he's been shot up bad."

Buell whipped his belt around his waist and buckled it. Grabbing his coat and hat, he pushed past the man. "Where?"

"The jail."

"I'm taking your horse. Mine's in there." He pointed at the barn, and then sprinted to the panting animal. Seconds later, he was galloping down the road towards Carlisle.

Stepping up on the boardwalk, Buell grabbed a man by the collar and jerked.

"Goddamn!" the man shouted as he landed on his butt. The scowl he wore vanished when he recognized Buell.

"Get out of the way," Buell bawled and pushed his way through the dozen men crowding the door to the jail. Inside, both deputies stood ashen-faced and silent as they stood over Doc Princher and a bloody Sheriff Staker. The lawman's chest lay bare, and the doctor was stuffing gauze into a bullet hole just below the sheriff's collarbone. Two other holes had already been plugged, both on the left side of Staker's belly. The first cell door stood open, and a mess of potatoes, carrots, gravy, and turkey lay strewn just outside on the floor. He knelt down beside Doc Princher. "He asked for me."

"He's not talking, Buell. He may never again."

Buell looked up at one of the deputies. "Were you here, Ford?"

The man shook his head slowly.

"You?" he asked the other one.

"I was down the street. Heard shots, but I couldn't tell from where."

"Dammit, Buell, do this another time," snapped Princher.

"Help me get this bandage under him. And be careful!" He glanced at the second deputy. "You. Help."

One on each side, Buell and the other man reached under until they touched hands. The sheriff's back was slick. As they started to lift, Staker eye's popped open to look directly at Buell. The bright red tip of his tongue wet his lips, and he took a shallow breath. He tried to speak, his voice less than a whisper. "Everybody shut up," Buell shouted. The jail fell silent. He leaned over Staker and put his ear to the man's lips.

"Bach—man."

Buell rose up again. "Bachman?" he asked and watched the sheriff's eyes. They focused for a second, and then Staker nodded once, his chin stopping to rest on his chest. "Did you see that? He nodded when I said Bachman."

"He passed out, Buell," Princher said through clenched teeth. "He doesn't even know you're here. Now lift, so I can get him to the infirmary."

CHAPTER 26

Buell nodded at the deputy standing in the doorway of the warehouse. He was shuffling his feet and wouldn't meet his eyes. Sherm Pederson stood just inside. "It was a simple question, Mayor," Buell said sharply.

"This is city business, and we'll take care of it. Keep your nose out." The mayor's head bobbed up and down, his face enflamed, and his voice squeaked every third or fourth word. He shot a furtive glance over his shoulder at the deputy.

Buell's scalp contracted. "I live here, and so does my pa. That makes it *my* business."

"We have two deputies, both experienced lawmen." The deputy winced. "And they'll find out the facts." The mayor looked past Buell.

Walt and two other men approached from behind to join them. "Ford," Walt greeted the deputy.

"Walt."

The mayor glowered at the three new men.

"Seems to me, Mister Pederson, that you'd welcome all the help you can get," Walt said.

"We're . . . investigating." The mayor's face flushed even redder.

"In here?" one of the men beside Walt said, and the deputy coughed.

"You've been told, Mace," the mayor said, and then abruptly turned to the deputy. "Go do something," he nearly shouted.

"Now listen, Sherm, we *were* asking around till you drug me over here. If you ask me, I think Mister Mace could help a lot. Sheriff Staker holds him in some regard."

"Right now, you work for me," Pederson said in a high voice. "You hear me!" He stormed out of the warehouse.

"Dammit, Ford, does that mean Staker died?" Buell asked.

The deputy stepped into the room. "Not as of an hour ago. I still work for the sheriff, and if I *had* to work for Sherm Pederson, I'd quit anyhow. We were doin' like you suggested, Mister Mace, asking everybody within sight of Main Street if they was open yesterday, and if they was, if they remembered seeing any of those islanders ride in. So far nothin'."

"It might have been only one, but I can't imagine Bachman comin' on his own—not his way."

"And yer sure the sheriff said Bachman?" Walt asked.

"Not a doubt. And it fits." Buell turned to the deputy. "Have you told the county sheriff about this, Ford?"

"Sherm said he'd do it."

"How well do you know the old man at the telegraph?"

"Percy? Real good."

"Ask him. And ask him to keep it to himself. Think he'll do that?"

"He'll tell me *if* he sent one, but I guarantee he won't tell me what it said. He's mum as a Mason about what's in a telegram."

"Just knowin' if it went out or not is enough."

"We don't have enough work to do?" Paisley said from the doorway and then came on in.

"We just had a visit from the mayor, Pa," Buell said. "He wasn't happy about me talkin' to Ford here."

"Petty little worm." Paisley shook his head. "I was just over to Doc's. He's a little more confident than he was yesterday. He said the sheriff making it through the night was a big step."

"Is the sheriff talkin'?" Ford asked.

"Oh, no. Doc says he's still real bad off. He got the bullet out of his chest, and the two in his side went right through. There was another shot he didn't see till he got all Loren's clothes off. It's in the hip—the bullet's still there."

"*In* the hip, Pa?" Buell shook his head.

"That's what he said. He can feel it but he can't move it—stuck in the bone."

"Did you see Staker?"

"Nope. Well, yeah, I could see him, but he was covered up. Why do ya ask that?"

"Ya think Doc would talk to me about it?"

"He's not real happy with gun-totin' men right now, Buell. I doubt it."

"I'm gonna go talk to the doc, whether he likes it or not," Ford said. "What do ya need to know, Mister Mace?"

"The size of the bullet in his hip. Not the exact size, just how it compares to the ones higher up."

"Ya think they're different, don't ya?"

The question surprised Buell. "Yeah."

"Which would mean there was probably more than one shooter."

"Damn, Ford, yer actin' like a real lawman," Walt said.

"You follow me real good, deputy," Buell said. "If the bullet stuck in the bone, I'd bet it was a twenty-two or maybe a twenty-five. A pocket gun, cheap, the kind a man down on his luck could afford. I know the hole in Staker's chest was a lot bigger than a twenty anything."

"I'll find out, Mister Mace. I better get back on the street, got a lot of folks to talk to. And just so ya know, we appreciate your help, and I know Sheriff Staker does too. See ya, Walt." He left.

"I need to talk to ya, Pa," Buell said. "Let's go to the office."

"Ya know we're ready to help if there's trouble," Walt said.

The other two nodded.

"I know that. With some luck, it won't come to town again." He followed his father out of the warehouse and down the dock.

Buell shut the office door and sat on the couch as his father settled down behind his desk.

"So, talk," Paisley said. "I feel like a green mule."

"There are a lot more people mixed up in this than I first thought."

"Mixed up in what? I saw some small-town shenanigans goin' on, but I never expected someone to shoot Staker." Paisley shook his head emphatically. "Never!"

"We have a fight between Blake Waldon and Ruben Bedell. Blake wants that property east of Venable's. And Blake owns Venable's, did ya know that?"

"I knew he had a stake."

"No stake—he owns it, and Venable. Waldon also tells the mayor what to do. He just proved that, and if what I think is true, the Lincoln County sheriff has been bought as well. We'll see that soon enough. And last, Waldon is behind the trouble you've had with the islanders." Buell nodded his head as he pictured something. "I think that little visit Bedell's boys made spoiled Waldon's comin'-out party. There were over forty men in that camp first time I saw it. Now there's eighteen, and ain't none of 'em looking too frisky."

"But what would Blake gain by having that bunch raise hell in Carlisle? He lives here too."

"People like him work best when there's lots of fussin' goin' on. They can do things without bein' noticed. Like gettin' Ruben Bedell killed or—" Buell paused a long time before he finished. "Or you, Pa."

"Me? Why on earth? Blake's always been my friend."

"He's not your friend. He doesn't have friends. Up until you were elected mayor you weren't a threat. Now you are, 'cause he knows damn well you can't be bought."

"But why shoot Staker?"

"Staker had Roscoe, and Roscoe knew something that was going to nut Waldon. He couldn't take the chance Roscoe would talk."

"Can you prove all this?"

Buell shook his head. "Not without Roscoe."

"What a mess. Want to know what I think?"

"That's why we're talkin'."

"I think we need to go to Judge Kingsley."

"He wants to put me in jail, remember?"

"But that was before all this."

"And all this's got me is Staker flat on his back where he ain't likely to put in a good word for me today. It is Friday, remember?"

"But Roscoe's gone."

"The judge issued a warrant, Pa. Staker told me Kingsley would follow the law, no matter what."

"So what do you intend to do?"

"I'm not gonna tell ya. All ya need to know is I'll be safe enough where I'm at."

"Dammit, Buell, I'd sooner see ya safe in jail."

"Don't look like jail is a very safe place, does it?" Buell stood and went to the door. "I hope Staker makes it. I'll be in touch." He left before his father could say any more.

Buell rode down the incline to Bedell's ranch just as the sun was setting and saw Andrew stride across the yard to the barn. The door rumbled open as he arrived.

The Scot took hold of Shadow's bridle. "What brings you out here?"

"Wu's cookin', what'n hell ya think?" He swung down and flexed his back. "That ride don't get no shorter."

"And it won't. Stayin' the night?"

"Or more. Gotta spare bunk?" Buell hooked the stirrup over the saddle horn and started to undo the cinch.

"More?" Andrew asked, and unbuckled the bridle. "Yeah, there's a bunk, but Ruben ain't gonna see that. Trouble?"

"Some. I just don't want to talk to the law right now." He winked at Andrew.

"Gotcha." Together they stripped the gear from the horse, and had just put Shadow in a stall when Ruben came in.

"I won't ask," Ruben said. "Can't say I'm surprised, but good to see ya just the same."

"Thanks. I'd like to squat for a few days. Got some thinkin' to do."

"Ya came to the right place for both." He patted the horse's rump. "There's a nice tight shed at the first line shack two miles south."

"Naw. He'll be fine here."

"C'mon to the house, then. You'll have to settle for roast beef tonight."

They had eaten in silence at the kitchen table, and now the supper dishes were cleared with Wu busy at the sink. "You can keep it to yourself if you'd like," Ruben said, "but I'd be a damn liar if I said I wasn't curious."

"You were right about Waldon."

"Let's go in the other room," Ruben said and stood. "Lot more comfortable." Buell followed him through the door and took the seat he'd used the last time. Ruben sat and leaned back. "So Blake made a move, did he?"

"More than one." Buell told him about the ambush, his narrow escape, and discovering the new pistol on Roscoe. Ruben remained passive and attentive as Buell told him about the visit to Venable's and Judge Kingsley's decision. His calm expression vanished when Buell told him about Staker.

"Son of a bitch," Ruben muttered, the first time Buell had heard him swear. "He had no reason to shoot Loren."

"Maybe the men who did it had a reason," Buell replied. "You sound like you expected the rest."

"Just say, it's playing out like I thought it might. I'm a little surprised they jumped you out on the road. Even more that they didn't just shoot you down."

"I could take exception that you didn't tell me that."

"But you won't. I've met you before, Buell. Several of you. You're hard to surprise."

"How'd you know your men scattered them horses?"

Ruben chuckled. "You're really good at that, Buell. You were supposed to think I didn't know."

"Of course ya knew. Andrew would kick a hornet's nest for you—ain't in him to ignore what ya say."

"Waldon was going to let that bunch do what he's scared to try himself—kill me. The rustling that was going on? That was just a way to get me out in the open. Real cattle thieves would've run off half the herd. So I decided to make it a little harder on 'em. And we did. Andrew says there are only sixteen left."

"Eighteen, by my count."

Ruben snorted. "No doubt you grabbed every one of 'em by the ear."

"Nearly. I used a spyglass."

"So what do you intend to do? Legally, you're wanted as of tomorrow morning."

Buell thought for a moment. "There are only a handful who will stand and fight, who'll follow Bachman or Roscoe. I'd like to see all of them with no place to sleep but on the ground."

"We can do that," Ruben said, "and will on two conditions."

"I don't like conditions."

"And I don't make 'em unless I have to. First, you can't be there—"

"I ain't gonna let—"

"I don't make conditions and then back off, Buell." The rancher leaned forward in his chair, his face stern looking. "And second, we don't touch them unless Roscoe or Bachman are seen, and I doubt Roscoe is still alive."

"I'll feel like a skunk, lettin' Andrew and the rest take on my scrap."

"Roscoe and Bachman are after me. It's more my problem than yours. You've just given me reason to take the fight to them again."

"What if Pederson sent a telegram to Lincoln County?"

"You read that right too. Didn't happen. Waldon wants a free hand."

"Why didn't you tell me you and him had a feud goin'?"

"Think about it." Bedell leaned back again and studied Buell.

Buell met his eyes for a moment and then looked into the fire for several seconds. "If I found out about it by myself, I'd know it for sure."

"Precisely." Ruben looked pleased. "A lot of people never learn that, Buell. Now, how about a mug of that buttered rum?"

CHAPTER 27

The day after Buell arrived at Bedell's, the clouds rolled in, pregnant with menace, and Mother Nature unleashed her fury on the area. Over two feet of snow fell before the raging storm moved east, leaving the frozen earth to contrast with a faded blue sky. And then the temperature plunged, and for the next six days any business outside was conducted infrequently and without dallying. Cribbage boards and card games wore away the daylight, and evenings were cut short as everyone sought the comfort of their beds.

The cold snap finally broke, and the day after saw a little thawing as the sun fought back. Buell was in the barn's large tack room helping Ruben mend a damaged harness strap when someone outside hollered. "Hey, Ford, ain't ya got better sense—don't answer that." Two men laughed.

Buell stood and watched the door. "It's not like they didn't know where I'd go."

"It would still just be a guess. If you don't want them to know you're here, they won't. You decide."

"If it was the county sheriff, I'd stay out of sight. Ford has something to say, and I hope it's not what I think."

Ruben put down the skiving knife he'd been using. "I've been expecting someone for the last couple of days."

"Let's go see." Buell headed for the door.

Deputy Ford, looking more like a fully loaded coatrack than a man, sat astride his horse, Andrew standing alongside. Ford spotted Buell as soon as he stepped out of the barn. "Mornin', Mister Mace, Mister Bedell." Ford raised his hand.

"Come on in here, Deputy," Ruben said. "Got a fire going and coffee that might still be fit to drink."

"Ya ain't gotta say that twice." Ford gigged his horse, crossed the yard, and rode through the door when Buell slid it open. Inside, he swung down, wincing as his feet hit the ground. "Still cold enough to freeze yer nuts off." He glanced at the half open tack-room door.

"Put your horse in a stall," Ruben said. "Gonna be here long?"

"No, sir. Left Deputy Skelton alone." He led the animal into an empty space and stepped out.

Buell slid a rail across the stall opening. "Looks like yer news ain't all that bad, Ford, else you'd've said right out."

"Mostly good news, I'd say." The deputy unbuckled a wide belt that held closed the masses of clothing he wore. "Ya said ya got some mud?"

"Come on in here," Ruben said and led Buell and Ford into the tack room. He pointed at the small stove set against the wall, and the half-frozen lawman eagerly went to it. The other two waited while he shucked two heavy wool coats and his gloves, and poured a tin cup full of steaming dark-brown coffee.

Ford took a careful sip. "Judge says he ain't wantin' ya to go to jail, Mister Mace." He nodded pertly.

"How's Staker?" Buell asked, his voice a little sharp.

"Oh yeah, sorry. Still down, but Doc says he'll mor'n likely make it. I thought so all along." He took a longer sip of coffee, his bare hands cupping the hot metal.

"Did Judge Kingsley say why he lifted the arrest warrant?" Ruben asked.

"Cuz Roscoe's dead," Ford said simply. "The day the snow stopped, his horse come into town. There was blood and such all over the beast. Doc says whoever the bits belonged to ain't feelin' no pain. I think it was brains."

"Ya look for Roscoe?" Buell asked.

"Too much snow. We'll let the buzzards find him for us. Good riddance, I say." He took another drink. "The city council is havin' a special meeting Monday evening and would like to talk to you, Mister Mace. I hope I ain't outta line, but I think ya ought to go. Word is they wanna hire ya. Me and the—"

"Is the council all agreed?" Buell asked.

"Well, not exactly all." Ford blushed a bit.

"There's not much latitude in the word *all*, deputy," Ruben said. "How many for and how many against?"

"Three are for ya." He smiled thinly at Buell. "But that's all ya need."

"Did the county sheriff ever get back to Staker?" Buell asked.

"Yep. Said he was too busy to go lookin' for a grave that might not exist."

"How about Staker gettin' shot? Did the mayor send that message like he said he was gonna?"

"According to Percy, no. I asked the mayor about it. He said Staker's gonna be all right and there ain't no reason."

Ruben shook his head slowly. "And how's he voting?"

"Mayor don't vote unless someone's missin' and the vote gets tied."

"And that's it," Ruben said. "No more news."

"No, sir. Mister Steele just—"

"Which Mister Steele, Ford?" Buell asked. "Simon or his pa?"

"*Mister* Steele." Ford wrinkled his nose. "The old one. Never thought of Simon as *Mister Steele*." He drained his cup and glanced at the pot. "Anyway, he said to make sure you know there's lots of people in town who'd like to see you in Staker's office. Me included. The sheriff gettin' shot like that, and then Roscoe's horse showin' up with brains all over its rump has got some folks mor'n a little bit jumpy."

"Remember our conversation about chess?" Ruben said to Buell.

"Most of it."

"How about the 'end game' part?"

"Yes'ir. I see what you're saying." Buell turned to Ford. "You talk Mister Bedell out of some oats for your horse, and I'll go see Wu Le about fixin' us something. All right with you, Mister Bedell?"

"Of course, of course. Have another cup of coffee, Deputy. Then feed your horse, and go see Wu in the kitchen."

Ruben followed Buell out of the barn, and they went into the ranch house by the back door. "I want to talk over a couple things before you leave. I'll wait in there," he said and pointed at the door to the big room. "Wu!" he shouted. "We got another customer." And he left without waiting for the Chinaman to appear.

Buell sat in his soft chair sipping coffee and thinking. The ride to Carlisle from Bedell's the day before had chilled him to his marrow. He'd delayed leaving the ranch to arrive in town right at sundown, so his arrival had gone mostly unnoticed. After putting his horse away, he'd stoked the stove, eaten a can each of potatoes and peaches, and gone to bed.

Next morning, he sat at the table nursing his third cup of coffee. His night had been spent in a whirlwind of memories: Tay's calm voice. "Sometimes the only thing you'll have is trust." But was it simply trust or trust someone? Typical of Tay, he'd left that part off. Buell had thought about it dozens of times and still the answer eluded him. Maybe the old man didn't mean trust some *one*, but some *thing*. His skill?

Arley had visited, too. Not surprising—Arley always seemed to be there when Buell felt alone. Straight-and-to-the-point

Arley. Buell remembered a scene inside the saloon their first night in Idaho City. A gambler had been giving a woman a bad time, and Buell meant to stop him. Arley had grabbed his arm. "Ain't no doubt *you* could hold your own with them, but don't be bettin' *my* ass without asking me first." Was he going to do what he had to without telling the town?

And Lacey, the quiet Texan who'd taught him to shoot, had warned him so many times against using a gun to settle a dispute. "Ya take care o' stuff like this with a chunk o' wood, 'n ya do it private." A gun was the last resort.

And what about his private demon? He shuddered as he half-expected the dark shadow to appear behind his eyes. It had been gone a long time, since the last winter in Idaho City, but he knew it could still be there, waiting. He glanced at the clock on the counter, ten after eight, and stood. Time to make a decision, but first he wanted to see Staker.

The six-bed hospital was on the east end of town, three streets off the main one. He walked, using the cold air to clear his head. Inside the double doors a lady in a light blue uniform sat at a desk. "Here to see Sheriff Staker, Mister Mace?"

Buell could not remember laying eyes on her before. "Uh, yes, ma'am. If he's up to seein' visitors."

"He'll be happy to see you—I know *I* am." Her tenuous smile seemed almost fearful, and she couldn't hold his eyes but for a moment. "Come this way." She got up, and Buell followed her into an open ward. Staker lay in the first bed on the right—his eyes shut. "Sheriff," she said and touched his foot.

Staker's eyes flashed open. "What!"

"Mister Mace is here to see you."

Staker looked past the blue dress and grimaced. "Buell." He looked back at the nurse. "Get a chair." She scurried off to the other end of the room and brought back a short stool. Setting it down, she winced an apology.

"That's fine, ma'am," Buell said. "I'm not gonna stay long." She hurried out.

"What did the council say?" Staker asked in a ragged voice.

"I haven't seen anyone yet. Got back last night. How's the leaks?" Buell tried to smile.

"Seems I'm gonna live. Sometimes I'm not so sure I want to. The one in my hip is a—" Staker gritted his teeth.

"Hurts some, I know. Wanna talk business?"

"Yep."

"Who were the shooters?"

"Shooters, plural." Staker smiled grimly. "Figgered you'd know."

"I reckon Bachman was one, the other—not sure. I just know there was two."

"Ned. That Negro you busted up. You thought it was Gus, didn't ya?"

"I'll be damned. I wondered where he went."

"Easy to be wrong." Staker's eyes bore the point home.

"Yeah, I thought about Gus. How many folks know who did it?"

"Nobody. Believe it or not, both Bachman and Ned have been in town since. They figger they've got us whipped. I didn't want Ford or Skelton to go against them till they had some experienced help."

"They could have come in here and taken care of you for good." Buell frowned.

"I've thought about that." Staker patted an obvious shape under the covers on his right side. "So, you ready to help your town out?" He coughed gently and pressed a cloth to his lips, then glanced at it before putting it back beside his hip.

"Bleedin' inside?"

"A little. Doc says it'll stop. Answer me, Buell."

"Is the town ready for my kind of help?"

"They're scared, son."

"They got a good reason to be. I've been tellin' you about that island bunch since I got here."

"It's not just the islanders, Buell." Pain appeared in the sheriff's eyes, but it wasn't reflected in his face. "The town's scared of you."

CHAPTER 28

The snowstorm the week before had wreaked havoc with Union Pacific's delivery schedule. When the morning train arrived Monday, Buell and the other four men working for Paisley were inundated with bales, boxes, and bags of every description. Three part-timers pitched in to help move the tons of freight off the dock and into the warehouse. Paisley sat at the door holding a list of manifests half an inch thick, furiously marking off items as they came through. "Fourteen B," he barked, and the man pulling a steel-wheeled cart hurried off.

Buell let the toe of his hand-truck settle forward, and Paisley noted the number on a coffin-sized wooden box. "That's got to be at least thirty items for Simon. Where's he gonna put it?"

"Beats me," Paisley replied. "I just take the shipment."

"What is it?"

"Steel posts and tools of all sorts. How full is fourteen?"

"This will do it, A *and* B. Next empty bay is seventeen. What time is it?"

Paisley pulled his watch from a side pocket of his vest. "Near enough noon. Put that away and we'll go eat. Tell the others." He got off the stool, put the stack of papers on it, and laid a large padlock on top. Buell tilted his load back and headed down the wide aisle between the orderly partitions.

A couple of minutes later, he pushed his truck to where Paisley waited and parked it against the wall. He jerked a thumb toward the gloomy interior. "They'll put away that last bit. I'm so hungry, my own cookin' sounds good."

"Why don't ya come over to Freda's and join the bunch."

"Naw, I always feel useless as half a hinge around them."

"Paul said he'd like to talk to ya, and John Lindstrom's gonna be there. I know what you think of him, but he's got a nose like a coyote, and he's straight as a lawyer *can* be."

Buell shook his head. "I reckon I'll see him tonight at that meeting."

"All the more reason to see 'im now. It never hurts to know what a man's thinking."

"And you think he's gonna tell *me*?"

"Sure he will. C'mon, they'll all be glad to see your ugly mug." Paisley stepped behind and nudged Buell along the dock and down the stairs to the street.

Buell felt the urge to turn around and leave when he saw the nearly full dining room. Then he spotted Simon beckoning, and his father's hand pressed into the middle of his back. "All right, Pa." He tried not to sound irritated. "I see 'im."

"Glad you decided to join us, Buell," Paul said as they took a seat.

"Indeed." The lines between John Lindstrom's eyebrows were reinforced once again, and he half-stood to offer his hand. "We haven't talked since Simon's wedding announcement." Buell's barely perceptible pause registered on the lawyer's face.

"Reckon I run with a different pack of dogs." Buell shook hands.

John settled back in his seat. "Interesting expression."

Buell glanced at Simon, who shrugged and reached for his coffee cup. "Hell, it ain't no secret, Mister Lindstrom. I don't fit, and I don't mind."

Paul cleared his throat. "I think you have a place in Carlisle, Buell. That's why I asked your pa to get you in here. Can we talk about Staker's offer?"

"You gonna vote for me?" Buell asked.

"Right to the point," Lindstrom said. "Good."

"Saves time."

"Yes, is the short answer," Paul replied. "Do you want to know why I changed my mind?"

"You changed because some other stuff changed. Stuff you didn't think would."

Before Paul could respond, a woman came by to take their orders. They all chose the Monday special—meat loaf—and she left.

"You're right, of course," Paul continued. "Up until now we've—the town as a whole, I mean—we've been able to take care of the odd troublemaker. There hasn't been a murder in Carlisle since a fight at Lancer's in seventy-four. Then all of a sudden, we've seen two men killed and Staker, almost."

Buell let out a tired sigh. "And folks reckon that's my fault."

"Some do," Paul replied. "I don't."

The answer surprised Buell. "I heard some time back that you and a couple others on the council were dead set against me."

"We didn't need you then. Now I think we do. But I'm just one vote of five. You're going to have some opposition tonight, maybe more than I think—we'll have to see. For now, there are two who will vote yes."

"See, I told ya, son." Paisley beamed.

Simon had been toying with his fork the entire conversation. "You ain't got nothin' to say, Simon?" Buell asked, and enjoyed the look of surprise on his friend's face.

"He's got his mind on the twenty-third," Paisley said.

"He's thinkin' about something all right, but I got a hunch it ain't his weddin'," Buell said. "Am I right?"

"Shows that much, does it?"

"To me? Yep."

"What're you two talking about?" Paul asked.

"I'll let him tell you, Mister Steele. Him and me have always seen things a little different." Buell snorted. "And he knows doin' it my way got us through mor'n once."

Simon offered a grudging smile.

"Now that you bring it up," Paul said, "what do you intend to do if the council decides in your favor?"

"What I have to."

"They're going to ask you to be a little more specific than that, Buell," Lindstrom said. "I understand what you meant about your and Simon's experience. I saw much the same thing myself many years ago. It's different now. There are laws, and they apply to lawmen as much as the people they serve."

"And that's been stickin' in my craw since the day Sheriff Staker asked me about takin' his job. He told me plain out that he was havin' trouble and didn't figger he could handle it much longer. What he meant was, he couldn't handle it *his* way, your way, the council's way. He wasn't even wearin' his gun when he went to the jail to take Roscoe his supper. Nobody saw that comin', did they? And I hear both Bachman and that black man have been to town since."

"What!" Lindstrom gasped.

"That's right. Staker told his deputies to leave 'em alone—and they *did*." Buell met the eyes of both Simon and Paul. "*I* won't.*"

"Both of those men have families," Paul said as color rose in his face. "I can understand why they—"

"Then they shouldn't be wearin' badges."

"Here comes our food," Paisley said, relief plain in his voice. "I'm hungry as a mother bear with twins."

That evening, Buell sat silently at the end of the long table as four members of the council entered the room. When he'd arrived, Paul Steele was already seated in the center chair. Doc Princher looked at Buell and scowled. Blake Waldon wouldn't meet his eyes at all, and Art Lancer nodded his head and whispered "Welcome" as he sat down in the chair next to him. Mayor Pederson huffed in after everyone else was sitting and strolled slowly to his seat at the far end.

"This special meeting of the Carlisle City Council is now in order." Paul Steele's commanding voice owned the small room. He rapped his gavel twice. "Jude Cody won't be here tonight. All the other members are present, so we have a quorum. There's only one item on the agenda. Sheriff Staker and Doc Princher here have decided that Loren will be unable to perform his duties for some time. The sheriff has submitted his resignation, and I move we table that for now. Second?" Lancer raised his hand. "Those in favor?" They all nodded. "Resignation is tabled. Now, it's obvious that we need someone who can take Loren's place. Do we need to discuss this, or do I hear a motion?"

Buell could hear resignation in the question.

"I don't like the idea at all," Mayor Pederson said.

"You've never seen an idea you liked that wasn't your own, Sherm," Doc Princher said.

Paul rapped his gavel. "Do we need someone to replace Loren, Sherm?"

"Of course."

"All right. We need someone. If not Buell, who?"

"What about Ford?"

"He's told me he's not interested. Same with Skelton. So who?" Paul stared down the table at the mayor. "Well?" Paul insisted when Pederson remained silent. "Then I move we offer Buell the job. Second?"

"Second," Lancer said immediately.

"Those in favor," Paul said and raised his right hand.

Lancer raised his and glared at Waldon.

"All right, those opposed."

Doc Princher and Waldon both nodded.

Paul sighed deeply. "Tied vote. Sherm?"

"I said no," he replied with a smirk.

"Motion denied." Paul rapped his gavel.

"Now what?" Lancer asked with a shrug.

"Good question, Art. Anybody?"

Waldon cleared his throat. "I move we make Sherm the acting sheriff and offer Buell a job as a deputy."

"Acting?" Doc Princher scoffed. "Now that's appropriate."

"Hold on just a minute, Doc." Sherm half stood up.

"Define *acting* Blake," Paul said.

"I don't know. Just not a regular sheriff. He wouldn't stay at the jail, or carry a pistol and things like that. He'd just fill the job."

Paul looked directly at Buell and then back at Waldon. "Would you vote for that if I suggested a special provision for Buell too?"

"Depends on the suggestion, of course."

"We hire Buell as a *special* deputy. Special in that he reports directly to this council."

"Isn't that a little irregular?" Doc said. "Deputies work for the sheriff."

"A sheriff who isn't a sheriff is a little strange too, don't you think? I heard no second on Blake's motion, so I move we make Mayor Pederson the acting sheriff, *and* Buell Mace a deputy reporting directly to me."

"You?" Doc Princher said.

"He can't report to a committee," Paul replied.

"Do I keep the sheriff job even after—" Pederson colored—"after Paisley Mace is mayor?"

"I see no reason now why you shouldn't, Sherm," Paul said. "Blake?"

Waldon looked confused. "Does Sherm vote?"

"Considering he's a candidate, no." Paul looked back and forth. "Agreed?" He nodded curtly. "The motion is to make Sherm acting sheriff with no office duties, and to hire Buell as a deputy reporting to the head of the city council. Second?"

"Second," Lancer said.

"In favor?" Paul raised his hand followed by Lancer and Waldon.

"Opposed?"

"This is going to lead to no good," Princher said. "I vote no."

"Motion carried." Paul banged the gavel and turned to Buell. "So what do you say?"

"I'd say there wasn't a lot of reason for me to be here," Buell said out loud while another thought shouted for an answer: why had Waldon voted yes?

"Will you take the job?"

"Workin' for you? Yep."

"Then stand and raise your right hand."

Jake was all smiles when Buell pushed through the door at Luger's Saloon. "I already heard. Congratulations, Deputy. Lemme see yer badge."

"Heard from who? It ain't been twenty minutes."

"There's not six people in Carlisle who don't know by now. Including those boys over there."

Buell followed his gaze to a table by the stove where four men sat, eyes downcast. "That some of Roscoe's bunch? Or used to be Roscoe's?"

"Yep. They were in last week with Bachman and that Negro."

"Have they been in since?"

"Nope. I get the impression they're here to keep an eye on things."

"Any trouble?"

"You say that like ya was wishin'." Jake chuckled. "Matter of fact, they've been quiet as snakes. Whiskey? Or can ya drink when yer on duty?"

"They didn't say. I'm not gonna stay, Jake. I wanted to stop by all four saloons in town before I go back to my place. Just to let 'em know what I expect. I've been down the street already, and I had a talk with Art before I left the council."

"And just what *do* you expect?"

"I expect to be called *before* trouble starts. Every one of you barkeepers know it when you see it."

"Like Bachman?"

"Especially him. I'm gonna go say hello to that bunch over there."

"Not for a minute, you ain't. Simon just walked past the window."

Buell turned around just as his friend came through the door.

"Pa just told me," Simon said as he joined him at the bar. "We had a good laugh. You and I both work for him now. Have you told your pa yet?"

"Nope. I'll see him in the mornin'."

"You gonna continue to work at the warehouse?" Simon asked.

"Have to until we can find someone to take my place. Which reminds me, what in hell ya doin' with all that buildin' stuff you've been orderin'?"

"I'm going to sell it. That's what I do." He leaned a little closer, and Jake dipped his head. "There's a business deal being made, and you know how that works. I'm not allowed to tell. Just say Carlisle is gonna get bigger real soon."

"Flour mills?" whispered Jake.

Simon started. "Where'd you hear that?"

"Barkeeps hear it all, Simon. I ain't gonna say nothin'."

"Well, don't. Pa would shoot me."

"But you didn't *say* anything."

"He'd still shoot me, Jake, I know it."

Buell smiled. "So, Simon, how many?"

"Dammit, Buell, nobody's supposed to know."

"Where the hell you gonna put another mill. Plus the silos?"

"Would you keep your voice down." Simon looked over his shoulder. "Just quit talking about it."

"He has a point, Simon," Jake said.

"I came in here to say congratulations, Buell, and I get *this*." Simon shook his head, his lips pursed. "I'm going back home." He stormed out, slamming the door.

"Guess we ain't s'posed to say anything," Jake said.

"What do you know?"

"Paul Steele and Lindstrom are angling for that property by Venable's. Word is the railroad will put in a spur there next spring. Makes that piece of ground worth a lot of money."

"I've got news for him. More folks know about them mills than he thinks. Who told you?"

"I'm a bartender, Buell." Jake winked. "I've got to get to work, and looks like your troublemakers have decided to leave."

Buell glanced up at the mirror just as the four men hurried out into the dark. Buell followed them.

CHAPTER 29

Buell stepped onto the boardwalk outside Luger's. "Hey!" The four cowboys were just about to step into the street by the hitching rail, and stopped. Nobody turned around as Buell approached them. "I want a word with one of you." All four faced him, and then three of them edged back half a step. Buell snorted. "Looks like they want you to do the talkin'." The man swallowed. "The rest of you, git on your horses and leave."

The man remaining glanced over his shoulder as his friends mounted and spurred their horse down the street. "Polecats," he muttered.

"Walk to the next street and turn right." Buell's hand moved a little closer to his pistol. The man spun on his heel and hurried to the corner. There he glanced back. "Turn right, I said." Buell followed him. "Now, into the alley and stop."

"Why'd ya pick me?" the man asked, his hands well clear of his gun.

"I didn't, your *friends* did. Might wanna remember that. Now turn around."

His hands still well away from his body, the man faced Buell.

"I want ya to lift yer pistol straight up out of the holster and drop it." When the man used only two fingers, Buell nodded. "You've done this before."

The cowboy just shrugged.

"I'm gonna ask you a couple of questions. Don't lie, and you can save yerself some pain."

"So I've heard."

"How many of you out there?"

" 'Bout a dozen, maybe fifteen. They come and go."

"Ya know Bachman?"

"Sure."

"Is he runnin' the place?"

"He thinks so."

"How about the one called Ned?"

"He's crazy. Stays in his hut mostly, but when he doesn't, someone gets cut."

"Who fixed you up with feed for your horses, and where'd that wagon come from?"

The man turned his shoulders just slightly and shifted one foot back. "I don't know 'bout that."

Buell studied his face for a moment. "Step back from yer pistol." When the man did, Buell put his own away, and took out his pocketknife. The cowboy watched, a puzzled look on his face. Then Buell picked up the man's weapon, and rotating the cylinder of the old Colt, flicked all the caps off. "I want you to give Bachman a message." He handed the pistol to the cowboy. "If I see him, I'll come up with a reason to kill him." He turned around and walked out of the alley.

For the next two weeks, Buell worked at the warehouse in the mornings, and then made himself visible around town until almost midnight. Three men on three separate occasions had tried him, and all three had spent the night in jail nursing a sore spot somewhere. He was slowly getting used to the idea of being the law in Carlisle.

He'd just settled back in his chair and propped his feet up, when the door to the jail opened and Simon came in. Buell knew what he wanted, had been expecting him, but the thought of actually seeing the deed done made his stomach queasy.

"Evenin', Simon. What brings you out after seven?"

"I'm getting married Saturday. You do remember, don't you?" Simon sat down on the stool.

"Yeah. Don't mean I have to look forward to it. Still four days away."

"The wedding is. The rehearsal is tomorrow, at six."

Buell's feet hit the floor with a thud. "What'n hell's so tricky about gettin' hitched that we have to practice it?"

"No sense argu—"

"I just stand there like a Judas Goat and—"

"If you'd sooner discuss it with Missus Kingsley, I can send her over."

"And you damn well would, wouldn't ya?"

"If it's me explaining it to her, or you—take a guess."

"All right, I'll be there. We ain't gotta wear a collar or nothin' like that do we?"

"Not tomorrow, but—"

"I can put up with it for the weddin'. You gonna go away for a week or so after?"

"Nope. You'd never guess what she wants to do. Wait until June, and then go see where I lived in the mountains. I'll never understand 'em."

"Don't surprise me a bit. Can I tempt you with a shot over to Luger's?" Buell shoved his chair back and stood up.

"Yeah, why not. But first, why aren't you surprised? She's never shown the least bit of interest in livin' rough."

"Then tell her no—start your marriage off right." Buell hurried out the door as Simon took a poke at him.

"Howdy, fellas," Jake said as Buell pushed the door shut and followed Simon across the room. The Wednesday crowd at Luger's was typical—there wasn't one. Jake stood leaning against the bar on one elbow, idly spinning a silver dollar. One other person stood at the far end, and three played dominoes at a table by the stove.

"Thought we'd come and keep ya company," Buell said. "I'll have a rye. He's buying." He tilted his head toward Simon.

"Better get him while ya can, I'd say." Jake took a bottle off the backbar and poured a glass nearly full. "Beer for you, I suppose," he said to Simon, and set the whiskey in front of Buell.

"Let me have a brandy—seeing as how I'm buying. Yourself too."

Jake charged the glasses and picked his up. "Not too late to get out of town."

"You're jealous, Jake. Admit it." Simon lifted his glass. "To the times we had in here."

"And there were some good ones," Jake said.

"Yep." Buell took a small sip.

"Unusually quiet, even for a Wednesday, isn't it?" Simon turned to face the empty room.

"New lawman in town. Ain't ya heard? Word is he lowered the mallet on one of them boys from the island."

Simon faced Buell again. "That true?"

"Bullshit. What do you expect from Jake?"

"Hey! That's what I hear. You sayin' it didn't happen?"

"I politely invited some of 'em to stay out of town. That's all."

"Looks like it worked," Simon said, then furrowed his brow. "I think everyone was a little shocked with all the shooting and . . . uh."

"And uh, what?" Buell put his drink down with a click, spilling a little.

"All the trouble. Maybe it was time for talking." Simon shrugged. "It worked."

"Lift your glass, Buell," Jake said, and wiped the bar beneath. "And no arguing, dammit."

"The only trouble, Simon, was them."

"I didn't mean it that way. I mean—I wasn't blamin' you."

"Doesn't matter, anyway," Jake said. "I'm just glad things have quieted down."

"Exactly right." Simon nudged Buell's arm. "Don't you think so? It's quiet. Sheriff Staker is getting better. We were talking just yesterday about how it's worked out."

"Who's we?"

Simon shrugged. "Pa and some business folks. Everyone's satisfied that you've been hired."

"Even Doc Princher?"

"Well, maybe not him. And there are a few others, but most are."

"Until we have some more trouble."

"No! They're happy with what you're doing." Simon tried to appear sincere, and failed.

"Next time you have one of them meetings, Simon, tell 'em something for me. I hope Staker gets well enough to take this job back, and I hope it stays quiet. But if it don't, I'll make you all a promise. I'll take care of the trouble, once . . . and for sure."

Simon looked down at his brandy and stood silent for several seconds before replying, "The town doesn't need trouble of either kind." His hand shot up. "Now let me finish. Everyone I've talked to—everyone—appreciates being able to walk down the street without running into an unwashed and surly transient."

"And what do you think brought that on?" Buell looked directly at Simon.

"They *know* what did." Simon couldn't meet his gaze. "And they accept that, and know you're going to have to put one or two in jail, maybe rough one up from time to time, but they don't want any more—" He looked trapped, and slightly fearful.

274

"Shootin'?" Jake suggested.

"Exactly, Jake," Simon replied quickly. "No more of that. That's not unreasonable, Buell."

"Yeah. It is." Buell shook his head. "You wanted to say killin', Simon. Why didn't ya? No! Let me tell *you*. This town wants a pack mule that's easy to ride. Ain't no such thing. Them boys out there on Sandy Island are the kind that was needed to make this place. They're tough and hard to get along with, just like a mule, and they still want gamblin', whiskey, and no rules." He made a sweep with his arm. "And it's a place like this they'll come to."

"Then they're going to have change, aren't they?" Simon said.

"There's the problem. For you *and* this whole damn town. You say something and expect it to happen. It's the mule thing again. Only way to make him do what *you* want is to make it hurt to do what *he* wants. More'n one mule has been beat to death learnin' that."

"You could be talkin' about yourself," Jake said.

Simon paled and stared nervously at Buell.

"That's what I like ya for the most, Jake. Ya say what ya think. What's the matter, Simon? You think I don't know that? Now, there's only one difference between me and that bunch out there. I can do what I've always done, only now you've made it legal." Buell's mouth suddenly felt dry so he picked up his drink and tossed it back.

"I don't think I've heard ya say that many words at one time in my whole life, Buell," Jake said. "And I agree with every bit of it."

"Simon don't, do ya?" Buell nudged his friend.

"You know how I feel and think about killing. Remember the camp by the river? You told me I had to grow some bark or go where I didn't need any."

"I didn't say that exactly, but yeah, I remember."

"Well, everything's changed."

Buell laughed out loud. "Think about that, Simon, what ya just said."

Simon looked baffled for a few seconds, and then irritated. "You don't need to throw that up to me. Dammit, I've got responsibilities now. There's more to think about than just me."

"I *didn't* bring it up, Simon."

"We can never have a normal conversation, can we?"

"Some things change and some don't."

Simon picked up his drink, looked at it a second, then put it back down. Fishing two dollars out of his pocket, he rattled them onto the bar. "I'll see you tomorrow. Six o'clock. G'night, Jake." He started across the floor.

"Thanks for the brandy," Jake said. Simon waved over his shoulder as he shut the door.

"Do you do that on purpose?" Jake asked.

"Sometimes."

"What was it that got brought up? Sure run him off."

"He said things have changed. He knows damn well they haven't. He's in another tight spot, and it kills him to admit I can take care of it—again. Matter of fact, he *won't* admit it."

"What happened by that river?"

"A thief was about to shoot Simon in his bed. I stopped him."

"And that's bad?"

"Simon has wondered ever since if it was worth it."

"Worth stayin' alive? That's crazy."

"Not bein' alive—owin' me for it."

At the first strains of *The Wedding March*, Buell felt the hundred pairs of eyes that had been fixed on him suddenly leave as one—the door to an anteroom opened and Sarah Kingsley stepped through. Those in front of her craned their necks, and a collective sigh rose from the congregation. She wore more silk than Buell had seen in his life, shimmering white, her sleeves puffed like clouds at her upper arm and then tapered to a snug fit at her wrists. Everywhere there could be lace, there was, and tiny pearls nestled in the fancy embroidery of her high collar and perfectly fitted bodice. Atop her head a yoke of silver held a gossamer veil in place and supported a long train of even more lace that trailed behind her. Buell felt a rush of pride.

He glanced at Simon as Sarah and Judge Kingsley turned the corner and started down the aisle. His lips were pressed tight together and white at the corners, beads of sweat stood proud at his hairline, and his eyes were those of a trapped fox. "You all right?" Buell whispered without moving his lips.

Simon's headshake was barely perceptible and his breathing more like panting.

As Sarah drew close, her soft smile apparent even behind the veil, her eyes fixed on Simon. Buell tipped his head down. "Want me to do it?" he asked quietly.

Simon choked, his head snapped around, and Buell gave him a big smile. For a second Simon's face flashed anger and then he softened. With a deep breath, he returned his gaze to the front and his breathing returned to normal. A long twenty minutes later, Simon and Sarah were man and wife, and Buell stood uncomfortably beside his friend in a reception line.

"What made you say that?" Simon asked.

"It didn't look like you was gonna make it."

"I'm not sure I would have. So thanks, Buell. Somehow your joke did it for me."

"What makes ya think I was joking?"

Before Simon could respond, the doors to the reception hall opened, and the first of over three hundred family members and guests began to file in. Buell gritted his teeth and offered his hand as Abby Steele hustled through the door with a wide-eyed Jeremy Princher in tow. Buell's collar got tighter.

CHAPTER 30

The discomfort of standing in a reception line hadn't faded much before Buell found himself in front of another group. Ten days later, on the morning of January second, 1877, he'd witnessed his father's swearing in. Then, at a special council meeting that evening, he'd found himself appointed as sheriff of Carlisle by a three to two vote. A protesting Sherm Pederson had been dismissed by a similar margin, with Waldon voting against him. He was still stinging from the slight when Buell walked into Lancers late afternoon of the next day. The stumpy little man sat at a table with Gus Swartz and two others whom Buell recognized, but didn't know.

Sherm stood as Buell passed. "We're going to be watching you," he said. "Don't think for a minute that this is done." Eight inches shorter and sixty pounds heavier than Buell, he puffed up like a toad.

Buell stopped and turned around. "Ya got my vote for balls, Sherm," Buell said, looking down at him. "Exactly what are you gonna be watchin' for?"

"You don't remember me, but I knew you when you were raising Cain before you left. Your kind don't change."

"You're right, we don't. Best keep that in mind. And I do remember you. You were following a couple of mules around back then too, weren't ya?"

Several men in the sparsely filled room chuckled, and one laughed out loud. "Sit down, Sherm. Yer being a damned

279

nuisance," someone called out.

Buell caught Gus's eye. "You behavin' yerself?"

"Does it look like it?"

"Just askin', Gus." Buell turned to walk on.

"We're not done, Mace!" Sherm shouted.

"I am," Buell replied without turning around, and walked over to a smiling Art Lancer.

"Good," Art said.

"He's got a burr stuck somewhere," Buell said and glanced up to see Sherm scowling at him in the mirror.

"He lost," Art said.

"I feel a bit sorry for him. What you and the council did was a little shaded. He *was* kinda promised a job."

Lancer winked. "Kinda."

"How do you politicians sleep?" Buell smiled when he said it.

"Better in"—Lancer took a short breath—"than out."

Buell had another look at the four men. "Gus turns up with the damnedest people."

"Bought."

"So I understand. Why did Waldon vote against Sherm yesterday?"

"Your pa."

"Is he dumb enough to think Pa will see that vote as a marker?"

"Dumber," Lancer said. "Work." He nodded his head down the bar towards a couple of men who were holding their empty beer glasses up.

"I'll see ya later, Art. I'm gonna have a talk with Sheriff Staker." Buell pushed away from the bar and headed for the door. Sherm watched him as he approached and was halfway to his feet when Gus reached over and grabbed the ex-mayor's arm. Sherm sat down abruptly. Buell stopped. "Looks like Gus don't want you sayin' any more."

Sherm's eyes blazed.

"Seems only fair you get a chance to do your new job, Mace," Gus said with a smirk.

Buell snorted. "Fair? From you? You forget how far back we go."

"I ain't forgot nothin'."

"Me either, Gus." Buell stared at him for several seconds and answered Gus's scowl with a slight smile. "You told me a while back that I'd better not think about being the law in Carlisle—remember? Well, Gus, now I *am*. Get used to it."

Five minutes later, Buell answered Staker's shouted invitation to open the front door and enter.

"The badge looks good on you." The gray around Staker's eyes made them appear sunken in his pale face. He lay half-reclined on a chaise, his right leg extended.

"Ya look like hell, Sheriff."

"I expected you to point that out. The bullet in my hip is giving me fits. Doc says I'll have to go to St. Louis or Omaha to get it out."

"So, why ya still here?"

"Would you go?" He paused a second. "I thought not. What brings you over here? Sit down—you make me tired just lookin' up at ya."

Buell sat. "I don't like to stir up trouble unless I figger on bein' around to meet it."

"I could say the obvious, Buell, but I won't."

"Good. I told ya this last summer that Carlisle was gonna have a fight sooner or later. Well, it's gonna be sooner 'cause I intend to get it over with when *I'm* ready. I just wanted to know how it's gonna set with you. You're still the sheriff, this badge be damned."

"I'm surprised to hear you say that, the badge part. I've been asking myself for months what it would take to make you fully accept the job. I knew it had to be something real personal, but I thought when you found the reason, you'd want the whole show. Was I wrong?"

"You spend too much time thinkin'. The islanders have been too quiet. Folks like Doc Princher and Jude Cody think that's a good sign. You and I know different, don't we?"

The sheriff shifted on the low couch and his gaze went to the floor for a moment. "Have you had a chance to dig through the Wants and Warrants file at the office?"

"Uh-huh. That's why I said that. Isaac Bachman, Lincoln County, New Mexico. No warrants, but the U.S. Marshal out there said he should have a dozen. The letter mentions a Negro too. No name, but he don't leave nothin' to wonder about— Ned's crazy as a rabid skunk, and he rode with Ike Bachman."

"Now you understand." Staker leaned against the back of the chaise and swung his legs onto the floor. "Dammit, that hurts."

"Did the mention of New Mexico strike you like it did me?"

"Sure. But I don't think Bedell is tied to Bachman."

"Maybe not tied, but connected. Maybe one owes the other something."

"And I thought about that too. No way of telling, unless Ruben or Bachman comes right out and says it." Staker laid his hand on his hip and winced.

"Ruben is gonna take another lick at 'em. Soon."

"What makes you think that?"

"I saw and heard some things when I was out there *visiting* just before you got shot. I'm surprised it hasn't happened already."

"You'd do him a favor if you told him not to."

"*Tell* Ruben Bedell something? All I hope is that he does a good job."

Staker groaned and shook his head. "He's stepping outside

the law, Buell."

"I know that. That's why I'm here."

The lawman sighed deeply. "I feel real strong about the law. You know that, don't you." He wasn't asking.

"Yes'ir. Do you still believe that justice done is justice?"

"You don't miss much, do you, son?"

"I try not to."

Buell's prediction that Ruben and his men would take another crack at Bachman and his bunch came to pass on a clear, cool night on the second of February. It was nearly midnight, and he'd just finished sending a noisy group of railroad workers back to their cabins. He was on his way to Lancer's door when Andrew and Red came in.

"First time I've seen the badge, Sheriff," Andrew said. "Very impressive."

Buell sniffed the air. "You smell like—" he sniffed again. "Like we better go to my office."

"We came in for a whiskey—or two." Red winked. "You kin join us."

"I don't drink in public when I'm working."

"B'gorry, the devil's got 'im," Red said, and poked Andrew on the arm.

"I can smell what you've been up to," Buell said. "You stink of coal oil and woodsmoke."

"Dealin' a bit of what's due," Andrew said. "C'mon over to the bar and we'll tell ya about it. We've done nothin' to be ashamed of."

Buell looked around the nearly empty saloon. "I don't want the whole town to hear a drunk's version of what they heard you say. I've got a bottle in my desk and the cells are empty."

"But there's nobody here." Andrew shrugged and looked over his shoulder.

"Four's more than I want." Buell waved at Lancer, and led the two cowboys out of the saloon.

While Andrew got a chair from beside the stove, Buell took out a nearly full bottle of rye whiskey and set it on the desk. He found two glasses and a coffee cup that he set beside it.

"When ya gonna learn to drink real whiskey?" Red said as he settled down on the stool.

"Irish whiskey?" Andrew chided. "Ye've no learned a thing in five hundred years of tryin' have ya? Now, Scot's whiskey—"

"This is what I've got." Buell put his hand on the bottleneck. "And I *can* put it back."

"No-no, don't be hasty," Red replied. "In a pinch, that'll do."

Buell poured the two glasses half full and sloshed a bit into the cup, which he then picked up. "There." He nodded at the two drinks. "Now tell me what you've been up to."

The two picked up their drinks, and Andrew sipped his. "We took a ride along the river this evenin', leisurely like." He chuckled. "Neighborly, we stopped by to see Mister Bachman and his friends. Brought some party favors 'n all. Ain't that right, Red?"

"Nothin' fancy, mind ya." Red grinned, and pointed at the bottle. Buell slid it over to him.

"Place looked almost deserted, so we just dropped them off and rode out."

"All right, you've had your fun," Buell said with a smile. "What's a party favor?"

"Ah, yes, not an American expression. Something to entertain folks at a party—little prizes and games. In this case, whiskey bottles full of lamp oil."

"I had to teach this ignorant Scot how to wrap them," Red added.

"And very clever it was," Andrew said. "He ties a rock to the side with a bit of cloth. Now that's a new one to me. A gobstopper made out of a rag I've seen."

"So you burned them out?"

"Every miserable shack and shanty. And a stack of hay."

"And nobody was there?"

Andrew winced. "In fact there was. Flushed like rabbits, they did. Me and Red stayed behind and watched from up the hill a bit. Ten minutes of scurryin' around, grabbin' bits of this and that, but nothin' they could do."

"No shooting?"

"The boss wanted them gone, unless—" Andrew glanced at Red. "We left the wagon we saw and the horses. Should be plain enough."

Buell leaned over the desk. "Did you see Bachman?"

"That'd be the *unless* part," Red said and smiled.

Andrew scowled at him. "Ya got a big mouth, Red." He looked back at Buell. "If Bachman was around, he was supposed to stay there."

"But you never saw him? Or the Negro?"

"Nope. I counted eight. About that same number of horses. How many should there have been?"

"Half again that. And everything burned?"

"Four men had already gotten on their horses and left by the time me and Red did. I'd say your problem there is gone."

"Do me a favor and don't mention this to anyone," Buell said and filled both their glasses again.

"Hadn't meant to," Andrew said.

"You're not going back to the ranch tonight, are ya?"

Red shrugged and looked at the cells. "Hate to waste good whiskey money on a bed."

"You're welcome to stay right in there. And here." Buell shoved the bottle toward Andrew. "A little party favor from the citizens of Carlisle."

Buell knew the next move would be Bachman's, but two weeks later the viciousness of the bushwhacker's attack shocked even him. It was early Monday afternoon when a young boy slammed open the jailhouse door and screamed, "Someone's dead, sir. They wants ya at home."

CHAPTER 31

Buell spurred his commandeered mount past several buggies and horseback riders on his way to his father's place. He slid to a stop at the front gate. A man standing there pointed toward the north side of the building. "Around back, Mister Mace," he said as Buell's feet hit the ground.

Buell rounded the corner of the house at a run and saw his father kneeling next to a prone woman. She lay beside a large wicker basket. Three white, flannel sheets hung from the clothesline in front of his father, and a chest-high spray of crimson ruined the one closest to Paisley. "Pa!" Buell shouted and hurried to them. "Ruth?" he blurted, not wanting to look.

"No," Paisley said, quiet and calm. "It's Missus Warren, Ruth's house help."

Buell scanned the back yard. "Where is she?"

"In the house with a neighbor."

"She all right?"

"Shaken up bad. She saw it from the back door."

Buell looked at the woman. Her kerchief was askew on her head, and Paisley had obviously smoothed her clothes. An irregular blotch of red the size of a dinner plate stained the dress between her breasts, and beneath her back her life's blood pooled. "Doc Princher?"

"I sent for him same time as you. No use, though."

The sound of hooves came from out front, and Buell waited until the first person rounded the corner. "Stay right there!" he shouted when he saw it wasn't the doctor. "And tell the rest to do the same."

"Who is it?" someone asked.

"Missus Warren," Paisley replied. "Someone go be with her kids."

"Where's her husband, Pa?"

"Widow. Four youngsters, oldest is only ten."

Buell stepped past the woman and studied the bloodied sheet—he found a round hole in the spatter. Pulling the line down a little, he stared out into the barren wheat field stretching to the west. He could see no cover except for a low patch of brush, but it was at least three hundred yards away. The last house on the west side of town was a quarter-mile up the road. "I'm gonna go see your neighbors. What's their name?"

"Pierson. They used to live out past Paul's old place. You'll recognize him."

Five minutes later Buell found the farmer in his toolshed. "A word, Mister Pierson," Buell shouted above the din of a hammer on steel.

A grease-smudged face was the last thing to appear as the man crawled from under a machine. "Oh. Buell Mace." He got to his feet, started to offer his hand, but instead used it to pull a rag from his back pocket. "Haven't seen ya since that." He pointed a grimy finger at Buell's badge. "I expect you'll do well. Official business is it?"

"Ruth's house help was shot about half an hour ago."

"Dammit, I knew something was up." Pierson wiped his hands on the rag, and then forcefully threw it onto a bench. "C'mon out here." Buell followed him outside and around back of the shed. "I heard a shot." Pierson pointed southeast. "Nothin' unusual about that, but then I saw a rider hightail it south. I thought he'd ride a bit, and then stop to take care of what he'd downed. He didn't. Just kept going straight until I couldn't see him no more."

"Could you show me exactly where?"

"Is the lady that got shot gonna be all right?"

"She died before she hit the ground."

"Aw, dammit, that's bad. Missus Warren, ain't it?"

Buell nodded his head.

"You can't miss where that fella was—a small sinkhole with some brush growin' around it. I'll go with ya—"

"I know where you mean. You've been a lot of help, Mister Pierson. Thank you." Buell reached out his hand.

The farmer glanced down at his own, and then shook Buell's. "I hope you find who did that, Sheriff. It's gettin' bad around here."

Buell rode directly to the sinkhole and dismounted. The sheets hanging on the line at his father's house were plainly visible, but as a continuous strip of white. At least a dozen men were now milling around, but it was hard to pick out any individual. The distance was easier to judge with people and buildings lending perspective, and his first guess had been way short—the range was at least four hundred and fifty yards. There was not a lot of sense in looking for the cartridge. Rifles accurate at that distance were very special and used by game hunters who reloaded the expensive shells—probably a fifty caliber. And it could even have been a muzzleloader.

He circled the brush and found the telltale pile where the horse had been ground-tethered. Tracks led in from the south and out, and he followed boot prints from there to the eastern edge of the brush. It took a few minutes of searching before he was certain where the man had lain in wait. Evenly spaced impressions of the shooter's elbows lined up with the scuffed dirt where the man had positioned his legs and feet. Buell could

picture it plainly, and his anger rose. Goddamn bushwhacker.
He spit on the ground, and was just about to return to his horse
when a glint of metal caught his eye. Just beyond the boot-
scraped ground lay an empty cartridge—Buell picked it up.

Stamped in the brass head was "45-75 WCF," and suddenly
he recalled the masked rider on the road from Bedell's pointing
a long-barreled rifle at him. There had been something odd
about the gun, a detail that hadn't quite fit. He looked at the
bottlenecked cartridge again. He hadn't recognized the weapon
the horseman held because he'd never handled one—it was Mr.
Winchester's new Model 1876. He dropped the cartridge in his
shirt pocket and went to his horse.

A small group of people stood alongside and behind a buckboard
wagon. Mrs. Warren lay in the back of it, her head on a pillow,
her body shrouded in a quilt. White showed around Doctor
Princher's mouth. "Violence begets more of the same, Sheriff.
Why on earth would someone shoot this gentle woman? She's
done nothing. Nothing!" The doctor picked up the reins and
slapped them across the backs of the team. People scrambled as
he jolted away, turned into the road, and headed for town.

Paisley shook his head sadly and then looked up at Buell.
"What did Pierson have to say?"

"He heard the shot and saw someone ride off. I found where
the man waited." He dug the brass out of his pocket. "And
this." He handed it down.

Paisley looked the shell over. "I've never seen one. Says it's a
Winchester though."

"Let me see that," a man asked and took the shell. "The very
latest," he said after a glance. "Steele's had two a while back.
Powerful. Way too rich for a workin' mule." The man handed it
up to Buell.

"How's Ruth?" Buell asked Paisley.

"She went over to the Warren place."

"Alone?"

"No. Her and another woman."

"I want you to keep her at home and inside for a few days," Buell said.

"Why on earth?"

"Doc said it right. Why someone like Missus Warren?"

Paisley suddenly started to tremble and his eyes went wide. "You think—"

"I do. Keep her out of sight for a few days." Buell reined his horse around and left as the knot of people tightened and started to talk. The vaguely defined, dark shape he hoped would never reappear flickered alive for a moment behind his eyes, and he suddenly felt cold all over—deadly cold.

A few minutes later, Buell thanked the man whose horse he'd taken, then walked down the street to Steele's Mercantile. Several people eyed him closely as he passed. He went in and found Simon in the storeroom. When he started to tell him what had happened, Simon stopped him.

"I heard already," Simon said. "That's horrible."

"Someone said you had the newest Winchester rifle. Still have them?"

Simon nodded, and Buell followed him out of the storeroom to a wall rack that held nearly a dozen rifles. Simon took one down. "Here ya go." He handed Buell the heavy gun. "Centennial model. We had two. I sold one." The color drained from Simon's face.

"To who?" Buell demanded.

"Blake Waldon. Same time he bought that Colt."

Buell felt cold. "Do you have shells for this?"

"Of course."

"Get me two boxes and I'll take this rifle."

"Now?"

"Yes, Simon. Now!"

His startled friend reached under the counter and put the shells on top. Buell grabbed both boxes and started for the door.

"What are you doing to do?" Simon hurried around the counter. "Where ya going, Buell?"

"You *know* where I'm going—to find Waldon."

Buell hurried down the street, ignoring inquisitive looks and half-started greetings. Mose looked up as he stormed into the barn. "I heard, Mister Mace. Who—"

"I'm in a hurry, Mose. Get my tack." Buell leaned the new rifle against the side of Shadow's stall, set the shells on the ground, and then hurried into his rooms. He was back with his binoculars in time to back the horse into the open for the blacksmith. Mose handed Buell the blanket, and a moment later tossed the saddle onto the animal's back.

"You cinch him," Buell said and took the bridle. A minute later, he dropped the glasses and shells into his saddlebag, stuffed the rifle into the boot, and walked Shadow into the street, almost running into Judge Kingsley.

"Hold on a minute, Buell," Kingsley said, not stepping aside. "Simon just told me you're going after Blake Waldon. Is that true?"

"Simon's got a big mouth."

"He's your friend too. If you're bound to get Blake, tell me why you should, and maybe we can do it within the law."

"You were gonna put me in jail, Judge, for something I *know* I didn't do." Buell's heart started to race. "It was plain as that beaver hat you're wearing that Roscoe was guilty, but Sheriff Staker had to take a bullet to make you believe it. You know both those things." He stepped closer to the older man. "Here's something you don't know. Waldon gave Roscoe the pistol he was going to shoot me with. Ask Simon. He also gave a man named Simpson a rifle like that one there," he pointed at the Winchester, "and he used it to kill a washerwoman. *Ask Simon.* That's all outside the law, Judge. It's why people like Waldon and Roscoe and Bachman are called outlaws. Now get out of my way."

Buell grabbed his saddle horn and swung astride the horse. "I'll bring Waldon back if he'll come without a fight. I'll give your law that much." Buell kicked Shadow lightly in the ribs and the eager horse moved past a gap-mouthed judge and up the street.

Venable's place looked deserted, the barn doors shut and the chimney over the office carrying no sign of smoke. Buell dismounted, whipped his reins across the rail, and tried the door. It opened, and he stepped into the unlit room. Jules Venable sat leaned back in his chair, his blank eyes fixed on a spot he'd see for eternity. Centered with obscene precision in the middle of his forehead, a powder-blackened hole leaked a thin trail of blood down the side of his nose. Jules had been executed; the acrid smell of his last call still hung in the air.

Buell stepped behind the desk to find an open floor-safe—it gaped emptily. He scanned the room. The two other chairs in the room stood upright; a ledger lay open on the desk alongside a few papers; an oil lamp sat undisturbed, but extinguished, on a table in the corner. The only thing out of order was the open stove door. Buell stepped closer and smelled burned coffee grounds just as he spotted the pot, lid off and empty, beside the stove.

He left the office and strode across the open ground in front of the barn, his eyes on the single window, his hand hovering close to his pistol. When he saw no movement, he shaded his face with one hand and looked through the window. A pair of frightened eyes stared back—eyes he'd seen before. "You in there alone?" he shouted. The old man nodded his head. "Go open the big door and come out."

A moment later one of the doors slid sideways, and the decrepit creature stepped out, wrapped in a blanket. "Where's Gus, old man?"

"Not here, sir. Nobody here." He hadn't yet looked at Buell.

"You hear shootin'? And don't lie."

"Yes'ir. I reckon it was Mister Waldon. He come over here right after that and told Gus to saddle a horse and go with him."

"Go where?"

The man finally looked up. "Didn't say—Sheriff." His eyes fixed on Buell's chest.

"Did Gus take a lot with him, like he was leavin' for good?"

The old-timer looked confused for a moment. "Gus didn't go. I mean he did, but not with Mister Waldon. He told him to bury his own witnesses. That didn't set too good with Mister Waldon." Rheumy eyes sought Buell's. "Jules is dead, ain't he?"

"Yes. Killed cold."

"Ya think I can stay here, Sheriff?" He blinked rapidly.

"You stand right there a minute." Buell stepped past him and entered the barn. Two workhorses stood in their stalls, head-down and hipshot; neither even looked up. He drew his pistol and climbed the loft ladder to the cold and empty expanse above. Seeing nothing, he descended to look in the tack room. It was empty except for harnesses—no saddles. He went back outside. "You can stay in there, old-timer. Nobody's gonna bother ya. And don't say anything about Waldon."

The man shrugged his blanket closer and turned without a

word. Slowly, the door rumbled shut and Buell crossed the yard to his horse.

Buell recognized Doc Princher's outfit when he arrived at his father's house. He tethered Shadow and went inside to find Paisley and the doctor standing in the kitchen. Buell told them what he'd seen and heard at Venable's, and then outlined what he suspected.

"Are you sure he's dead?" Doc Princher asked grimly.

"Seen enough to know."

"I find that easy to believe. Trouble follows you."

Paisley glanced at the closed bedroom door. "Let's not talk in here." He turned and left the kitchen.

"What you said is not fair, Doc," Paisley said when they were all three in the parlor. "If Waldon is behind this, it started long before Buell got here."

"Doesn't matter when or why. It's here," Buell said, "and you hired me to take care of it."

"By shooting everyone you see spitting in the street?" Princher said sarcastically.

"If spitting is a problem, Doc, I'll take care of that too."

"And *I* didn't vote for you," Princher said emphatically.

"I know that. But you and your kind will be real quick to push me out front when the shootin' starts."

"There are judges and courts to take care of this, *Sheriff*."

"Not if all the witnesses are dead." Buell turned his back on Princher. "Is there a small town or something south of here, Pa?"

"No towns—too far off the river and the railroad. There's an abandoned stage way-station about six miles a little east and south, and an old ranch a mile west of that, but it's been burned flat."

"The man who shot Missus Warren rode south. If it's who I

295

think it was, I won't be long. And if I'm lucky, I'll find three or four polecats in the same hole."

"Then you'd better take one of the deputies along." Paisley sounded worried.

"I've seen enough widows today. I'll go alone."

CHAPTER 32

Finding the abandoned way-station might have been difficult but for a wisp of smoke. Buell tied Shadow in a patch of low scrub brush on the north side of a slight rise, then walked to the crest with his binoculars. A dirt-roofed hut with a lean-to attached on the left side sat in the bottom of a shallow east-west gully. A precarious-looking shack with half a roof joined the soddy on the right. Buell thought a stable. Part of a pole corral, the back third missing completely, stood useless about twenty yards farther west. The whole place showed many years of neglect. A thin trail of blue smoke rose from a foreshortened chimney. Buell trained his glasses on the two side-buildings.

The one on the east was too low to hold a horse and appeared empty except for a small stack of crudely broken wood. That explained the missing corral sections. The shed on the west held at least one horse. The animal stood broadside in the open-ended structure, a sorrel with four stocking feet—Buell's breath caught in his throat. "Not this time, you lyin' son of a bitch," Buell muttered. The horse wore a bridle, but carried no saddle; sure sign of an uneasy man, but one not really afraid of being found. Buell studied the front of the station. To the right of a wood-slab door a small window filled with something other than glass blocked any light.

The door, supported by a single hinge at the top, stood slightly ajar. As he watched, someone lifted it up and back, out of the way. Simpson stepped into the light wearing only a tan shirt, baggy wool pants, and clumsy looking shoes. He hugged his chest while he scanned the hillside in front of the station, looking directly, but fleetingly, at Buell before hurrying to the end of the lean-to where he relieved himself.

He finished with the unmistakable shrug, and then picked up an armload of wood on his way back to the door. He disappeared for a few seconds, then came back out, grabbed the edge of the door, and pulled it shut. A moment later a rush of sparks blazed out of the leaning chimney. Was Simpson stoking the fire for supper?

Taking a leak in his shirtsleeves meant he'd been there long enough to get the interior warm. Or, someone else was there before him and had since left. Will they be back soon, and who were they? Bachman? Waldon? How about Gus? Bachman was from the same place as Ruben Bedell—a troubled place where fights were short and bloody, but where grudges kept forever. There was a feud between Bedell and Waldon. Ruben had said as much, but was it over the feedlot, or was Waldon using something brought all the way from New Mexico—something like an unsettled score between Ruben Bedell and Ike Bachman? And the crazy Negro? Jake said he and Bachman had been to town after Staker was shot. Bachman was running out of friends.

He trained the glasses on the chimney again. Shimmering waves of heat danced above the pipe. Simpson was busy. Buell rolled over on his back and scanned the rolling plain behind him for several minutes. Anyone riding his way would sooner or later rise into view—nothing appeared. He settled back on his stomach, and thoroughly glassed the valley to the west. Finally satisfied, he went back down the gentle slope, untied Shadow, and headed him toward the lowering sun.

Forty minutes later, he found a small stand of scruffy trees where he hid his horse. The low-angled sun ceased giving up its heat, and the chill made his shoulder ache. One time, a coat had almost cost him his life, but after thinking for a bit, he untied his from behind the saddle and shrugged into it, leaving the front open. He pulled the heavy rifle out of the boot, then methodically jammed a dozen cartridges past the loading gate. Working the lever down and back, he lowered the hammer and shoved one more round into the magazine. What did he need to see or hear from Simpson to prove he was the shooter? Would just the sight of the rifle be enough? Hefting the weight of the gun, he tried to remember what he'd seen when Roscoe had stopped him. Had Simpson been carrying a rifle like this? It had been a large one. Did Waldon give both Roscoe *and* Simpson new weapons? He glanced down at the shiny badge pinned to his shirt, buttoned his coat, and started along the overgrown road.

The smoke appeared leisurely again—a cooking fire. Keeping his eye on the front door, Buell approached the stable, careful where he put his feet, until he reached the open front. "Hey, horse," he whispered and reached out his hand. The animal turned to look at him with soft eyes, unafraid. Buell stroked the horse's muzzle. "Good horse," he murmured and looked over its back to the interior of the shelter. "What's the bastard feedin' ya, boy?" The animal shook its head and Buell grabbed its muzzle again. "Stand here quiet, okay?"

Stepping past the beast, he went to the shoulder-high window and peeked around the edge. The frame was intact, the hole covered with three rough boards fastened on the inside and caulked with rags. He could hear someone muttering, and moved to the ramshackle door. Buell saw Simpson through a crack by the frame.

An oil lamp hanging over the table lit the side of the man's face as he sliced strips off a slab of bacon. A three-quart pot sat on the right side of the stove—the warming spot, and nearer the two stove lids sat a black skillet. Simpson stopped slicing, went to the stove, and gave the kettle contents a gentle stir with a wooden spoon, then went back to cutting.

Buell searched as much as he could see of the interior—no rifle. A heavy coat lay on top of a two-tiered bunk bed; a floppy hat hung from the bedpost. Two sets of saddlebags lay on the bottom bunk. He *did* have company. Then, with a grunt, Simpson stabbed the knife tip into the table, picked up the stack of bacon slices, and went to the stove. Buell counted the nine strips of bacon Simpson dropped into the pan to sizzle. Simpson then stood and poked lazily at the meat, muttering to himself—obviously a man alone and at ease.

Buell stepped to the other side of the door, took another peek at the man, and caught hold of the edge. Then, he hiked the front edge of the door off the ground, and in the same move, stepped past it and inside. Simpson poked the bacon a couple more times before turning around. His face went as pale as a bean sack, and he dropped the fork in the dirt.

"Not who you expected, eh?" Buell hauled the hammer full back and trained the rifle on him.

"Wha—where—where'd you come from?" His gaze dropped to the Winchester.

"Recognize it, do ya?" Buell looked around the place. There was another bed to his left and another pair of bags on the straw tick. Nine pieces of bacon, three saddlebags—three men. "You armed?"

"No." Simpson eyed the Winchester nervously. "Where'd you get that rifle?"

"Same place you got it."

Simpson swallowed hard. "It was none of my doin'. I'm just looking for—"

"I've heard that before, remember?"

"He's dead, ain't he?" Simpson sounded cautiously hopeful.

"Who?"

"Bachman."

Buell knew Simpson had said more than he meant to as soon as he spoke. He unbuttoned his coat and turned back one side. "He is, and you're going to Carlisle."

Simpson's eyes fixed on the badge. "Bachman did it," he blurted. "He gimme the rifle for just that one time, when I went with Roscoe. I didn't shoot then—remember? I didn't shoot ya." He tried to wet his lips. "Soon's I saw him again, he took it back. I ain't seen it since then, so don't be tryin' to blame her shootin' on me."

Buell nodded slowly to hide his rage. "Did he have it when he left here?" he asked evenly.

"Yes—I mean, I didn't—he wasn't here. There's just me . . ." his voice trailed off as his eyes drifted to the two pairs of saddlebags on the bunk, and Buell's loaded question dawned on him.

Buell pointed his rifle at the two pots on the stove. "When will they be back?"

"They?"

"Yeah. Bachman and Waldon."

Simpson's shoulders slumped. "He ain't dead, is he?"

"Not yet."

"I swear, Sheriff—"

"I didn't mention no woman gettin' shot."

Simpson's face paled in the yellow light. "But ya got my rifle and—"

"Which means ya give it to Bachman when he left."

Confusion clouded the man's face. "But—"

Buell backed away from the door. "Go outside real slow, to your horse."

"My coat."

"You won't need it. Move." Buell raised the muzzle to eye

level. Simpson shuffled across the dirt and into the failing light outside. Buell followed him, the muzzle of the rifle centered on Simpson's spine, and then kept close watch as Simpson placed a blanket and saddle on the horse.

Simpson paused. "What if I tell the judge all I know?" He was looking into the back of the lean-to.

"You're gonna hang."

The man's back stiffened and he took a deep breath.

"Get on with it," Buell said quietly.

Simpson stepped back slightly, and then stooped to reach the cinch strap hanging on the other side of the horse. Suddenly, he grabbed at his ankle, and lunged sideways—Buell pulled the trigger. The horse reared, slamming its head into the ceiling. The sound of splintering wood and the animal's terrified shriek masked Simpson's gasp. Buell jumped out of the way as the horse threw off the saddle and bolted west down the road. Simpson sagged to the ground, blood spurting from under his arm. He fell over on his back. Buell kicked a derringer pistol out of his hand. The dying man managed to meet his eyes for a moment, his head rising slightly off the ground. Then, he took one last shuddering breath and went limp.

"I was hopin'," Buell muttered, and turned to watch the horse disappear in the gloom.

Buell untied what reins the horse had left behind, and then carried the saddle and blanket around to the back of the lean-to. Returning, he grabbed Simpson's shirt and dragged him out of sight as well, going back to kick dirt over the spilled blood. Back inside the soddy, he turned the lamp up a little, and set it on a table that stood under the boarded window. The smell of bacon and beans reminded him he hadn't eaten since early morning, so he scooped a plate full, laid four strips of bacon on top, and dragged a chair to the head of the single bed. Leaning his rifle against the wall, he sat down and began to eat.

He hadn't been finished with his plate of beans for very long when he heard the lazy cadence of a walking horse. He stood, lifting the rifle as he did, and backed into the corner. Turning his head back and forth, he made out the direction and cussed under his breath—it was coming from the west. Why in hell? Had Shadow kept quiet like he usually did? He heard only one horse, and its pace never varied until it stopped and he heard the creak of leather. He imagined the rider loosening the cinch and, as expected, heard the saddle come off and then the animal sidestepping into the shelter.

Seconds later, the door opened and the slim figure of Ike Bachman dragged it shut again. Going straight to the stacked beds, he threw his hat on top, and then leaned a long rifle against the end. He went to the stove. "Where'd that dumb bastard get off to," he muttered and lifted the wooden spoon from the bean pot.

"To hell, if I'm any judge," Buell said and ratcheted a shell into the rifle's chamber.

Bachman spun around as his hand moved to the butt of his gun. He jerked away as though the handle were red-hot. He stared wide-eyed at Buell's Winchester for a second and then chuckled. "You're like a cockroach. Always showin' up where ya ain't wanted. Where's Simpson?"

"Who's with ya?" Buell asked and stepped out of the corner. "And where's he at?"

Bachman glanced at the door. "Make ya nervous, does it?" His eyes narrowed. "Good."

"Step past the stove, away from that bunk. I want a look at that rifle."

"Sure." Bachman sniffed. "Just like any other rifle."

The muzzle of Buell's gun followed Bachman as he moved almost nonchalantly to the foot of the single bed. Buell then went to the bunk and reached for the weapon. It was the twin of the one he held. "I think this rifle was used to kill a woman today," he said. "We're going to go to Carlisle, and you're gonna explain to the judge why you have it."

Bachman reached up and felt the rough scar above his right ear. "I don't think so."

A chill crept up Buell's back. "You sayin' ya won't go?"

"I'm sayin' one of us ain't leavin' here alive."

The blast from the Winchester slammed into Buell's ears as the front of Bachman's coat ballooned out and dirt cascaded from the ceiling. With a look of amazement, Bachman clutched at his chest and started to sit down on the bed. He missed the edge and tumbled onto the hard-packed floor. "Ya—killed me," he said matter-of-factly, studied his bloodied hands for a few seconds, and started to struggle for breath. "Cock . . . roach," he wheezed and closed his eyes against the falling debris. Buell watched carefully until the man's chest quit heaving. A dark form danced behind his eyes.

The buckskin horse didn't like Bachman anymore, stepping sideways every time Buell tried to lay the dead man across his back. Buell solved the problem by backing the horse into the lean-to and soon managed to have both men strapped to the fidgeting animal.

Two hours later, after several stops along the way to rearrange the gruesome load, he rode into Carlisle and met the puzzled looks of the people still moving around in the streets. He went straight to the stable and led both horses inside. "Go get Doc Princher." He ordered the first man to follow him. He had Shadow unsaddled and eating a measure of oats when the doctor burst through the man-door.

Princher paled when he saw the limp men draped over the buckskin's saddle. Placing a finger on Bachman's neck, he paused only briefly before hurrying around the horse to

Simpson's head. A moment later he faced Buell over the horse's rump. "Is this your *only* solution? Kill them all?"

"It's the one *they* chose, Doc."

"But it's the one that suits you best, isn't it?" Princher's face flushed, his eyes flashing.

"I won't argue that." Buell unstrapped the dead men's saddlebags. "I'll need these for a bit. If we find these men have kin, and I doubt it, we'll send their things along." He threw the bags down and hauled Simpson's rifle out of its boot. He jabbed the lifeless man in the hip. "This one admitted he shot Missus Warren."

"And the other one?" the doctor demanded.

"He didn't know *what* to do." Buell turned and walked out of the stable, pushing his way through the gathering crowd.

CHAPTER 33

The sight of two dead men slung over the back of a horse ignited a storm of controversy such as Carlisle had never seen. People were either demanding that Buell be fired, or publicly thanked—nothing in between. Three days later, Mayor Mace called a special meeting of the council, closed to the public. Buell was not invited.

The chamber seemed too small to contain the animosity Paul Steele felt circulating the room. He sat at one end of the table, a silent Art Lancer on his right, Paisley Mace on his left, while an animated Jude Cody and Doc Princher sat at the other end. The recorder sat behind a small desk near the door, pen poised. Doc Princher had just declared Buell persona non grata, and Paisley was half out of his chair, his fists bunched.

"This special meeting will come to order," Paul Steele shouted and slammed the gavel down hard. "Now!" Doc Princher scowled at him and then slumped back in his chair. Paisley regained his seat. "I don't like Buell not being here one bit," Paul said, "But it's the rule that any member can so stipulate. For the record, is that what you asked for, Jude?"

"It is," Jude Cody replied. "I'll make no bones about it; he scares the hell out of me, and if I say what I want to say, I don't want him hearing it."

Steele looked at the stenographer. "So noted." He took a deep breath. "Blake Waldon could not be reached. Members present constitute a quorum. On the agenda is the question of continuing the services of Buell Mace. Each member can now make a statement. We'll start with you, Jude."

Jude stood, grim faced. "Buell Mace is a cold-blooded killer."

Paul grabbed Paisley by the arm and squeezed hard. "A little less would be better, Mister Cody," Paul said. "You can state your position without an accusation like that."

"He can say what he likes," Princher challenged. "I intend to."

"Jude has the floor, Doc. You're out of order."

"Don't tell me about order, Paul. You've all made a mess of this and we'll—"

Paul slapped the table with his hand, making the gavel jump. "One more word, Doc, and it'll be the last one you'll have tonight. I mean it." Princher's face flushed and the veins along the side of his neck bulged. "Go ahead, Jude," Paul said.

"I just know we've had five confirmed killings, with a sixth alleged and our sheriff mortally wounded. We know three have come at Buell Mace's hand, and Sheriff Staker's shooting and I believe Missus Warren's death as well can be partially blamed on him. That leaves only the cause of Jules Venable's death unresolved, and I think Buell is somehow involved in that as well. I want the badge *you* gave him removed, and it made plain he's not welcome in Carlisle." Pale around the mouth, he sat down and stared at his hands.

"Art? You want to speak?"

Art remained seated. "Buell—saved—us all." He took three long slow breaths. "He stays."

Paul waited several seconds, and then looked at Princher. "Doc?"

Princher stood. "I've known Buell Mace for twenty-seven years. I've closely witnessed his behavior for twenty of those, his formative years. Buell Mace is"—he looked directly at Paisley—"a pathological killer."

Paul caught hold of Paisley again. "You'll have your turn, Mace," he said firmly.

"From his assault on David Steele on the playground as a child, to his cold-blooded murder of a Kansas drover at age sixteen, and reports I've heard since he came back of an indiscriminate slaughter of Indians in Dakota Territory, he's shown, and still shows, a total disregard for human life. From what I've read, it's not something Buell chose, it's how he was born—his brain isn't normal. My duty as a doctor is to point that out because there's nothing medicine can do for it. Based on that diagnosis alone, Buell Mace should not be allowed to carry a badge, and should probably be disarmed completely. I take no joy in this, Paisley." He sat back down.

"Mace," Paul said quietly.

A pale Paisley Mace stood straight up for a moment, and then leaned forward, his fists planted on the table. "How old are you Jude? Twenty-nine—thirty?" He waved his answer away. "You've been in Carlisle less than four years. Just long enough to make ya think you can talk for the younger people. You weren't here to fight the Indians, or put up with the railroad workers. You never saw the teamsters, the gamblers, the whores, the buffalo hunters, or the drovers. You've never seen neighbors stand shoulder to shoulder to kill grasshoppers, or pitch in and harvest by hand forty acres of wheat for a man who's been hurt. You don't know a goddamn thing, Jude, and are in no position to be judging a real man's character."

He turned his eyes on Doc Princher. "You take no joy, Doc? You *have* no joy. You're old and dry and bitter. You fail to mention *why* Buell kicked David in the head—David Steele was intent on breaking Simon Steele's neck. Deny it. And you decide to leave out the reason Buell had to shoot that filthy piece of crap in Lancer's saloon. He was defending a woman's honor—at sixteen, he was doing what any man should do. You remember who that woman was?" He looked down at Paul for a second. "And Lancer here will tell you, the Kansan goaded him and the Kansan drew first. Your last claim is so outrageous, I can't believe you said it. Those Indians he massacred? It was a story, Doc, pure imagination, and told for the fun of it to a young girl over supper—to Abby Steele and the whole family. No doubt Samantha heard it from her and when she told you, *you* heard what you wanted. Five dead? How about Ruben Bedell's rider? He doesn't count? And what about Missus Warren? You said it yourself Doc, 'Why her?' Buell told me afterward it wasn't meant to be Missus Warren, it was meant to be Ruth. Do you hear me?" Paisley shouted. "Ruth! And Buell found the son of a whore who did that—I hope he made him suffer. Next might be your son or *your* wife, Doc. Or one of your kids, Jude. You should all get down on your knees and thank God we have a man willing to do what none of us dare to do ourselves." He glared down the table. "Buell stays," he muttered and sank onto his chair.

Paul Steele stood and studied the faces of his fellow councilmen. All but Jude Cody met his gaze. "I'd trust my family to Buell Mace's care without hesitation. I can say no more than that. He stays and I so move." He sat back down.

"Second," Art said.

"Those in favor of sustaining Buell Mace as sheriff of Carlisle raise their hand."

Paul raised his hand and Lancer did the same. "Those opposed."

Doc Princher lifted his hand and shook his head. "No."

Jude Cody's hand barely left the table as he muttered, "No."

Paul looked at Mace. "Tie vote."

"He stays," the mayor said.

"The ayes have it. Buell stays where he is. There being no other item on the agenda, this meeting is adjourned." He glanced at the recorder whose forehead was wet with sweat. "So note it." He banged the gavel and dropped it on the table.

Buell watched his father scan the saloon and finally see him. Paisley started across the floor, weaving in and out of the tables. Buell turned to Jake. "As fast as he's movin', I'd say I still got my job, more's the worse."

Paisley was breathing heavily, his face flushed. "I've never been so ashamed—of a couple of men—in my life," he puffed.

"Just two?" Buell asked and stepped around to stand at the end of the bar.

"Wanna beer, Mister Mace?" Jake asked.

"Sounds good." Paisley leaned against the bar and wiped his brow with his handkerchief.

"Well. What did they say?" Buell asked.

"Majority wants you to stay."

"Let me guess. Princher and that Cody fella don't."

"Yep. Cody I can understand, but Doc's another case. He just don't like you, son. I'm afraid I let him have both barrels over it, too."

Jake set a full glass of beer on the bar, and Paisley eagerly quaffed half of it. For the next fifteen minutes, with Jake hurrying off and back again to listen, Paisley told Buell what had gone on in the meeting. "When Blake Waldon gets back, the vote might well go the other way," Paisley finished.

"If Waldon ever comes back, I'm going to arrest him," Buell said.

"For what?"

"I'll come up with something. Do you think Sheriff Staker would still be up for a visit?"

Paisley pulled out his watch. "I'd think so. If his lights are still on in the front room, try him."

"I'll see ya in the mornin' then. I see half a dozen folks in here who'd like to hear what went on in the meeting. Go tell 'em, Mister Mayor." He punched his father lightly on the shoulder and left.

Staker's lights had not been on, and Buell had gone back to the stable where he'd spent a restless night. Going to work early the next morning was a relief, despite the temperature being below zero. He ate a hurried breakfast in Mrs. Luger's kitchen, an agreement he'd made with her only the week before—she was busy making bread and left him alone.

At the jail, he got a good fire going in the stove, and had just put the coffeepot on top when steps sounded on the boardwalk outside. He watched the door open slowly and then the old man from Venable's barn stepped halfway in and stopped. "Kin I have a word, Sheriff?" he asked, hugging himself against the cold.

"Not if you're standin' in the damn door. Come in and shut it."

The man moved like he'd been jabbed, and pushed the door shut. He wiped a drop of mucous off the tip of his nose with a dirty sleeve and sniffed. "Cold," he said.

"Get over here by the stove. Sit down if you've a mind to. We'll have coffee in a few minutes." Buell hooked the chair by the wall with his toe and dragged it closer. "Ya got a name, old-timer?" He walked over to his desk and leaned against it.

"Ted Keys." He crossed the room, sat down on the chair, and held out his hands to the heat.

"What ya got on your mind this mornin', Mister Keys?"

The codger sniffed another shiny drop up his nose. "Did ya mean yerself when ya told me not to talk about Blake Waldon?"

Buell stood up straight. "Has someone asked?"

"Someone wanted to."

"Who was askin' about Waldon?"

"Nobody. It was him lookin' for me, I think."

When he paused, Buell nodded. "And?"

"I heard a horse last night, middle of the night, so I went to the window to see what was goin' on. Waldon and that black mare of his was at Venable's office. He went in for a few minutes, lit the lamp, and then come out with it. When he headed for the barn, I hid."

"Why do you think he might be looking for you?"

"I'm old and I'm slow, but I'm not addled jist yet. Folks don't seem to notice me much, so I hear lots of things. That skinny fella that was laid out at the undertaker, the one you brought in? I saw Mister Waldon give him a new Winchester. Same time, he handed a new Colt's pistol to the one they called Roscoe. I hear tell that washer lady was killed with a long-shootin' gun."

"Why would you think the two things have something to do with each other?"

"Cuz Waldon told the skinny one he'd better not miss Bedell this time. The fella said he'd practice some."

Buell eyed the man for a moment and felt slightly sick to his stomach. He gingerly touched the side of the coffeepot. "How do you know he was looking for you?"

"He hollered my name. Said he'd help me find a place to live. And then he looked all over, even in the loft. I was hid good. After a bit, he left cussin'."

"Do you have a place?"

"To hide? Sure."

"No. A place to stay."

"Nope. And with Jules gone, I don't have a way of makin' no money."

"When did ya eat last?"

Keys caught a sudden rush from his nose on his sleeve and wiped it on his leg. "Couple days, I guess. That coffee sure

312

smells good."

Buell grabbed his cup off the desk and got another from a shelf by the stove. Pouring one nearly full, he handed it to Keys. "Sugar?" He pointed at a large bowl on the same shelf.

"I like sugar," Keys said eagerly, and when Buell held the container in front of him, he scooped five spoons full into the steaming cup.

Buell took a sip of his own and then set the cup on his desk. "Do you know the deputies?"

Keys stirred his cup for a few seconds and then looked up. "I know 'em both."

"I'll tell 'em you're gonna stay here today. Don't go out. There's a slop bucket under the cots in the cells if ya have to do that. Tonight, I'll take you over to my place. Mose will find you a place to bed down."

"I like ol' Mose. Him and me go back a bit. We gonna get Blake Waldon?"

"One way or the other, old-timer. Now, drink that while I go get you a bite to eat."

After telling the deputies about Ted Keys, Buell went to Sheriff Staker's place. His hail was answered immediately, and he went in to find Staker sitting in the kitchen, his right leg straight out. Buell crossed the sitting room and leaned against the door jam. "Well, looks like ya intend to live."

"I appreciate the encouragement, Buell. I was about to send the army after you." Staker sounded a little agitated. "I need to know what the hell you're doing."

"A lot more than I ever thought I could, if ya want to know."

"Paul Steele said the council voted to keep you on."

"Only because Pa was voting."

"No sign of Waldon?"

"I haven't seen him." Buell knew he'd hesitated too long.

"Spill it." Staker's eyes flashed. "I've talked to Judge Kingsley, so I know what you think."

"That old-timer who stays at Venable's barn come to the jail early this morning. Waldon was there last night lookin' for him—called his name and searched the barn good. I reckon Waldon has figgered out there are only two more people who can witness against him. The old-timer would be the easiest to take care of."

"You're talking about Ted Keys. Used to be a coach driver till he tipped one over and broke his back. What'd he have to say?"

"He saw and heard Waldon give Bachman and Roscoe the Winchester and that Colt, just like I said. He also told me four days ago that he saw Waldon come out of Venable's office a couple of minutes after hearing a shot. Waldon come to the barn and told Gus to saddle up and go with him. Gus told him to go to hell."

"Ted is sure of all this?"

"I'd like to see someone try to shake him."

"Why didn't you tell someone about this sooner? We could have a warrant out for Waldon."

"And let him hide behind the law? His kind don't deserve that."

"They all deserve to be heard, Buell."

"I don't see it that way, Sheriff. Ya don't wait for a rabid dog to bite."

"Where's Ted now?"

"He's over at the jail eating."

"Eating? What? I don't understand."

"He hadn't eaten for two days. I got some stuff from Freda. I'll have Mose find him a place to stay until I run Waldon down."

"That doesn't sound like a man who doesn't care about this town."

"Don't make too much of it." Buell stood away from the door.

"What do you intend to do now?"

"Track Gus and Blake Waldon down."

"You don't have the legal or moral authority to shoot them on sight, Buell. You must see that."

"Is that what you think I do?" Heat rose in Buell's face. "Goddammit, Sheriff, every time I talk to folks like you and Simon and the judge, I feel like I have to—to—" He spun on his heel and stormed through the sitting room.

"Dammit all, Buell," Staker shouted. "That's not what I meant at all."

Buell banged the door shut behind him and headed for the stable.

An hour later he lay in the same spot he'd lain three days before and studied the old station. Waldon's black mare was in the shed, but well back inside, invisible to anyone without a glass. There was no smoke coming from the chimney, but the pile of wood he'd seen before was gone. He was still stinging from Staker's words.

How many men had he killed? The Kansan. And then, that gambler—no, then David Steele, both men rotten at the soul, and both tried him first. Then the gambler at Amos's place. No—before that, the drifter at the river. He'd tried to bushwhack Simon and got caught lookin'. And then the gam—no, after the bushwhacker, the Indian. Sharp Knife. The name came to him so easy. He'd mutilated Knife, emptied his Remington into his face after shooting him in the chest with the fifty caliber Sharps. And then the gambler, or? Buell dropped his face into the crook of his arm and closed his eyes. No wonder they thought what they did.

A vague shape, dark and sinister, passed slowly behind his

eyes, and he sensed its power—the demon he'd first seen as a young boy. The demon that had made his head pulse deliciously after he'd kicked David in the ear. The demon that later used him, drove him to do things he didn't remember afterward, horrible things. But that devil was gone, driven away by something he never recognized, something that released him from its power. And he'd promised himself then that he'd never give in to its influence again.

He raised his head and peered through the binoculars. Waldon was down there. The man had tried to kill someone his father cherished. That was the same as trying to kill his father. Waldon didn't deserve to live. Slowly he retreated and went back to Shadow.

Buell tied the horse west of the stage station, in the same place as before. He then followed the faint track to the ramshackle buildings. Soon he peered through the crack in the door at the unlit room. He sensed someone inside and listened for a while, his eyes straining to see in the dim light.

Drawing his pistol, he caught the edge of the door, jerked it back, and leapt inside. Bright sunlight lit the interior, and the lump on the single bunk moved, then a tousled head appeared from under the pile of blankets.

Buell cocked the pistol and stepped close, jamming the muzzle into the side of Waldon's neck. "Get your hands out!" He jabbed hard. With a grunt, Waldon pushed back the covers and laid both hands on top. "I'm arrestin' you for plannin' to murder Ruben Bedell and for killin' Jules Venable. Get up slow." He stepped back, his pistol aimed at Waldon's face.

Blake Waldon never said a word, from the time Buell rousted him out of bed until he slammed the door on his cell in Carlisle two hours later.

Ted Keys did: "Ya can't disrespect a man cuz he had some bad luck, Blake. Now yer gonna get yer comeuppance. Jules was hard, but he understood. Gus was a bully, but he knew 'bout folks like me, too. You are just plain mean and rotten to the core."

"You'll get your chance later, Mister Keys," Buell said, and moved him away from the cell. "Do you still want that place I mentioned?"

"No. I'll be okay out to Venable's. The place still needs muckin' out, and the stock needs feedin'. Someone will take it over, and until then I can borrow a few dollars to get by." He paused for a moment. "Yer a good man, Sheriff," he said and walked away.

A sensation swept over Buell that he hadn't felt since an old-timer in Idaho City had said much the same thing. And as then, he wasn't sure he liked the feeling.

CHAPTER 34

That evening, as Buell was making one last check, Waldon had finally said something. He wanted to talk to the new lawyer. Buell had passed the request on to Judge Kingsley, and then gone to Luger's to have a quiet drink before he made the rounds to the rest of the saloons. Simon found him there.

"So, what's the big grin for?" Buell asked. "Ya look like a fox who's found a hole in the chicken wire."

"I'm just glad you brought Waldon in, instead of"—he shrugged—"shooting him. I guess that's the only way to say it."

"That would be it, Simon. Not the blood-drinkin' crazy man the Methodist ladies talk about, huh? What ya havin'?"

"I'll take a shot of your brandy." He waved his hand when Jake looked their way. "Judge Kingsley asked me if I could find out how many of those new Winchesters had been sold in this part of Nebraska."

"Can ya?"

"Easily. I'll send a telegram tomorrow. I think with what you have to say about Simpson's confession, and what the man at Venable's saw and heard, Blake Waldon will go to Lincoln for a long time."

"And that's good enough for you, ain't it?"

"Yes, Buell, it is. That should end this."

"Hello, Simon. What ya havin'?" Jake asked and leaned on the bar.

"He's gonna drink my stuff, Jake. I guess somehow that

makes sense."

"Your stuff? Oh, yeah." He reached under the bar and brought out a nearly full bottle of brandy. "Ya think Waldon's gonna get off, Simon?" He poured a drink. "Half the people here do."

Buell's scalp prickled.

"I don't think so. There's too much against him."

"I saw Gus," Jake said nonchalantly.

"Where!" Buell nearly spilled his drink. "When?"

"He walked past my place about an hour ago. Looked in the window for a minute, and then moved on." He stepped back from the bar. "What?"

"Why didn't ya say so?" Buell demanded.

"I didn't know you was lookin' for him."

"Damn, Jake, how can you be that stupid and still manage to keep breathin'." Buell let out an exasperated puff and shoved his way out of the saloon.

He spent the next hour looking in all the saloons, eating places, stables, and any other place that came to mind as he searched. He found both deputies and told them to be on the lookout as well, then went back to the jail to check on Waldon again. Until well past midnight, Buell prowled the darker places around Carlisle and finally went home to bed.

The next day, Buell stood looking through the iron door and into the jail cell. "Then you're going to have to talk quiet, cuz I ain't lettin' him out of there," he said and rattled the door. "And I'm not leavin' the jail with you in there."

"My client has the right to private counsel, Sheriff." The Cincinnati lawyer wore a striped coat and matching trousers, patent leather shoes, and spats. His oily hair was cut short on the sides and parted right down the middle.

"You've got it as private as you're gonna get, lawyer."

The man scowled and bent closer to Waldon.

Over the course of the next two hours, Buell began to wish he'd goaded Waldon into something, anything. Blake's insolent looks and occasional chuckle as he talked quietly with his lawyer made Buell's blood hot.

Finally, the smug slicker stood up and tapped on the iron bars with his walking stick. "I'll be leaving now, Constable," he said.

The temptation to kick him in the ass was strong as the lawyer pranced out of the cell and past Buell. He crossed to the door and turned around. "You'll be out of there by noon, Mister Waldon," he said, and walked out the door, leaving it open.

Buell went over and slammed it shut, then spun around. "You aren't goin' anywhere, Waldon. Take my word."

Just before noon, Judge Kingsley walked into the jail and handed Buell an official-looking piece of paper. "That's a *pro forma* transfer order from the federal court in Lincoln. Either you or one of your deputies will escort Blake Waldon to Lincoln, where you will turn him over to a U.S. marshal."

Buell was unable to talk, instead staring down at the stiff paper and seeing nothing.

"He's been charged with felony murder, Buell. His lawyer argued that he's not safe here, and cited your performance with Simpson and Bachman."

Buell continued to look at the fancy lettering.

"Do you understand?"

"No! I hear what you're saying, but *no*, I don't understand. That lawyer got this done a little too easy, seems to me. And what's *pro forma*?" He glared at the judge.

"A formality, something already made up. I just filled in the names. You are ordered to put him on the first train east. That's six-forty this evening."

"It's not noon, Mace, but it'll do," Waldon crowed from his cell.

Buell spun around and charged against the cell door. "Shut up, Blake, or—"

"Or what?" he said with a sneer, and then looked at Judge Kingsley. "I don't want to be left alone with this maniac. My lawyer said I can demand that."

"Let's go outside, Buell," the judge said, opened the door, and followed Buell through it and into the bitter cold. "I know this sits wrong, but I'm asking you to have a little faith in what *I* believe in."

"How will you sleep, knowing Jules Venable was shot in the face from six inches away? Will you be able to look at the Warren kids when Waldon is set free and heads for California or Chicago?"

"I trust he will be found as guilty as I think he is. It's what I have to do, Buell. You gained a lot of respect by bringing him in to face a trial. I hope that helps." He pulled his scarf tighter around his neck, stepped off the walk, and crossed the street.

Buell avoided talking to anyone, even cutting Paisley off when his father tried to stop him in the street. About noon, he saddled Shadow and rode out to the way station, brazenly cresting the low hill in front at a canter, hoping to see Gus make a run for it. The door stood ajar, just as he'd left it two days before, and he went back to town. He was at his desk brooding when the door burst open and Ted Keys stumbled in, out of breath. "I saw Gus." He coughed, his breath rattling in his throat.

Buell stood up and hurried around the desk. "Where?"

"I was poking around in the alley behind the general store. I heard a door open and made myself scarce. Gus come out, walked right past me and into the street that goes in front of your place. I got to the end of the alley just as he went in. I run over here as fast as these old legs would move." His nose was running like a downspout.

"Did he have a gun—rifle or pistol?"

"Gus never carries either." He edged toward the door. "I'll make myself scarce now, if ya don't mind."

"Thanks, Ted." Buell grabbed his coat off the hook, jammed his hat on, and rushed out the door.

Striding past the street the stable was on, he circled around behind it and carefully opened a little-used door in back of the barn. The leather hinges silently offered no resistance and he stepped inside. Gus stood facing the double doors, obviously waiting. Maybe Keys hadn't made himself as scarce as he thought. Buell scanned the stable for any sign of the old man, then lifted his pistol clear of the holster, and started to walk, Gus unaware of his presence.

Not so Shadow. The horse turned in his stall and nickered— Gus spun around like a roped calf. "Might have known you'd find a back way, Mace."

Buell continued forward until he could see the forge. Mose stood motionless against the bench. "Get out of here, Mose." Buell pointed at the door with his revolver. Mose needed nothing further; he walked through and slammed it shut.

"You have some explainin' to do," Buell said. "I want you to walk ahead of me to the jail." He motioned with the pistol again.

"I've waited a lot of years for this, Buell. We're gonna find out just how brass your balls are."

"I'm not foolin', Gus."

"Neither am I. You've always thought of me as big and stupid. Well, I've got a secret for ya. My pa thought the same thing and I let 'im. I was able to take enough from him to live pretty good for a while. Wasn't just me, though. The *respectable* folks around here didn't mind either. As long as they got a share, they'd help me steal the church offering. Simon caught on and didn't have the sense to keep his mouth shut, so he got burned. But from then on the bastards I'd helped skim cream, suddenly discovered righteousness. Oh, they'd still use me when it suited them. They're still doing it. Waldon did. That lawyer Lindstrom did." He chuckled. "Don't believe it?" he said and then almost whispered, "Simon did." He laughed out loud. "You ought to see your face. You don't want to hear it, but you know it *can* be true."

"I've let you have your say, Gus. Doesn't change a thing. You're going to jail."

"For what? Name one thing I've done. Knocked your hat off in the alley? Yeah, I know you think that was me. Think about it." He held out an enormous hand. "I'd have taken your head off." Gus spit in the dirt. "You just didn't like my company, Buell. Just like I don't like yours."

"I'm done listenin'."

"And I'm done talkin'. Can you shoot an unarmed man? I never doubted your ability with that pistol of yours, but I've always wondered what you'd do without it."

Buell could see the determination build in Gus's eyes, saw him shift his weight ever so slightly to his right foot, and watched the fingers of his left hand loosely curl. He'll lead with his left foot. The thought had no more been born than Gus took a long stride forward and swung his massive fist at Buell's head. Buell's swing, which started a split second before, carried the Remington across the distance just ahead of Gus's hand and cracked into his right eyebrow. The big man sagged to his knees, and then leaned forward on his open hands. Buell blinked in disbelief. The blow would have stunned an ox. He took a step back, a cold chill shooting up his back. *For God's sake, don't get up, Gus.*

★ ★ ★ ★ ★

Footsteps sounded outside on the walk, then stopped, and Buell shook the bloody image of Gus from his head to watch the jailhouse door. It opened, and Ruben Bedell stepped in.

"Your father said you weren't entertaining visitors," Ruben Bedell said as he shut the door. "That include me?"

"I'm not sure. Try me."

"I've heard what's happened." He glanced at the chair by the stove.

"Sit down, Ruben. Coffee?" Buell stood.

"Sure, if you're going to have some." He hung his hat by the door, unbuttoned his heavy coat, and dragged the chair over to Buell's desk.

Buell poured two cups and handed one to the rancher. "I wish I had a few more answers," he said as he sat back down.

"Maybe I can help. Actually, it's the reason I came to town. A wagonload of men came to the ranch day before yesterday— six of 'em. They were cold, hungry and desperate—islanders. Interesting how much a man will tell you when he's afraid of dying."

"You made them talk?"

"They were more than willing to talk in exchange for a steak and some spuds. Did you ever make the connection between Ike Bachman and me?"

"I did. Why didn't you just tell me?"

"It was a personal thing. I take care of my own business. He and his friends took their opportunities, and I took mine. I knew it would eventually turn out the way it did. What I didn't know was Waldon's side in it. I knew he was fairly aggressive, and I've had to use the law a couple of times over that property he wanted. You've heard about that as well, right?"

Buell nodded.

"What I couldn't imagine was him going so far as having me

324

shot to get what he wanted. But that was what he was doing, and Bachman was pleased to take his money. Plus, he paid those cowboys to raise hell here in town. He told them to take every opportunity to make cattlemen and anyone associated with them look bad. He thought he could influence the city council to prohibit a feedlot being built on my property."

"Did you know Paul Steele was lookin' at the ground as well?"

"Sure. And he would have been tough to best in a business deal, but he'd have fought fair."

"Why did Waldon send Roscoe after me?"

"He didn't. *You* earned that visit. Waldon thought he could neutralize you by making you sheriff, and then put pressure on you through the council. He didn't know you like I came to."

"What about Gus?" Buell felt a twinge of regret.

"I was sorry to hear about that. But knowing him, I don't expect he gave you any choice. Everybody used Gus, and I mean everybody." He looked directly at Buell.

"Even you?" Buell's scalp tingled.

"Even me. He could move without being watched. He was a familiar face, and nobody expected much of him. He was the perfect informer."

"But Waldon used him too. So did John Lindstrom. Even Simon, so I hear."

"I told Gus they'd ask him to do things, and I told him to go ahead, long as there wasn't killing involved. Me knowing, and them not, gave me a big advantage. Simon's a different matter. He just wanted peace and quiet, and sometimes that's a hard position to defend. He tried to talk Gus into just getting out of the area. And I think Gus did for a bit, but something drew him back."

"He wanted to die, Ruben. I saw it clear as day."

"I'm not surprised to hear that. He was jealous of you, always had been. Did you think of that, or did you know it?"

"I guess I knew it."

"A jealous man is an inferior one, Buell. And worse yet, he knows it. Can you imagine living with that day in and day out?"

"No, sir, I can't."

"Gus decided he couldn't either. This last affair is going to be a test for you. You know that."

"I'm through with it. I sent a telegram to Texas two weeks ago. I got an answer back. An old friend of mine has a place, a saloon. I'm welcome there anytime."

"Far be it from me to judge, but I can tell you you're wanted and needed here. After the shock has worn off, and this gets talked about around town, the folks here are going to see what you've done. Not many will thank you outright, but you'll know what they're feeling. Think on your decision, Buell, and if you need a place to clear you head a bit, the ranch is three hours away." Ruben put his empty cup on the desk and got up. "I think you know all I know. That bunch out at the ranch will be available for Waldon's trial—I'll see to that." He buttoned his coat, retrieved his hat, and left.

Two weeks later, Buell sat at his desk and laboriously wrote a half-page letter to Pat Lacey in Uvalde, Texas, and told him he'd be staying in Carlisle for a while. He also mentioned his appointment as sheriff just so his old mentor could see how absurd life can be. He scrawled his signature, folded the paper, and stuffed it in an envelope.

The sun's feeble rays still made him squint as he pulled the door shut and started down the boardwalk. By the time he'd made it to the post office and back out, a dozen people had greeted him, while only two or three chose to ignore him.

"Buell," someone hollered from across the street. He turned to see Walt Garner veer off the walk and cross the road.

"Howdy, Walt. How's the freightin' business?"

"A lot better with the snow gone—still cold though." He shaded his eyes. "Ya gonna go to Missus Luger's for noon?"

"I still have a hard time with that. Thought I'd go to my place, and put my feet up."

"Some are expectin' ya to make an exception." He winked broadly.

"That kind of invitation usually means I'm gonna get embarrassed."

"I know what ya mean. That's why I stopped ya. The folks who think they count around here have decided to say thanks." Color rose in his neck and spread to his cheeks. "No offense."

"None. I know who ya mean."

"Well, they're expectin' you to walk by and are gonna shanghai ya. Drag you in there. Don't seem quite fair to me, even though I think ya deserve a lot of credit. Lots of folks do."

"You gonna be there?"

"Do I look like I count?" Walt punched him lightly on the arm. "I have an errand to run. I'll be eatin' on the dock with the boys like always."

"Thanks for the warning, Walt. Say hello to Mose and the rest."

Walt gave him a wave and headed down the street. Buell turned around and started for his place, taking a roundabout way past Lancer's. He appreciated Walt's word of caution, but what Walt had said about the men Buell used to work with meant much more. They represented the people who stood to lose a lot by losing just a little. They'd understood the danger. People who depend on each other, share the burden of hard times, and celebrate the good together, know to accept the need for harsh action. And they did.

Buell approached the man-door from the unusual direction, the wan sun on his face. The noon flood of people on Main Street was in full flow, and he stopped for a moment to watch.

It was good to see people come out after the long winter. He even saw a parasol, defiantly colorful and nearly useless. More for show than anything, but that was good. He lifted the latch, hauled the door open, and went inside, pulling it shut behind. By habit, he glanced at Shadow's stall, and the black and white tail twitched slightly as the horse recognized his presence. He then started for his room, and stopped cold—the door was ajar.

As he knelt on the dirt floor holding his chest, he tried to remember if he'd even seen him approach. Did it matter? He winced as another spasm constricted his breathing and decided it didn't. How many times since he'd seen Doc Princher had he reminded himself to *look* to the right? He hadn't today, and now he was paying for it.

The strike hadn't been painful at first, the thrust forcing his lungs to expel their contents in a single whooshing breath—a reaction to being stabbed through, he thought. The pain came, hot and fierce, when Ned had jerked the short blade out and stepped back.

"To'd ya," the black man had said with a flash of white teeth, then turned to walk away, out the back door Buell had used to ambush Gus.

Buell had sagged to the floor, at the same spot where Gus has fallen. Justice? He coughed, and tasted a mouthful of blood—salty and raw. He spit it out, then wondered if Arley had felt what he was feeling right now. Was he scared? Of what? Buell decided he wasn't. Tuning slightly sideways, he got his legs out from under him and stretched out in front. That felt better. The light faded for a moment and he blinked it back to full again. Not a good sign, he thought. Better not do that again.

Simon glanced over his shoulder and smiled to himself. This is what Buell needed. Mrs. Luger's was full: Paul Steele, John

Lindstrom, Judge Kingsley, Paisley Mace, Art Lancer, Jacob Luger, and his son Jake, Mister Moir, and over thirty others sat impatiently and watched Simon watch up the street. Ten minutes passed, and then Simon held up his hand. The café went silent. Simon pushed open the door and grabbed.

"Did you see Buell when you walked past the jail?" he asked the startled teamster.

Walt looked around the room, his eyes wide. "So many," he said.

"Well, did you?"

"I reckon I let the cat out. I told him you might be layin' for him. He went around the back way to his place."

"Oh, dammit, Walt," Paisley said. "How long ago?"

"Not mor'n four or five minutes. I'm sorry now," he said looking over the crowd.

"No matter," Simon said. "I'll go get him." He pushed past the driver, hurrying to the corner and down the street to the stable.

"Buell!" he shouted as soon as he entered the barn. "Get your lazy butt—what in hell! Buell!" He charged across the floor and slid to his knees. "Good Lord, Buell, you're bleeding bad. Let me see." He pulled a blood-soaked hand away and gasped. "Say something." Buell slowly turned his head. A red bubble formed on his lips and then popped. Simon scrambled to his feet and raced to the door. "Get Doc Princher!" he hollered at the top of his lungs. Half a dozen people at the corner stopped and looked. "Go get the doctor," he screamed, "Now!"

Back at Buell's side, he caught hold of his shoulders and lowered him to the floor, holding his friend's head in his lap. "Who?" he whispered. Buell just shook his head. Simon glanced at the door. "You'll be okay. Doc's coming." Again, Buell shook his head. And then he reached for Simon's hand, the grip wet and sticky.

"Closer," Buell whispered and Simon bent lower. "Gone. My time. The devil's due." He met Simon's eyes for a moment, then Buell's stuttered shut.

Simon looked up to the sound of the door opening. Someone poked their head in. "Get Doc Princher, you dumb bastard!"

ABOUT THE AUTHOR

Wallace J. Swenson was born and raised in a small rural town in southeast Idaho. From the very beginning, he lived a life of hard work supported by a strong family. He was taught by example the value of honesty and loyalty, and it is about such that he wrote. His family numbered ten, and though poor in a material sense, he considered himself blessed beyond measure in the spiritual. He resided with his wife of fifty-plus years, Jacquelyn, near where both were born, and close to all their children and grandchildren. He intended to live there the rest of his life as he was allowed to breathe and spend that time putting down on paper the dozens of stories that whirled around inside his head. He did just that. Wallace J. Swenson died suddenly in February of 2015. He left a literary legacy that this book is a small part of.

The employees of Five Star Publishing hope you have enjoyed this book.

Our Five Star novels explore little-known chapters from America's history, stories told from unique perspectives that will entertain a broad range of readers.

Other Five Star books are available at your local library, bookstore, all major book distributors, and directly from Five Star/Gale.

Connect with Five Star Publishing

Visit us on Facebook:
https://www.facebook.com/FiveStarCengage

Email:
FiveStar@cengage.com

For information about titles and placing orders:
(800) 223-1244
gale.orders@cengage.com

To share your comments, write to us:
Five Star Publishing
Attn: Publisher
10 Water St., Suite 310
Waterville, ME 04901